BESTSELLING AUTHOR COLLECTION

In our 2011 Bestselling Author Collection, Harlequin Books is proud to offer classic novels from today's superstars of women's fiction. These authors have captured the hearts of millions of readers around the world, and earned their place on the bestseller lists with every release.

As a bonus, each volume also includes a full-length novel from a rising star of series romance. Bestselling authors in their own right, these talented writers have captured the qualities Harlequin is famous for—heart-racing passion, edge-of-your-seat entertainment and a satisfying happily-ever-after.

Don't miss any of the books in this year's collection!

D1040332

Trade 1/2 176

Casper, Wyoming

**Praise for *New York Times* and *USA TODAY*
bestselling author Diana Palmer**

"Palmer demonstrates, yet again,
why she's the queen of desperado quests for
justice and true love."
—*Publishers Weekly* on *Dangerous*

"Diana Palmer is a mesmerizing storyteller
who captures the essence of what a
romance should be."
—*Affaire de Coeur*

"Nobody does it better."
—*New York Times* bestselling author
Linda Howard

**Praise for *USA TODAY* bestselling author
Kathie DeNosky**

"DeNosky's keen touch with family drama and
enduring love makes for a great read."
—*RT Book Reviews* on *Expecting the Rancher's Heir*

"Kathie DeNosky finishes up her Lonetree
Ranchers trilogy with a true winner… Readers
will race to the delightful conclusion, only to
regret that there are no more pages to turn."
—*RT Book Reviews* on *Lonetree Ranchers: Colt*

BESTSELLING AUTHOR COLLECTION

New York Times and *USA TODAY* Bestselling Author

DIANA PALMER

Nelson's Brand

TORONTO NEW YORK LONDON
AMSTERDAM PARIS SYDNEY HAMBURG
STOCKHOLM ATHENS TOKYO MILAN MADRID
PRAGUE WARSAW BUDAPEST AUCKLAND

If you purchased this book without a cover you should be aware that this book is stolen property. It was reported as "unsold and destroyed" to the publisher, and neither the author nor the publisher has received any payment for this "stripped book."

Recycling programs
for this product may
not exist in your area.

ISBN-13: 978-0-373-18492-7

NELSON'S BRAND

Copyright © 2011 by Harlequin Books S.A.

The publisher acknowledges the copyright holders
of the individual works as follows:

NELSON'S BRAND
Copyright © 1991 by Diana Palmer

LONETREE RANCHERS: COLT
Copyright © 2003 by Kathie DeNosky

All rights reserved. Except for use in any review, the reproduction or utilization of this work in whole or in part in any form by any electronic, mechanical or other means, now known or hereafter invented, including xerography, photocopying and recording, or in any information storage or retrieval system, is forbidden without the written permission of the publisher, Harlequin Enterprises Limited, 225 Duncan Mill Road, Don Mills, Ontario, Canada, M3B 3K9.

This is a work of fiction. Names, characters, places and incidents are either the product of the author's imagination or are used fictitiously, and any resemblance to actual persons, living or dead, business establishments, events or locales is entirely coincidental.

This edition published by arrangement with Harlequin Books S.A.

For questions and comments about the quality of this book please contact us at Customer_eCare@Harlequin.ca.

® and ™ are trademarks of the publisher. Trademarks indicated with ® are registered in the United States Patent and Trademark Office, the Canadian Trade Marks Office and in other countries.

www.Harlequin.com

Printed in U.S.A.

CONTENTS

NELSON'S BRAND 7
Diana Palmer

LONETREE RANCHERS: COLT 271
Kathie DeNosky

For Kathryn Falk and Melinda Helfer of
Romantic Times with love

NELSON'S BRAND

New York Times and *USA TODAY* Bestselling Author

Diana Palmer

DIANA PALMER

The prolific author of more than one hundred books, Diana Palmer got her start as a newspaper reporter. A multi–*New York Times* bestselling author and one of the top ten romance writers in America, she has a gift for telling the most sensual tales with charm and humor. Diana lives with her family in Cornelia, Georgia.

Visit her website at www.DianaPalmer.com.

Chapter One

He was very noticeable, and he knew it. He also had a pretty formidable reputation locally with women and he didn't usually turn down blatant invitations. But the wide-eyed scrutiny he was getting from the woman at the corner table only irritated him tonight. The past six months had been difficult, and he'd been drinking too much and womanizing too much...or so his family kept saying. Not that he was listening to them much these days. Not when he knew that they weren't really his family.

She wasn't hard on the eyes. He gave her one

encompassing glance that took in everything from the French plait of black hair at her nape, down high, firm breasts under a soft white blouse, to a small waist and full hips and long elegant legs in tight jeans. She was sitting at a corner table, a little away from it on one side, with his half brother Dwight, and Dwight's fiancée, Winnie. He didn't know her name, but he was pretty sure that she was Winnie's out-of-town houseguest. Pryor, Wyoming, was a small town, and news traveled fast when anyone had company.

He took another sip of his whiskey and stared at the small shot glass contemplatively. He drank far too much lately. When he started staying out late at night and couldn't remember anything about it the next morning, he needed to take another look at his life, he thought bitterly. Dale Branigan had caught him in a weak moment and now she was hounding him for dates. Not that she was bad-looking, but she reminded him of the excesses that were taking him straight to hell, according to Dwight.

He glanced toward Dwight's disapproving face, so unlike his, and deliberately raised the shot glass to his thin lips with a mocking smile. He drained it, but when the bartender asked if he wanted another, he said no. It wasn't Dwight who stopped him. It was the expression on that woman's face who was sitting with Dwight and Winnie. There was something quiet and calming about her face, about the oddly compassionate way she was looking at him. What he'd thought was a flirting stare didn't seem to be one. As he met her eyes across the room, he felt a jolt of pure emotion run through him. Odd. He hadn't felt that before. Maybe it was the liquor.

He looked around. The bar was crowded, and there weren't many women around. Thank God Dale wasn't here to pester him. Frequently on a Friday night, he drove up to Billings for a little entertainment. Tonight, he wasn't in the mood. He'd overheard a chance remark from one of his men and his quick temper had cost him a good mechanic. It was his nature to strike out when he was angry. With a soft, cold laugh he considered that he'd probably inherited that trait from his father. From his *real* father, not the man who'd been married to his mother for more than twenty years. Until six months ago, his name had been Gene Nelson and he was accepted by everyone as Hank Nelson's son. But six months ago, Hank Nelson had died—ten years after Gene's mother— and he'd left a will that was as much a confession as a bequeath. It had contained the shocking news that he'd adopted Gene at the age of four.

Gene realized that he was idly sliding the shot glass around on the bar and stopped. He paid for the drink and turned toward the door.

Dwight called to him and he hesitated. His younger half brother was the head honcho at the Triple N Ranch now. That was the biggest blow to his pride. He'd been the eldest son. Now he was the outsider, and Dwight was the rightful heir. That took a lot of getting used to after thirty years.

He cocked his hat over one eye and strode toward Dwight's table, his lean, dark face rigid, his pale green eyes like wet peridots under lashes as thick and black as the straight hair under the gray Stetson.

"You haven't met Gene, have you, Allison?" Winnie asked, smiling. She was blond and petite and very pretty. Her fairness matched Dwight's, who also had blond hair and blue eyes, a fact that had often puzzled Gene. Their sister Marie was equally fair. Only Gene was dark, and he alone had green eyes. His mother had been a blue-eyed blonde, like Hank Nelson. Why had he never connected those stray facts? Perhaps he'd been dodging the issue all along.

"No, we haven't met," Allison said softly. She looked up at Gene with hazel eyes that were his instant undoing. He'd never seen eyes like that.

There was something in them that made him feel warm inside. "How do you do, Mr. Nelson?" she asked, and she smiled. It was like sunshine on a cloudy day.

He caught his breath silently. She'd called him Mr. Nelson, but he wasn't a Nelson. He straightened. What the hell, it was the only name he'd ever known. He nodded curtly. "Miss…?"

"Hathoway," she replied.

"Are you on your way back to the ranch?" Dwight asked, his tone reconciliatory, hesitant.

"Yes."

"I'll see you there, then."

Gene let his eyes fall to the woman again, to her gentle oval face. Her eyes and mouth were her best features. She wasn't really pretty, but she had a glow about her. It grew as he looked at her unsmilingly, and he finally realized that she was blushing. Strange response, for a woman her age. She was out of her teens; probably in her mid-twenties.

"Gene, are you coming to the barbecue tomorrow night?" Winnie asked.

He was still staring at Allison. "Maybe." His head moved a little to the side as he looked down at Allison. "Are you Winnie's houseguest?" he asked her, his voice slow and deep, without a noticeable accent.

"Yes," she said. "Just for a couple of weeks, I mean," she stammered. He made her nervous. She'd never felt such an instant attraction to anyone.

Unbeknownst to her, neither had Gene. He was having a hard time trying to drag himself away. This woman made him feel as if he'd suddenly come out of a daze, and he didn't understand why. "I've got to get home," he said, forcing the words out. He nodded curtly and left them, his booted feet heavy on the wood floor, his back arrow-straight.

Allison Hathoway watched him go. She'd never seen anyone quite as fascinating as the departing Mr. Nelson. He looked like a cowboy she'd seen in a movie once, tall and lean and lithe, with wide shoulders and narrow hips and long, powerful legs. She, who had little if anything to do with men, was so affected by him that she was still flushed and shaking inside from the brief encounter.

"I didn't think he was going to stop," Dwight said with a rueful smile. "He avoids me a lot these days. Marie, too. Except to start fights."

"It isn't getting any easier at home, is it?" Winnie asked her fiancé, laying a small hand on his.

Dwight shook his head as he curled his fingers around hers. "Gene won't talk about it. He just goes on as if nothing has happened. Marie's at the end of her rope, and so am I. We love him, but he's convinced himself that he's no longer part of our family."

Allison listened without understanding what they were talking about.

"Is he much older than you, Dwight?" she asked.

He lifted an eyebrow, smiling at her interest. "About six years. He's thirty-four."

"But he's not a man to risk your heart on," Winnie said softly. "Gene's just gone through a bad time. He's hurt and he's ready to lash out at anybody who gets too close."

"I hate to agree, but she's right," Dwight replied quietly. "Gene's gone from bad to worse in the past few months. Women, liquor, fights. He threw a punch at our mechanic and fired him this morning."

"The man deserved it," Winnie said quietly. "You know what he called Gene."

"He wouldn't have called Gene anything if my brother hadn't started acting like one of the hands instead of the boss," Dwight said angrily. "He hates the routine of working cattle every day. He had the business head and he was good at organization. I'm not. I was better at working cattle and taking care of the shipping and receiving. The will reversed our duties. Now we're both miserable. I can't handle the men, and Gene won't. The ranch is going to pot because he won't buckle down. He drinks on the weekends and the men's morale is at rock bottom. They're looking for excuses to quit or get fired."

"But…he only had one drink at the bar," Allison said softly, puzzled, because one drink surely wasn't that bad.

Dwight lifted a blond eyebrow. "So he did. He kept glancing at you, and then he put down the glass. I was watching. It seemed to bother him. That's the first time I've known him to stop at one drink."

"He always used to," Winnie recalled. "In fact, he hardly ever touched the stuff."

"He's so damned brittle," Dwight sighed. "He can't bend. God, I feel for him! I can imagine how it would be if I were in his shoes. He's so alone."

"Most people are, really," Allison said, her hazel eyes soft and quiet. "And when they hurt, they do bad things sometimes."

Winnie smiled at her warmly. "You'd find excuses for hardened criminals, wouldn't you?"

she asked gently. "I suppose that's why you're so good at what you do."

"At what I *did*," Allison corrected. Her eyes fell worriedly to the table. "I don't know that I'll ever be able to do it again."

"You need time," Winnie replied sympathetically. "That's all, Allie. You just need time."

"Something I have in common with your future brother-in-law, I gather," came the reply. Allison sighed and sipped her ginger ale. "I hope you're right."

But that night, alone in bed, the nightmares came again and she woke, as she always did these days, in a cold sweat, trying not to hear the sound of guns, the sound of screams.

She wrapped her white chenille bathrobe around her worn white gown and made her way to the kitchen. Winnie was already there. Her mother was still in bed. Mrs. Manley was no early bird, even if her daughter was.

Allison's long black hair was around her shoulders in a wavy tangle, her hazel eyes bloodshot, her face pale. She felt dragged out.

"Bad dreams again, I'll bet," Winnie said gently.

Allison managed a wan smile. She accepted the cup of hot black coffee Winnie handed her as they sat down at the kitchen table. "It's better than it was," she said.

"I'm just glad that you came to us," Winnie replied. She was wearing an expensive pink silk ensemble. The Manleys were much better off financially than the Hathoways had ever been, but Mrs. Manley and Allison's late mother had been best friends. As they grew up, Winnie and Allison became best friends, too.

They'd all lived near Bisbee, Arizona, when the girls were young and in school. Then the Manleys had moved to Pryor, Wyoming, when Mr. Manley took another job with an international mining concern. The Hathoways had been reassigned and Allison had gone with them to Central America.

The last few weeks could have been just a bad memory except that Allison was alone now. She'd called Winnie the minute she'd landed in the States again, and Winnie had flown down to Tucson to pick her up. It had been days before Allison could stop crying. Now, at last, she was beginning to heal. Yesterday was the first time Winnie had been able to coax her out among people. Allison was running from the news media that had followed her to Tucson, and she didn't want any attention drawn to her. She'd successfully covered her tracks, but she didn't know for how long.

"The barbecue is tonight. You have to come," Winnie told Allison. "Don't worry," she added quickly when the taller girl froze. "They're all rodeo people that Dwight's introducing me to. Nobody will bother you."

"Dwight's brother said he might be there," Allison murmured.

Winnie groaned. "For God's sake, don't tempt fate by getting too close to Gene. You've just come through one trauma; you don't need another one."

"I know." Allison cupped her cold hands around her coffee cup and closed her eyes. "I suppose I'm pretty vulnerable right now. It's just the aloneness. I've never been really alone before." She looked up and there was faint panic in her face.

"You'll never be alone as long as the Manleys are alive," Winnie said firmly. She laid a warm hand over Allison's forearm. "We all love you very much."

"Yes, I know. Do you know how much I care for all of you, and how grateful I am for a place to stay?" Allison replied sincerely. "I couldn't even go back to the house in Bisbee. Mom and Dad rented it out… Well, before we went to Central America." She faltered. "I was afraid to go near it even for possessions, in case somebody from the press was watching."

"All the furor will die down once the fighting stops," Winnie assured her. "You're being hunted because you have firsthand information about what really happened there. With the occupation forces in control, not much word is getting out. Once the government is well in power, it will become old news and they'll leave you alone. In the meantime, you can stay with us as long as you like."

"I'm in the way. Your marriage…"

"My marriage isn't for six months," Winnie reminded her with a warm smile. "You'll be my maid of honor. By then, all this will just be a sad memory. You'll have started to live again."

"I hope so," Allison replied huskily. "Oh, I hope so!"

Back at the Nelson place, Gene had just gone into the house to find his half sister, Marie, glaring at him from the living room. She looked like Dwight, except that she was petite and sharp-tongued.

"Dale's been calling again," she said irritably. "She seems to have the idea that she's engaged to you."

"I don't marry one-night stands," he said with deliberate cruelty.

"Then you should make that clear at the beginning," she returned.

His broad shoulders rose and fell. "I was too drunk."

Marie got up and went to him, her expression concerned. "Look at what you're doing to yourself," she said miserably. "This is your home. Dwight and I don't think of you as an outsider, Gene."

"Don't start," he said curtly, his pale green eyes flashing at her.

She threw up her hands with an angry sigh. "You won't listen! You drink, you carouse, you won't even pay attention to the lax discipline that's letting the men goof off half the time. I saw Rance with a bottle in broad daylight the other day!"

"If I see him, I'll do something about him," he said, striding toward the staircase.

"And when will that be? You're too busy having a good time to notice!"

He didn't answer her and he didn't look back. He went upstairs, his booted feet making soft thuds on the carpet.

"What about Dale? What do I tell her if she calls again?" she called after him.

"Tell her I joined a monastery and took vows of chastity," he drawled.

She chuckled. "That'll be the day," she murmured as she went back into the living room. At least he had been sober when he got home last night, she thought. And then she frowned. Not his usual style on a Friday night, she pondered.

It wasn't until later in the morning, when Dwight told her about his meeting with Allison, that his behavior registered.

"You mean, he looked at her and put the shot glass down?" Marie asked, all eyes.

"He certainly did," Dwight replied. Gene had gone out to check on the branding. Considering the size of the ranch and the number of new calves, it was much more than a couple of days' work. "He couldn't seem to keep his eyes off her."

"Is she pretty?" Marie asked.

He shook his head. "Nice. Very sweet. And a passable figure. But no, she's no beauty. Odd, isn't it, for Gene to even notice a woman like that? His tastes run to those brassy, experienced women he meets at rodeos. But Allison seemed to captivate him."

"If she influenced him enough to keep him sober on a Friday night, I take my hat off to her," Marie said with genuine feeling. "He was like his old self last night. It was nice, seeing him that way. He's been so different for the past few months."

"Yes. I know it's hurt him. I never realized how much until I saw him coming apart in front of my eyes. Knowing about his real father has driven him half-mad."

"We can't help who our parents are," Marie said. "And Gene wouldn't be like that man in a million years. Surely he knows it?"

"He mumbled something about never having kids of his own because of his bad blood, one night when he was drinking," Dwight confided. He sighed and finished his coffee. "I wish we could find some way to cope with it. He has no peace."

Marie fingered her coffee cup thoughtfully. "Maybe he can find it with our Miss Hathoway," she mused, her eyes twinkling as they met his. "If she had that effect from a distance, imagine what it could be like at close range?"

"Except that she isn't Gene's kind of woman," he replied, and began to tell her all about the quiet Miss Hathoway.

Marie whistled. "My gosh. Poor kid."

"She's an amazing lady," he said, smiling. "Winnie's very fond of her. So fond that she'll discourage her from even looking at Gene, much less anything else."

"I can see why. The angel and the outlaw," she

murmured, and smiled gently. "I guess I was day-dreaming."

"Nothing wrong with dreams," he told her as he got up from the table. "But they won't run a ranch."

"Or organize a barbecue," Marie said, smiling. "Good luck with the books."

He groaned. "I'll have us in the poorhouse in another few months. If Gene was more approachable, I'd ask him to switch duties with me."

"Could you do that?"

"No reason why not," he said. "But he hasn't been in a listening mood."

"Don't give up. There's always tomorrow."

He laughed. "Tell him." He left her sitting there, still looking thoughtful.

Chapter Two

"Are you sure this looks all right on me?" Allison asked worriedly as she stared into the mirror at the low neckline of the strapless sundress Winnie had loaned her for the barbecue. They'd spent a lazy day at home, and now it was almost time to leave for the Nelsons' Triple N Ranch.

"Will you stop fussing? You look fine," Winnie assured her. "You've been out of touch with fashion for a while. Don't worry, it's perfectly proper. Even for Pryor, Wyoming," she added with a mischievous grin.

Allison sighed at her reflection in the full-length mirror. The young woman staring back at her looked like a stranger. Her long, dark hair was loose and wavy, framing her lovely oval face to its best advantage. She'd used mascara to emphasize her hazel eyes and she'd applied foundation and lipstick much more liberally than usual. Too, the off-the-shoulder sundress with its form-fitting bodice certainly did make her appear sophisticated. Its daring green, white and black pattern was exotic and somehow suited her tall, full-figured body. The strappy white sandals Winnie had loaned her completed the outfit.

Winnie modeled dresses for a local department store, so she was able to buy clothes at a considerable discount. She knew all sorts of beauty secrets, ways of making the most of her assets and downplaying the minor flaws of face and figure. She'd used them to advantage on her houseguest. Allison hardly recognized herself.

"I always knew you'd be a knockout if you were dressed and made up properly." Winnie nodded, approving her handiwork. "I'm glad you finally gave in and let me do my thing. You'll have the bachelors flitting around you like bees around clover. Dwight has a friend who'd be perfect for you, if he just shows up. He'll be bowled over."

"That'll be the day." Allison laughed softly,

but she was secretly hoping that one particular bachelor named Gene might give her at least a second glance. She didn't know what kind of problems he had, but knowing that he'd been hurt, too, gave her a fellow feeling for him. It wasn't good to be alone when you were in pain.

"You're a late bloomer. Trust me." Winnie dragged her out of the bedroom and down the hall to the living room, where her mother was waiting. "Mom, look what I did to Allie," she called.

Mrs. Manley, a tall, graying woman, smiled as she turned to greet the two young women. "My, what a change," she said. "You look lovely, Allie. I wish your parents could see you."

Allie sobered. "Yes. So do I, Mrs. Manley."

"Forgive me," the older woman said. "Your mother and I were best friends for thirty years. But as hard as it is for me, I know it must be ten times harder for you."

"Life goes on," Allie said. She sighed, spreading her long, elegant fingers over the full skirt of the dress. "Isn't this a dream? I don't know how to thank you and Winnie for letting me stay with you. I really had nowhere else to go."

"I'm sure you have plenty of friends besides us, even if they are spread around the world a bit," Winnie chided. She hugged Allison. "But I'm still your best one. Remember when we were in seventh grade together back in Bisbee and we had to climb the mountain every day after school to get to our houses?"

"I miss Arizona sometimes," Allison said absently.

"I don't," Mrs. Manley said, shaking her head. "I used to have nightmares about falling into the Lavender Pit." She shuddered delicately. "It suited me when Winnie's father changed jobs and we moved here. Of course, if I'd known he was going to have to travel all over the world, I might have had second thoughts. He's gone almost all the time lately."

"He'll retire next year," Winnie reminded her.

"Yes, so he will." Mrs. Manley smiled and changed the subject. "You two had better get going, or you'll be late. The barbecue's at the Nelsons'?"

"Yes. Dwight invited us." Winnie grinned. "I'll have to make sure he doesn't toss me into the corral with those wild horses and ride off with Allie."

"Small chance when you're engaged." Allison grinned.

Winnie drove them to the Nelson place in her small Japanese car, a sporty model that suited her.

Allison could drive, but she didn't have a current license. Where she'd been for the past two years, she hadn't needed one.

"Before we get there," Winnie said with a worried glance at Allison, "remember what I said and don't get too close to Gene. I don't think he'd let you get near him anyway—he's pretty standoffish around shy little innocents. But I wasn't kidding when I told you he was a dangerous customer. Even his brother and sister walk wide around him lately."

"He can't be that bad," Allison said gently and smiled.

"Don't you believe it." Winnie wasn't convinced. She scowled. "You watch yourself."

"All right. I will," she promised, but she had her fingers crossed beside her. "Is he by chance a jilted man, embittered by the faithlessness of some jaded woman, or was he treated horribly by his mother?" she added dryly.

"Gene doesn't get jilted by women, and his mother was a saint, according to Dwight," Winnie recalled. "A really wonderful woman who was loved by the whole community. She died about ten years ago. His father was a small-time rancher with a big heart. They were happily married. His... father died about six months ago."

Allison wondered at the hesitation in Winnie's voice when she talked about the late Mr. Nelson. "Do you know what's wrong with Gene, then?" she persisted.

"Yes. But I can't tell you," was the quiet reply. "It's not really any of my business, and Dwight's already been asked too many questions by the whole community. I don't mean to sound rude, and I trust you with my life," Winnie added, "but it's Gene's business."

"I understand."

"No, you don't, but Dwight may tell you one day. Or Marie."

"Is Marie like Gene or Dwight?"

"In coloring, she's like Dwight, blond and blue-eyed. Gene's…different. More hardheaded. Fiery."

"I gathered that. Doesn't he ever smile?"

"Sometimes," Winnie said. "Usually when he's about to hit somebody. He isn't an easygoing man. He's arrogant and proud and just a little too quick on the trigger to be good company. You'll find all that out. I just don't want you to find it out at close range, the hard way."

"I can take care of myself, you know," Allison mused. "I've been doing it in some pretty rough places for a long time."

"I know. But there's a big difference in what

you've been doing and a man-woman relationship."
She glanced at Allison as she turned into a long,
graveled driveway. "Honestly, for a twenty-five-
year-old woman, you're just hopelessly backward,
and I mean that in the nicest possible way. It isn't
as if you've had the opportunity to lead a wild life.
But you've been criminally exposed in some ways
and criminally sheltered in others. I don't think
your parents ever really considered you when they
made their plans."

Allison laughed gently. "Yes, they did. I'm just
like them, Winnie. I loved every minute of what
we all did together, and I'll miss it terribly, even
now." Her eyes clouded. "Things happen as God
means them to. I can cope."

"It was such a waste, though...."

"Oh, no," Allison said, remembering the
glowing faces she'd seen, the purpose and peace
in the dark eyes. "No, it was never a waste. They're
still alive, in the work they did, in the lives they
changed."

"I won't argue with you," Winnie said gently.
"We've kept in touch and remained friends all
these long years since we were in school together
in Bisbee. You're still the sister I never had. You'll
have a home as long as I'm alive."

Tears sprang to Allison's big eyes. She hurriedly

dashed them away. "If the circumstances were reversed, I hope you know that I'd do the same thing for you."

"I know," Winnie said. She wiped away a tear of her own.

There was a crowd of cars in the front driveway at the Nelsons' after they'd wound their way up past the towering lodgepole pines and aspen trees to the big stone house, backed by jagged high mountains.

"Isn't it just heaven?" Allison sighed involuntarily. "Wyoming is beautiful."

"Yes, it certainly is. I can happily spend the rest of my life here. Now, Allie, you aren't planning to sit behind bushes all night, are you?" she muttered. "The whole idea of this party is to meet people."

"For *you* to meet people," Allison emphasized. "You're the one who's getting married, not me."

"You can take advantage of it, all the same. These are interesting people, too. Most of them are rodeo folks, and the rest are cattlemen or horse breeders."

"You're making me nervous," Allison said, fidgeting in her seat as Winnie parked the car behind a silver-gray Lincoln. "I don't know anything about rodeo or horses or cattle."

"No time like the present to learn," Winnie said easily. "Come on. Out of there."

"Is this trip really necessary?" Allison murmured, swinging her long, elegant legs out of the car. "I could stay in the car and make sure it doesn't roll down the hill."

"Not a chance, my friend. After all the work I've put in on you today, I want to show you off."

"Gloating over your artistry, I gather?" Allison primped. "Well, let's spread me among the peasants, then."

"I'd forgotten your Auntie Mame impersonation," Winnie winced. "You really have to stop watching those old movies. Don't lay it on too thick, now."

"Cross my heart and hope to die," Allison agreed. She drew an imaginary line across her stomach.

"Your heart isn't down there," Winnie said worriedly.

"Yes, it is. The only thing I really love is food, so that's where my heart is. Right?"

"I give up."

Allison followed her friend up the wide stone steps to where Dwight Nelson waited on the porch, his blond hair gleaming in the fading sunlight.

"There you are!" he chuckled, and swung

a beaming Winnie up in his arms to kiss her soundly. "Hello, Allie, glad you could come," he told the other woman and suddenly stopped, his eyes widening as he stared at her. "Allie? That is you, isn't it?"

Allison sent a dry look in her friend's direction. "Go ahead. Gloat," she dared.

"I did it all," Winnie said, smiling haughtily. "Just look. Isn't she hot?"

"Indeed she is, and if I hadn't seen you first…" Dwight began.

Winnie stomped on his big foot through his boot. "Hold it right there, buster, before you talk yourself into a broken leg. You're all mine, and don't you forget it."

"As if I could." Dwight winced, flexing his booted foot. "You look gorgeous, Allie, now will you tell her I was kidding?"

"He was kidding," Allie told Winnie.

"All right. You're safe, this time." Winnie slid her arm around Dwight's lean waist. "Where's Marie?"

"Around back," he said, grimacing as he glanced toward the sound of a local band beyond the arch in the surrounding wall. "Gene's out there."

"Gene and Marie don't get along," Winnie told Allison.

"That's like saying old-time cowboys and old-time Indians don't get along." Dwight sighed. "Fortunately the guests will keep them from killing each other in public. Mother used to spend her life separating them. It was fine while Gene was abroad for a year on a selling trip. We actually had peaceful meals. Now we have indigestion and a new cook every month." He pursed his lips. "Speaking of food, let's go see if there's any left." Dwight glanced over their heads toward the driveway. "I think you two are the last people we expected."

"The best always are, darling," Winnie said, smiling up at him with sparkling affection.

Allison had to fight her inclination to be jealous, but if anyone ever deserved happiness, Winnie did. She had a heart as big as the whole world.

She followed the engaged couple through the stone arch to the tents that had been set up with tables and chairs positioned underneath it to seat guests. A huge steer carcass was roasting over an open fire while a man basted it with sauce, smiling and nodding as two women, one of whom Winnie whispered was Marie Nelson, carried off platters of it to the tables.

Other pots contained baked beans and Brunswick stew, which were being served as well, along with what had to be homemade rolls.

"It smells heavenly," Allison sighed, closing her eyes to inhale the sweet aroma.

"It tastes heavenly, too," Dwight said. "I grabbed a sample on my way around the house. Here, sit down and dig in."

He herded them toward the first tent, where there were several vacant seats, but he and Winnie were waylaid by a couple they knew and Allison was left to make her own way to the long table.

She took a plate and utensils from the end of the table, along with a glass of iced tea, and sat down. Platters of barbecue and rolls, and bowls of baked beans and Brunswick stew, were strategically placed all along the table. Allison filled her plate with small portions. It had been a long time since she'd felt comfortable eating her fill, and she had difficulty now with the sheer volume of food facing her.

Gene Nelson was standing nearby talking to a visiting cattleman when he saw Allison sit down alone at the table. His eyes had found her instantly, as if he'd known the second she'd arrived. He didn't understand his fierce attraction to her, even if she did look good enough to eat tonight. Her dress was blatantly sexy, and she seemed much more sophisticated than she had in the bar with Dwight and Winnie. Winnie was a model, and he knew she had some liberated friends. He'd even dated Winnie once, which was why Dwight's fiancée had such a bad opinion of him. Not that he'd gotten very far. Dwight had cut him out about the second date, and women were so thick on the ground that he'd never given Dwight's appropriation of his date a second thought. That might have added to Winnie's disapproval, he mused, the fact that he hadn't wanted her enough to fight for her. It was nothing personal. He'd simply never wanted any woman enough to fight for her. They were all alike. Well, most all alike, he thought, staring helplessly at Allison, with her long, dark hair almost down to her narrow waist.

He sighed heavily as he watched her. It had been a while since he'd had a woman. His body ached for sensual oblivion, for something to ease the emotional pain he'd been through. Not that he remembered much about that supposedly wild night with Dale Branigan that had kept her hounding him. In fact, he hardly remembered it at all. Maybe that was why his body ached so when he looked at Allison. These dry spells were hell on the nerves.

Allison felt his gaze and lifted her hazel eyes

to seek his across the space that separated them. Oh, but he was handsome, she thought dizzily. He was dressed in designer jeans and a neat white Western shirt with pearl snaps instead of buttons. He wore a burgundy bandanna around his neck and hand-tooled leather boots. His head was bare, his hair almost black and faintly damp, as if he'd just come from a shower. He was more masculine and threatening than any man Allison had ever known, and the way he looked at her made her tingle all over.

She shouldn't encourage him; she knew she shouldn't. But she couldn't stop looking at him. Her life had been barren of eligible men. It was inevitable that she might be attracted to the first nice-looking bachelor she met, she told herself.

If that look in her eyes wasn't an invitation, he was blind, Gene thought, giving in to it with hardly a struggle. He excused himself, leaving the cattleman with another associate, and picked up a glass of beer and a plate and utensils before he joined Allison. He threw a long leg over the wooden bench at the table and sat down, glancing at the tiny portions on her plate.

"Don't you like barbecue?" he asked coolly, and he didn't smile.

She looked up into pale green eyes in a lean

face with a deeply tanned complexion. Her eyes were a nice medium hazel flecked with green and gold, but his were like peridot—as pale as green ice under thick black lashes. His black hair was straight and conventionally cut, parted on the left side and pulled back from a broad forehead. He had high cheekbones and a square chin with a hint of a cleft in it. His mouth was as perfectly formed as the mouth on a Greek statue—wide and firm and faintly chiseled, with a thin upper lip and an only slightly fuller lower one. He wasn't smiling, and he studied Allison with a blatantly familiar kind of scrutiny. It wasn't the first time a man had undressed her with his eyes, but it was the first time it had affected her so completely. She wanted to pull the tablecloth off the table and wrap herself in it.

But that wouldn't do, she told herself. Hadn't she learned that the only way to confront a predator was with steady courage? Her sense of humor came to her rescue, and she warmed to the part she was playing.

"I said, don't you like barbecue?" he repeated. His voice was like velvet, and very deep. The kind of voice that would sound best, she imagined, in intimacy. She started at her own thoughts. She must be in need of rest, to be thinking such things about a total stranger, even if he was lithe and lean and attractive.

"Oh, I like barbecue," she answered with a demure smile. "I'm just not used to having it cut off the cow in front of me."

He smiled faintly, a quirk of his mouth that matched the arrogant set of his head. "Do tell."

"Do tell what?" she asked with what she hoped was a provocative glance from under the thick lashes that mascara had lengthened.

He was a little disappointed at her easy flirting. He'd rather expected her to be shy and maidenly. But it certainly wouldn't be the first time he'd been mistaken about a woman. He lifted a thick eyebrow. "Give me time. I'll think up something."

"A reason to stay alive," she sighed, touching a hand to her chest. "I do hope you aren't married with six children, Mr. Nelson. I would hate to spoil the barbecue by throwing myself off the roof."

His eyes registered mild humor. "I'm not married."

"You must wear a disguise in public," she mused.

He studied her with pursed lips for a minute before he picked up his plate and glass and came around the table. Her heart skipped when he sat down beside her—very close. He smelled of soap and cologne, potent to a woman who wasn't used to men in any form.

"You didn't come alone, I suppose," he mused, watching her closely. "Let me get a few bites of this under my belt so that I'll have enough strength to beat your escort to his knees."

"Oh, I don't have one of those," she assured him, hiding her nervousness in humor, as she always had. "I came with Winnie."

"That spares my knuckles." He was flirting, too, but she appealed to him.

"Have you known Winnie a long time?" he asked pleasantly.

"Yes," she said. "We've been friends since we were kids, back in Arizona."

Winnie had never mentioned her, but then, he hadn't been around Winnie that much since she'd become engaged to Dwight. And these days, he had very little to say to Dwight.

"You said at the bar that you'd only be here a couple of weeks. How long have you been in Pryor?"

She smiled faintly. "Just a few days. I'm looking forward to a nice visit with Winnie. It's been years since we spent any time together." She couldn't very well tell him that the length of her stay depended on whether or not she could keep anybody in Pryor from knowing who she was and why she was here. She'd successfully ducked the media since her arrival. She didn't want them after her again.

"Have you done much sightseeing?" he asked, letting his eyes fall to her bare shoulders with bold interest.

"Not yet. But I'm enjoying myself. It's nice to have a vacation from work."

That sounded odd, as if she'd forced the words out and didn't mean them. One pale eye narrowed even more. His gaze slid over her curiously, lingering on the thrust of her breasts under the low neckline. "What do you normally do—when you aren't visiting old friends?" he asked.

"I'm a vamp," she murmured dryly, enjoying herself as she registered his mild surprise. It was like being an actress, playing a part. It took her mind off the horror of the past months.

"No, I won't buy that," he said after a minute. "What do you really do?" he persisted, fingering his glass.

She lifted her own glass to her lips, to give her time to think. He didn't look stupid. She couldn't say anything that might give her away to Winnie's neighbors, especially her future brother-in-law.

"I'm in the salvage business," she said finally.

He stared at her.

She laughed. "Oh, no, I didn't mean used cars and scrap metal and such. I'm in the human salvage business. I'm..." she hesitated, searching for something that wouldn't be a total lie.

"You're what?" he asked.

He was dangerously inquisitive, and almost too quick for her. She had to throw him off the track before he tripped her up and got at the truth. She lifted her eyebrows. "Are you by any chance the reincarnation of the Spanish Inquisition?"

"I don't even speak Spanish," he said. He smiled slowly, interested despite his suspicions. "How old are you?"

"Sir, you take my breath away!" she exclaimed.

His eyes fell to her mouth. "Is that a request?" he murmured, and there was suddenly a world of experience in the pale eyes that skimmed her mouth, in the deepness of his soft voice.

Her hand trembled as she put down the glass. He was out of her league and she was getting nervous. It didn't take a college degree to understand what he meant. "You're going too fast," she blurted out.

He leaned back, studying her through narrow eyes. She was a puzzle, a little mass of contradictions. But in spite of that, she appealed to him as no one else had in recent years.

"Okay, honey," he said after a minute, and smiled faintly. "I'll put on the brakes." He took another bite of barbecue and washed it down with what looked and smelled like beer.

"How old are you?" she asked without meaning to, her eyes on the hard lines of his face. She imagined that he had a poker face when he wanted to, that he could hide what he was feeling with ease. She knew his age, because Dwight had told her, but it wouldn't do to let him know that she'd been asking questions about him from the very first time she saw him.

He glanced at her, searching her wide, curious eyes. "I'm thirty-four."

She dropped her eyes to his chin and farther down, to his broad chest.

"Too old for you, cupcake?" he asked carelessly.

"I'm twenty-five," she said.

His dark brows drew together. He'd thought she was younger than that. Yes, she had a few lines in her face, and even a thread or two of gray in her dark hair. Nine years his junior. Not much difference in years, and at her age, she couldn't possibly be innocent. His heart accelerated as he studied what he could see of her body in the revealing dress and wondered what she'd look like without it. She was nicely shaped, and if that beautiful bow of a mouth was anything to go by, she was probably going to be a delicious little morsel. If only she wasn't best friends with Winnie.

He studied her again. She really was a puzzle. Young, and then, suddenly, not young. There had been a fleeting expression in her eyes when he'd asked her about her profession—an expression that confused him. He had a feeling that she wasn't at all what she seemed. But, like him, she seemed to hide her emotions.

"Twenty-five. You're no baby, are you?" he murmured.

Her eyes came up and that expression was in them again, before she erased it and smiled. Fascinating, he thought, like watching an actress put on her stage makeup.

"No. I'm no baby," she agreed softly, her mind on the ordeal she'd been through and not really on the question. She didn't realize what she was saying to him with her words, that she was admitting to experience that she didn't have.

He felt his body reacting to the look in her eyes and he stiffened with surprise. It usually took longer for a woman to affect him so physically. He wouldn't let her look away. The electricity began to flow between them and his eyes narrowed as he saw her mouth part helplessly. She was close, and she smelled of floral cologne that drifted up, mingling with the spicy scent of barbecue and the malt smell of his beer.

His gaze dropped to the cleft between her breasts and lingered there, on skin as smooth and pink as a sun-ripened peach. His chest rose and fell roughly as he tried to imagine how her breasts would feel under his open mouth...

The sudden shock of voices made the glass of beer jerk in his lean hand.

"Did you think we'd deserted you?" Dwight asked Allison, echoing Winnie's greeting. "I see you've found Gene," he added, patting the older man on the shoulder as he paused beside him. "Be careful that he doesn't try to drag you under the table."

"Watch it," the older man returned humorously. But his eyes were glinting, and he knew that Dwight wouldn't mistake the warning even if it flew right past his new acquaintance.

Dwight understood, all right, but he didn't do the expected thing and go away.

"You don't mind if we join you, do you?"

"Of course not," Allison said, frowning slightly at Gene's antagonism. She glanced from him to Dwight. "You two don't favor each other a lot."

There was an embarrassed silence and Winnie actually grimaced.

"No, we don't, do we?" Gene's eyes narrowed as they glanced off Dwight's apologetic ones. "We all share the same mother, but not the same father." He leaned back and laughed coldly. "Isn't that right, Dwight?"

Dwight went red. "Allison didn't know," he said curtly. "You're always on the defensive lately, Gene."

The past few months came back to torment him. He stared at his half brother with eyes as cold and unfeeling as green stone. "I can't forget. Why should you be expected to?"

"You're family," Dwight said, almost apologetically. "Or you would be if you'd stop lashing out at everybody. You're always giving Marie hell."

"She gives it back." Gene swallowed his drink and put the glass on the table. His eyes went to a silent, curious Allison. "You don't understand, do you, cupcake?" he asked with a smile that was mocking and cruel. "I had a different father than Dwight and Marie. I was adopted. Something my mother and stepfather apparently didn't think I needed to know until my stepfather died six months ago."

She watched him get up, and her eyes were

soft and compassionate as they searched his. "I'm sorry," she said gently. "It must have been very hard to find it out so suddenly."

He hated that softness in her eyes, that warmth. He didn't want compassion from her. The only thing he might ever want from her was that silky body, but this was hardly the time to be thinking about it. He glared at her. "I don't want pity, thanks."

"Gene, for God's sake," Dwight ground out.

"Don't worry. I won't spoil your party." He caught a strand of Allison's dark hair and tugged it. "Stay away from me. I'm bad medicine. Ask anybody."

He grabbed his beer and walked away without another word.

Allison's eyes followed him, and she almost felt his pain. Poor, tormented man....

"Don't make the mistake of feeling sorry for him," Dwight told her when Gene was out of earshot. "Pity is the last thing he wants or needs. He has to come to grips with it himself."

"Where is his real father?" Allison asked quietly.

He started to speak, but before he could, a smaller, female version of Dwight slammed down into a chair beside Winnie.

"So he's gone," Marie Nelson muttered. "Dwight, he's just impossible. I can't even talk to him…." She colored, looking at Allison. "Sorry," she said. "You must be Allison. Winnie's been hiding you for days, I thought she'd never introduce us!" she said with a smile. "I didn't mean to start airing the family linen in public. You'll have to excuse me. Gene always sets me off."

"What's he done now?" Dwight groaned.

"He seduced my best friend," she muttered.

"Dale Branigan is not your best friend," Dwight reminded her. "She's a divorcée with claws two inches long, and if anybody got seduced it was Gene, not her. It's not his fault that she won't realize it was a one-shot fling for him."

"I don't mean Dale," she sighed. "I meant Jessie."

"Gene's never been near Jessie," Dwight said shortly.

"She says he has. She says—"

"Marie," he said, calling her by name for the first time and confirming Allison's suspicions, "Jessie couldn't tell the truth if her life depended on it. She's been crazy about Gene for years and it's gotten her nowhere. This is just a last-ditch effort to get him to marry her. I'm telling you, it won't work. She can't blackmail him to the altar."

"She might not be lying," Marie said, although not with as much conviction as before. "You know how Gene is with women."

"I don't think you do," Dwight said. "Jessie isn't even his type. He likes sophisticated, worldly women."

Marie leaned back in her chair with a sigh. "Poor Jessie."

"Poor Jessie," Dwight agreed. "Now say hello to Winnie."

"Hi, Winnie," Marie greeted belatedly, and smiled. "It's nice to see you again. And I'm glad Allison could come," she added, smiling. She didn't add what Dwight had said about the effect she had on Gene. Now that she'd seen it for herself, she was intrigued. There was indeed something very special about Miss Hathoway, and apparently Gene had noticed it.

"Thank you for inviting me," Allison replied sincerely. "I wouldn't want to impose."

"You aren't. How do you like Wyoming?"

"Very much. It's beautiful."

"We think so." Marie studied her curiously. "Winnie's very secretive about you. You aren't a fugitive Hell's Angel or anything, are you?" she teased, trying not to give away what Dwight had told her about the other woman.

"I don't think so," Allison said, leaning forward to add, "but what if I have memory failure and I've got a motorcycle stashed somewhere?"

"As long as it's a Harley-Davidson, it's okay." Marie grinned. "I've always wanted to ride one."

"Horses, okay. Motorcycles, never." Her brother grinned. "She's a former rodeo champion, or did I mention it?" he added.

"Are you, really?" Allison asked, all eyes.

"Gene, too," Marie said, sighing. "He was world champion roper one year, before he hurt his hand. He doesn't compete anymore. He's bitter about so many things. I wish he could stop blaming Dwight and me. We love him, you know. But he won't believe any of us do."

"Maybe he'll come around someday. It's a blessing that he has so much to do that he doesn't have time to brood," Dwight added. "We supply broncs and bulls for rodeos," he told Allison. "It's a full-time job, especially since we're always shipping or receiving livestock. The paperwork alone is a nightmare."

"It sounds complicated. And dangerous," she added, thinking about the wildness of the animals involved. She wasn't a rodeo fan, but she'd seen the kind of animals cowboys had to ride in competition when she and Winnie had lived in Arizona.

"Working around livestock is always dangerous," Dwight agreed. "But it goes with the territory."

"And we have a good safety record," Marie chimed in. "Have you ever seen a real rodeo, Allison?"

"Yes," Allison nodded. "Once, when Winnie and I were little."

"I remember the candy better than I remember the rodeo," Winnie laughed. "I imagine Allie does, too."

"I'm afraid you're right," Allison agreed.

"We'll make a fan of you, if you stay here long enough," Dwight promised. "How about some music, Marie? We might as well drag the band out of the barbecue and make them work."

"I'll get them started."

The dancing was fun, but by the time Allison and Winnie went home, Gene Nelson hadn't made another appearance and Allison was disappointed. She was fascinated by him, despite what she'd heard about his reputation. He liked sophisticated women, and tonight she'd pretended to be one. But he'd walked away and left her. She sighed miserably. Even when she was pretending to be a siren, she was still just plain old Allison, she thought dully. It was too much to hope for, that a man like Gene would give her a second glance.

With determination, she smiled and danced and socialized. But her heart wasn't in it. Without the elusive Mr. Nelson, everything had gone flat.

The elusive Mr. Nelson was, in fact, feeling the same way. He'd had to force himself to leave the barbecue, because he'd wanted to dance with Allison. But getting involved with her would only create more problems and he'd had enough. He thought about going into town to the bar, but that felt flat, too. He was losing his taste for liquor and wild women. Maybe he'd caught a virus or something.

He strolled past the bunkhouse, hearing loud laughter, led by the redheaded Rance. It was Saturday night, and he couldn't forbid the men liquor on their own time. But one of these days, he was going to have to confront that venomous rider. He'd been needling Gene for days. The man was sweet on Dale Branigan, and fiercely jealous of Gene. He could have told him there was no need, but it wouldn't have done any good.

He kept walking, his mind still on the way Allison had looked in that sundress. He paused to check two of the sick calves in the barn, marveling at how much he'd changed in just one day and one night. Maybe it was his age, he thought. Then a picture of Allison Hathoway's soft hazel eyes burned into his brain and he groaned. With a muttered curse, he saddled a horse and went out to check on the night herders—something he hadn't done in months.

Chapter Three

Allison wasn't comfortable talking to Winnie about Gene Nelson, but she was too curious about him not to ask questions. He'd warned her away himself, telling her that he was bad medicine. But she was attracted despite the warnings. Secretly she wondered if it could be because of them. She'd led a conventional life all the way, never putting a step wrong. A renegade was bound to appeal to her.

"You can't get involved with him," Winnie said quietly when Allison couldn't resist questioning her the next day.

"He didn't seem like a bad man," Allison protested.

"I didn't say he was," Winnie replied, and her expression was sympathetic. "In fact, there isn't a nicer man than Gene. But he's gone wild since he found out about his father. You heard what Marie accused him of yesterday. She wasn't kidding. Gene makes no secret that he has only one use for a woman, and he's done a lot of hard drinking and hard living in the past few months. Because everybody around Pryor knows it, just being seen with him could ruin your reputation. That's why I don't want you to go out with him. I'd never begrudge you a little happiness, but Gene could cost you your respectability. And that's something you can't afford to lose, my friend, in your chosen vocation."

"Yes, I know," Allison murmured. Her heart sank. Winnie was drowning all her dreams. "You said that Gene didn't know about his real father?"

"No. He was just four when his mother divorced his father and married Hank Nelson," Winnie said, startling her. "Until six months ago, when his stepfather died, he never knew that he wasn't a blood Nelson."

Allison's tender heart ached for him. "Poor

man," she said huskily. "How terrible, to find out like that!"

"It's been terrible for all of them," Winnie said honestly. "Don't get me wrong. Dwight and Marie don't feel any differently now than they ever did about Gene, but it's changed everything for him. He worshiped Hank."

"No wonder he's embittered," Allison said softly.

"None of that," Winnie murmured dryly. "Your soft heart will be your undoing yet. Now let's talk about something besides Gene. I don't think he's got a soft spot anymore, but he could hurt you if you tried to find it, even for the best of reasons."

"Yes, I know," Allison replied. "I sensed that, too. But you don't need to worry," she added with a sad smile. "I'm not the type of woman who could appeal to a man like him. He's very handsome and suave. I'm just…me."

"You weren't yourself at the barbecue," her friend murmured tongue in cheek. "You were light and flirtatious and carefree. Gene has no idea who and what you really are, and that kind of secret is dangerous to keep."

"Any kind of secret is dangerous to keep," she replied with a gentle smile.

"Amen. Just trust me and keep your distance."

She patted Allison's hand gently. "Don't underestimate your own attractions, my friend. You're a knockout when you dress up, and that warm heart of yours attracts everyone, including men like Gene."

"It never has before," Allison sighed. "Well, not the right kind of men, anyway."

"One of these days the right man is going to come along. If anybody deserves him, you do."

Allison smiled. "Thanks. I could return the compliment. I like your Dwight very much."

"So do I."

"Will you live with his family when you marry?"

"No," Winnie returned, grateful for the change of subject. "There's another house on the ranch, where Dwight's grandfather used to live. It's being remodeled, and we'll live there. I'll take you to see it one day, if you like."

"I would."

Winnie smiled. "You're so much better than you were when you first came here," she said gently. "Is it easing off a little?"

Allison nodded. "Every day, thanks to you and your mother."

"That's what we both hoped. Dad will be home soon, and then we can do some sightseeing. You know I'm hopeless at finding things, and mother hates to drive distances. There's a lot of history around here."

"I know. I read all the books I could find about northern Wyoming before I ever dreamed I might actually come here." She lowered her eyes. "I had hoped it would be for a happier reason, though."

"So did I." Winnie sipped coffee. "What do you want to see?"

"The nightly rodeo in Cody," came the immediate reply. "Not to mention the historical center there. And there's a place called Shoshone Canyon just outside it, on the way to Yellowstone…"

"Shoshone Canyon gives me the cold willies," Winnie said, shivering. "It's eerie, especially when you have to come across the dam to Cody, through the mountain tunnel. I only have to go that way when we're coming back from Yellowstone National Park, thank God. Cody is northwest of here, so we can avoid the canyon altogether."

"You chicken, you," Allison gasped. "I'd love it!"

"I imagine you would. Well, we'll go when Dad gets back, but I'll wear a blindfold."

"I'll make sure you have one," Allison laughed.

There was no more mention of Gene Nelson, even if he did seem to haunt Allison's dreams.

Then, all at once, she seemed to run into him everywhere. She waved to him in town as he drove by in his big Jeep, and he waved back with a smile. She saw him on his horse occasionally as she drove past the ranch with Winnie, and he seemed to watch for her. When she and Winnie visited Dwight, he sometimes paused in the doorway to talk, and his green eyes ran over her with frank curiosity as he joined in the conversation. It always seemed to be about cattle or horses or rodeo, and Allison never understood it, but then it didn't matter. She just loved looking at Gene.

He noticed that rapt stare of hers and was amused by it. Women had always chased him, but there was something different about this one. She was interested in him, but too shy to flirt or play up to him. Ironically that interested him more than a blatant invitation would have.

He began to look for her after that, despite his misgivings about getting involved. She stirred something inside him that he didn't even know he possessed. It was irritating, but he felt as if he'd been caught in an avalanche, and he couldn't stop it.

A few days after the barbecue he noticed Winnie's car going past the ranch, with a passenger, on the way in to Pryor. And he'd found an excuse to go into town himself. To get a new rope, he said. The ranch had enough ropes to furnish Pancho Villa's army already, but it was an excuse if he really needed one to appease his conscience.

That was how Allison came upon him, seemingly accidentally, in Pryor that afternoon while she was picking up some crocheting thread for Mrs. Manley and Winnie was having a fitting for her wedding gown.

He was coming out of the feed store with what looked like a new rope in one lean hand. He'd been working. He was wearing stained jeans with muddy boots and dusty bat-wing chaps. A worn and battered tan Stetson was cocked over one pale green eye, and he needed another shave, even though it was midafternoon. He looked totally out of sorts.

In fact, he was, and Allison was the reason for his bad humor. All the reasons why he should snub her came falling into his brain. It didn't do any good, of course, to tell himself that she was the last complication he needed right now. Miss Chic Society there wasn't cut out for ranch life or anything more than a wild fling, and he was beginning to feel his age. Instead of running around with wild women, he needed to be thinking about a wife and kids. Except that kids might be out of the question, considering the character of his real father. His expression hardened. Besides that, considering his reputation with women, it was going to be hard to find a decent woman who'd be willing to marry him. This wouldn't be a bad time to work on improving his image, and he couldn't do that by linking himself with another sophisticated party girl. Which Miss Hathoway seemed to be, given her performance at the barbecue.

Of course, it wasn't that easy to put the brakes on his interest. Now here she stood, looking at him with those big hazel eyes and making his body ache. And he'd initiated the confrontation.

"Hello, Mr. Nelson," she said, smiling at him. "Out looking for a lost cow?" she added, nodding toward the rope in his hand.

His eyebrows arched. "I came in to buy some new rope, Miss Hathoway." He was irritated at having told a blatant lie.

"Oh." She stared at it. "Can you spin a loop and jump through it?"

He glared at her. "This," he said, hefting it irritably, "is nylon rope. It isn't worth a damn until you tie it between the back bumper of a truck and a fence-post and stretch it."

"You're kidding," she said.

"I am not." He moved closer, looking down at

her. She was at least average height, but he still had to look down. She seemed very fragile somehow. Perhaps her lifestyle made her brittle.

He searched her soft eyes. "Did you drive in?" he asked so that she wouldn't know he'd followed her to town.

"Yes. With Winnie," she said. "She's trying on her wedding gown."

His thick eyebrow jerked. "The wedding will be Pryor's social event of the season," he said with faint sarcasm. The thought of the wedding stung him. Dwight was a Nelson, truly his father's son. Dwight had inherited the lion's share of the business, even though Gene couldn't complain about his own inheritance. It was just that he'd been the eldest son all his life. He'd belonged. Now he didn't. Dwight and Winnie's wedding was a potent, stinging reminder of that.

"It hurts you, doesn't it?"

The gentle question brought a silent gasp from his lips. He stared down at her, caught completely off guard by her unexpected remark. The compassion in those eyes was like a body blow. She almost seemed to glow with it. He couldn't have imagined anyone looking at him like that a week ago, and he wasn't sure he liked it even now.

"Haven't you got someplace to go, Miss Hathoway?" he asked irritably.

"I suppose that means you wish I did. Why are you wearing bat-wing chaps in the northwest?" she asked pleasantly. "And Mexican rowels?"

His eyes widened. "I used to work down in Texas," he said hesitantly. "What do you know about chaps?"

"Lots." She grinned. "I grew up reading Zane Grey."

"No better teacher, except Louis L'Amour," he murmured. His pale eyes slid down her body. She was wearing jeans and a white shirt, short sleeved, because it was June and warm.

"No hat," he observed, narrow-eyed. "You know better, or you should, having lived in Arizona. June is a hot month, even here."

She grimaced. "Yes, but I hate hats. It isn't usually this warm, surely, this far north?"

Those hazel eyes were casting spells. He had to drag his away. "We get hot summers. Winters are the problem," he said, nodding toward the distant peaks, snow covered even in the summer. "We get three and four feet of snow at a time. Trying to find calving cows in that can be a headache."

"I expect so." Her eyes went to his thin mouth. "But isn't summer a busier time?"

He looked down at her. "Not as much so as April and September. That's when we round up cattle."

"I guess that keeps you busy," she said softly.

"No more than anything else does," he said shortly. He had to get away from her. She disturbed him. "I've got to go."

"That's it, reject me," she said with a theatrical sigh, hiding her shyness in humor. "Push me aside—I can take it."

He smiled without meaning to. "Can you?" he murmured absently.

"Probably not," she confessed dryly. She searched his eyes. "Winnie warned me to stay away from you. She says you're a womanizer."

He stared down at her. "So? She's right," he said without pulling his punches. "I've never made any secret of it." His eyes narrowed on her face. "Did you expect a different answer?"

She shook her head. "I'm glad I didn't get one. I don't mind the truth."

"Neither do I, but we're pretty much in the minority. I find that most people prefer lies, however blatant."

She felt momentarily guilty, because she was trying to behave like someone she wasn't. But she knew that her real self wasn't likely to appeal to him. She couldn't help herself.

Gene saw that expression come and go on her face and was puzzled by it. He glanced past her, watching Winnie in the doorway of a shop, talking to another woman.

"You'd better go," he said abruptly. "Your watchdog's about to spot you talking to me." He smiled with pure sarcasm. "She'll give you hell all day if she sees us together."

"Would you mind?" she asked.

He nodded. "For Dwight's sake, yes, I would. I don't want to alienate Winnie before the wedding." He laughed curtly. "Plenty of time for that afterward."

"You aren't half as bad as you pretend to be," she remarked.

He sobered instantly. "Don't you believe it, cupcake," he replied. "You'd better go."

"All right." She sighed, clutching the bag of thread against her breasts. "See you."

"Sure." He walked past her to his black Jeep and he didn't allow himself to look back. Pursuing her had been a big mistake. She was Winnie's best friend, and Winnie was obviously determined not to let her become one of his casual interludes. He had to keep his head. He had more than enough problems already, and alienating his future sister-in-law wasn't going to solve any of them. That being the case, it might be wise, he told himself sarcastically, if he stopped following her around!

Allison was calm by the time Winnie finally joined her. "My dress is coming along beautifully," she said. "Did I see you talking to someone?"

"Just passing conversation. I got your mother's thread," Allison said, evading the curious question gracefully. By the time they got back to the car, Winnie had forgotten all about it.

But Allison couldn't forget about Gene. When she was invited, along with Winnie, to supper at the Nelson home two days later, it was almost as if Fate was working in her favor.

She wore a plain gray dress with a high neckline and straight skirt, gently gathered at the waist with a belt. It wasn't a sexy dress, but when she wore it, it became one. She did her hair in a neat French plait and put on makeup as Winnie had taught her. When she finished, she looked much less sophisticated than she had at the barbecue—a puzzling outcome.

"I don't look the way I did before," she told Winnie after they'd said good-night to Mrs. Manley and were on the way to the Nelsons'.

"You look great," Winnie corrected. "And tonight, will you please be yourself?"

"Why? Are you hoping that Gene Nelson might keep his distance if he sees what a frump I really am?" she murmured dryly.

"He seems to be doing that all by himself," Winnie reminded her. "I'm not trying to be difficult, honestly I'm not." She sighed worriedly. "I just don't want to see you hurt. Gene…isn't himself these days."

"What was he like before?" Allison asked softly.

Winnie laughed. "Full of fun. He always had his eye on the ladies, but he was less blatant with it. Now, he's reckless and apparently without conscience when it comes to women. He doesn't really care whom he hurts."

"I don't think he'd hurt me, though, Winnie," she said.

"Don't bet on it," the other woman replied. "You put too much faith in people's better instincts. Some people don't have any."

"I'll never believe that," Allison said firmly. "Not after what I've seen. Beauty often hides in the most horrible places."

Winnie's eyes were gentle as they glanced toward her friend. She didn't know what to say to Allison. Probably nothing would do much good.

She'd just have to hope that Gene was out, or that, if he was home, he wasn't interested in Allison.

It was late afternoon, and still light. A gentle flutter of rain greeted them as they arrived in front of the Nelson house and darted up the steps to the front door.

"You're early," Marie stammered, flustered and wild-eyed when she opened the door for them. She swept back her blond hair. "Oh, gosh, do either of you know anything about first aid? Dwight had to run to town for some wine, and Gene's ripped open his arm. I'm just hopeless…!"

"Where is he?" Allison asked, her voice cool and professional-sounding. "I know what to do."

"Thank God!" Marie motioned them along behind her, down the long hall toward the bedrooms.

"I think I'll wait in the living room, if you don't mind." Winnie hesitated, grimacing. "I'm as hopeless as Marie is."

"You won't be alone long," Marie promised her. "I can't stand the sight of blood, either! He's in there, Allison," she added, nodding toward an open bedroom door. "You can hear him from out in the hall."

"I'll look after him," Allison assured her, leaving Marie to keep Winnie company while she ventured into the room.

Muttered curses were coming from the bathroom. Allison moved hesitantly past the antique furniture in the cream and brown confines of the room, certain that it was Gene's. The bed was king-size. There was a desk and chair in one corner and two chairs and a floor lamp in the other, beside a fireplace. The earth tones and Native American accent pieces suited what she knew of Gene Nelson.

But she didn't have time to study his taste in furnishings. She pushed open the bathroom door, which was already ajar, and walked in. The bathroom, like the bedroom, was done in beige and brown with a tile floor and a huge glass-fronted shower with gold fittings. There was a Jacuzzi, too. But it was the vanity sink that caught her eye. Gene was standing in front of it, in clothes similar to those he'd been wearing in town. His shirt was off and one brown, hair-roughened forearm was cut from elbow to wrist and dripping bright red blood into the marble sink.

"That needs stitching," she said.

He turned, his green eyes darker with pain, his lean face hard and without a smile. "What the hell do you want?" he asked, irritated because he'd been thinking of her when he'd gone too close to one of his few horned cows and had his arm ripped for his pains.

"A Ferrari and a house on the Riviera," she said. She moved close, trying not to stare blatantly at the broad, bronzed chest with its thick wedge of hair that ran down his flat stomach and under the heavy brass belt buckle that secured his jeans. He was beautifully male, so striking that she had to drag her eyes away.

"You know what I mean," he returned shortly.

"Marie and your future sister-in-law are squeamish. I'm not. Let me see, please." She scanned the things he'd dragged out of the medicine cabinet and proceeded to gently bathe the long gash with soap and water before she used a strong disinfectant and then an antibiotic cream. "I guess you'll scream if I suggest the local hospital emergency room?" she asked as she worked.

He stared down at her bent dark head with mingled emotions. He'd hoped to be gone before she and Winnie arrived, but he hadn't counted on letting his mind wander and getting himself gored. "I've had worse than this," he replied.

She looked up into his searching eyes, trying to ignore the beat of her pulse and the difficulty she was having with getting her breath. She was too involved with hiding her own reactions to notice his racing pulse and quick breathing. "At least it's stopped bleeding. I don't suppose you have any butterfly bandages?"

"What?" he murmured, lost in her eyes.

"B…butterfly bandages," she stammered. She dragged her eyes down to his forearm. "Never mind. I'll make do with these."

Her hands felt cool on his hot skin. He watched her work, marveling at the ease and confidence with which she put the dressing in place.

"You've done this before, haven't you?" he asked.

"Oh, yes," she said, smiling reminiscently. "Many times. I'm used to patching up people." She didn't add anything to that. It was too soon to talk about her past yet.

"You're good at it. That feels better."

"How did it happen?"

He chuckled softly. "I zigged when I should have zagged, cupcake. Now that you've gotten that one under control, care to have a go at this one?"

She put the last piece of adhesive in place and lifted her eyes. "Which one?" she asked.

He pointed to a smaller gash on his chest that was still bleeding.

"I guess your shirt was a total loss," she murmured dryly, trying to stop the trembling of her hands as she began to bathe the scratch. His chest was warm under her fingers, and she loved the feel of that thick hair as she worked through it to the cut. Her lips parted on quick, jerky breaths. He was hurt. She had to keep that in mind, and not let herself lose control like this.

"My shirt and the denim jacket I was wearing over it," he murmured. The feel of her hands on him was giving him problems. His body began to tense slowly as he watched her clean the cut. "If you try to put a bandage on that, I'm leaving," he added when she'd stopped the bleeding.

"I…I guess adhesive tape would hurt when it had to come off, with all that…hair," she faltered, her eyes helplessly tracing the muscular lines of his torso with involuntary delight.

The way she said it was faintly arousing. He ran a hand over the thick mass of it, nodding absently. "Just put some antiseptic on it, honey, and we'll let it go, okay?"

"Okay." *Honey.* No man had ever called her that in such a deep, sexy way, so that her toes curled inside her shoes. She took the antibiotic cream and put a little on her fingers. But when she began to rub it gently over the cut, he flinched and her fingers paused on his body.

"Did it hurt?" she whispered, puzzled by the heavy beat of his heart under her hand and by the sudden fierce glitter of his eyes.

"Not the way you mean," he said curtly. He felt hot all over, and when she lifted her face, he could see the same awareness there. He couldn't let this happen, he told himself firmly. He had to stop it now.

But she smelled of flowers, and he loved the touch of those gentle hands on his bare skin. Involuntarily he traced her long, elegant fingers, simultaneously pressing them deeper into the hair on his chest so that they caressed the hard muscle. His eyes lifted to hers, holding them in a silence that was suddenly tense and hot with promise.

She looked younger tonight, in that gray dress with her hair in a braid at her back. Despite the makeup she'd used, she looked country fresh. He liked her better this way than in that sexy dress she'd worn at the barbecue. He almost said so, but he managed to bite back the comment in time.

"It's…stopped bleeding," she whispered. But she was looking into his eyes, not at the cut.

"So it has," he replied.

The hand that was caressing the back of hers moved her fingers slowly over a taut, flat male nipple, letting her feel the effect her touch was having on him. He pressed it close and hard, his whole hand covering hers as the silence continued.

She smelled leather and a faint breath of hay on him, pleasant scents that mingled with the aftershave he wore. Her heart was beating madly, and under her fingers she could feel the fierce pulsation of his own.

"Gene," she whispered unsteadily.

The sound of his name on her lips was his undoing. He couldn't help himself. He bent slowly, his eyes on her soft mouth, no other thought in his mind except possession.

His hands moved up to frame her face, warm and strong on her cheeks as he tilted her head to give him total access to her parted lips.

She didn't make even a pretense of resisting. Her hands rested lightly, with fascination, on the hard, warm contours of his chest, spearing into the thick mat of hair that covered it. She could taste his breath, warm on her mouth, and she wanted him to kiss her with an almost feverish desperation. There had never been a man she'd felt this kind of attraction to. Just once she wanted to taste him. Just…once…

Her eyes closed. She stood on her tiptoes to coax his mouth the rest of the way while the world vanished around her. She heard the sharp intake of his breath and felt his hands contract and his mouth almost touched hers.

And just then a sharp, feminine voice broke into the tense silence with all the subtlety of an explosion.

Chapter Four

"Allison, is he all right?"

Winnie's voice hit Gene with the impact of a sledgehammer. He jerked back from Allison even as his hard mouth touched hers, his face going as rigid as the arousal he barely kept her from feeling.

He whirled away, grabbing his shirt and jacket. "Yes, he's all right," he called, irritated. He didn't know which bothered him the most—the interruption or his weakness.

"Oh. Sorry!" Winnie stammered.

There were fading footsteps. "My God, does she think I'm in any condition to ravish you?" he asked angrily, running a restless hand through his thick, straight hair.

Allison was still getting her breath back. She leaned against the vanity sink, her trembling hands behind her. "You don't understand," she said softly, wondering if she could find the right words to explain Winnie's protectiveness.

He turned, glancing at her irritably until his searching gaze fell to the taut nipples pressing against the soft fabric of her dress. His breath sighed out heavily. "Are you what you seem to be, Allison?" he asked unexpectedly, resignation in his tone. His eyes lifted back to capture hers. "Are you modern and sophisticated?"

"Why do you want to know?" She sidestepped the question.

His eyes narrowed and stabbed into hers. "Because there's no way on earth I'm getting involved with you if you aren't."

Her heart ran wild. "Do you want to get involved with me?" she asked huskily.

"My God, can't you tell?" he demanded. His chest rose and fell roughly. "I've barely touched you, and I'm on fire!"

That made two of them, but she didn't imagine he could tell how she felt. She wanted to get close to him. If she told him the truth, he wouldn't come near her. If she kept her secret, there was a slight chance that he might drop his guard, that she might get to see the real man, the hurting one. As for anything more, perhaps they could agree to some ground rules that would protect her until she could tell him the truth.

"I'm not modern enough to jump into bed with any man who asks," she said simply, and met his eyes bravely. "I like to know what I'm getting into first."

His chin lifted with faint arrogance. "You're cautious, then. So am I. I won't rush you. But I don't want a platonic relationship."

"Neither do I," she said, but with her eyes averted.

He hesitated. Something didn't ring true about what she was saying, but he couldn't quite put his finger on it. He wondered if this wasn't lunacy. A woman was the last complication he needed right now, and he hadn't forgotten that her best friend was marrying his brother. There were at least ten good reasons for keeping his distance, but none of them mattered when he was around Allison. He seemed to have been alone for a very long time. When he was with her, the aching loneliness vanished.

"Suppose we go to a movie tomorrow night?" he asked.

"Winnie won't like it."

"I'm not asking Winnie," he replied easily. "Or anyone else. Just you and me."

"Could we go to Cody? Isn't there a rodeo there every night?"

He smiled slowly. "Every night during the summer," he corrected. "We'll save that for another time. But we can detour through Cody, if you like. The nearest movie house is in Billings."

"Montana?" she exclaimed. "But that's over a hundred miles away!"

"No distance at all out here, cupcake."

"I suppose not. It's like that in Arizona, too, but I'd forgotten." She stared at him quietly, her heart still beating wildly. "I guess you supply animals to the rodeo in Cody, too?"

He nodded. "That one and any number of others." He studied her for a long moment. "You'd better get out of here. I need a shower before we eat."

"All right."

"Unless you'd like to stay and scrub my back?" he mused, a wicked gleam in his eyes.

"It's much too early for that sort of thing," she

told him and left with a demure glance from under her lashes.

He was smiling when she left the room, but she wasn't. She wondered what she was letting herself in for, and how she thought she was going to keep a man like that at bay. If he really was the womanizer everyone said he was, she'd be in over her head in no time.

"He's as good as new," Allison assured the two women when she joined them in the living room. "Almost, anyway. The cut on his arm really needed stitching, but he won't go to a doctor."

"That's Gene," Marie said wearily. "It's been so hard for him. I wish Dad had never left that letter. It would have been so much kinder not to have told him after such a long time. Let's go on into the dining room. Gene won't be long, I'm sure, and we can drink coffee while we talk."

She led them into the dining room, where a cherry table was set under an elegant crystal chandelier. The floor was oak, highly polished, and the walls were wood paneled. It was the most elegant room Allison had seen in years. They sat down and busied themselves with coffee for several minutes before Allison finally voiced the question that had been nagging her.

"Why did your father leave a note for Gene?" she asked curiously.

Marie shook her head. "Nobody knows. Dad was honest to a fault, and he was a deep thinker. Maybe he thought Gene had the right to know. His real father is still alive, even if Gene would rather die than go to see him. Heritage, health, so many things depend on knowing who your real parents are. I think that he planned to tell Gene before he died. That would have been Dad's way. He certainly wouldn't have wanted him to find out the way he did. It's hurt Gene so badly."

"I suppose it's been difficult for you and Dwight, too," Allison said gently.

"You can't imagine. We don't care who Gene's real dad is. Gene is our brother and we love him. But he can't accept that," Marie said. "He's still trying to come to grips with it. I wonder sometimes if he ever will. Meanwhile, he's just hell to live with."

"Is he staying for supper?" Winnie asked with a worried glance at Allison.

"Yes," Allison said. "At least he said he was."

"Don't look so worried," Marie told Winnie, grinning at her expression. "He'll be nice because Allison's here. I think he likes her."

"God forbid!" Winnie said. "You know how he is with women!"

"He won't hurt Allison," Marie said. "Don't be such a worrywart."

"I hope you're right. Anyway," Winnie sighed, "he's involved with Dale, isn't he?"

"No, he isn't," Gene said from the doorway. He lifted an eyebrow at Winnie's shocked face as he joined them, freshly showered and shaved, dressed in a white shirt and dark slacks. He looked wickedly handsome, and Allison's heart raced at the sight of him.

"Sorry," Winnie began.

Gene lifted a careless hand, stopping her before she got started. "I'm not going to gobble up your houseguest," he said quietly. "But she'll be safer with me than some of the other yahoos around here, especially at night," he added with a meaningful stare. "I'll take care of her."

"Okay. I suppose you're right." Winnie sighed softly. "It's just that…" She glanced toward Allison, grimacing. "Well…"

"She's your best friend," Gene finished for her with a faint smile. "No problem. I won't hurt her, Winnie."

"Will you stop?" Allison asked Winnie on an exasperated laugh. "I'm twenty-five."

"Yes, but..."

"What are we having for dinner?" Allison interrupted, arching her eyebrows at an amused Marie.

"Duck," Marie returned. "And if I don't take the orange sauce out of the microwave, we'll be having it without sauce! Excuse me."

Before Winnie could say anything else to Gene and Allison, Dwight was back with the wine. But all through dinner, Gene's eyes kept darting to Allison's, as hers did to him. Whatever there was between them, it was explosive and mutual. She hoped she wouldn't have cause to regret giving it a chance.

Over dinner, she learned that Gene was a wizard with figures and that his taste in books ran to mysteries and biographies, while he took a conservative stand on politics and a radical one on ecology. She discovered that he enjoyed a lot of the same things she did, like winter sports and the Winter Olympics, not to mention science fiction movies. He was droll and faintly sarcastic, but underneath there had to be a sensitive caring man. Allison wanted to flush him out.

He pulled her aside while Winnie was saying good-night to Dwight and Marie.

"I'll pick you up at five tomorrow afternoon,"

he said. "We'll need to get an early start. It's a long drive."

"You're sure you want to?"

"No," he said curtly, and meant it. He'd never wanted involvement with her, but things seemed to be out of his hands for once. Out of control, like his life. He shifted his stance, putting the past away from him. "We'll have dinner in Billings," he continued, searching her eyes slowly, "before the movie starts. There's a nice restaurant in one of the hotels."

"Okay." She smiled shyly. "I'll look forward to it."

He only nodded. He didn't want to admit how easily he could echo that sentiment. In the past, being a loner had had distinct advantages. He didn't want to have to account for his time or have restraints put on his freedom. Dale had tried that tack, and Jessie, God bless her, was as thick as a plank. One smile and Jessie was hearing wedding bells.

Allison's soft voice caught his attention again and he glanced to where she and Winnie were laughing with Marie over some television program they'd apparently all seen as they said good-night at the front door.

He waved in their general direction and went

up to his room. He wondered if Winnie was going to talk Allison out of tomorrow's date. If she did, it might be the best thing for both of them, he decided.

But Winnie didn't manage that, despite the fact that she coaxed and pleaded all the way home that night.

"Your reputation…!" she concluded finally, using one last desperate argument.

"It will survive one or two dates," Allison said firmly. "Oh, Winnie, he's so alone! Can't you see it? Can't you see the pain in his eyes, the emptiness?"

Winnie pulled up in front of her house, turned off the engine and the lights with a long sigh. "No. I don't suppose I'm blessed with your particular kind of empathy. But you don't know what it's like with an experienced man. You've hardly even dated, and Gene has been around. If you drop your guard for a minute, he'll seduce you, you crazy little trusting idiot!"

"It takes two," Allison reminded her.

"Yes, and I can see sparks flying between the two of you the minute you're together! Allie, it's an explosive chemistry and you don't have the faintest idea how helpless you'd be if he turned up the heat!"

"Aren't you forgetting how my parents brought me up?" Allison asked gently.

"No, I'm not," Winnie replied tersely. "But I'm telling you that ideals and principles have a breaking point. Sexual attraction is physical, and the mind doesn't have a lot of control over it."

"I can say no," Allison replied. "Now let's go and watch some television. Okay?"

Winnie started to speak, but she realized it was going to be futile. It was like trying to explain surfing to an Eskimo. She could only hope that Allie's resolve was equal to Gene Nelson's ardor when it was put to the test.

Gene pulled up in the yard at exactly five o'clock the next afternoon. He was wearing gray slacks with a Western shirt and a bola tie, a matching gray Stetson atop his head and hand-tooled gray boots on his feet. He looked elegant, and Allison's heart skipped when he came in the front door behind Winnie.

She looked good, he mused. She had on a pretty lilac vintage shirtwaist dress with a flowery scarf, and her hair was loose, hanging down her back like a wavy dark curtain almost to her waist. The dress clung gently to her slender body in just the right places, enhancing her firm, high breasts and narrow waist. She had it buttoned up right to her throat, but it only made the fit more sexy to Gene, who assumed that the prim fashion statement was a calculated one. He smiled gently, liking her subtle gesture.

Allison, unaware of his thoughts, smiled back. "Is this dressy enough, or should I wear something else?" she asked. "I'm not used to fancy restaurants."

"You look fine," Gene assured her.

"Indeed you do. Have fun," Winnie said gently. She glanced at Gene. "Take care of her," she said worriedly.

"No sweat." He linked Allison's soft hand in his and led her out the door, leaving an unconvinced Winnie behind.

"Why is she so protective of you?" Gene asked when they were out on the main highway in his sleek black Jeep.

Allison studied him from the comparative safety of her deep bucket seat. "She thinks you're too experienced for me."

He raised an eloquent eyebrow. "Am I, cupcake?" he asked with cynical mockery.

She laughed softly. "Probably. But you don't scare me."

"Give me time." He draped his hand over the

wheel casually. "You haven't asked which movie I'm taking you to."

"No, I haven't. Is it a good one?"

"I don't know. I don't see movies too much these days. This one is supposed to be about the cattle business. But if it follows the trend, it'll be about people taking their clothes off to discuss gene splicing and cloning of pedigree cattle."

She laughed involuntarily at the disgust in his voice. "You don't think much of 'modern' films, I gather?"

"No. Too much skin, not enough substance. Sex," he replied with a glance in her direction, "should not be a spectator sport."

"You're right," she said, averting her eyes to the darkening skyline. She was glad of the dimly lit interior of the Jeep, so that he couldn't see the slight embarrassment the remark caused her.

They drove in silence for a few minutes. He took a detour to let her see a bit more of Wyoming, going north and west several miles out of the way so that she could see one of the area's most fascinating sights.

When he mentioned that they were traveling through Shoshone Canyon, Allison didn't need to be told that, because the eerie sound of the wind and the gnarled outcroppings of rock in their desert colors gave her cold chills. She remembered what Winnie had said about the area, and she almost asked Gene about it, but the tunnel through the mountain came into view ahead and her curiosity vanished in sheer fascination at the engineering job it must have been to put that long tunnel through solid rock.

Once they were through the tunnel, it was just a little way into Cody. Gene pointed out the famous Buffalo Bill Cody museum and the rodeo grounds on the way through the small city, adding that one of the first water systems in the West had been funded by Bill Cody with labour provided by the Mormons.

"Why, this looks like southern Arizona!" Allison exclaimed as she looked out the window when they were driving north out of Cody.

"Yes, it does," he said. "But when we go through the Pryor Mountains and head into Montana you'll see the difference in the terrain. Wyoming is mostly jagged mountains, and southern Montana is mostly buttes and rolling grassland." He smiled at her. "I love both. I could happily spend the rest of my life in Billings, but I suppose I've gotten too used to Wyoming."

"Where were you born?" she asked.

His face hardened and his lean hands gripped

the wheel convulsively. "My birth certificate says Billings, Montana," he replied tersely. "I suppose that's where my mother and her…husband lived at the time." He didn't add that he'd never had occasion to look at his birth certificate in all those years—even when he'd joined the service, his mother had provided records to the authorities. Why hadn't he ever questioned it? It wasn't until after Hank Nelson died that he'd seen all the paperwork—the birth certificate with the name he was born under and the adoption papers. God, it hurt to realize how easily he'd accepted the lies….

Allison hesitated. She could tell that it was like putting a knife into him to answer the question. But his own avoidance of the subject had surely added to his discomfort.

"You don't like to talk about it, do you?" she asked quietly.

"No," he said honestly.

"When a splinter gets under the skin," she began carefully, "pulling it out at once prevents it from doing too much damage. But when it's left inside, it festers and causes infection."

His eyes sliced through her. "And that's what my past is, do you think? A splinter that's embedded?"

"In a manner of speaking," she replied. Her eyes fell to the firm set of his lips. "I imagine it was the shock of your life to find out who your father was in such a way. But I agree with Marie. I think your stepfather meant to tell you and kept putting it off until it was too late."

His pale green eyes flashed. He didn't like being reminded of it, but what she said made sense. It was just the newness of discussing it, he supposed. He wouldn't let Marie or Dwight talk about it around him. He couldn't really understand why he hadn't already cut Allison dead. He knew instinctively that she was sensitive enough that one hard word would stop her. He just couldn't seem to speak that one hard word. The idea of hurting her didn't appeal to him at all.

They drove into Billings, along the wide streets, and Gene pointed out the landmarks.

"The airport sits on the Rimrocks," he added, nodding toward his left as they turned toward the hotel. "Yellowstone Kelly's buried up there, and the old graveyard is down the hill from the grave."

"I'll bet I could spend a whole day just looking around Billings," she remarked.

"Billings is big, all right," he agreed, his eyes on a traffic light up ahead. "And the surrounding area is full of history."

"Yes, I know," she said excitedly. "The Custer Battlefield is somewhere nearby, isn't it?"

"Over near Hardin," he said. "I'll take you there one day if you like."

Her heart jumped. He made it sound as if they were headed for a real relationship, not just a quick flirtation. She stared at his profile with a feeling of slow warmth building inside her.

"I'd like that very much, Gene," she said softly.

He was grateful that the traffic light changed in time to distract him, because the expression on her face could have hypnotized him. He'd never seen such warmth in a woman's eyes. It drew him like a blazing fire on a snowy night.

"You shouldn't look at me that way when I'm trying to drive," he said curtly.

"I beg your pardon?"

He glanced at her as he pulled into the hotel parking lot, mentally praying for an empty spot. She looked blank, as if the remark didn't register.

"Never mind," he murmured, his keen eyes on the last space, where a car was backing out. "The answer to a prayer," he chuckled.

"The parking spot?"

"You bet," he agreed. "The food here is something special, as you'll see, so it's usually crowded on weekends."

He pulled into the vacated parking spot and parked. The night air was warm and the city smelled of anything but exhaust fumes. Perhaps it was its very spaciousness.

"This doesn't look like Arizona, but it's just as spread out," she remarked, staring around her with interest.

"Most Western cities are," he said. He escorted her into the lobby and then into the elevator. They rode up to the restaurant near the top of the building and were seated by a window overlooking the Yellowstone River and the railroad tracks. A freight train was barreling through the darkness and Allison's eyes followed it wistfully.

"Do you like trains?" he asked, glancing down at the passing train.

"Oh, yes," she said with a sigh. "I used to dream about having an electric train set of my very own, when I was little. But I was taught that there were many things more important than toys."

He smiled gently. "Such as?"

She returned the smile. "A pair of shoes for a neighbor's little girl who didn't have any. Glasses for a seamstress who was the sole support of three children. Insulin for a diabetic who could barely afford to pay rent."

He had to search for words. He hadn't expected that reply. "Taught by whom? Your parents?"

She nodded. She looked down, toying with

her utensils. "They were…very special people." She had to bite down hard to keep the tears back. Nightmare memories flashed through her mind.

Gene didn't miss the sudden look of panic on her face. His lean hand crossed the table and caught hers, enveloping it tightly. "You can tell me about it later," he said quietly.

His compassion startled her. Her lips parted as she met his pale green eyes and searched them, while her fingers curled trustingly into his. "It's still fresh, you see," she whispered huskily.

"You lost them recently?"

She nodded. Words couldn't get past the lump in her throat.

"So that's why you're here," he said, thinking aloud. "And why Winnie's so protective of you."

She didn't disagree. There was so much more to it than that, but she couldn't talk about it just yet. Instead her fingers curled against the firm, comforting strength of his.

"If it helps, I know what you're going through," he said. His voice was as comforting as his clasp. "You'll get past it. Take it one day at a time and give yourself room to grieve. Don't shut it inside."

She took a steadying breath and forced a smile. "Look who's telling whom not to shut it inside," she said, meeting his gaze.

He laughed softly. "Okay. Point taken." The smile faded and he frowned with real concern as he studied her wan face. "Want to give this a miss and go back to Winnie's?"

Her lips parted. "Oh, no, please," she faltered. "I'm okay. It was just…sometimes I think about them and it hurts. I'm sorry. I didn't mean to spoil your evening."

"What makes you think you have?" he asked quietly. "I know how it feels to hurt inside. You don't have to hide it from me."

She took a steadying breath and smiled. "Thank you."

He shrugged. "No sweat. Are you hungry?"

She laughed. "Yes."

"Good. So am I."

Their waitress made an appearance, almost running to keep up with the demands on her, apologetic as she deposited a menu and then took their order. Gene found that Allison shared his taste in food, because she ordered a steak and salad and coffee, just as he had. He grinned.

"Coffee will poison you," he reminded her after the waitress had left it and gone off to the kitchen.

She put cream and sugar into hers. "As long as it doesn't cripple me, I'll be okay," she said. "You're drinking it, too," she pointed out.

"Of course. I didn't say it would poison *me*."

Her face beamed as she studied him. "I noticed."

He grinned at her. "I hope you also noticed that I'm not drinking."

"It's hard to miss," she confided. "You're turning purple."

"I'll survive," he replied.

Just then, the waitress brought their orders and then they were too busy eating to talk. Allison hadn't realized how hungry she was. She ate, but, with every bite, her eyes were helplessly on Gene Nelson's dark face.

Chapter Five

The theater wasn't crowded, so Gene and Allison had a whole row to themselves, away from the few other people in the audience. Gene put his Stetson atop one folded seat and stretched his long legs, crossing one over the other while the previews ran. Allison munched the popcorn he'd bought her and tried to pay attention to the screen.

It had been a long time since she'd seen a movie, because there hadn't even been a television set where she and her parents had spent the past few years. She was behind the times in a lot of ways, and the fact was really brought home to her as the story unfolded. As Gene had predicted, despite the fact that the story was supposed to deal with cattle ranching, most of it seemed to take place in bedrooms. She watched, red-faced, during one particular scene replete with heavy breathing and explicit material.

Gene glanced at her expression with faint curiosity. That wide-eyed gape couldn't be for real. Nobody who had a television set could be shocked these days. Of course, it could be seeing a scene like this with him, a comparative stranger, that made her nervous. She might not be all that experienced, even if she'd been with one or two men. Funny how it disturbed him to think of her being with any man at all except himself.

He reached for her hand and drew it gently into his, resting it on his muscular thigh. She resisted for a few seconds, until the contact began to weaken her and she gave in.

His long fingers played with hers, teasing between them while things heated up on the screen. He lifted them to his lips and began to nibble at her fingertips with slow, sensual intent.

Allison had never been exposed to this kind of thing. She felt his lips against her fingers and almost gasped at the sensations she felt when he nibbled them.

She tried to draw back her hand, but he held it in a firm, gentle grasp. What was happening now on the screen had her rigid with disbelief.

Gene glanced down at Allison, watching her reaction to the screen. Her expression was one of astonished awe, and something scratched at the back of his mind, only to be gone before he could let it in. Her fingers clenched around his unconsciously and he returned the pressure.

"Amazing what they can get away with, isn't it?" he murmured deeply, keeping his voice low. The nearest people were three rows away, so there was little danger of being overheard. His thumb rubbed slowly across her damp palm, pressing the back of her hand into the powerful muscle of his thigh. The sensation rocked him, because it was such an innocent contact. He looked back at the screen, all too aware of her warm touch. His chest rose and fell heavily as he watched the couple on the screen. "Does it embarrass you?" he asked quietly.

"Yes," she moaned, giving in to honesty.

"I thought you said you were a modern girl," he murmured, and he smiled, but it was a kind smile.

"I thought you said sex shouldn't be a spectator sport," she returned.

He chuckled at the riposte. "Touché." The screen suddenly drew their attention as the sounds grew louder and more frantic and finally ended in breathless cries of simulated ecstasy.

Allison was almost trembling by now. Gene felt stirred himself. It had been a while between women. He looked down at Allison with fascination as he felt the shiver go through her. She had to be very sensitive to react so fiercely to a love scene.

His hand absently moved hers up his thigh, until he realized what he was doing and felt the almost frantic restraint of her hand.

"Sorry," he murmured dryly as he released her fingers and watched them retreat to her lap. "I guess it got to me more than I realized."

"They shouldn't show things like that," she faltered, still red-faced and unsteady.

"I couldn't agree more. I didn't realize it would be this explicit." He stood and tugged her along with him, ignoring the curious glances of much younger couples.

"They think we're crazy to leave, don't they?"

she asked as they walked through the lobby to gain the street.

"No doubt. But they're a different generation. Come to think of it," he added as they reached the dark sidewalk, "so are you."

"I'm only nine years younger than you are," she protested.

He smiled down at her, the coolness of the night air calming his heated blood. "Almost a generation, these days," he observed. He slid his hand into hers and clasped it gently, his head lifting as he heard the first strains of Mozart in the distance. "If you don't care for explicit sex, how about soft music and ice cream?"

"Soft music?"

"There's an ice-cream social, complete with orchestra concert, in the park on summer nights," he explained. "Come on. I'll show you."

He helped her into the car and drove down to the enormous city park she'd seen earlier, with its ancient towering cottonwood trees and lush grass. Tables and chairs were set up for visitors, although plenty of the guests were sprawled on blankets or quilts on the dry grass. It was like something out of a fantasy, and Allison was enchanted.

"How delightful!" she exclaimed.

Gene lifted an eyebrow and smiled as he led her from the car into the throng, past where the symphony orchestra played magnificently. This was very much his kind of affair, and it touched him that Allison should find it so enjoyable, which she very obviously did.

"I have to admit that this is much more my scene than risqué movies," he mused. "Doing it is one thing, but watching other people do it—or pretend to—doesn't really appeal to me."

She averted her eyes, clinging to his strong lean hand as he led her to one of the tables where homemade ice cream was being dished up.

"I guess you know enough about it already, if what people say about your reputation is true," she said quietly when they were standing in line.

He turned to look down at her, worldly knowledge in his pale eyes. "Are you fishing for a denial?" he asked in a voice that sent goose bumps down her spine. "What they say about me is true. I've never made any secret of it. I've just been a little less discreet in the past few months."

She felt nervous. He'd never looked more like a predator, and she was feeling more threatened by the minute.

He moved closer to her as the line caught up and

surged forward. His reputation had never bothered him before. It bothered him when Allison looked at him in that threatened way. "What about you?" he asked just above her ear. "You don't talk about your private life very much."

"There's not a lot to tell," she confessed.

His lean hand traced her shoulder lazily, an action calculated to disturb her. It didn't fail. Her breath caught audibly, and he felt a surge of desire for her that made his knees go weak.

"I don't believe that." He caught her waist with both hands and held her lightly in front of him while the queue moved ever closer to the ice cream. "What flavor do you like?"

"Vanilla," she said at once, because whenever that rare treat had been available, vanilla was invariably all that was offered.

"I like chocolate myself."

"Most men do, I think," she recalled with a smile, remembering how her charges, even the oldest of them, grumbled about the lack of that flavor.

His fingers tightened. "Something you know from experience?"

She put her hands over his to support them. "I suppose, in a way," she agreed.

"How experienced are you?" he asked.

"That's a question a gentleman doesn't ask," she chided, trying to make a joke out of it. And fortunately, before he could pursue the matter, they reached the ice cream.

The orchestra played many familiar pieces, and Allison found herself sitting beside Gene on the grass on a quilt they'd borrowed from a younger couple nearby.

Gene had mentioned that they'd come up from Wyoming, and the young man—much thinner and fairer than Gene—had grinned and asked, "Came up especially for the music, did you?"

"To tell you the truth, we came up for a movie," Gene replied ruefully. "But we left."

The young woman, a vivid redhead, put her hands over her mouth and giggled with a shy glance at her companion. "The one about cattle ranching?" she asked.

"That's right," Gene agreed.

"We left, too," she said in a very country-sounding drawl. "My daddy would skin me alive if he knew I'd been to such a film, so I made Johnny leave. He liked it," she added with another meaningful look.

"It's life," the boy replied. "We're getting married in two months, after all, Gertie."

"Johnny!" She went scarlet and jumped up. "I'll get us some more ice cream!"

"Virgins," Johnny sighed and then smiled with pure joy.

That smile bothered Gene. He'd never known a virgin, not in all his life. He'd certainly never dated one. But part of him envied that young boy, to be going into a marriage with a woman who'd saved such a precious part of her life for him. He'd never have to wonder about his wife's ex-lovers or how he compared, because there hadn't been any. He'd be the only one, at first anyway, and all her first times would be with him.

He looked down at Allison with speculation. How would it be, he wondered, if she were that fresh and untouched? His eyes ran slowly down her body and he tried to picture himself with her in bed, slowly teaching her things he'd learned. Would she be shocked? Or would it all be old hat to her? He'd found that experienced women tended to be inventive in bed, and uninhibited. That was a definite plus. But it must have been special, too, to be able to teach those responses to a woman, to touch her and hear her cry out with pleasure and know that no other man had ever seen or heard her in ecstasy.

The thoughts bothered him. Surely Allison was experienced, at her age, and she could certainly flirt with the best of them. He sighed. Anyway, what could he expect from a casual interlude like she was going to be? It was just going to be sex, nothing more, and daydreams had no part in this.

As the music built and the last of the ice cream began to disappear, Gene suddenly became aware of time. It was almost a three-hour drive back to Pryor at night, and they were going to be later than he'd expected.

"I hate this, but we have to go," he told Allison after checking his watch. "We've got a long drive back."

"We saw your Jeep," Johnny remarked. He smiled. "Nice wheels. We're starting out in an ancient pickup. But it's tough," he added, "and that's what you need on a ranch."

"Tell me about it." Gene grinned. "We've got a twenty-year-old Ford pickup that I still use to haul calves. Nothing wrong with a classic vehicle."

Johnny beamed. "You bet!"

Gene shrugged. "Starting out is fun. Everybody does it."

"You two married?" Gertie asked.

"No chance," Gene chuckled. "She'd run a mile if I asked her."

"Too bad. You look good together." Gertie leaned against Johnny with love beaming out of her face as she looked up at him.

"So do you two," Allison said gently. "God bless."

"You, too."

"Thanks for the loan of the quilt," Gene added, neatly folding it before handing it back. He didn't want to think about how he and Allison looked together, and marriage was the last thing on his mind. He was glad Allison hadn't made an issue of his reply to Johnny's question. She seemed almost relieved that he'd made a joke of it. Maybe she was marriage-shy, too. That would make things easier.

"Our pleasure. Drive carefully."

Gene nodded. He took Allison's hand and walked her back to the Jeep.

"That was fun," she said. "Thank you."

He looked down at her. "We'll do it again sometime," he said noncommittally.

He opened the passenger door for her, but as she moved into the space he'd made, he turned unexpectedly so that his body was touching hers, one hand holding the door, the other on the cab, so that she was trapped.

"I like the dress," he said. "Lilac suits you."

"Thank you," she replied. His proximity was working on her like a drug. She felt her breath catch as she drank in the clean, cologne-scented warmth of his tall, fit body close to hers.

He bent one leg, so that his knee brushed past her thigh to rest against the seat. The contact brought him even closer, his body shielding her from onlookers in the park.

His breath was warm as his head bent, his glittery eyes meeting hers in the light from the park. "I'll be too busy for a few days, but on the weekend we could go sightseeing up around the Custer Battlefield. And next Tuesday night, we'll go up to Cody for the rodeo if you like."

"Yes," she said without hesitation. She searched his lean, dark face with pure pleasure. "I'd like that very much." Allison was surprised at the effect he had on her. He wasn't even touching her and her body was tingling.

He smiled, because he could read her expression very well indeed. He bent a little closer, so that she could feel his breath on her mouth. She could almost taste him.

"So would I, cupcake," he said softly. He let his eyes drop deliberately to her mouth and stared at it until he heard her breath catch and saw her lips part in helpless response. He leaned just a little closer. "We'd better go," he whispered, letting his breath brush her mouth. It was exciting to tease her; she responded to it so deliciously. She made him feel like the first man who'd done this with her, and his ego soared.

Just as she was beginning to tremble with anticipation, he drew back slowly, still smiling, and gently handed her into the cab. As he went around to the driver's side, his eyes gleamed with unholy delight. The one advantage of experience was that it could recognize capitulation. He was going to stay away from her for a few days and build the tension between them before he made another move. Calculation, surely, but it would be for her benefit, too. Their first time would be explosive.

He got in and started the Jeep. "It'll warm up in a minute," he said, watching her wrap her arms around her breasts.

She smiled thankfully, trying to hide her nervousness. "I didn't think it would get chilly at night."

"Now you know."

"I sure do!" she agreed with a laugh, and shivered until the heater began to blow warm air.

She leaned her head back against the seat and Gene turned on a country-and-western radio station. The drive back to Pryor was very pleasant, despite the fact that they talked very little. She felt safe with him. Comfortable and safe, even through the excitement he generated in her. She wondered if earlier he'd wanted to kiss her and had drawn back because of the crowd. Or was he playing with her? She didn't know. She sighed silently, wishing she had just a little more experience of men to draw on.

They pulled up at the Manley house. It was dark, except for the porch light, and when Allison glanced at the Jeep's clock, she was amazed to find it was three o'clock in the morning.

"I told you we'd be late getting home," Gene mused, watching her catch her breath as she looked toward the dash. "At least they don't seem to be worried about you," he added, nodding toward the darkened windows.

"Don't you believe it," she replied with a gentle smile. "The lights may be off, but I'll bet Winnie isn't asleep. She's like a mother hen sometimes."

He turned in his seat and unfastened her seat belt and then his, leaning back as one dark hand went out to tease the hair at her throat lazily. "Do you need one?" he laughed softly.

She felt her body tingle. All evening it had been a war of nerves with him, from the way he'd played with her hand in the theater to the way he'd looked at her in the park and that almost-kiss as he'd helped her into the Jeep to come home. Now she was at fever pitch, and she wanted his mouth more than she'd ever imagined she could want anything.

"No, I...don't think so," she said unsteadily. Her eyes fell to his mouth hungrily.

He saw that rapt stare and his heart jumped. She was easy to read for a sophisticated woman. Perhaps it was the first time she'd reacted so strongly to a prospective lover, and that made him proud. It was one thing to turn a virgin's head, but quite another to make an experienced woman nervous and unsure of herself.

His fingers moved to her cheek and traced it lightly and then settled at her jaw while his thumb dragged across her soft mouth in a savagely arousing motion.

She actually gasped, her eyes widening as they met his in the dim light from the dash.

"You don't wear much makeup, do you?" he asked deeply. The feel of her mouth was exciting to him. His thumb rubbed more insistently at her lips, parting them against the pearly white of her teeth. "I'm glad. I don't like layers of lipstick on a woman's mouth when I kiss it."

She felt hot all over. Winnie had warned her about Gene Nelson's expertise and she hadn't understood. Now, suddenly, she began to. She wanted to pull his fingers away from her mouth, she wanted to pull them closer, she wanted to run!

He saw and felt that reaction, registering it with a little curiosity and a lot of pride. He smiled softly as he caught a handful of her long hair with his other hand and pulled her face under his with easy mastery.

"Bite me," he breathed as his mouth dragged against hers in brief, arousing kisses. She tasted mint and coffee and ice cream and pure man as he played on her attraction to him in the smouldering silence that followed. She couldn't breathe properly. Her fingers bit into his broad shoulders, feeling the steely tautness of the warm muscle as his teeth nibbled at her lower lip.

He lifted his head a fraction and looked into her dazed hazel eyes, his own pale green ones bright with arousal. "Bite me," he repeated gruffly, his fingers contracting in her hair to force her face back up to his. "I like it rough," he breathed into her open mouth. "Don't you?"

She didn't know how she liked it or what he expected of her. She could barely think at all and the words didn't really register. She moved closer, not needing the impetus of his strong hand in her hair to force the movement. She felt him stiffen a little as she slid her arms around his neck with a helpless moan and pushed her mouth hard against his.

The kiss was sweet and heady. His lips parted hungrily and he pressed her head back into his shoulder with the sheer force of his ardor. He made a sound deep in his throat. The taste of her was making him drunk. He couldn't remember the last time he'd felt like this in a woman's arms. Her soft, eager response tested his control to the limits. For an experienced woman, she was purely lacking in seductive skills, unless this rapt submission to his mouth was some kind of feminine tactic.

At any rate, he was too involved to care. He shifted her, bringing her across his hard thighs to lie in his arms while his mouth began to invade hers.

She struggled faintly and he drew away, his breath shuddering out against her moist, swollen lips.

"What is it?" he asked, his voice almost betraying him with its deep, drowsy huskiness.

She swallowed, trembling at the feel of his hard thighs under her. Something had happened to him while they were kissing, something masculine that was totally out of her experience, and she was shy and a little frightened.

When she tried to shift away, he understood, but he only smiled mockingly. "Is this a problem?" he murmured, one steely hand pressing at the base of her spine to hold her against his raging arousal.

She gasped and stiffened in his arms.

"Too much too soon, Allison?" he murmured, his pale green eyes narrowing as they met hers. "At any rate, I can't help it."

"Please," she said, flustered, and tried again to move away. He held her, firmly but gently. She knew she probably sounded like an outraged virgin—but that was what she was.

"You're twenty-five," he said solemnly. "Too old for little-girl games." His hand contracted again, deliberately, and he watched her face flush, her eyes widen. Odd, that reaction, because it actually seemed genuine. Not that it could be. He refused to believe that.

"Gene," she protested breathlessly, because incredibly the evidence of his need kindled something comparable in her. She'd never felt that knotting in her lower belly, the rush of warmth, the weak trembling that made her helpless.

He bent toward her, his lips poised just above hers, tempting them. He whispered something then, something so explicit and softly threatening that she actually gasped. When her lips parted, his moved sensuously between them, his tongue probing tenderly past her teeth as if to emphasize what he'd just said to her.

The combination of seductive whisper and equally seductive action tore a shocked moan from her throat. What he was doing to her mouth was… outrageous! Crude, and suggestive and…

She shivered. Her eyes opened to find him watching her while his tongue probed and withdrew in a soft, gentle, subtly arousing rhythm that she was utterly helpless to resist.

And while his tongue touched and tasted, one lean hand was riding up her rib cage to tease around a swollen breast. Even through three layers of fabric, the sensation was devastating. He held her gaze the whole while, intoxicated with the way she responded to it, with the look on her face, the shocked, almost terrified fascination in her misty, dilated eyes. When his thumb suddenly stroked her taut nipple she shuddered and moaned sharply.

He lifted his head, because he liked that. He wanted to see if he could make it happen again. And he did. Again and again, the sound of his fingers faintly abrasive against the fabric of her bodice unnaturally loud in the cab of the Jeep. His hand became more insistent on her soft body, openly caressing now as she gasped for breath and stiffened in his arms, lying helplessly against him and without resistance.

"Yes, it feels good, doesn't it?" he breathed, pride and faint arrogance in the way he was watching her. "You're very, very aroused, little Allison," he said softly, turning his attention to the hard tip of her breast, so very visible through her thin dress. "And just so you won't forget until I see you again…"

Before she realized what he meant to do, he bent and put his lips over the hard nipple and suddenly closed his teeth on it.

She gasped and pushed at him frantically, shocked and frightened by the intimacy.

He lifted his head, frowning, because her reaction puzzled him.

"My God," he breathed. "You don't surely think I meant to hurt you?"

"Di...didn't you?" she whispered shakily, all eyes.

He touched her gently, soothing the place his teeth had been, noticing that she flinched at even that light caress. "I'm sorry if I frightened you," he said tenderly. "Evidently you're used to gentler men altogether."

"Well, yes, I am," she faltered. It was true, too, but not in the way he meant it. She was still shivering from the force of what he'd made her feel. She'd never been so helpless. She couldn't have stopped him, no matter what he'd done to her, and now she realized what Winnie had been trying to tell her.

"I'm not a gentle lover," he said quietly, searching her eyes. "I've never had to be. My kind of woman can match my passion move for move, and it's always been rough and wild because I like it that way." He drew in a slow breath, and his hand flattened over her breast suddenly, in an almost protective gesture. "It never occurred to me before that some women might find that kind of ardor intimidating."

"I'm sorry," she said softly. "I didn't quite know what to expect."

Why in God's name he should feel guilty, he didn't know. But he did. He bent and kissed her with noticeable restraint, almost with tenderness. "Next time," he whispered at her lips, "I'll be a little less wild with you, and a hell of a lot gentler. The last thing I want is to make you afraid of me."

She searched his dark face with wonder. He seemed as surprised by what they'd shared as she did. But he wasn't inexperienced. Shouldn't it have been routine to him to make love to a woman and experience those feelings? She wished she could ask him, but that would mean admitting her naïveté. And once he knew how innocent she really was, he'd never come near her again. He'd said so.

She tried to relax, to carry on the fiction of sophistication. But the blatant masculinity of his body against her made her uneasy.

"I'm not afraid," she said.

He moved his hand away from her breast and lightly touched her mouth, liking the way she lay so softly in his arms, her long hair draping around her shoulders, her eyes gentle and trusting now. She was a woman who needed tenderness, and he was angry with himself for the way he'd treated her. What had been natural with other women seemed out of place and crude with her. He remembered what he'd whispered to her, and winced now, wishing he could take it back.

"What is it?" she asked, having seen that change of expression.

"I said something pretty crude to you a few minutes ago," he said with quiet honesty. "I'm sorry. I suppose I'd forgotten that a woman with some experience can still be a lady, and deserves to be treated like one. The next time I make love to you, it won't be like this."

He moved her gently out of his arms while she was still absorbing the shock of what he'd said.

He went around the cab and helped her out, holding her arm protectively as he escorted her onto the well-lit porch. He looked down at her and his eyes fell suddenly to her dress. He smiled ruefully.

"Good thing Winnie's not up," he murmured.

She followed his gaze and flushed. There was a very obvious dampness on her dress around the nipple that no engaged woman would mistake the reason for.

He cupped her face in his hands and held it up to his eyes, smiling indulgently at her. "Don't worry, no one will see it. Next time," he breathed, bending to her mouth with agonizing slowness, "we'll make sure the fabric is out of the way before I put my lips on you."

She gasped and he smiled against her mouth as he kissed it. His body went rigid instantly, drawing a shocked gasp from his own mouth.

"God, you excite me!" he said roughly, drawing back. "I'd better get out of here before I shock us both. I'll call in a day or so and we'll set a time for that trip to Hardin. By the way, you can tell your mother hen that I won't keep you out this late again."

"I will." She was holding his arms for support. It wasn't easy to let go. She didn't want to be away from him for a minute, much less two days. "Well, good night. I enjoyed the dinner and the concert."

"Not the movie?" he murmured dryly, smiling at her faint flush. His smile faded as he looked down into her eyes. "Never mind. I think I'm getting too old for careless passion." He touched her mouth with a long forefinger. "I would be tender with you," he said huskily. "I know enough to give you heaven. And when the time comes, I will. That's a promise."

Before she could get her breath or her wits back, he'd turned and was on his way back to the Jeep, his lean-hipped stride holding her eyes against her will. He was so good to look at, and what she felt with him was terrifying. She knew then, hopelessly, that she'd give him anything he asked for. She couldn't even run. The pull of attraction was too strong to fight. She watched him drive away without looking back and wondered sadly if this was how it would be when it was over, and he was going out of her life for good.

Gene knew she was still standing on the porch, but he didn't wave. He was teeming with new and confusing emotions that he really didn't want to explore too fully. His planned seduction was going sadly awry. His conscience was getting in the way.

Allison unlocked the door and went inside, half afraid that Winnie was going to see her. Impulsively she grabbed up a sweater from the clothes tree in the hall and slipped it on, pulling it over her breasts. And in the nick of time, too, because Winnie appeared in the hall as she was on the way to her room.

"About time, too," Winnie said worriedly. "Where have you been?"

Allison told her, making light of the date and raving over the symphony.

"So that's all it was," Winnie relaxed. She smiled ruefully. "I'm sorry. I know I'm overreacting. But he's so potent, Allie. So much a man…"

A sudden, horrible suspicion grew in the back of Allison's mind. "Is he?" she probed.

Winnie grimaced. "I guess you'd better know. I dated Gene before Dwight cut him out. It was innocent; I never slept with him," she emphasized. "The thing is, I would have," she confessed miserably. "And he knew it. That's why I warned you. Gene takes what he wants, but he has nothing to give in return. You're playing a very dangerous game. I'm no Snow White, and I could have survived an affair with him—if I hadn't fallen so hopelessly in love with Dwight. But you're very innocent, Allie. I don't think you could live with yourself. Especially after your upbringing."

"I'm not sure I could, either," she confessed on a hard sigh. "He's…very potent."

"So I see."

The amused drawl brought her eyes down and she noticed then that the sweater had fallen open.

She went scarlet, wrapping it protectively over her breasts.

"Don't look so hunted," Winnie said gently. "I understand. A man like that is too hard to resist. You can't be blamed for being human. But to keep seeing him is asking for trouble."

"I know." Allison looked down at the floor. "I... think I'm falling in love."

Winnie bit her lower lip. "He can't help being the way he is. But he isn't a man who knows how to love. Or commit himself to a long-term relationship."

Allison looked up with haunted, sad eyes. "There's still a chance."

"And you're too hooked to listen to warnings, aren't you?" her friend replied gently. She hugged Allison to her with a sigh. "Try to keep your head, at least."

"I'll do that. Complications are the last thing I need."

"At least you know about precautions," Winnie sighed, smiling at Allison's flush. "Your training may come in handy before you're through. Okay, no more lectures. Go to bed. Is the wild man coming back?"

"Yes. Sometime in the middle of the week. He's

taking me to see the Custer Battlefield. Then next week, we're going to the rodeo in Cody," she said.

Winnie just shook her head.

Allison changed into her nightgown, awed and frightened by the way it had been. Her first intimacy with a man, and she couldn't even admit it to him. She wondered if he'd have been different with her, had he known how naïve she was. Probably he'd have done what he swore at the beginning—he'd have left her strictly alone. He'd been honest about his opinion of innocence; that he wanted no part of it. She felt guilty about hiding hers, but she was falling in love. Even if he got angry at her later, she had to have a chance. He might fall in love with her, too, and then it would be all right.

Except that in the meantime he might seduce her, she thought worriedly. His ardor was unexpected and so was her helplessness. She'd never experienced those sensations, and they were addictive.

She tried to push it out of her mind when she went to bed. But she felt as if her body had scorched the sheets by morning. She'd never had such erotic dreams in all her life, and they were full of Gene.

Chapter Six

Gene was surprised by the force of his attraction to Allison. He'd meant to wait a few days before he saw her again, to give her time to miss him, to enhance her response to him. But he found himself thinking about her all too much. By the second day, the tables had suddenly turned on him and *he* was missing *her*.

He gunned the Jeep into the Manley driveway, smiling when he saw Allison out digging in Mrs. Manley's small flower garden near the porch steps. She was wearing Bermuda shorts and a pink tank top, her long black hair in a ponytail, and she looked charming. He cut off the engine and climbed out of the big vehicle, his bat-wing chaps making a leathery rustling sound as he walked toward her.

"They've put you to work, I see," he drawled.

Allison flushed and smiled shyly, getting to her feet. She'd just been daydreaming about him, and here he was! "Hi!" she said, her whole face radiant with the greeting.

His heart jumped a little. "Hi, yourself," he murmured, moving closer. His eyes fell from her firm breasts down her narrow waist to softly flaring hips and long, elegant legs. She even had pretty feet, encased in brown leather thongs. "Nice legs," he murmured with a wicked glance.

"Thank you," she stammered. "Are you looking for Winnie and Mrs. Manley? They had to run to the store…."

"I came to see you, cupcake," he said softly, his wide-brimmed hat shadowing his eyes as they searched hers. "But I hardly dared hope I'd find you alone."

She felt her heart race. "Did you?" she whispered.

He tipped her chin up and bent his head unexpectedly, brushing his mouth with lazy expertise over her parted lips. "No, that won't do," he breathed, his voice deep and slow as he reached for her. "Come close, little one."

He enveloped her in his muscular arms and drew her against his body as he bent again. This time the kiss was longer, harder, but so different from the way he'd kissed her two nights ago. This one was gentle, full of respect and warmth. She reacted to it with all her heart, sliding her arms under his and around his lean waist, loving the way his mouth played with hers and teased around it between kisses.

"Very nice," he mused when he lifted his head. It was much better like this, gentle and sweet, so that she responded and didn't fight or draw away. He liked it when she wasn't frightened. "Dessert, in the middle of the day," he added, teasing. "You taste sweet."

She laughed softly, her hazel eyes adoring him. "I just ate a cinnamon bun."

"And that wasn't what I meant," he murmured. "Does tomorrow suit you to drive up to Hardin? We can leave about nine, if you like."

"Oh, yes," she said, already excited.

"Good. I'll make sure I'm free. Wear jeans and boots. There are rattlers in that area. I don't want you hurt."

Her smile widened. "I will," she promised,

surprised and pleased that he was concerned about her. Being with him shot her through and through with pleasure.

He drew his forefinger down her nose. "Don't get sunstroke out here. What are you doing?"

"Weeding Mrs. Manley's flowers," she said. "I hate just sitting around. I hate talk shows and I can't do handicrafts. I like working."

The women he usually escorted liked to preen and put themselves on display. He scowled as he thought about it. Not one of them would like getting her hands dirty digging in a garden. His eyes slid over Allison's soft face and lingered there. His mother had been an enthusiastic gardener, too.

"Do you have a garden where you live?" he asked suddenly.

Her smile faded and she averted her eyes to the spade she was using. "Yes, I had a vegetable garden," she said. "But it…was ruined."

"I'm sorry. I don't think Winnie's mother grows vegetables."

"No, she's a flower enthusiast," Allison replied. She looked up at him again, smiling as she studied the way he looked in his working clothes, very lean and lithe and Western. Very masculine, too, as he stood with his hands on his hips, his Stetson low over his eyes. "You look like an ad for a Western vacation," she said involuntarily. "Very, very handsome."

He chuckled. "That's it, hit me in my weak spot."

She laughed, too. "You could have phoned. About Hardin, I mean."

"I know." He touched her soft mouth lightly. "I wanted to see you. Don't overdo. I'll pick you up at nine."

"Okay," she said, her voice low and gentle.

He winked at her, but he didn't touch her again. He pulled his hat lower over one eye and strode back to the Jeep. He didn't look back as he drove away. She had a feeling that he never did, and it just vaguely disturbed her. It was a reminder that he wasn't a committing man. And he was used to walking away from women without looking back.

But by the time he picked her up the next morning, she'd convinced herself that she was going to be the one exception to his rule. He did at least seem to be different with her since the other night, when she'd drawn back from his overwhelming ardor. Maybe he sensed her innocence and wasn't put off by it. She laughed silently. More likely, he'd decided that roughness might put her off him, and he was soft pedaling his raging desire until he could coax her into satisfying it. She had to be realistic, but it was difficult when she was so vulnerable to him. That had to be mutual, though, she told herself. Otherwise, why would he have come all the way to the Manleys' to see her, when he could have phoned? She tingled with the delicious possibilities.

He was dressed in jeans and boots and a brown-and-white patterned Western shirt, the familiar Stetson cocked over one eye. Allison had dressed similarly, with a beige tank top under a blue-and-brown striped shirt. She laughed at the way they matched.

So did Gene. He helped her into the truck, jamming a Caterpillar bibbed cap down over her hair, which she'd pulled up in a soft bun. The cap came down to her eyebrows. "You can fix that. There's an adjustable strap in the back," he told her as he drove. "I figured you'd forget your hat."

She beamed. He was taking such good care of her. She looked at him, her heart overflowing with warm feelings. "Thanks," she said softly, and adjusted the plastic strip.

"I have to take care of my best girl," he said softly. The strange thing was that he meant it. She was the best girl he'd ever taken out. She wasn't demanding or petulant or sulky. She reminded him of bright summer sunshine, always cheerful.

She became radiant as she heard the words, blushing. It got worse when he reached out and tangled her fingers in his as he drove.

"Miss me?" he asked gently.

"Oh, yes," she said, not bothering with subterfuge.

He glanced at her, his eyes lingering on her rosy cheeks and soft, parted mouth before he forced his gaze back to his driving. "That goes double for me." His fingers clenched in hers. "You're good medicine, sunshine."

"Medicine?" she teased.

"Up in this part of the world, medicine means more than drugs. The Plains Indians used to 'make medicine' before battle, to protect them and help their spirits find the way to the hereafter. There was good medicine and bad, equally potent. They filled small rawhide bags with special talismans to protect their bodies from their enemies. Good medicine," he added, smiling as he glanced at her. "But I'd have hell stuffing you into a rawhide pouch."

She laughed. "I expect it would be uncomfortable, at that." Her eyes adored him. "Thank you for taking me to the battlefield. I've wanted to see it all my life."

"My pleasure. I don't think you'll be disappointed."

She wasn't. There was a museum and guided tours were available. She noticed that Gene avoided the groups of tourists as they meandered along the paved walkway up to the graves in their wrought-iron square and the tall monument on which was carved the names of the soldiers who died at the spot.

"We're standing on Crow land," he explained, nodding down the ridge to the small stream that cut a deep ravine through the green grass. Beyond it was a large stand of trees and an even larger body of water. "Through there was the encampment. Several Native American tribes came together to form an army of several thousand. This fenced area is where the last stand was made. Custer died here, so they say, along with his brother and brother-in-law and nephew. He was shot through the left breast and the temple."

"I read somewhere that he committed suicide."

He shook his head. "I think that's unlikely. If you read his book, *My Life on the Plains*, you get a picture of a man who is definitely not the type for suicide. One authority on him thinks he was shot down in that ravine, through the left breast, and brought up here to the last stand position by his men. A bullet wound was found in his left temple. The Indians usually shot their enemies at close range to make sure they were dead. It was reported that after a buckskinned soldier was wounded in the ravine, the soldiers lost heart and seemed not to fight so hard. If it was Custer who got shot, then it would explain that near rout. His men were young and mostly inexperienced. Few of them had ever seen Indians on the warpath."

"I guess it would be scary," she said, looking up at him with fascination.

"You don't know the half of it, cupcake. Plains Indians in full regalia were painted—faces, surely, and bodies. Even the horses were painted. Add to that the death cry they all yelled as they went into battle, and the eagle bone whistles they blew, and you've got a vision of death terrifying enough to make a seasoned trooper nervous."

He stopped and looked out over the rolling buttes and high ridges and vast stretch of horizon. "My God," he breathed, "no wonder they fought so hard to keep it. Look. Virgin land, untouched, unpoisoned by civilization. God's country."

"Yes. It really is beautiful," she said.

The wind was blowing hard and he slid an arm around her, drawing her close. "Want to walk down to the ravine?" he asked.

"Could we?"

"Surely. There's a trail. Watch for snakes, now."

He led her down the deceptively long path to the ravine, stopping at each place that marked where men had fallen in battle. He seemed familiar with all of them, and the history. He stopped for a long moment beside one marker.

"My great-great-uncle," he said, smiling at her expression. "Surprised? Now you know how I knew so much about the battle. His wife kept a journal, and I have it. The last entry was the night before he set out with Custer's 7th for the Little Bighorn. He probably kept a journal all the way here, too, but the Native tribes scoured the battlefield after the fight, and took everything they thought they could use. Watches, pistols, clothing, even saddles and boots were carried off. They threw away the soles of the boots and used the leather to make other things out of."

"Tell me about your great-great-uncle," she said, and listened attentively while they walked back up from the steep banks of the ravine. He held her hand tightly, speaking at length about the battle and its historical controversies.

He took her to the museum when they were through. She wandered through the souvenir shop afterward, oohing and aahing over the exquisite beadwork on the crafts. She paused by a full-length warbonnet and sighed over a war lance. It was amazing to consider how terrifying these same things would have been to a woman only a hundred years before. Gene insisted on buying her a pair of beaded earrings for her pierced ears. On the way home, he explained the wearing of earrings by the various Plains tribes and how you could tell warriors of each tribe apart by their hairstyles and earrings.

"It's just fascinating," she said.

Gene glowed with pride. None of his dates had ever liked to hear him hold forth about the battle. Allison not only listened, but she seemed to be really interested. He learned as they drove back that she was a student of Native cultures herself, and she seemed to have a wealth of knowledge about the Mayans. He listened to her on the way back, absorbing little-known facts about the Mayans.

"You're good," he said when he drove up in front of the Manley house just after dark. "Damned good. Where did you learn all that?"

She smiled wistfully. "I just read a lot and kept my ears open, I guess," she said, neglecting to add that she'd climbed over Mayan temples where she and her parents had been assigned. The smile faded as the memories came back. "I had a good time, Gene. A really good time. Thank you."

He drew her to him. "So did I." He searched her eyes in the dim light from the dash. "We'll say our good-nights here," he said softly, letting his eyes drop to her mouth. "The way we kiss might shock them."

As he whispered the words, his lips slowly parted hers. They didn't take, they coaxed this time. Moist, aching pressure teased her mouth open in a silence that grew with strained breathing. He moved, so that her head fell back against the seat, and his face followed hers, his mouth still teasing, provoking, tantalizing until she was trembling.

"You set me on fire," he groaned as the need finally broke through. The pressure of the kiss pushed her head hard into the back of the seat, and she felt him shiver as his tongue slowly thrust past her teeth. He groaned again, one lean hand sliding down her throat to her breast under the shirt, over the thin tank top. "Stop wearing bras," he managed unsteadily. "They just get in my way."

She opened her mouth to speak, but no words came out. He was kissing her again, and this time his hand slid boldly right under the fabric. His thumb rubbed tenderly over her hard nipple, his moist palm cupping the firm underside of her breast. She moaned and he lifted his head.

"Satin and velvet," he said, his eyes glittery as they met hers. He deliberately pulled her tank top and bra out, so that he could look down at her taut, bare breast. "Yes," he said huskily, but without touching her this time. "You look as I knew you would. Pretty breasts. Tip-tilted and exquisitely pretty."

Her lips parted, but she was beyond shock. She shivered and actually arched toward him, so aroused that she wanted his mouth on her, there.

But he saw what she didn't—the curtains moving at the window. He released her reluctantly and lifted his head. "I can't touch you there," he said quietly. "Not now. We have an audience."

"Oh," she stammered, all at sea.

He lifted his invading hand back to her cheek and searched her eyes for a long moment. "We'll be good together," he said quietly. "You know it, too, don't you?"

She should tell him, she thought. She should... "Yes," she replied instead.

He nodded. "I won't rush you," he said. "But I won't wait a great deal longer, either. It's been too long for me."

She didn't know what to say. She shifted a little, still on fire in the aftermath of his ardor.

"Good night, sweet thing," he murmured, kissing her closed eyelids. "You're very special."

He drew back then and helped her out of the Jeep, keeping his arm around her as they walked back to the porch.

"Your guardian angel is hanging back," he mused, smiling down at her. "Is she giving up?"

Her heart leaped. "Sort of. She's engaged, you know."

He cocked an eyebrow. "So she is." He tapped her cheek. "I'll never be," he said suddenly. "You know that, don't you? I enjoy being with you, and physically, we burn each other up. But I won't lie and promise you happy ever after. I'm a confirmed bachelor."

Her heart didn't want to hear that. She forced a smile to her mouth. "Yes, I know."

He nodded slowly, searching her eyes. He couldn't let her get her hopes up. Marriage was definitely not on his agenda. He was still having hell coping with his past. And there was one very good reason why he didn't want to procreate. Bad genes could be passed on. He shifted. "Good girl. I'll pick you up tomorrow night and we'll go to the rodeo. I know I said next week, but I don't want to wait that long. Do you?"

She shook her head. "No. Not really," she confessed.

"Then I'll come for you at six." He nuzzled her face and kissed her softly. "Good night, pretty thing."

She smiled up at him a little wanly. "Good night. Thanks for the trip, and my earrings."

He twitched them, watching them dangle. "They suit you. See you tomorrow."

He was gone at once, without another kiss and still without looking back. She went into the house, smiling as Winnie came to meet her.

"We're just putting supper on the table," Winnie said. "Have fun?"

"Oh, yes. He knows a lot about the Custer Battlefield, doesn't he?" she asked.

"Indeed he does. Did he bore you with it? Marie says he drives them crazy spouting history."

"But I love it!" Allison said, surprised. "History is one of my hobbies. I found it fascinating."

Winnie's eyebrows went up. "My, my, imagine that." She grinned. "Way to go, tiger. You may land that feisty fish yet. Come on. I'll feed you."

The remark gave Allison hope, and she needed it. Her conscience was bothering her. She really should tell Gene the truth. If only she could be sure that he wouldn't turn around and walk away from her for good.

The next day, Allison decided that the best thing to wear to a rodeo—since her one pair of jeans was in the wash—was a blue denim skirt with sporty pull-on pink sneakers and a pink T-shirt. But she wore a lightweight rose-patterned sweater with it, because she hadn't forgotten how cool it had been in Billings after dark. She pulled her hair into a ponytail and tied it with a pink scarf. Then she sat down to wait for Gene, because she'd dressed two hours early for their date. Every few minutes she involuntarily checked her watch. The instrument was so much part of her uniform when she worked that she felt naked without it. Despite the innovations in modern medicine, a watch with a sweep second hand was about the most advanced equipment for pulse monitoring available in the primitive areas where she and her parents had worked.

Winnie's mother had been invited to a baby shower for a friend's daughter, and Winnie was going out with Dwight. They left just a few minutes before Gene arrived. True to her word, Winnie didn't make a single remark about the date. She just hugged Allison and smiled sympathetically. That was no surprise. Winnie was in love herself, so she certainly understood how it felt.

Gene arrived exactly on time. He was dressed for a casual evening, in jeans and hand-tooled black leather boots with a blue Western shirt and a turquoise-and-silver bola. He wore a new black Stetson tonight with a moccasin headband, and he was freshly shaved and showered.

He smiled down appreciatively at the way she looked in her skirt and T-shirt with her silky black hair in a ponytail. His body had given him no peace for the past few days, going over and over the sweetness of Allison's response to him and the joy he'd felt in her company. They shared so many common interests that he actually enjoyed talking to her. Not that the way they exploded when they touched was any less potent. Not for worlds would he have admitted how much he'd looked forward to tonight. Looking at her made him feel good. Being with her was satisfying and sweet. And, unfortunately, addictive. He was going to have to do something about it; the sooner the better. She couldn't be staying much longer, and she was beginning to interfere with not only his work, but his sleep. He found himself thinking of her constantly, wanting to be with her. He was acting like a lovesick boy and he didn't want to disgrace himself by letting anyone know. The sooner he got her out of his system physically, the sooner he could get back to normal and deal with his worst problems.

The odd thing was that since Allison had been around, he hadn't worried so much about his parentage or that will that had changed his life. In fact, he was more at peace than he'd ever been. She gave him the first peace he'd had in weeks. Months. He felt as if there was no problem he couldn't overcome when he was with her. And that was disturbing. Really disturbing.

He pushed the thoughts to the back of his mind. "You look cute," he murmured dryly. "I like the T-shirt."

It read Women's Revolutionary Sewing Society. She'd found it in an out-of-the-way shop, and she loved it. She grinned up at him, her eyes warm in her oval face with its exquisite peaches-and-cream complexion. "It appealed to my sense of the ridiculous. Do you really like it?"

"I like the way you fill it out better," he said quietly, his eyes admiring her breasts and darkening with memory. "Is that skirt going to fall off without a belt?" he added, frowning at the way it fit in the waist—very loosely.

"I've lost a little weight in the past few weeks," she said noncommittally. "But it will stay up. I couldn't find my belt."

Of course not. It was still in Central America, along with most of her other belongings. That brought back vivid memories of how she'd left foreign surroundings, and how the media had followed her. Being seen in public could put her in jeopardy, but it was unlikely that Gene would introduce her to anybody from the press. She relaxed, shifting restlessly as she pushed the worries to the back of her mind.

He glanced around. "Where's Winnie?"

"Out with Dwight. Didn't you know?"

He laughed curtly, and without any real humor, his lean face full of mockery, his pale green eyes narrow and cool. "Dwight doesn't discuss his social life with me these days."

She moved closer to him, and because of the heels on his boots and the lack of them on her sneakers, she had to look up a lot farther than usual. He smelled of spicy cologne, a fragrance that made her pulse race almost as much as being close to him did. "He might, if you didn't make it so difficult for him," she said gently, and with a smile that took the sting out of the words.

He'd have thrown a punch at any man who dared

say something like that to his face. But somehow it didn't offend him when Allison said it. One corner of his thin, disciplined mouth twitched and his eyes sparkled with faint amusement as he looked down at her.

"You standing in a ditch?" he asked unexpectedly. "Or did you get wet and shrink overnight?"

She laughed, her whole body on fire with life and love and his company. "I'm wearing sneakers."

"Is that it?" He looked down at her feet in pink tennis shoes. "Dainty little things," he mused.

"Nobody could ever describe *your* feet that way," she replied with a meaningful glance at his long boots.

"I throw away the boots and wear the shoe boxes," he agreed pleasantly. "Mrs. Manley isn't here, either?" he added, glancing around.

"She went to a baby shower."

He drew a slow breath, feeling a contentment he could hardly remember in his life stealing over him as he stared at her. "No lectures from your mother hen before she left with Dwight?"

She shook her head.

He chuckled. "She really has given up!"

"Yes." She searched his face quietly, loving every strong, lean line of it, its darkness, its masculinity. She could have stood looking at him all day.

His eyebrow jerked. Her delight was evident, and it made him bristle with pride. "We'd better go," he said after a minute.

"Yes."

But he didn't move, and neither did she. His eyes fell to her mouth, its pale pink owing nothing to lipstick. He caught her by the waist and drew her lazily against him, bending to brush his lips softly over hers in a delicate kiss that aroused but didn't satisfy. She tasted of mint and he smiled against her soft mouth, liking the hungry, instant response he got. Her arms moved up to hold him and he half lifted her against him in an embrace that made her think inexplicably of Christmas and mistletoe and falling snow, because she was warm and safe.

He wasn't thinking at all. The feel of her in his arms had stopped his mind dead. Everything was sensation now. Warm, soft breasts flattened against him, the floral scent of her body, the trembling eagerness of the soft lips parting under his rough mouth. His body stiffened as the first wave of desire hit him.

He forced himself to lift his head. He had to catch his breath, and she seemed similarly occupied. He searched her wide, stunned eyes for a long moment, until his heartbeat echoed in his ears like a throbbing drum.

Her face was beautiful. Her exquisite complexion was softly flushed, her lips were swollen and moist from the long, hard contact with his mouth. Wisps of black hair trailed around her rosy cheeks, and her hazel eyes looked totally helpless.

"It might be a good idea if we go, while we still have a choice," he murmured ruefully. He put her back on her feet and let her arms slide away from his neck. God, she was potent!

"Yes, it might," she agreed gently, equally affected and having a hard time dealing with it.

He waited while she locked the door and escorted her to the Jeep. "If you stick around long enough, I'll buy a car," he murmured when they were driving off.

"I like the Jeep," she protested. "And it must come in handy on the ranch."

"It does," he had to agree. He glanced at her, frowning. So many secrets, he thought. She was mysterious, and he had a terrible secret of his own, about his real father. It would be better for both of them if he took her back to Winnie's and didn't see her again. But he couldn't seem to force himself to do that. Whatever happened, he had to have her,

even if it was only one time. He knew instinctively
that it would be different with her than it ever had
been before; that it would be a kind of ecstasy he'd
never known. He ached for her now. It was too late
to stop it.

He'd been having more trouble sleeping lately
than he ever had in his life—and more cold
showers. He opened the window, needing air, and
glanced at Allison.

"Do you mind?" he asked.

She leaned her head against the seat and studied
his face warmly. "No."

"It'll keep me awake. I haven't been sleeping
well. Too many things on my mind."

"What things?" she asked gently.

"Life, Allison."

The sound of her name on his lips made her
tingle. She liked the way he said it.

"It's been difficult for you, I know," she replied.
"The important thing is that you'll get through it.
Nothing lasts forever. Not even pain."

He scowled, darting a glance in her direction.
"Don't bet on it," he replied.

Her eyes fell to his firm jaw, to the cut of his
lips. She liked his profile. It was strong, like the
man himself. "It's early days yet, though," she
reminded him. "You can't expect to have your life

torn apart and put back together overnight. I don't imagine that waiting comes easily to you."

He smiled in spite of himself. "No. It doesn't." He was quiet for a minute before he spoke again. "But in this case, I don't have a lot of choice. Are you impatient, Allison? Or do you find it easy to wait for the things you want?"

"I was always taught that patience was among the greatest virtues," she said simply. "But sometimes it's very difficult to stand back and not try to force things into place. Accepting things isn't much easier," she added, thinking of her parents.

He nodded. "I guess we're all human, aren't we, cupcake?" he asked quietly. "And there are times when it seems that we can't manage any control over our own destiny."

"You don't go to church, I guess," she asked softly.

He shook his head. "No." His face hardened. "I can't believe in a God who torments people."

"He doesn't," she said. "We do that to ourselves. He watches and helps when we ask Him, but I think we're somewhat responsible for our own destinies. When we have choices, we make them. Life takes care of the rest."

"And where does God enter into it?"

"He gave us free will," she said, smiling. "Otherwise, Eve would never have handed Adam that delicious, succulent juicy apple."

He burst out laughing. "Do tell?" he chuckled.

"Besides, there are other forces at work in the world. Balance means evil exists with good. Sometimes it's hard to win against the darker forces." Her eyes clouded. "That doesn't mean you quit trying. You just work harder."

"You sound like a minister we used to have," he mused without looking at her, which was a shame. The expression on her face would have fascinated him. "He wasn't a bad sort. I used to enjoy listening to him."

"What stopped you from going to services?" she asked, curious.

"I don't know," he shrugged. "I guess it was because it didn't seem to make any difference. Going to church didn't solve my problems."

"It doesn't solve them. It helps you cope with them," she said with a gentle smile. "Being religious doesn't automatically make you immune to hard times and hurt."

"That's what I discovered for myself. I expected miracles."

"Miracles are all around," she said. "They happen every day."

"Do they really?" he asked, unconvinced.

"Oh, yes." She could have told him that she was one. That she was alive was truly through divine intervention. She glanced out the window. "We aren't going through Shoshone Canyon again, are we?" she asked, changing the subject delicately.

"No. I took you on a wide Western detour to show you the canyon and the tunnel. We're going northwest straight into Cody this time. Have you ever been to a rodeo?"

"Once or twice, down in Arizona. It's very dangerous, isn't it?"

"More than one cowboy has lost his life in a rodeo arena," he agreed. "All it takes is one small lapse of concentration, or carelessness. You can be gored by a bull, kicked by a horse, trampled, bitten, thrown so hard you break a bone... It's no game for city cowboys."

"Have any tried?" she asked, curious now.

He chuckled softly. "We had this guy from back East at one of the Cody rodeos last year," he began. "He'd been riding those mechanical bulls in bars and figured he was plenty good enough for a hick rodeo. He signed up and paid his entrance money. They put him up on one of the bulls we'd supplied. Old Scratch, by name." He grinned at her. "There he sat, waiting for the buzzer and for the gate to open, when the announcer gave Old Scratch's history and mentioned that in seventy-eight rides, not one cowboy had stayed on him until the horn sounded. The look on that dude's face was worth money."

"What happened?" she prompted.

"He and the bull parted company two seconds out of the chute. He broke his arm and one rib. Last I heard, he'd given up bull riding in favor of his old job—selling shoes at a department store back home."

She gasped. "Oh, the poor man!"

"Poor man, hell. Anybody who thinks riding almost a ton of bucking beef is a picnic ought to have his rear end busted. It's no game for shoe wranglers."

She studied Gene's lean, hard face and let her eyes fall to his tall, fit body. "Do you ride; in rodeos, I mean?" she asked.

A smile touched his thin lips as he shot a quick glance her way. "Do you think I'm too old, cupcake?"

She smiled back. "No. I was just curious. I guess what you do at the ranch takes up most of your time."

"It used to," he recalled bitterly. "Until control of it passed to Dwight."

"Dwight doesn't seem like the kind of person who'd take over everything," she said slowly, not wanting to offend him. "I'm sure he was as upset as you were by what came out."

He scowled. She hit nerves. "I guess he was, at that," he said in a slow, even tone. "He inherited the business side of the ranch, which he hates, and I wound up with the day-to-day operation of it, which I hate. I don't mind physical labor, you understand, but while I'm helping load cattle into trailers, Dwight's committing financial suicide with the accounts."

"Haven't the two of you talked about that?" she probed.

He tilted his hat across his brow. "There's Cody up ahead," he said, discouraging any further comment.

When he parked the Jeep and helped her out, it occurred to him that he'd told her more about himself than he'd shared with anyone in recent years. And in return, he'd learned nothing—not one damned thing—about her. He looked down at her steadily as they waited in line for tickets.

"You don't talk about yourself, do you?" he asked suddenly.

She lifted both eyebrows, startled by a question

she hadn't expected. "Well, no, not a lot," she admitted.

"Is it deliberate?"

She shrugged. "I can't learn very much about other people if I spend my time talking about myself."

He tugged at her long ponytail mischievously. "I'll dig it out of you before I'm through."

"I'm shaking in my boots," she assured him.

"You aren't wearing boots."

"Picky, picky," she said, and laughed up at him. He was easily the most physically impressive man in the line, and the handsomest, to her at least.

"Well, hello, Gene," a soft, feminine voice drawled beside them, and a striking raven-haired beauty with flashing blue eyes attached on to his arm.

"Hello, Dale," he replied with a stiff nod.

"It's been months. Why haven't you called me?" the woman asked. She was dressed in rodeo clothes, with a white Stetson and matching boots. She was beautiful and younger than Allison by about three years.

"If I'd had anything to say, I would have," Gene replied curtly, irritated by Dale's possessive manner and the blatant way she was leaning against him.

Dale's blue eyes glared at Allison. "Is she the reason?" she demanded, giving the older woman a hard appraisal. "She's hardly a beauty, is she?"

Gene took her arm roughly and moved her aside, his eyes as threatening as his cold tone. "Get lost. Now."

Dale tore away from him, glaring back. "You weren't so unfriendly once."

He gave her a mocking, icy smile. "I wasn't sober, either, was I?"

She all but gasped. Realizing that they were attracting attention, she turned and stormed off toward the back of the arena.

"I'm sorry about that," Gene told Allison, angry that she'd been embarrassed and hurt by Dale's harsh remarks.

Allison only nodded. So his conquests weren't in far-flung cities. She had a glimpse of how it might be if she married someone like him, and had to be constantly reminded of his wildness. Only a few months ago, the woman had said, and he was already resentful at having to see her again. Allison shuddered, thinking that she might have just seen herself in the future. She couldn't look up at Gene again. She was afraid of what she might give away.

But he sensed her discomfort. When they were

seated in the bleachers waiting for the first event to start, he stared at her until she looked up.

"I'm sorry," he said curtly. His pale green eyes searched her wan face quietly. "That couldn't have come at a worse time, could it?"

"She's very pretty," she voiced involuntarily.

"Yes. I was drunk and she was willing, and I thought that would be the end of it. But she's tenacious. I'd forgotten that she was entered in the barrel-racing competition tonight."

"Is she good?" Allison asked.

He glared at her. "In the saddle, or in bed?" he asked, taking the question at face value.

She averted her eyes. "In the saddle, of course."

His face hardened. "You take some getting used to," he said after a minute. "I always expect sarcasm from a woman. It's hard to acclimate to honesty."

"Maybe it's your choice of women that's at fault," she replied, trying to smile. Hearing him talk so casually about one of his conquests made her uncomfortable.

He had to admit that Allison wasn't like any of his other women. She appealed to a lot more than his senses. He scowled, because that bothered him. He clenched his hands togther as he stared toward the chutes. "Okay, honey, here we go," he said, nodding toward the announcer, who'd just started speaking.

It was the best rodeo Allison had ever seen. Gene knew most of the contestants and most of the livestock, so he pointed out the strongest riders in each competition and the worst bulls and broncs.

"Now that son of a mustang leaped flat-footed into the backseat of a convertible on a neighboring ranch," he informed her as one of the worst bareback broncs trotted away after unseating his would-be rider. "He doesn't belong to us, and I'm glad. He's a really bad customer. All but unridable and bad-tempered to boot. I've been kicked by him a time or two myself."

"You said you didn't ride," she remarked.

"Not often," he corrected. "Now and again when I've had a beer too many, I get the old urge to try to break my neck in the arena," he chuckled.

That didn't sound encouraging, either, as if he liked to go on binges. Allison knew so little about men and their habits. She really had led a sheltered life.

"Look, here comes one of ours," he said, nudging her. "That's Rocky Road. He can outbuck most of the others hands down."

Sure enough, the bronc unseated his rider in jig time and sashayed off without a care in the world.

The cowboy he'd unseated slammed his hat down in the dirt and jumped on it repeatedly while the audience laughed at the unexpected entertainment.

Allison laughed with him. She really couldn't help it.

"Oh, the poor man," she choked.

"You pay your money and take your chances," he said without much real sympathy. "It happens to all of us. The name of the game is to keep down the number of winners. A rodeo exists to make money, not to give it away, you know."

"I guess I didn't think. But I still feel sorry for the men who lose."

"So do I, actually."

The next man stayed on and Allison thought he'd done extremely well, but he didn't score at all.

"He didn't get thrown!" Allison protested on the man's behalf.

"The horse didn't buck enough, honey," Gene explained patiently, and then went on to point out that a cowboy was judged on much more than just staying on the horse's back.

"It's so complicated." She shook her head.

"That's the name of the game," he replied. He smiled down at her. "If you watch rodeo enough, you'll get the hang of seeing how it's judged. That's an art in itself."

She smiled back at him, tingling from head to toe at the warm, intimate look in his eyes before they averted back to the action down in the arena. She couldn't remember when she'd felt happier or more alive. Especially when Gene appropriated her hand and clasped it warmly in his while they watched the rest of the competition.

The last of the bareback bronc riding finished, with the winner and second and third places announced. Then came barrel racing, and the woman named Dale was competing. Allison noticed that Gene didn't applaud or pay much attention to the pretty young woman in the arena. He didn't even react when his ex-lover won the race. Dale Branigan, they announced, and Allison stared down at the younger woman with envy. She was pretty and young and full of the joy of life as she reacted to her win by jumping in the air and giving out a loud, laughing yell. So that was the kind of woman who attracted the taciturn man at her side: young, aggressive, eager for intimacy and fancy-free. She didn't really have much of a chance. That might be a good thing, considering how he seemed to treat women he'd slept with. She felt suddenly sad. She was daydreaming, and it was no good. He might be wonderful to kiss, and delightful as a companion, but it was all just means to an end, she was sure of it. The thought depressed her terribly, although Gene didn't seem to notice. He was quiet after the barrel racing.

He felt Allison's gaze, but he didn't meet it. Seeing Dale again had disturbed him. He remembered very little of the night he'd spent with her, and now he was ashamed of his part in it. The old Gene wouldn't have had any qualms at spending the night in the arms of a pretty, willing woman. But since he'd been taking Allison places, the ease of his old conquest disturbed him. He couldn't sort out the confused feelings he was entertaining for Allison, or the guilt she aroused in him sometimes. She seemed to look for the best in everyone and everything, as if she wouldn't even admit the existence of evil in people. She was caring and kind and gentle, and sensuous in a strange, reserved way. He was surprised at her inhibitions when he kissed and held her intimately, and he wondered why her own conquests hadn't taught her more. Perhaps she'd been sleeping with the wrong men. He thought about sleeping with her himself, and his body vibrated with excitement. It would be like having a virgin, he thought, and his heartbeat increased fiercely. He didn't dare look at her until he got himself under control again.

Unaware of his thoughts, Allison concentrated

on the arena. But there seemed to be a distance between Gene and herself, and she didn't understand why.

In no time, the competition was over, the prizes awarded and it was time to go home. Allison followed Gene down from the bleachers, noting his dark scowl as he saw Dale coming toward them with her award.

"Going to congratulate me?" she asked Gene, apparently having recovered from her bad humor, because she was smiling seductively.

"Sure. Congratulations." He slid an arm around Allison's shoulders and drew her close, glancing down at her possessively. "We thought you were great, didn't we, cupcake?" he added, his voice low and caressing for Allison.

She smiled with difficulty, going along with the pretense. "Yes." She looked at the younger woman with kind eyes. "You were very good."

Dale shifted restlessly under that warm, easy smile, which showed no trace of antagonism or hostility. She didn't know how to react to a woman who didn't behave like a spitting cat. "Thanks," she said uneasily. "Going to the dance?" she added.

"We might," he said.

"Going to introduce me?" she persisted, nodding toward Allison.

"This is Allison Hathoway," he said, glancing down at her. "She's an old friend of Winnie's. You know Winnie—she's engaged to Dwight."

"I know her. Nice to meet you. I'm Dale Branigan." She extended a hand and shook Allison's firmly, her blue eyes unwavering. "Are you just visiting?"

Allison nodded. "For another week or so," she said, hating to put into words how little time she had left. But she couldn't impose much longer on the Manleys, and she had to go to Arizona and finish tying up the loose ends of her parents' lives. It was a task she didn't anticipate with pleasure.

Gene stiffened. He hadn't realized how soon she planned to leave. It disturbed him to think of her going away, and he didn't understand why.

Allison felt the sudden stiffening and looked up at Gene just as he glanced down at her. The tension exploded between them so that it was almost visible. Dale said something and left and neither of them noticed her departure. Allison's lips parted under the force of the shared look, the impact like lightning striking. Her heart raced.

"Do you want to go to a dance with me?" he asked huskily, his body suddenly on fire. "It would mean going home very, very late."

"Yes." She spoke without hesitation. She didn't

want to go home yet; she didn't want to say good-night to him. She wasn't considering the dangers of being seen in public or giving the media any clues to her whereabouts. She wanted to be held in his arms, for as long as possible. She was too much in love to care about the consequences anymore.

Gene was feeling the same thing. His world had just narrowed to the woman beside him. "All right," he said curtly. "To hell with the consequences. Come on."

Chapter Seven

The dance that followed the rodeo was in a local bar and grill, and nothing fancy by city standards. It was very casual, with men and women both in jeans and Western hats, in what looked like a converted barn.

Gene ordered two beers, ignoring Allison's grimace, and seated them at a small round table near the dance floor. There was a live band and no shortage of dancers. The place was packed with celebrators from the rodeo.

"But…" she protested when Gene put the mug of foamy beer in front of her.

"Taste it first," he coaxed gently. "It won't hurt you. One beer isn't going to do much damage, and I've ordered some sandwiches to go with it. Okay?"

She sighed, still reluctant.

He leaned toward her, one lean forefinger tracing patterns on the back of her hand while his eyes held hers. "I like beer. I'll taste of it when we leave here." His gaze fell to her mouth. "If you taste of it, too, it won't bother you when we make love."

Her lips parted and her heart jumped. "Tonight?" she stammered, because he looked as if he meant business this time.

"Tonight, Allison," he said huskily. He caught her eyes again and held them, his whole body throbbing with anticipation. She was staring back at him just as intently and he felt his body react fiercely. He leaned closer, his lips almost touching hers as he spoke. "There's a line cabin between here and the house," he breathed. He caught her chin and tilted it tenderly so that his thin lips could brush lightly over hers in a whisper of rough persuasion. "I promise you, I'll be gentle. It will be exactly the way you want it, all the way."

She tried to speak, but his teeth closed on her lower lip, tugging, and before she could get a word out, the moist warmth of his mouth buried itself in hers. She was so sweet. He could hardly breathe for his need of her. He hadn't meant to let it go this far, but once he felt her mouth under his, he couldn't stop.

He wasn't the only one. Allison shivered with reaction. Her mouth answered his, blind to where they were, deaf to the people and music around them, hopelessly lost in him. Nothing mattered except being in his arms. She'd been alone so long, been through so much. Surely she could be given this one, sweet night! To lie in the arms of the man she loved and be cherished, just one time. The temptation was overwhelming. And he'd said he'd be gentle. That had to mean he cared. Hadn't he told her at the beginning that he was always rough because that was the way he liked it—and now here he was putting her wants before his. He had to care, a little.

When he lifted his head, they were both breathing roughly. He had to force himself to draw away. With a jerky movement, he reached for his mug of beer and all but drained it.

"I didn't mean to do that, yet," he said unsteadily. He stared at her solemnly, his eyes lingering on her delicately flushed face with its exquisite complexion. Her eyes were misty, a little dazed, and her mouth was swollen and parted from the long, hard kiss. Just the sight of her knocked the breath out of him.

"It's all right," she said huskily.

He averted his gaze and found himself looking at Dale, who was dancing stiffly with a plain, lanky man wearing a red shirt. She gave him a pouting, accusing look before she turned her attention back to her partner.

Allison followed the cold stare of his eyes. "She's very pretty," she remarked quietly.

He turned, his gaze glittering. "Yes. But she wanted more than I could give her."

Was she like that, too, Allison wondered, wanting more than he had to give? It didn't seem to matter. She was too hopelessly in love with him to let it matter tonight. Soon she'd be alone again, for the rest of her life. Just this one night, she prayed silently. And then the thought bored into her mind—be careful what you ask for…you might get it.

She quickly lowered her gaze to her own beer. She cupped her hands around the frosty mug and lifted it to her lips, making a face when she tasted it.

She looked over at Gene. They came from different worlds. He wouldn't understand her hang-ups any more than she could understand his lack of scruples with women. She'd told a lie and now it was catching up with her. Despite the fact that he'd opened up to her, that they were getting along well together, she was still afraid to tell him the truth about herself. But would it matter—if he were gentle? She flushed.

Her eyes searched his stern expression. There was a different man that he kept hidden from the world. She caught glimpses of him from time to time, behind the sarcasm and tough facade. She wanted a glimpse of the lonely, wounded man he was hiding.

A sudden cry split the noise of people and music, and suddenly everything around them abruptly stopped.

"What is it?" Allison asked, frowning as she looked toward the bar.

He turned in his seat and stood. "Oh, boy," he murmured. "Somebody broke a beer bottle and cut his hand half off. Dale's new beau, Ben, no less."

Allison got up without a word and went to the hurt man. She smiled at Dale and then at the cowboy, who was holding his hand and shivering with pain while Dale tried ineffectually to stem the flow of blood.

"Let me," she said gently, taking the cloth from Dale's shaking hands. "I know what to do."

She did, too. Gene watched her with fascination, remembering how efficiently she'd patched him up. He wondered where and why she'd gotten her first-aid training. She was good at it, calm and collected and quietly reassuring. Even Dale relaxed, color coming back into her white face.

"That should do it," she said after a few minutes of applied pressure. "Fortunately it was a vein and not an artery. But it will need stitches," she added gently, cleaning her hands with a basin and cloth the bartender had provided after she'd put a temporary bandage over the cut. "Can you drive him to the hospital?"

"Yes," Dale said. She hesitated. "Thanks."

"That goes double for me," the cowboy said with a quiet smile of his own, although he was still in a lot of pain. "I could have bled to death."

"Not likely, but you're welcome. Good night."

They left, and Allison noticed that Dale gave Gene a long, hurting look even as she went out the door with her wounded cowboy. Poor thing, she thought miserably. Maybe she'd look like that one day, when Gene didn't want her anymore.

Without sparing her a glance, Gene led Allison out onto the dance floor. "Full of surprises, aren't you?" he mused. "Where did you learn so much about first aid?"

"I had a good teacher," she said noncommittally, smiling up at him.

He scowled down at her. "I can't dig anything out of you, can I?" he asked quietly. "You're very mysterious, cupcake."

"There's nothing out of the ordinary about me," she laughed. "I'm just a working girl."

"When are you leaving the Manleys'?" he asked suddenly.

She lowered her eyes to his broad chest. "Next week. I don't want to, but I need to," she said. "I've got a lot to do."

"Where?"

"In Arizona," she said.

"Is that where you work?"

She hesitated. "I guess it's where I'll be working now," she replied. She didn't want to think about it. Life was suddenly very complicated, and the worst of it was going to be leaving here and not seeing Gene Nelson again.

He sighed half angrily. One lean arm pulled her closer and he turned her sharply to the music, so that his powerful leg insinuated itself intimately close to hers.

She stiffened a little and he slowed, pausing to look down at her.

"Don't fight it," he said huskily. "Life's too short as it is, and what we've got together is magic." And with that, he caught both her arms and eased them under his and around him while his circled her, bringing her totally against him.

"Gene," she protested weakly.

"This is the way everyone else is doing it, if you want to look around us. Put your cheek on my chest and give in."

She knew it was suicide, but she couldn't help her own weakness. She moved close to him with a long sigh and laid her cheek against his hard chest. Under his blue shirt she could feel the warmth of his body and the rough beat of his heart. He smelled of soap and cologne and starch, and the slow caress of his hands on her back was drugging.

They moved lazily around the floor as the lights dimmed and the music became sultry. Everyone was relaxed now, a little high from the beer and revelry, and when Gene's hands slid down to her lower spine and pulled her intimately to him, she didn't protest.

His lean, fit body began to react to that closeness almost at once. He felt himself going rigid against her, but he didn't try to shield her from it. It was too late, anyway.

He lifted his head and looked down into her eyes while they danced. She looked a little nervous and uncertain, but she wasn't protesting.

His eyes fell to her breasts, lingering on them. With a low murmur, he drew his hands up her back to her rib cage and slowly, torturously moved her toward him so that her breasts brushed sensuously against his hard chest, making the tips suddenly hard and swollen. He could feel them even through the fabric, and when she trembled, he felt that, too.

His eyes lifted to hers, and held them as his hands moved again, down, down, until they reached her hips. He lifted her gently and her thighs brushed his, hard.

Her breath caught. She flushed, because even an innocent couldn't mistake what he was feeling and what he wanted now. But the worst of it was that she wanted it just as much. She was caught in a sensual daze and her body ached. She wanted him to kiss her. She wanted his hands on her body to soothe the burning ache he'd created. She wanted…him.

He stopped dancing and stood with her in the middle of the dance floor, his pale eyes glittery as they searched hers. "I want to take you out of here," he said huskily. "I can't stand much more of this."

"Yes," she whispered. She knew what he was saying, and part of her was ashamed and frightened and reluctant. But she cared too much to refuse him.

"All right." He let her move slowly away from him, but he didn't let her go. "I need a minute, cupcake," he said softly. He pulled her back into his arms, but so that their legs didn't touch. He drew in deep breaths until he could get his body back in control so that what he felt wouldn't be on public display. Then, gently, he led her off the dance floor and out the door to the Jeep, ignoring the sandwiches he'd already paid for that had just been placed on their table. Food was the very last thing on his mind right now.

"Did you enjoy the rodeo?" he asked on the way home. He hadn't touched her or said anything vaguely romantic since they'd left the bar. Allison was still in a daze, and her body was on fire to be held close to his. But she tried to keep that to herself.

"I enjoyed it very much," she said. "I never realized the events were so complicated."

"It helps when you know a bit about it," he said. He was nervous. Imagine that, he thought with graveyard humor, and with his reputation. But Allison wasn't like other women he'd made love to. She was very, very special, and he wanted this to be like no other time for her. He wanted to give her everything.

He pulled off the main road and drove toward the ranch, but there was a dirt track that led into a grove of trees by the creek, and he took that one instead of the ranch road that led home.

Allison felt herself tensing, because she knew instinctively what was in that grove of trees down the road. But she didn't say a word. She'd committed herself back in Cody. It would be cowardly and cruel to back down now. Of course, that was only an excuse to appease her conscience, and she knew it. She looked at the man beside her and knew that she'd do anything he asked of her. No one had ever been so gentle and kind to her, no man had ever made her feel so special. He'd rescued her from a kind of limbo that she'd been in ever since her parents death.

"The line cabin is down there," he said, trying not to show how desperately he needed her or how nervous he was. "It's old. Probably the oldest building still in use on the place. The men stay here during the winter when they have to keep up with the outlying herds."

"I see."

He pulled up in front of a small, darkened cabin that looked like something out of a history journal and cut the engine and the lights. "It doesn't look like much, but it's pretty well kept."

He got out and helped her out, then led her up the porch to the front door and inside. She felt oddly light-headed, probably, she thought dizzily, the result of the beer and no food.

"See, we even have electricity," he mused, turning on a small lamp.

The cabin was only one room, with a small kitchen, a fireplace and two chairs, and a neatly made bed with a blue-beige-and-red-patterned quilted coverlet over it. Just the thing, Allison thought, for a cowboy on his own in the winter.

"The bed linen is washed weekly, even if nobody stays here, and we keep a supply of food in the kitchen," he told her. He turned, his gaze slow and warm on her face as he took off his Stetson and tossed it onto a chair. She looked so young, he thought, watching her. So sweet and vulnerable and hungry for him. His heart raced.

Without another word, he unfastened his bola and unsnapped the buttons down the front of his shirt with a dark, lean hand.

Her breath caught in her throat as he pulled

the shirt out of his jeans and opened it. His chest was darkly tanned and thick with curling black hair. He moved toward her with a faintly arrogant expression, as if he knew how exciting and sensuous he was without the trembling of her body and the sudden parting of her lips to tell him.

He caught her cool hands and brought them under the lapels of the open shirt, pressing them palm down on his warm, rough chest. The sensation was incredible. He shivered. "Feel me," he said huskily, moving her hands around. He drew her to him and bent to her lips, pausing just above them to tease them, torment them, while he let her hands learn the contours of his torso. It was sheer heaven, the feel of those soft, warm fingers on his taut body. He felt himself going rigid all at once and didn't even try to hold back.

"Allison," he groaned as he bent to her mouth. "Oh, God, I've never wanted anyone so much!"

The wording weakened her, because she knew how he felt. Odd, with his reputation that he could be so vulnerable to an innocent like her. Of course, she thought uneasily, he didn't know she was innocent. His hands were moving over her back and she hesitated for just one second with maidenly fear of the unknown. Then she relaxed as the kiss began to work on her, his exploring lips making her mouth soft and eager for its moist, warm touch.

All at once, the wanting broke through his control. His tongue shot into the dark softness of her mouth in a rhythm that was staggeringly sensual and arousing. She gasped in shocked pleasure. But there was more to come.

His lean hands caught the backs of her thighs and lifted her up to his aroused body in a sharp, quick rhythm that made her knees go weak and shaky. Sensations of hot pleasure rippled through her lower belly like the tide itself. She shuddered all over and grabbed his arms to keep from toppling over at the feverish need she felt. She cried out under his mouth, and he made a deep, satisfied sound in his throat.

He bent, lifting her totally against him, her feet dangling as his hands suddenly brought his hard thighs between her legs and pressed her intimately to him.

She moaned harshly, clinging, almost in tears from the sudden fury of her desire of him. She knew in the back of her mind that this was wrong, that she was letting him go too far, but she was helpless from the hot surge of passion he'd kindled in her. She'd never known such pleasure.

Her mouth answered his, giving him back the

deep kiss as hungrily as he offered it. He felt his own body begin to tremble and he knew there was no way he could stop now. It had gone too far.

He fell onto the bed with her, shivering with need, his hands trembling as they slipped her out of her sweater and T-shirt and the filmy bra she wore under them. He didn't stop there, either. While he was at it, he unsnapped the skirt and kissed his way down to her thighs while he smoothed the rest of her clothing down her body and tossed it aside with her shoes.

She lay nude under the slow, insistent brush of his hard mouth. His hands explored while his mouth learned every soft curve of her in a silence that grew hotter with her soft cries of pleasure and the helpless movements of her body on the springy mattress.

He lifted his head while his fingers brushed expertly over the hard crests of her breasts and he looked into her eyes with pure masculine need. She was shivering, her eyes wide and glazed, her lips parted under hopelessly gasping breaths. Her long legs were moving helplessly on the bed in little jerky motions. Yes, he thought feverishly, and he touched her gently where she was most a woman, deliberately adding to her helplessness as shocks of pleasure lifted her hips and closed her eyes.

He didn't question why she should be so easily and quickly aroused, or why her eyes opened in something like faint shock when he threw off his shirt and boots and socks and started unzipping his jeans with quick, economical movements. He didn't question why she lifted up suddenly on her elbows and gasped when he turned, his blatant arousal the crowning glory of a body that some women had called perfection itself. His mind was buried in the desire for her that had made him shudder at just the sight of that creamy pink body with its firm, soft breasts and exquisite figure, lying there waiting for him, trembling.

He straddled her hips arrogantly, watching her watch him with wide, almost frightened eyes.

"You can take me, if that's what you're frightened of," he said gently, levering down so that his body slowly overwhelmed hers, his elbows catching his weight. "A woman's body is a miracle," he whispered at her lips. "Elastic and soft and vibrant with life." His mouth brushed hers in tender little contacts that aroused like wildfire while his hands smoothed down her body, his thumbs hard on her belly, rough, making some unbelievable sensations kindle with each long pass of his hands. She shivered under his warm mouth, her nudity and his maleness almost forgotten until his knee began to ease between her long legs.

"Shhh," he whispered when she tensed. "Don't do that. I want you just as badly, but if you tense up, it's going to hurt."

She swallowed. It would hurt anyway, but it was too late to tell him that, because his hips were already probing delicately at hers.

He kissed her face with trembling, aching tenderness, while his lean hands gently positioned her hips. "One, long, sweet joining," he whispered into her open mouth. "That's what I want first, before I even begin to love you." His thumbs pressed into her belly again, making her shiver. He smiled tenderly against her lips. "Now lift up against me, very, very slowly," he whispered. He lifted his eyes to watch. He'd never wanted to watch before, but this was like no other time in his life. Her eyes were wide, almost frightened. "Shhh," he breathed, achingly tender as he began the slow, downward movement of his body. "Shhh. Be one with me, now," he whispered. She tensed and he smiled, sliding one hand between them to gently caress her flat belly. "Yes, just relax and let it happen. Don't close your eyes," he said huskily. "Watch me. Let me watch you. I want...to see you...take me!"

His teeth ground together and Allison was so shocked by what he was saying and doing that she forgot to be afraid. His powerful body was tanned all over, except for that pale strip across his lean hips, and she saw his eyes dilate, his teeth clench, his face contort with wonder. She could feel the shudder that went through him, she could actually see him lose control.

It was what made it bearable when he suddenly cried out and pushed into her body with helpless, driving urgency. The pain was scalding, like being torn with a hot knife, and she both stiffened and dug her fingers into his arms, weeping suddenly as he hurt her.

But she was too ready for him for it to last long. Gene felt the barrier give, somewhere in the back of his mind, although it didn't register through the blinding throb of pleasure that ran down his backbone and sent him wild in her arms. He buffeted her with a total, absolute loss of control, borne of too many months of abstinence and his raging hunger for her. A loaded gun wouldn't have stopped him.

Allison wept silently for her lack of resistance. He was going to hate her. He couldn't not know what she was, now.

Seconds later, he stiffened and cried out, and

Allison watched his corded torso lift as his hips enforced their mastery of her, watched his face contort in the unmistakable mask of fulfillment. His voice throbbed hoarsely as he cried her name once, twice, and then like a prayer, his body convulsed in a red fever of blinding ecstasy.

It hadn't hurt as much as she thought it would. He was lying on her heavily now, his body drenched in sweat, his mouth against her bare shoulder. Still flushing from what she'd seen, she stroked his damp, black hair absently, her eyes wide and shocked as she stared at the rough wood of the ceiling. Despite everything it was so sweet to lie and hold him like this, so close that they were still one person. The embarrassment and pain and shame would follow, she knew, and would be almost unbearable. But for these few seconds, he was helpless and in need of comfort, and she held him to her with tender generosity, her eyes closing as she whispered her love for him silently, without a sound.

Gene got his breath back and lifted his head to look at Allison. Her eyes opened slowly and she blushed. There was something in those soft hazel eyes that hurt him. He'd failed her all the way around.

He accepted the knowledge with shame and a

kind of helpless pleasure as his eyes slid down to her breasts, still hard-tipped because he hadn't satisfied her. He would have been more than willing to do that, because she'd given him heaven. But it would be too soon for her, after the ordeal of her first time. First time. He shivered. A virgin. He was her first man.

The thought humbled him. He bent and started to kiss her soft mouth, but she turned her head, and then he saw it. The shame. The fear. He took a sharp breath and rolled away from her, standing up to dress quietly, with cold efficiency. It had never been like that, he thought bitterly; it had never been so urgent that he couldn't wait for his partner. He couldn't even blame the beer, because he hadn't had that much. And he knew damned well he hadn't satisfied Allison. There hadn't been time. Besides that, he thought, horrified as he turned to look at her, she'd been unnaturally tight and afraid and now he knew that he must have hurt her terribly. They said no man could tell, but even without glancing at that faint stain on the coverlet, he knew. Somehow, he thought he'd known from the beginning. And if his own guilt wasn't enough, she wouldn't even look at him. She made him feel like less than a man.

He looked away while she put on her own

clothes with trembling hands. When he turned again, she was sitting on the edge of the bed with her hands folded on her thighs, her eyes downcast, her thin body trembling.

The most beautiful experience of his life, and he'd cost her not only her chastity but any pleasure she might have had, all because he'd been selfish. She looked as if what she'd done was some unforgivable sin to boot. Her downcast, defeated expression made him hurt. His guilt and self-contempt spurred his temper, and he exploded with rage.

He reached out and grabbed her arms, jerking her roughly to her feet. "Damn you," he said icily, shaking her none too gently. His blazing eyes made her flinch. "You lied to me! You told me you were experienced, when all the time you were a virgin!"

She all but cringed, closing her eyes. Neither of them saw or heard the shadowy figure on horseback who'd heard that furious accusation. The rider moved a little closer and spotted them through the window, a sarcastic smile on his mouth. He didn't hesitate. He abruptly turned his mount and stealthily rode away.

"Why did you do it?" Gene was demanding.

"I wanted to get to know you," she said dully.

"Well, you did, didn't you?" he asked with deliberate cruelty, and a meaningful glance at the stain on the coverlet.

Her eyes dropped on a hurting moan. Tears were rolling down her cheeks without a sound. She stared at his throat, watching the pulse throb there. She deserved the anger, so she didn't fight it. He was right. She'd lied and let him think she was experienced and because of it, he hadn't felt any need to hold back physically. Now he'd seduced her and she only had herself to blame. Worse than that, she hadn't taken any precautions or asked him to. One time might not be anything to worry about, of course, but there were no guarantees. And she still had to live with her guilt and shame, with her conscience.

He let go of her abruptly, savagely ashamed of his own uncharacteristic behavior. He didn't think he'd ever be able to look at her again without hating himself.

Allison, of course, didn't realize that his anger was directed at himself, not at her. She thought he surely must hate her now, and she couldn't bear to meet his eyes.

He noticed, with bitter pain. "We'd better go," he said coldly.

He turned out the light and jerked open the door, helping her inside the Jeep with icy courtesy before he went back to lock the cabin. He got into the Jeep without a single word, and that was how he drove home.

When he pulled up at the Manleys' house, she got out without assistance, clutching her purse, and she didn't say anything or look back as she went up onto the porch. Shades of Gene Nelson himself, she thought with almost hysterical humor. Wasn't he the one who never looked back?

But apparently he wasn't going to let her get away with it that easily. He went with her, staying her hand as she started to unlock the door.

"Are you all right?" he asked tersely, forcing the words out.

"Yes." She didn't look up. Her soul was tarnished.

He took off his Stetson and ran a hand through his hair. "Allison," he began hesitantly. "What I said back there..."

"It doesn't matter," she replied numbly. "I have to go in now. I'm sorry about...about what happened. I've never had alcohol before."

"And that was why?" he asked with a mocking laugh. "You were drunk?" Deny it, he was thinking. For God's sake, tell me it was because you loved me!

But the silent plea passed into the night. She unlocked the door. "Goodbye, Gene," she said gently, even now unable to blame him for something she'd encouraged to happen.

"Isn't that a little premature?" he asked hesitantly.

"I'll be leaving in the morning," she said without looking at him. "You won't have to worry that I'll…be like Dale and hound you…" Her voice broke and she got inside fast, closing and locking the door behind her.

Gene stood staring at the closed door for a long moment. He felt empty and alone and deeply ashamed. What had possessed him to attack her, as if the whole thing was her fault? She was a gentle woman, with a soft heart and a heavy conscience, and it bothered him that she'd looked so torn when he let her go. She talked about religion a lot and church, and he wondered if she believed sleeping around was a mortal sin. It amazed him that he hadn't seen through the act, that he'd really believed she was experienced, when everything pointed the other way. If he'd kept his head, he'd have known in time that she was innocent, and he could have stopped. But he didn't know, and he hadn't been rational enough to control his raging desire. A desire that he still felt, to a frightening degree. Allison. He felt her loss to his very soul.

In a few days she'd become an integral part of his life, his thoughts. He wasn't sure if he could go on living when she left Pryor. Could half a man live?

He turned and went back to the Jeep, cursing himself all the way. She'd leave and he'd never have the opportunity to apologize. Not that she was completely blameless, he told himself. It hadn't been all his fault. But what had motivated her? Had it been desire? Loneliness? Curiosity? Or had there been some feeling in her for him? She was a virgin and she'd given herself. Would she really have done that, being the kind of person she was, unless she cared deeply? His heart leaped at the thought of Allison loving him.

Of course, she was twenty-five and modern, he reminded himself grimly. Maybe she was just tired of being a virgin. He didn't like to consider that last possibility. And even if she had begun to care about him, she surely wouldn't now. His cruelty would have shown her how fruitless that would be. He climbed into the Jeep, started the engine, threw the car in gear and pulled out of the yard. This time he stopped the car, and he looked back. It was the first time in his life that he ever had. But darkened windows were all that met his hungry gaze. After a moment, he pulled the Jeep back onto the road and drove home.

Inside the house, Allison had made it to her room without being seen by Winnie. She took a shower, with water as hot as she could stand it, to wash away the scent and feel of Gene Nelson. She washed her hair as well. Her body felt bruised and torn, but she couldn't bring herself to tell Winnie what had happened. She was going to have to invent an argument or something to explain her sudden departure. But whatever happened, she couldn't stay here any longer. Even the horror of the past few weeks and the fear of being hounded by the media were preferable to ever having to see Gene again. He hated her. She'd made him hate her by lying to him. He must feel terrible now, too, knowing the truth about her. He'd said he didn't play around with virgins, and she'd made a liar out of him.

She lay down, but she didn't sleep. Her mind went over and over that painful episode in the line cabin until she was utterly sick. The worst of it was that Gene was right. It was her fault. She'd ignored Winnie's warnings about Gene and the danger of physical attraction. Now she understood, too late, what it was all about. She'd never dreamed that she could be so hungry for a man that principles and morals could be totally forgotten. Now she knew. She wondered if she'd ever be able to forget what she'd done. Loving him didn't seem to excuse her behavior, or justify her submission anymore.

She got up before daylight and packed. The phone rang long before she dressed and went downstairs, but apparently it wasn't for her, because she wasn't disturbed.

She put her hair up in a bun and dressed in her sedate gray dress with matching high heels for the trip to Arizona. With a glance at her too-pale face in the mirror, she went in to breakfast and pasted a smile on her lips.

But there was no one there. She searched the house and found a scribbled note from Winnie. "Gone to hospital," she read. "Dwight hurt in wreck."

She caught her breath. Poor Winnie! And poor Dwight! She picked up the phone and called the hospital immediately, having found the number in the telephone directory.

She got the floor nurse on Dwight's ward and talked to her. After introducing herself, she explained about Dwight and Winnie and the nurse was sympathetic enough to tell her what had happened. When she hung up, she knew it was going to be impossible for her to leave. Dwight was in intensive care and he might die. She was trapped. She couldn't leave Winnie at a time like this, even if it meant having to endure Gene's hatred in the process.

Chapter Eight

Winne came home at lunch, red-eyed and wilted, supported by her worried mother.

"Oh, Winnie, I'm so sorry," Allison said, hugging her friend warmly. "Is there any change?"

"Not yet." Winnie wept. "Allie, I can't bear to lose him! I can't!"

"Head injuries are tricky," Allison said quietly. "He's in a coma, but that doesn't mean he won't come out of it. I've seen some near-fatal injuries that recovered fully. Give it time."

"I'll go mad!" the blonde wailed.

Allison hugged her again. "No, you won't.

Come on, I've made lunch. I'll bet you're both starved."

"I certainly am," Mrs. Manley said gently. She smiled at Allison. "Bless you for thinking of food. We really hadn't."

"I can understand why. What happened?"

"Nobody knows. The car he was driving went down a ravine. They only found him early this morning. Gene and Marie are at the hospital. Gene looks really bad," Winnie said.

Allison averted her face before anyone could see that she did, too, and make any embarrassing connections. "I'll pour the coffee," she said.

She didn't want to go to the hospital with them, but Winnie pleaded, so she did.

When they walked into the waiting room, only Marie was there, and Allison thanked her lucky stars. She hugged Marie and murmured all the comforting things she could think of. Then she went in search of the floor nurse she'd talked to on the phone, while Winnie and Mrs. Manley sat with Marie.

Tina Gates was in charge of the intensive care unit, a twenty-two-year veteran of nursing arts. She welcomed Allison and showed her through the ward, pausing at Dwight's bed.

"He's bad," she told Allison. "But he's a fighter,

like the rest of his family, and strong-willed. I think he'll come out of it."

"I hope so," Allison said gently, staring at Dwight's unnaturally pale face. "My best friend loves him very much."

"Sometimes love is what it takes." She continued the tour, and they came back to Dwight's cubical when they finished. "If you ever want a job, we've got a place for you," she told Allison. "Help is hard to get out here, and you're more qualified than even I am. I never had the opportunity to go on and get my degree in nursing arts."

"I was lucky," Allison said. "My parents sacrificed a lot for my education. It's important work, and I love it. I don't know that I could get used to the routine in a hospital. I'm too accustomed to primitive conditions. But I appreciate the offer, all the same."

"I'll repeat it at intervals, if you promise to consider it," Tina promised, smiling. "This is pretty country, and there are some nice folks here. You might like it."

"I already do. But I made a promise to my parents that I'd carry on the work they did," Allison said finally. "I don't like to break promises."

"Actually, neither do…look!"

Tina went quickly to Dwight's side and watched

him move restlessly. His eyes opened and he groaned.

"Head…hurts," he mumbled.

"Hallelujah!" Tina grinned. "If your head hurts, Mr. Nelson, it means you're alive. I'll get Dr. Jackson right now!"

"I'll go and tell Winnie. Dwight, I'm glad you're back with us," she said gently, touching his arm where the IV was attached. "They'll give you something for the pain. Just try to relax and don't move around too much."

He looked up at her, licking dry lips. "Gene?" he whispered.

Her face closed up. "Do you want to see him?"

"Yes."

"I'll try to find him. Rest, now." She patted his hand and walked out, all nerves.

Gene was in the waiting room when she came out. He stiffened as she approached, but Allison pretended not to notice. After the night before, it was all she could do to stay in the same room with him without breaking down and crying.

"He's out of the coma," she said, talking to Winnie and Marie. "They're getting the doctor. I think he'll be all right."

"Oh, thank God!" Winnie burst out, and Marie

laughed and cried as the two women hugged each other.

"Your first-aid training qualifies you to make prognoses, does it?" Gene drawled suddenly with cold mockery. Having her deliberately ignore him had hurt him terribly.

"First-aid training?" Winnie asked, frowning. "Gene, she's a registered nurse, didn't she tell you?"

Gene scowled. "A nurse!"

"A graduate nurse, with a college degree," Winnie said. "You didn't tell him?" she asked Allison.

Allison's eyes warned her not to give anything else away. "There was no need to," she said simply. She didn't want him to know about the life she'd led. "Dwight is asking for you," she said.

"He wants to talk business," Winnie muttered. "Well, that can wait. I want to see him first. Marie, come on, we'll go together."

"But the doctor..." Allison began.

"We'll ask first," Winnie promised, dragging a smiling Marie along with her.

Allison was left alone with Gene, who shoved his hands into his pockets.

"A nurse. No wonder you were so good at patching people up," he said absently. Even Dwight's miraculous return to consciousness didn't quite register through the shock. He glared at her. "How many other secrets are you keeping?" he asked bitterly. She hadn't trusted him at all. Did everyone know things about her that he didn't?

"Enough, I suppose," she said, folding her hands in front of her. She turned away from him and stared out the window.

"I thought you were leaving today."

"So did I. Don't worry. This is just a temporary setback. The minute Dwight's off the critical list, I'll be on the next plane out."

His eyes narrowed. Was that what she thought? That he couldn't wait to get rid of her? Seeing her did play havoc with his conscience, but probably it was worse for her. Why hadn't she told him she was a qualified nurse? And what were those other secrets she was keeping? She hadn't shared anything with him, except her body, and she hadn't enjoyed that. It would haunt him forever that he'd taken his pleasure at her expense. Poor little thing, all she'd given him since they met was tenderness and concern and compassion. And for that, he'd given her a nightmare experience that would scar her.

Guilt was riding him hard. It was the first time in memory that he'd ever hurt a woman in bed, and he didn't like the feeling. His teeth ground together. If only she'd told him! He'd have made her glory in that sweet sacrifice. Of course, he had to admit that it could have been worse. He'd aroused her totally, and he'd treated her like a virgin, as if maybe subconsciously he had known. A man without scruples could have done her a lot more damage. He frowned, thinking about Allison in bed with some other man. It made him livid with jealousy.

"A nurse, of all things," he said curtly, glaring at her. "It's a miracle that you reached your present age intact. Don't they teach you anything about sex in nurses' training?"

She went scarlet and wouldn't look at him. "It isn't the same as reading about it," she said stiffly.

His jaw clenched. "No doubt. You little fool, if I'd known, I could have made you faint with the pleasure! God knows, I had the experience to give you that. I hurt you. My conscience is giving me hell. Damn it, Allison, if I'd known, I could have stopped!"

She turned, her eyes shy but knowing. "Could you, Gene?" she asked sadly.

He averted his eyes to the wall. No, of course he couldn't have. But it made him feel better to think so. "Dwight will have to have around-the-clock nursing when he comes home. He's got some internal injuries and a busted rib besides the concussion."

"It shouldn't be too difficult finding someone," she said slowly, although she had her doubts after what Tina Gates had said about the shortage of nurses around here.

He whirled and stared at her. "He likes you." Was he out of his mind, he wondered? The very last thing she'd agree to was a job that put her near him. But the thought was intriguing. Having her in his home, near him, being able to look at her whenever he liked would be so sweet. He caught his breath at the very thought of it.

Allison was catching her own breath. She didn't want to be near him, not at any price. "No," she said hastily. "No, I can't do it. I have to go back to Arizona."

He moved toward her, and she backed up a step, afraid to be close to him again. What had happened once was never going to be allowed to happen again.

Gene stopped. He understood that timid retreat. He'd hurt her, mentally and physically. She had every right to be intimidated by him.

"Dwight needs you," he said softly. Charm had never meant much to him before, but if he could lure her home with him, he might have a chance that she'd begin to trust him. "Winnie would be grateful," he coaxed. "And so would Marie and I."

"You needn't pretend that you want me around, Gene," she replied miserably. "You can find someone else to sit with Dwight."

"He has nothing to do with you and me," he said after a minute, his eyes narrow and steady on her face. "He's my brother, honey. I love him."

That got to her when nothing else had. She clasped her hands tightly together. "I thought you'd decided you weren't part of his family anymore," she murmured.

He sighed. "So I had. Until I heard he'd been hurt. Strange how nothing else seems to matter when someone's near death. I thought of all the good times we had as kids, all the games we played together, all the mischief we got into." A faint smile came to his thin lips. "Even if there wasn't much blood tying us together, we were the best of friends. Marie and I fight, but we'd die for each other. I guess I've been living inside myself without a thought to how it affected them." He looked straight at her. "It's still hard for me. But I think we can work it out now, if I don't have to worry about somebody to take care of Dwight. The hospital is short staffed."

"Tina told me," she said. She wrapped her arms around her breasts and turned away, head bent.

He moved closer, keeping some distance between them so that she wouldn't feel uncomfortable. "You can't regret what happened any more than I do, sweetheart," he said unexpectedly, and in a tone that made her legs tremble. "I'm sorry."

Her eyes closed. "It was my fault, too," she replied huskily, shaken by his compassion and the soft endearment. "Can we…not talk about it anymore, please?"

"Can I assume that since you've had medical training, you knew how to take care of yourself after what we did?" he persisted, holding his breath while he waited for her reply. He knew he hadn't taken any precautions, and he was pretty sure she hadn't. But he wanted to know.

She didn't look at him. "It wasn't a dangerous time of the month, if that's what you're asking," she said, coloring.

He let out a heavy sigh. "Allison," he said softly, "that wasn't what I asked."

She bit her lower lip. "I think it's too late to do anything now," she said, averting her gaze to the window.

"I see." He moved again, towering over her. "A

few weeks, then…until we know for certain?" he asked quietly.

She didn't look up, but she nodded.

He started to speak, but anything he said would be the wrong thing now. His shoulders lifted and fell in a strangely impotent gesture and he moved back to the chairs.

The thought of a child scared him to death. He couldn't imagine what they'd do if they'd created a life together during that frenzied coupling. He didn't want a child to suffer for his lapse. He was terrified because of his father's character, sick at the thought of passing those genes onto a child. It wasn't rational, but it was how he felt. God, there couldn't be a child!

But even as he dreaded that thought, his eyes sought Allison and he scowled thoughtfully. She had a built-in maternal instinct. He could imagine her with a baby in her arms, suckling at her breast…

The sudden, fierce arousal of his body made him gasp audibly. God, what a thing to trigger it! But the more he thought about Allison's slim body growing big with a child, the worse it got. He got up from the chair and left the room without another word, leaving Allison to stare after him with sad curiosity. He couldn't imagine what was wrong with him!

Dwight was glad to see him, and Gene was relieved that his baby brother wasn't going to meet his maker just yet. He looked at the face so like his, and yet so unalike, and smiled indulgently as he held the other man's hand tightly for a minute.

"Need anything you haven't got?" he asked.

Dwight smiled through a drugged haze. "Not really, thanks. You handle things for us while I'm here, okay? I think I've made a real mess of the books."

"You don't know what I've done to the daily routine with the livestock," Gene confessed with a grin.

"Dad sure fouled us up, didn't he?" Dwight groaned. "I know he never meant it to wind up this way. He knew I couldn't handle finances. Why saddle me with it?"

"We'll never know," Gene replied. "We just have to make the best of it."

"No, we don't. We can go back to the way we were doing things before Dad died. If we both agree to it, we can have a contract drawn up and the will won't be binding. I've already asked our attorneys."

"You didn't mention that to me," Gene reminded him.

Dwight shifted. "You weren't ready to listen. I know it hit you hard, finding out about the past. But I figured when you were ready, we could talk about it." He winced. "Head hurts real bad, Gene."

"I know." He patted the younger man's shoulder. "I'm trying to talk Allison into nursing you at home. Would you like that?"

He smiled weakly. "Yes. They'd let me go home earlier if I had my own nurse."

"Did you know she was one?" Gene asked, scowling.

"Sure. Winnie told me. And about her parents. Incredible, that she got out at all, isn't it…? Gene, I need a shot real bad."

"I'll go and ask for you," Gene replied, puzzled about what Dwight had started to say. What about Allison's parents? Had there been anything unusual about the way they died? And what was that about it being incredible that Allison got out? Out of where? What? He glowered with frustration. Well, he was going to find out one way or the other. He was tired of being kept in the dark.

Winnie asked, and so did Marie, if Allison

would nurse Dwight. It had been hard enough to refuse Gene, but there was no way she could refuse Winnie. What she didn't know was how she was going to survive a week or more under Gene's roof when Dwight went home.

"You've been different lately," Winnie said several days later, when Allison had put some things into a small bag to take to the Nelson home.

"Different, how?" she hedged.

"Quieter. Less interested in the world. Have you and Gene had a fight? Is that it?"

"Yes," Allison said, because it was easier to admit that than to tell the truth. "A very bad falling out. I was going to leave the morning that Dwight got hurt."

"Oh, Allie." Winnie sat down on the bed where Allison was folding clothes. "I'm sorry. But if Gene wants you to stay with Dwight—and Marie said it was his idea—he can't be holding a grudge."

"He has a lot of reasons to hold one," Allison confessed. She lowered her eyes to the floor. "It's better that I don't see too much of him, that's all."

Marie's eyes narrowed. "Would this have anything to do with Dale Branigan?"

Allison lifted her head. "How did you know about her?"

"Everybody knows about her." Winnie grimaced. "She's been after Gene for a long time—just like most of the single women around here. But she was more blatant with it, and she's a very modern girl. Gene wasn't the first or the last, but she's persistent."

"Yes, I noticed."

"I gave you a bad impression of Gene at the start," Winnie began. "I just wanted to protect you, but I wasn't quite fair to him. Gene can't help being attractive, and I hear he's just plain dynamite in bed. Women chase him. They always have. But since he met you, he's not as wild as he was—he's calmed down a good bit. It's just that he can't shake his old reputation, and I didn't want yours damaged by it."

"Thanks," Allison said quietly. "I know you meant well." She managed not to blush at Winnie's remark about how Gene was in bed. She knew all too well that he was dynamite, and if she hadn't been a virgin, maybe it would have gone on feeling as sweet as it had when he was just kissing and stroking her body.

But maybe that really was all sex was supposed to feel like, for a woman. Maybe it was the preliminary part that made women give in. She sighed. If that was what sex felt like, she wasn't in any rush to experience it again, despite the brief pleasure that had led to it.

Winnie drove her over to the Nelson house, where Dwight was tucked up in bed with every conceivable amusement scattered around him. He had his own TV, DVDs, all the latest movies and a veritable library of the latest bestsellers.

"Talk about the man who has everything," Allison said, smiling at him.

"Not quite everything," Dwight said with weak humor. "My head could use a replacement."

"You'll get better day by day. Don't be too impatient. I'll take very good care of you."

"Thanks." He hesitated, staring up at her with his vivid blue eyes. "I get the feeling that you and Gene are having some problems. In view of that, I really appreciate the sacrifice you're making for me," he added.

She smiled wanly. "Gene and I had a difference of opinion, that's all," she said, trying to downplay it.

"In other words, he tried to get you into bed and you said no." He chuckled when she went scarlet. "Good for you. It will do him good to have the wind knocked out of him."

She didn't say anything. Let him think what he liked. She couldn't bear having anyone find out what had really caused her difference of opinion with Gene. It was a godsend that he was out with the cattle, and she didn't have to see him until she'd settled in.

Winnie was there for supper, visiting with Marie while Allison got Dwight up and ready for the meal that would be served on a tray in his room.

"Gene won't be in until late," Marie said as she helped Winnie and Allison fix a tray. "I'm sorry this had to happen to Dwight, but it's a good thing, in a way. It's brought Gene to the realization that he's still part of this family. I wouldn't take a million dollars for that. He's actually being civil to me, and he's been wonderful to Dwight."

"Sometimes it takes a near tragedy to make us appreciate what we have," she agreed. "You two have a nice supper. I'll come down and get something later. I'm not really hungry right now."

"Okay," Marie said, and smiled. "There's plenty of stuff in the fridge, and if there's anything you need in your room, let us know."

"I'll do that. Thank you, Marie."

"No. Thank *you*," the other woman replied, impulsively hugging her. "You don't know what a load you've taken off our minds."

"Yes, she does," Winnie said warmly, smiling at Allison. "She's very special."

"I'm leaving." Allison laughed. "See you later."

She arranged Dwight's tray and sat down by the bed while he maneuvered his utensils through a pained fog.

"Isn't Gene home yet?" he asked.

She shook her head. "Marie said he'd be late," she replied, hating to talk about him at all.

Dwight caught that note in her voice. He studied her curiously. "You haven't told Gene anything about yourself. Why?"

She couldn't answer that. In the beginning it had been because she didn't want to scare him off. Now, she didn't see any logic in it. She'd be gone soon and Gene wanted no more of her.

"I don't know," she told Dwight. "I suppose the way I've lived has taught me to keep things to myself. My parents were the kind of people who didn't like whiners. They believed in honor and hard work and love." She smiled sadly. "I'll miss them all my life."

"I miss my father that way," he replied. "So do the others. Gene, too. Dad was the only father he really knew."

"What about Gene's real father?" she asked softly.

He started to speak and hesitated. "You'd better ask Gene that," he said. "He and I are getting along better than we have in a long time. I don't want to interfere in his business."

"I can understand that. Can I get you anything?" she asked.

He shook his head. "Thanks. I think I could sleep a little now."

She straightened his pillow with a smile. "I'll get something to read and be nearby if you need me. You've got medicine for the pain. Please don't be nervous about asking for it if you need it. Your body can't heal itself and fight off the pain all at once in your weakened condition. All right?"

"You make it sound simple."

"Most things are. It's people that complicate it all. Sleep well."

Winnie came up later to check on him, and volunteered to sit with Dwight while Allison went down to get herself a sandwich.

Marie had gone to a movie with one of her friends since Allison and Winnie were staying with Dwight. She had, she told them, needed the diversion. It had been a traumatic few days.

Allison understood that. She'd had a pretty traumatic few days herself.

She went downstairs and fixed herself a sandwich in the kitchen. She ate at the kitchen table, liking the cozy atmosphere, with all Marie's green plants giving the yellow and white decor of the room the feel of a conservatory. She was just starting on her second cup of hot black tea when the back door opened and Gene came in.

He looked tired, his face under his wide-brimmed hat hard with new lines. He was wearing dusty boots and jeans and bat-wing chaps, as he had been that day Allison had met him in town, but despite the dust, he was still the most physically devastating man Allison had ever met.

He paused at the table, absently unfastening his chaps while he studied her. She was wearing the gray dress he'd seen her in several times, with her hair up and no makeup, and she looked as tired as he felt.

"Worn-out, little one?" he asked gently.

His unexpected compassion all but made her cry. She took a sip of hot tea to steady herself. "I'm okay." She glanced at him and away, shyly. He was incredibly handsome, with that lean dark face and black hair and glittering peridot eyes. "You look pretty worn-out yourself."

He tossed his Stetson onto the sideboard and smoothed back his black hair. "I've been helping brand cattle." He straddled a chair and folded his arms over the back. "Got another cup?"

"Of course." She poured him a cup of steaming tea. "Want anything in it?" she asked.

He shook his head. "Thanks." He took it from her, noticing how she avoided letting her hand come into contact with his. But he caught her free hand lightly, clasping it in his as he searched her face. "Can't you look at me, sweetheart?" he asked when she kept her eyes downcast.

The endearment went through her like lightning. She didn't dare let him see her eyes. "Let me go, please," she said, and tugged gently at her hand.

He released her with reluctance, watching her as she went back to her own chair and sat down. He no longer had any doubts about her reaction to him. He wrapped his lean hands around his cup and flexed his shoulders, strained from hours in the saddle and back-breaking work as they threw calves to brand them.

"How's Dwight?" he asked after a minute.

"He's doing very well," she replied. "He's still in a lot of pain, of course. Winnie's sitting with him right now. Marie's gone to a movie."

"I haven't said it, but I appreciate having you stay with him. Especially under the circumstances."

She sipped her tea quietly, darting a quick

glance up at him. He was watching her with steady, narrow, unblinking eyes. She averted her gaze to her cup again.

"I'm doing it for Winnie," she said finally.

"That goes without saying." He put his cup down and folded his arms over his chest. "How long will it take, do you think, before he's on his feet again?"

"I don't know," she said. "You'd have to ask the doctor about that."

He watched the steam rise from his mug, not really seeing it. He'd driven himself hard today, trying not to think about Allison and what he'd done. But it hadn't worked. Here she was, and sitting with her was the first peace he'd known all day. She had a calming effect on him. She made him feel at ease with himself and the world around him. It was a feeling he'd never known before. His emotions had gone wild with Hank Nelson's death and the subsequent revelations about his past.

He thought about his real father and the shame it would bring on him to have people know what kind of parent he'd had. But the sting of that knowledge seemed to have lessened. Now he could look at Allison and none of the anguish he'd known seemed to matter anymore. All he could think about was how it had been with her during the time they'd spent together, her softness in his arms, her gentle voice full of compassion and warmth. But he'd killed all that. He'd reduced what they were building together into a feverish sexual fling, without meaning or purpose. That was how she was bound to see it, and it wasn't true. He'd used women before, of course he had, but Allison wasn't an interlude. She was…everything.

He looked at her with soft wonder. She couldn't know how she'd changed him. She probably wouldn't care, even if she knew it. The more he saw of her, the more he realized how genuinely kind she was. He'd never met a woman like her. He knew he never would again.

"I've been a fool about my family, Allison," he said suddenly, his dark brows knitted together as he stared at her. "I think I went mad when I found out how I'd been lied to all these years. Hurt pride, arrogance, I don't know. Whatever it was, I've just come to my senses."

"I'm glad about that," she replied. "You have a nice family. They shouldn't have to pay for things they never did."

"I've come to that conclusion myself." He picked up the cup, but didn't drink from it. "Are you going to be able to forgive what I've done to you?" he asked suddenly.

Her heart jumped at the question. But in all fairness, she couldn't let him take all the blame. Nobody held a gun on her and made her do it, she knew. That one lapse could have cost her her career as a missionary if anyone had found out about it, but she couldn't have blamed him totally even then. She was pretty lucky that they hadn't been seen at that line cabin, she supposed. "You didn't do anything that I didn't invite," she said dully. "It doesn't matter."

Her reply caught him on the raw. "You might have my child inside your body, and it doesn't matter?" he asked icily.

She flushed. "It isn't likely," she said stubbornly.

He set the mug down again and his chest rose and fell roughly. Even now she wouldn't put all the blame on him. His lean hand speared across the table and gently slid into hers, holding it warmly. "I'm sorry I made it into something you'd rather not remember," he said solemnly. "It shouldn't have been like that, your first time. The least a man owes a virgin is satisfaction. All I gave you was pain."

She colored furiously and drew back her hand. "I have to get back to Dwight," she said huskily. "Good night, Gene."

She stood, but so did he, moving around the

table so fast that she didn't see him coming until he had her gently by the shoulders, his tall, fit body looming over her.

"Do you hate me?" he asked abruptly. "No subterfuge, no half-truths. I need to know."

She swallowed. "No. I...don't hate you."

He let out a heavy sigh. "Thank God." He bent and brushed his mouth over her eyelids, closing them with aching tenderness. His hands held her, but not in any confining way, and he didn't move a fraction of an inch closer or threaten her mouth with his lips.

"Good night, little one," he said softly, lifting his head. There was something new in his eyes, in his voice, in the way he touched her. He knew it and was stunned by it. Women came and went in his life, but this one spun a cocoon of love around him and made him whole. He wanted her as he'd never wanted anything else. But it wasn't going to be easy. His eyes fell to her stomach and darkened. A child. He found the thought of a child not nearly as frightening as he had. He could almost picture a little boy with dark hair and green eyes, following him around. A miniature of himself in small blue jeans and little sneakers. His heart lurched. Allison would be wonderful with a child. And maybe genes weren't so important. Maybe it wouldn't matter about his father. But the manner of the child's possible conception bothered him and he frowned.

His hands contracted. "A baby shouldn't be made like that," he said huskily. "Not as a consequence. It should be planned. Wanted. God in heaven, why didn't I stop?"

He let go of her all at once, and turned, leaving the kitchen like a wild man. He sounded bitter and furiously angry. Probably he hated her. She couldn't blame him for that. He might even think she'd deliberately done without precautions to trap him into a marriage he didn't want. Tears stung her eyes. All the same, he'd been worried that she might hate him, and that gave her a little solace. She finished her tea, emptied the pot and cleaned it, washed the few dishes and went back up to sit with Dwight.

Chapter Nine

The next day, Allison went outside for the first time since she'd been in residence, to clear her head while Marie spent a few minutes with her brother.

It was a beautiful day, warm and sultry, and there was so much to see. Puppies and kittens, ducks and chickens were everywhere, not to mention the bulls and cows and steers and horses. Corrals were spaced beyond the house and its small kitchen garden, down a dirt road. She strolled along in her jeans and yellow T-shirt with her long hair drifting on the breeze. Even with all that had happened, she loved it here. But she knew her stay was limited—she had to think about leaving.

She'd been given some time off to cope with her parents' death, and avoid the press, but soon she'd have to go back to work. It was a good thing that she'd face that problem in Arizona and not here, because there was a morals clause in her contract. But nobody knew, she reminded herself. Nobody knew except Gene and herself.

She was worrying about Gene's sudden avoidance of her today when a voice hailed her from the corral.

She turned, frowning, to find a lean, wickedly smiling redheaded cowhand leaning against the fence. His eyes gave her a lazy appraisal and there was something vaguely insulting about the blatant way he sized her up.

"Miss Hathoway, isn't it?" he drawled. "Thought I recognized you."

She started. *Recognized her?* "Were you at the barbecue?" she asked, trying to be polite.

The man laughed, weaving a little as he pushed himself away from the fence. He approached her and she could smell the whiskey on his breath. "No, I don't get invited to that sort of socializing.

I meant, I recognized you from the other night. In the line cabin. You were there with the boss."

Her face went stark white. She was quite literally at a loss for words.

He laughed unsteadily, moving closer, but she backed away before he could reach for her. That had obviously been his intention, because he looked surprised that she avoided his outstretched hands.

"No stomach for a common ranch hand, is that it?" he jeered. "You were hot enough for the boss. Of course, he's got money."

"Please!" she cried huskily, scarlet in the face that she and Gene should have been seen—like that!

"The boss won't have much to do with you these days, though, will he, Miss High and Mighty?" he taunted. "I heard what he said. Mad as hell that you were a virgin, wasn't he? Not his usual kind of woman, for sure, he likes 'em worldly. Now me," he said, stalking her again, smiling, "I like innocents. I'd take my sweet time with you, pretty thing, and you wouldn't be looking like the end of the world afterward. He must have been in one hell of a rush. You weren't in there ten minutes."

Allison put her hand to her mouth and turned, running wildly for the house with tears in her eyes.

She didn't know what to do. It terrified her that the cowboy might tell someone else what he knew. At least he hadn't seen them, or she knew he'd have taunted her with that, too. But he knew! He'd overheard what Gene said! And now he'd spread that horrible gossip around. She could imagine having her name bandied around the bunkhouse all night. And that wasn't the worst of it. What if it got around the community? Her reputation would be lost forever and her job along with it. The least breath of scandal attached to her name would cost her everything. She hadn't considered the potential for disaster, but now all her mistakes were coming home to roost.

She went back into the house and stayed there, taking a few minutes in her room to wash her face and get her nerves back together before she went to Dwight's room to check on him. It was almost time for his medicine.

If she'd hoped nobody would notice her turmoil, she was doomed to failure.

"What's wrong?" Winnie asked, concerned. "Allie, you're so pale!"

The temptation to tell her friend was great, but it wouldn't be fair to share the burden now. Winnie had enough to worry about with Dwight. She forced a smile. "I feel a little queasy," she said.

"I think it was the sausage I had for breakfast. I love it, but sometimes it upsets my stomach."

"Tomorrow, you'll have steak," Dwight said with a weak smile. "I promise. Tell Gene to shoot you a cow."

She started just at the mention of Gene's name. How could she face him, ever, after what that terrible man had said? How would he react if he knew one of his men was making crude remarks to her? She sighed. After the way he'd walked away from her so angrily that night in the kitchen, he probably wouldn't say anything. He might think she deserved it. After all, he'd been very vocal about Dale Branigan and his contempt for her after he'd slept with her.

She gave Dwight his medicine and put on a fairly convincing act from then on. But when she was alone in her room, she cried until she thought her heart would break. She was paying a very high price for the one indiscretion of her life, and learning a hard lesson about how easy it was to tarnish a heretofore spotless reputation. She thought about how hard her parents had worked to invest her with a sense of morality, and she'd let them down so badly. Maybe it was as well that they'd never have to know about her downfall. But she could have talked to her mother about it, and there would have been no censure, no condemnation. Her mother was a loving, gentle woman who always looked for the best in everyone. She cried all the harder, missing her.

For the next few days, she didn't go outside at all. But inevitably, Winnie noticed it and asked why. Allison made up a story about not wanting to be out of earshot of Dwight. But Winnie told Marie. And Marie told Gene.

He alone knew that Allison might simply be avoiding him. But he'd been away from the ranch for a couple of days on business, and that wouldn't explain why she was staying inside while he was gone. He almost said something to her about it. Her abrupt departure from any room he entered stopped him. She obviously wanted no part of his company, so he forced himself not to invade her privacy. All the while, he was cursing himself for what he'd done to her. Even he, a relative stranger, could see the change in her since that night in the line cabin. She was almost a different person, so quiet and shy that she might have been a mouse. She never entered into conversations with the rest of the family, or laughed, or did anything except be professional as she charted Dwight's progress and talked to the doctor who checked on him several times a week. She didn't look at Gene or speak to him, and when he tried to make conversation with her, she found a reason to go somewhere else. His pride and ego took a hard blow from her attitude, even if he understood it. Women had never avoided him. Quite the contrary. Of course, he'd never hurt anyone the way he'd hurt Allison.

Winnie and Marie finally browbeat her into going into Pryor with them to shop. She felt fairly safe about going there, sure that she wouldn't run into anyone who knew her.

She was wrong. Dale Branigan was shopping, too, in the boutique where Marie and Winnie took Allison. She caught sight of the older woman and with a purely cattish smile, Dale maneuvered closer.

"Nice to see you again, Miss Hathoway," she said. "Ben's doing nicely, thanks to your quick thinking at the bar that night."

"I'm glad to hear it," Allison said pleasantly.

Dale gave the other woman's gray dress a demeaning scrutiny, shrugging when she realized how much prettier she was in a pink sundress that flattered her figure.

"I hear Gene's gone off you after that one night," she said out of the blue.

"I beg your pardon?" Allison asked reluctantly.

"After he slept with you in the line cabin," she

said carelessly, smiling at Allison's gasped shock. "Didn't you know? It's all over town. You can't expect a man like Danny Rance to keep his mouth shut. He's a bigger gossip than most women. He really laid it on thick about you and Gene. Too bad. You should have held out for a wedding ring." She sighed theatrically. "By the way, there's a reporter in town. He's looking for some woman missionary who escaped from Central America in a hail of bullets. Someone said she'd left a trail that led here."

"Really?" Allison's hands were shaking. "Well, it could hardly be me, could it?" she asked huskily.

Dale laughed. "Not if you're giving out with Gene, it couldn't," she said mockingly. "Hardly a missionary's nature, is it?"

"Hardly. Excuse me." Allison went out the door and got into the car without a word to Marie or Winnie. She sat in shock, her body shaking, her face paper white as she tried to cope with what that malicious woman had said to her. She was branded. Really branded. She'd never get her job back. She'd have no place to go. Her family was dead, and now she was almost certainly going to lose the only work she'd ever wanted to do. It was inevitable that the reporter would track her to the Nelson place, inevitable that Dale or someone like her would relate the whole sordid story of her one-night stand with Gene. She'd given in to temptation and lost everything. If she'd had a lesser will, she'd probably have gone right off a cliff. She didn't know what she was going to do. Oh, please, God, she prayed silently. Please forgive me. Please help me!

Winnie and Marie belatedly noticed her absence and came looking for her.

"Are you all right?" Winnie frowned. "I saw Dale Branigan talking to you. What did she say?"

"Something about Gene, no doubt," Marie said heavily as they started the drive home. "She's so jealous it's sick. I'm sorry, Allison, I should have hustled you out of there the minute I saw her."

"It's all right. She was just…telling me something I already knew."

"There's a reporter in town," Winnie said uneasily. "That was what she said, wasn't it?"

"Yes. I may have a few days before he finds me," she said with defeat in her whole look. "It doesn't matter anymore. I don't have anything left to lose."

"What are you talking about?" Winnie demanded. "You've got your job, your future…!"

"I don't have anything." Allison pushed back

wisps of hair with shaking hands. "I've ruined my life."

"How?"

Allison just shook her head and stared out the window. She was too hurt and upset to even talk.

When they got back to the ranch she went to her room and locked the door. She couldn't face anyone just yet.

"What's wrong with her?" Marie asked quietly when she and Winnie were drinking coffee while Dwight slept. "Something's upset her terribly. I wonder what Dale said to her? Could it just be the reporter who's got her upset?"

"I don't know." Winnie sipped coffee, aware of the front door opening and closing. "Surely, Gene won't let him come here, will he?"

"I won't let who come here?" Gene asked abruptly, taking off his work gloves as he paused in the doorway.

"That reporter," Marie said. "The one who's looking for Allison."

He scowled. "What reporter? And why is he looking for our houseguest?"

Winnie hesitated. She exchanged glances with Marie and grimaced. "I guess you'd better hear it all. Allison isn't going to tell you, but someone needs to. You'd better sit down."

He sprawled in the armchair next to the sofa and crossed his arms over his chest. "All right," he said, his green eyes solemn. It would be almost a relief to know it all. He'd had a feeling from the very first that Allison wasn't what she seemed, although he had one strong premonition that he wasn't going to like what he found out.

"Allison and her parents were sent to Central America to set up a small clinic in one of the rural provinces," Winnie began. "It was a war zone, and inevitably, two opposing factions threatened the village."

"What were they doing in Central America?" Gene interrupted.

Winnie blinked. "Why, they were missionaries."

Gene's face went several shades paler and his jaw clenched. "All of them?" he asked in a choked tone. "Allison, too?"

"Yes," Winnie replied, confirming his worst fears.

He ran a hand through his hair, his eyes blank. Now it all made sense. No wonder she'd been so naïve, so trusting. He closed his eyes. If the guilt had been there before, it was almost unbearable now. A missionary. He'd seduced a missionary! "Finish it," he said stiffly, opening his eyes to glare at her.

"They were taken prisoner," Winnie said slowly. "Allison's parents were shot to death right beside her, and the firing squad had taken aim at her when the opposing force marched in and spared her. She was smuggled out of the country by international peacekeepers. She has information that nobody else has, and that's why the media's been after her. She came here to heal, Gene."

He'd gone rigid during that revelation. When Winnie finished, he got up out of his chair without a word and went out the front door. He didn't want anyone to see what he felt at the thought of bullets tearing into that gentle, loving woman. He felt something wet in his eyes and kept walking while stark terror ran over his body like fire. Incredible, Dwight had said. No. Not incredible. A miracle. Allison believed in miracles, she'd told him once, and now he knew why. She was alive because of one.

The sound of approaching voices disturbed his thoughts. He wasn't really listening, it was just some of the hands heading into the bunkhouse for lunch. But then one loud, slurred voice caught his attention.

Rance, he thought angrily, drinking again. He'd warned the man once. Now he was going to have to do something about it. The hands knew he wouldn't tolerate alcohol during working hours.

Just as he started around the barn toward the bunkhouse, he heard what Rance was saying.

"She wouldn't give me the time of day," the man snarled. "Can you imagine that? She didn't mind rolling around in that line cabin with the boss, but she was too good to let me touch her. Dale hates her guts, and I can see why. Well, it's all over town about the high and mighty Miss Hathoway and Nelson, and before I'm through…"

His voice trailed off as the object of his venom walked into the bunkhouse with an expression on his face that made the rest of the men scatter.

"Now, boss," Rance began hesitantly, because he knew the set of the older man's lean body and the glitter of those green eyes from long experience.

"You son of a…!" The last word was muffled by a huge fist as Gene knocked the cowboy to the floor and dived after him. They demolished chairs in the struggle, but it was no contest. Gene was quicker and more muscular than the young cowboy, and he had the advantage of murderous anger.

He pulled Rance up from the floor and knocked him through the open bunkhouse door and out into the dirt, and was going after him again when one of the older hands stepped in front of him.

"He's had enough, boss," the man said gently, keeping his voice low and calm. "You got the point across. No need to tear his arms off. None of us listened to his venom. A blind man would know that Miss Hathoway's a lady."

Gene was breathing heavily. He looked from the half-conscious man on the ground to the one who was speaking, his green eyes hot and wild. He took a deep breath to steady himself. "If anyone else asks, Miss Hathoway is my *fiancée*," he emphasized the word, looking at each cowboy's face individually with an expression that was calm and dangerous all at once. "I may deserve that kind of malicious gossip, but she doesn't. She's a missionary. A man who *is* a man doesn't belittle a woman of her sort!"

The men looked shamefaced. They stood uncomfortably congregated with downcast eyes.

"Rance told some reporter she was here," one of them said. "We did try to reason with him, Mr. Nelson, but he was half lit and out for blood. Dale Branigan fed him a lot of bull about you and he's sweet on her; not to mention him drinking like a fish half the time when you didn't see him."

"He can be sweet on her from a closer distance

from now on," Gene said, trying to cope with all the new developments at once. He'd been lax on the job a lot. It was just coming home to him how much time he'd spent wallowing in self-pity over his parentage while he let his stepfather's ranch go to hell. Well, there wouldn't be any more of that. He stood over Rance, watching the man open a swollen eye to stare up at him with evident fear.

"Get off my land," Gene said coldly, and without raising his voice. "If I see you again, I'll break your neck. I'll send your check along in care of Dale Branigan. But if you're counting on a little romance with her, you'll have to get past Ben Hardy. He's all but engaged to her, in case you didn't know."

Rance looked shocked. "Ben...?"

"She played you for a fool, didn't she?" Gene asked with a mocking smile. "You poor stupid fish, that will be all over town by tomorrow, too. I promise you it will, along with the news of my engagement to Allison and the damage you tried to do to her reputation."

Rance dragged himself to his feet, considerably more sober now. He wiped blood away from a cut lip and shivered a little with reaction and muscle strain as he reached for his hat and put it back on.

"No need to beat a man half to death over some woman," Rance said angrily.

"No need to make her out to be a tramp because she won't let you touch her, either," Gene said dangerously, his temper kindling again. "You're finished in Pryor, Rance. I'll see to it, no matter what it takes."

Rance straightened. "I've had my fill of Wyoming, anyway," he said shortly. "You can have it."

He hobbled into the bunkhouse to pack. Gene turned on his heel and walked away, ignoring the murmurs of comment from his men as he stalked toward the house with blood in his eye.

He went straight up the staircase without a word to Marie and Winnie, who'd been standing speechless at the window, watching the byplay.

Dwight was asleep when he peeped in the door, so he went straight along to Allison's room.

He knocked and waited for her to answer. It only took a minute. She was surprised to see him, and he wondered absently if she'd have opened it if she'd known it was him. She looked terrible.

He rubbed his fist against the corner of his mouth, feeling the cut there as he stared down at her furiously. "Why didn't you tell me what Rance was saying about you?" he demanded without preamble. "Why didn't you tell me what you'd gone through in Central America, and what you and your parents were doing there?"

She was looking at his bruised, cut face, hardly hearing the words. "You're hurt," she said worriedly. "What happened to you?"

"I've been out in the backyard beating the hell out of Rance before I fired him," he said icily. "And I enjoyed it. Does that shock you? I wish I'd hit him twice as damned hard!"

"You know...all of it?" she asked hesitantly.

"All of it," he assured her. His broad chest rose and fell jerkily. "Oh, God, why didn't you trust me?" he asked huskily. "Why didn't you tell me the truth?"

Her eyes fell to his shirt buttons. "I couldn't. It hurt too much to talk about it, at first. And then I knew you'd take off like a shot if you knew, well, what I did for a living. I lied because I wanted to be alive, just for a little while. I wanted to be someone else, I wanted to be like other women, to be...loved." She almost choked on the word and her eyes closed. "But I had no right."

"Do you think I did?" he groaned. He stepped into the room and slammed the door, jerking her hungrily into his arms. He held her against him, rocking her gently, folding her to his heart in a silence that was broken only by the sound of her soft weeping.

"The worst of it is that I was so wrapped up in my own problems that I was blind to your character," he said bitterly. "I deliberately overlooked all the telltale signs of your innocence because I wanted you so badly. I deserve to be shot!"

"But, I wanted you, too," she whispered at his ear, feeling his cheek warm and rough against hers as he held her. "It's not all your fault. You were hurting. I understood."

"That doesn't excuse it. And to have that redheaded vermin gossiping about you in town!" he groaned. "I'm sorry."

"I won't be here much longer," she reminded him miserably. "And if that reporter just doesn't find me..."

His arms tightened. "It won't matter if he does," he said curtly. "I've just told the men that we're engaged. I'll make sure that gets around town. Dale will wind up with egg on her face from her damned gossiping."

"Engaged?" she gasped. "But I can't!"

He drew back, scowling. "Why can't you? You're a missionary, not a nun. Marriage is permissible."

"But not like this, Gene," she said quietly, her hazel eyes sad and regretful. "Not to spare my reputation. It will be all right. I'm a qualified nurse. I can still get a job."

His eyes searched her face, down to her soft mouth. "Marriage is a job, isn't it? Dwight and I are switching responsibilities, and we'll both be happier. That means I'll be home more. I can spend time with you and the kids."

She flushed. "There aren't any kids."

His lean hands smoothed down her hips and one of them lightly touched her belly. "Yet."

She shivered and tried to pull away.

But he held her, gently, firmly. "I know. I hurt you, didn't I? Your first time was a nightmare that you don't want to repeat, especially with me."

She nodded slowly, without looking at him.

He bent and suddenly lifted her in his hard arms, his eyes searching her frightened ones as he carried her toward the bed.

"If I can make you want me, in spite of what happened before, will you agree to marry me?" he asked softly.

"But, I don't…!" she protested.

He covered the frantic words with his mouth, gently this time, using every shred of skill he possessed to coax her set lips into a shy response.

He laid her down on the coverlet and stretched out beside her, his lips teasing hers in a gentle, exquisite kind of exploration. His fingers traced her cheeks, pushing back the wispy strands of long black hair that had escaped from her bun while the seconds lengthened into minutes.

"I like your hair long and loose," he breathed against her yielding mouth, one lean hand disposing of pins and combs before he arranged her loosened mane of hair around her flushed face.

She looked up at him nervously, her body already taut from the threat of his, her memory all too vivid of the last time.

"There's a barrier," he whispered deeply, holding her eyes while he traced a long forefinger around the swollen contours of her mouth. "It's called a maidenhead. It protects a woman's chastity. The first time, it has to be disposed of, and that's why I hurt you. It won't ever be like that again. Now that I know how innocent you really are, I'll make a meal of you, Miss Hathoway. When I've finished, fear is the last thing you'll feel when you look at me."

She colored. "I'm a nurse," she reminded him, trying to sound worldly. "I do know something about my own anatomy."

He brushed her open mouth with his. "I was in

too much of a hurry to wait for you. I lost my head. I won't lose it with you again until I've satisfied you."

"Please," she moaned, "you mustn't talk to me like this!"

"You're my woman," he said, lifting his head to hold her eyes. "We're lovers, Allison. We're going to be married. You'll have to face the implications of that, sooner or later."

"I won't marry you!"

"Like hell you won't marry me," he said with quiet determination. He searched her eyes. "I'm sorry," he said as he bent. "But this is the only way, now."

She didn't understand what he meant at first. He covered her mouth with his and his hands smoothed down her body while he built the kiss from a slow caress to a blazing, raging statement of intent. She shivered as the heat exploded in her body when his mouth suddenly went down hard over her breast and began to suckle it through the fabric of her dress. She arched and gasped, at the same time that one lean hand found the fastening of her jeans and slipped expertly inside against warm flesh.

"Gene, you can't!" she whimpered.

But he touched her intimately then, and his

mouth became as insistent and rhythmic as the hand invading her privacy with such slow, sweet mastery. She began to shiver. Her eyes closed. She couldn't fight this sweet tide of pleasure, she couldn't! She heard her breath shuddering out in little gasps, felt her body lifting, yielding itself to whatever he wanted. His face nuzzled under the fabric of her blouse and nudged her bra aside so that he could find the hard, aching tip of her swelling breast, hot and moist against the silky bare flesh.

"Gene," she whispered, her voice breaking on his name as he quickened the rhythm and increased the insistence of his mouth on her body. "Gene! Oh, Gene, please—!"

Her voice broke and he gave her what she begged for, feeling her release with pride and indulgent pleasure. He lifted his head and watched her convulse, her face a study in rigid ecstasy, her body completely his. She wept afterward, and he comforted her, kissing away the tears, lightly caressing her trembling body until she was completely still in his arms.

"That's what it feels like, Allison," he said softly, holding her shocked eyes. "That's what it was like for me, that night in the cabin. I wanted you to know, because next time, I'll give you this same pleasure with my body. Only it will be an agony of a climax, I promise you. This will be nothing by comparison."

She blushed as she met his eyes. "Why?"

He kissed her nose. "I told you. I want you to marry me."

"You don't have to go that far to spare my reputation, or salve your own guilt. I told you, I don't blame you...Gene!" she gasped sharply.

His body had levered over hers in midsentence and he'd coaxed his way between her long legs, so that she felt him in blatant intimacy, became shockingly aware of the power and need of his body.

He moved deliberately, balancing himself above her on his forearms, smiling down at her with the slow, deliberate shifting of his lean hips.

"Say, yes, I'll marry you, Gene," he instructed very slowly, "or I'll peel you out of those jeans right now and make you scream like a banshee under me. If you think your reputation's in shreds already, wait until that unholy crew in the bunkhouse hears the noises I drag out of you now."

She shivered, because she was vulnerable and he knew it. Worse, the window was open, she glanced at it and saw the curtains moving.

"Better say it quick, cupcake, before I get too

involved to roll away," he said huskily and pressed his lips down hard over hers. "It's getting worse."

Yes, it was, and her face registered her knowledge of it. She swallowed, sensations in her lower belly making her hot and weak all at once. Her legs trembled under his. "You can't do that…to me," she protested. "Marie and Winnie—"

"Are downstairs," he said, "and the door is closed. Neither of them is likely to walk in without an invitation since they know I'm up here with you," he said in a deep, husky tone. "Open your legs, Allison," he whispered, his mouth poising over hers to brush at it with soft, sensual intent. His own long, powerful legs began to edge out and she felt him against her in a hot daze. She gasped softly and looked up into his glittering green eyes, feeling a kindred recklessness. With a faint moan, she let him shift her legs, let him fit his lean body intimately to hers while he watched her face with unblinking intensity. His jaw tautened and she felt his body swell even more in the stark closeness. She shivered.

His hand went between them and ripped open his shirt and pushed hers up, easily unclipping her bra and moving it out of the way. He looked down as he brushed his hair-roughened chest blatantly over the hard tips of her breasts and watched her shiver with reaction. His hips began to move upward over hers, throbbing with building passion as his eyes bit into hers.

"Tell me you don't want to be filled," he whispered at her lips. "Filled hard, and deep."

She made a helpless sound and shivered again, totally helpless.

His hands went to her jeans, and then to his own, and seconds later, she felt his muscular, hair-roughened nudity against her softness with a sense of wonder. His body echoed the soft shiver of hers.

"Are you going to let me?" he whispered, drawing his hips against hers.

"We shouldn't...Gene," she choked.

"Yes, we should," he whispered tenderly. His hands smoothed down her silky hips, under her thighs, and he lifted them, eased them apart with such gentleness that she couldn't find a single protest.

He moved then, fitting himself to her in a silence that smoldered with promise.

She looked straight into his eyes and gasped softly as he began to possess her, with exquisitely gentle movements.

"Yes," he whispered tenderly. "You see? It doesn't hurt. No, don't tense up. That's it," he coaxed. He took her mouth under his and cherished it. "That's it, little one. I'm only going to love you. Isn't that what you said you wanted? To be loved?"

She'd meant another kind of love entirely, but this was heaven. She wondered if he'd ever been so tender with anyone else, but he moved then, and she couldn't think anymore.

He probed her body softly. "Yes, watch my eyes, Allison. You watched me, that night. Now I want to watch you."

As he spoke, he moved, slow and easy movements that brought them first into stark intimacy, and then into contact, and then totally together. She gasped as she felt her body absorbing his, stunned with the ease of his passage, the readiness of her own body. She stared into his eyes with wonder, trying to feel guilt and shame, but she couldn't. She couldn't have imagined the expression on his lean face in her wildest dreams. His eyes were soft and warm, full of secret knowledge and tenderness and excitement.

He moved lazily against her, smiling as he settled on her body in a soft rhythm that lifted her very slowly to an ecstasy she'd never dreamed possible.

She cried out and pushed at his chest, frightened, but he continued the steady rhythm, increasing it now, his breathing suddenly changing as he watched her eyes.

"Don't look away," he said huskily. "I'm going to watch. Now, Allison. Now, little one. Now. Now!"

She made sounds she'd never made in her life as the sensations gathered and suddenly exploded. She wept in what sounded like anguished pain, her breath trapped in her throat, her face contorted like her convulsing body. He went with her every step of the way, only giving in when she was almost exhausted. He laughed even as his body corded over hers, laughed through the vicious ecstasy that suspended him above her in a shuddering anguish of satisfaction.

He ground out something and went rigid before he collapsed on her body, his heartbeat shaking both of them. He trembled, as she did, long afterward.

"I really should have closed the window," he murmured dryly, feeling the heat in her cheeks. "Don't curl up. We're too far from the bunkhouse and the living room for anyone to hear you, and Dwight's asleep. Did it hurt this time?" he asked, smiling as he lifted his head to search her eyes, knowing the answer already.

She swallowed. "Oh, no," she whispered. She

was still trembling a little, and so was he. They were both drenched with sweat, but her body felt deliciously boneless, although it still tingled with pleasure. "No, it was…" She searched for the right word as she looked into his soft eyes. "It was beautiful."

"That's how it should be," he breathed at her ear, gathering her legs in the muscular cage of his as he kissed her tenderly. He lifted his head. "I hope you weren't disappointed this time."

"You were…watching," she whispered, coloring. "Couldn't you, well, see?"

"I saw, all right." His face hardened with the memory and he kissed her roughly. "I've never watched before. I've never been satisfied like that before, either. If you don't marry me, so help me, I'll move in here with you until I shame you into saying yes."

She swallowed. "Gene…"

He brushed back her damp hair. "Your conscience will beat you to death over this," he said quietly, drawing her gaze along their bodies until she flushed and averted her eyes. "I didn't force you or coerce you. It was mutual. We've got a lot going for us. I want to live with you, cupcake."

"Sex wouldn't be enough for you," she whispered sadly. "And you'd have a long time to regret it."

"I won't regret it." He brushed his mouth over her eyes. And he knew he wouldn't. He was awash with new feelings, with a tenderness he'd never experienced before. He studied her quietly. "You'll be everything I ever needed, or wanted. I'll take care of you until I die. And someday, somehow, I'll make you glad you said yes."

Those words echoed in her mind long after they'd dressed and gone downstairs to announce their engagement. Allison couldn't decide if she believed him or not; if she dared to believe him. Because it sounded very much as if more than physical need was the basis for the proposal. About that, only time would tell.

Chapter Ten

"I just can't believe it," Marie said later, smiling at Allison. "I never thought I'd live long enough to see Gene married. Imagine that, my footloose, fancy-free brother not only willing, but anxious to tie the knot! And to someone I really like!"

"I'm glad of that," Allison said, but her eyes were troubled.

Winnie was upstairs with Dwight, and Gene had gone back out to work after a brief lunch. Marie was still getting over the shock of what Gene had announced so matter-of-factly.

Marie stared at her for a moment. "There's

something more, isn't there?" she asked gently. "Forgive me for prying, but I know my brother very well and I've learned quite a bit about you. Something happened that night that Rance gossiped about, and you think Gene is only marrying you to appease his conscience. That's it, isn't it?"

Allison started to deny it, but there really wasn't any point. She stared down at her hands folded in her lap. "Yes."

"Gene has a conscience," Marie continued. "But nothing could make him marry a woman in cold blood, not even that. You'd better believe that it isn't guilt on his part."

"There could be a baby," Allison said painfully, amazed that she could talk to Marie this way when she couldn't bring herself to tell Winnie about it.

Marie smiled. "Gene loves children," she said simply. "So do all the rest of us. A baby would be the sweetest kind of surprise."

Allison fought tears and lost. She put her head in her hands and wept bitterly. "I've trapped him, all because I got in over my head," she moaned. "Whatever his motives, inevitably he'll hate me!"

Marie hugged her warmly. "No, I don't think so. Not the way he's been acting since you've been around. You've changed him. All the bitterness and mockery are gone. He's gentler, less volatile."

"Mr. Rance wouldn't agree with you," Allison said with a watery smile.

"Mr. Rance deserved what he got," Marie said shortly. "I don't feel sorry for him. Now you cheer up," she told Allison. "No more regrets. You're the first sister-in-law prospect Gene's ever presented me with, and I'm not letting you escape!"

Marie's enthusiasm was catching. Allison went back up to sit with Dwight in a brighter mood altogether. If she had doubts, she kept them to herself.

Gene led her off into the study later that night, after they'd had supper, and closed the door.

She was nervous, and he smiled gently at the expression on her face.

"Don't look so threatened," he said, his green eyes twinkling at her. "The couch is too short, and the desk would be hell on your back."

She blushed, her eyes like saucers as they met his.

He moved toward her, indulgent and smiling. "How can you still blush?" he asked, drawing her gently to him. "You wide-eyed little innocent."

"Not so innocent now," she said quietly.

He bent and kissed her softly. "It won't do much

good to ask you not to beat your conscience to death. But try not to go overboard. God made us human, little one," he said, his voice deep and caressing as he searched her eyes. "He gave us physical pleasure to ensure the perpetuation of the species."

"And He gave us responsibility not to make a mockery of it, or twist it into something bad," she replied miserably.

He framed her wan face in his lean hands and studied her. "You believed in me when no one else did," he said. "You weren't put off by my reputation or intimidated by my temper. You gave yourself to me more than any other reason because you knew how desperately I needed you." He sighed heavily. "Allison, what we did, that night at the cabin and today, was as natural as breathing. It isn't hateful to want someone, especially when it goes beyond a physical need."

"Did it, though?" she asked sadly.

He nodded. "Yes. This afternoon, it most certainly went beyond desire."

"You were...so tender," she whispered.

He drew her against him and enveloped her in his arms, resting his cheek on her dark hair. "It's going to be that way every time, from now on," he said. His arms tightened as he felt her warmth and softness so close to him. His body reacted predictably and he laughed. "My God, feel that," he whispered at her ear.

"Stop," she protested in a flutter.

"You're a nurse. You should know that I can't stop it."

"That wasn't what I meant." She buried her face in his chest and felt him suddenly go stiff and catch his breath.

His hands moved slowly into her hair. He drew her mouth against him, through the shirt, and his breathing became ragged. "Allison," he whispered huskily. His eyes closed. He'd never felt so vulnerable, or minded it so little.

"You like that?" she whispered hesitantly.

"I like it a lot." He eased a lean hand between them. "But I'd like it on my bare skin more, sweetheart," he said, unfastening buttons as he spoke. "Push my shirt out of the way and put your mouth on me," he whispered sensuously.

"We shouldn't," she protested weakly. "What if…"

"We're going to be married," he said at her forehead. "A piece of paper and the right words aren't going to bind us any closer than our bodies already have. You're mine now. I love being part of you, feeling you share my pleasure. Is it really so frightening to let me love you now?"

"It isn't...frightening," she confessed. She rubbed her hands flat against his hair-laden chest, up and down in a sensual pattern.

He drew her mouth to his warm skin, feeling her lips search through the mat of hair to the hard muscles of his chest and he caught his breath, tautening involuntarily.

It was intoxicating, she thought dazedly, smoothing her hands over him while her mouth lifted and touched. He smelled of spicy cologne and the touch of his body was all of heaven.

Her hands smoothed down to his belt and his lips brushed her closed eyelids. "Lower," he whispered. "I want you to touch me."

She hesitated. She was curious, but all her inhibitions were protesting.

"I belong to you as surely as you belong to me," he said quietly. "Aren't you curious about the differences between your body and mine?"

"Well, yes," she confessed hesitantly.

His lips parted against her eyebrows. "Then find them out for yourself."

She lay her cheek on his chest and slowly let her cool, nervous hands trespass past the wide belt. He jerked a little at the unfamiliar touch, and she hesitated, but his hands trapped hers when she tried to pull them away.

"It's all right," he whispered against her temple. "I'm no more used to this than you are."

"You're experienced…" she protested.

"Not in this, I'm not," he replied, surprisingly. "What we've done together is totally new for me, up to and including this. Haven't you realized that I'm not playing some sophisticated game with you?" he asked. "Allison, I'm as helpless as you are when we make love. Your touch is just as exciting and potent to me as mine seems to be to you."

"I didn't realize that," she whispered. Under her softly questing hands, his body was powerfully male and very, very responsive. He gasped and she felt his body shudder. "Did I hurt you?" she breathed.

"No," he said, his voice faintly choked. "I'm sensitive there."

"Oh."

"Don't stop," he whispered, searching for her lips with his mouth. He opened it to a slow, deep kiss that seemed to have no end, glorying in her tender exploration of him. He guided her hand to the zipper and groaned helplessly when she touched him under the fabric. They wound up on the couch in a tangle of arms and legs, fighting their way into each other's arms through a sea of uncooperative clothing.

She shivered, her breasts flattened in the thicket of hair on his warm chest, swelling as he traced them with his thumbs while they kissed.

"When are you going to marry me?" he whispered into her open mouth.

"Whenever...you like," she managed unsteadily.

"Friday?"

"That's only three days away," she said huskily.

He smiled against her mouth. "I know." He lifted his head and looked down where her body was lying across his lap, her torso bare against his. "And not a minute too soon." He tugged at her lower lip with his teeth, in a sensual throbbing fantasy that made him dizzy. "Make a baby with me, Allison," he whispered, easing her down onto the sofa as he lifted his head to hold her hazel eyes in thrall. "Here. Now."

"Gene...!" she exclaimed when he moved.

But it was already too late for second thoughts, because he joined them with a minimum of fuss and smiled gently into her shocked eyes as he began to move sensually and with expert knowledge of her body.

"Yes, that's it," he whispered when she ground her teeth together and gasped. "Only don't cry out when I satisfy you," he added with a slow, sensual smile, "because the walls aren't that thick and the door isn't locked. Do you hear me? Bite my chest or kiss me when it happens, so that the sound doesn't penetrate the walls. God, you're noisy," he whispered as she began to bite back the sounds. "One day I'll make love to you deep in the woods and you can scream for me. Yes. Yes. That's it, lift up to me." His hands gripped her hips and pulled her to him in a ragged, rough rhythm. "Yes. Yes!" His eyes closed and he began to shudder, then they opened straight into hers and his body impaled her fiercely. She felt the spiraling rhythm explode into ecstasy and rocked her slender body.

"I want a son!" he bit off in her ear, and his hands clenched on her hips and ground her into him as he shuddered against her.

It was the most unbelievable pleasure she'd ever shared with him. He collapsed against her and she clung to him, trembling in the aftermath.

"God, that was good," he whispered hoarsely at her ear. His arms contracted, riveting her to him. "Did you hear what I said, just at the last?"

"Yes." She drew him closer. "You whispered that you wanted a son," she said, shivering.

"I meant it. A son. A daughter. Our child." He lifted his head and searched her eyes, his sweaty hair hanging down onto his broad forehead, his green eyes glittery with spent pleasure. "It's exciting to make love like this. I never wanted children before. But it's all I think about when I'm with you."

She reached up and touched his mouth. "I can never say no to you," she whispered. "It's… frightening."

"It's your inhibitions," he corrected. He kissed her softly and moved away, smiling indulgently at her embarrassment as she rearranged her clothing while he fastened his own. "Feverish, isn't it?" he asked wickedly. "Hot and wild and out of control. You're every dream I ever dreamed. I don't know how I lived this long without you."

"Are you sure it isn't just physical?" she asked after a minute, really worried.

He brought her face up to his and kissed her gently. "If it was only physical, why would I want to make babies with you?" he whispered tenderly.

She smiled, her heart in her eyes, and laid her head against his chest. "Then I'll marry you whenever you say, Gene."

He hesitated. "There's something I have to tell you, before you commit yourself," he told her a minute later. "A secret I've held back. I should have told you before we ever got involved. I can't ask you to live with me unless you know it."

She lifted her head. "It won't matter. What is it?"

"My father," he began slowly, watching her face closely, "my real father, I mean…is in prison."

Her eyes didn't waver. She smiled up at him. "I'm sorry about that. But what does it have to do with my marrying you?"

He let out the breath he'd been holding. "My God," he ground out. He caught her up roughly and held her close enough to bruise her, his eyes closed as he rocked her against him. "My God, I was scared to death to tell you…!"

"But why?" she asked gently.

"You might be afraid of our children inheriting bad blood," he said curtly. "My father is a thief. From what I've been able to find out, he's been in trouble with the law all his life."

She nuzzled her face against him, feeling warm and safe and secure. "Environment plays a big part in shaping a person's character," she said drowsily. "I get sleepy when you love me. Is that natural?"

His breath caught. "When I love you," he repeated in a slow whisper, feeling the words to his bones. His eyes closed and he held her closer, shivering. Love her. Love her. It *was* loving. Why hadn't he realized it? "My God."

"Is something wrong?" she asked, her voice puzzled.

"No. Not a single thing." He drew back and searched her eyes, holding them while he looked for more secrets, hoping that he'd hit on the right one. "How do you feel about me, sweetheart?" he asked gently.

"I...I want you," she stammered, embarrassed.

He shook his head slowly. "Sex wouldn't be enough for you. Even good sex. Not with your background. Try again."

She hesitated. It was hard to lay her heart down in front of him, but clearly that was what he wanted.

He brushed his thumb over her soft lips. "It takes a lot of trust, doesn't it? But I trusted you enough to tell you the most painful secret I have."

That was true. He had. She was the one lacking in trust, not him. She drew a slow, steadying breath and looked up at him. "I love you, Gene," she said simply.

"Do you?" he asked huskily.

The expression on his lean, hard face made her confident. "With all my heart," she whispered.

He traced the soft contours of her mouth with

fingers that were faintly unsteady. "Forever, little one," he breathed, bending to her mouth.

Tears stung her eyes as she closed them. "Forever!"

He kissed her with aching tenderness and picked her up in his arms, sitting down in an armchair with her in his lap. He tucked her face into his throat and sat just holding her close for a long, long time before he finally leaned back with a heavy sigh, still cradling her close.

"Now, you're going to tell me about your parents."

She shivered. "I can't."

"You can. We're part of each other now. There's nothing you can't share with me. Tell me about them."

She lay quietly for a minute. Then she began to speak. She told him about the countries where they'd lived, the conditions of unspeakable poverty they'd endured.

"They never let it get them down," she told him. "They were always sure that things would get better. If we ran out of supplies, they were confident that new ones would come in time. And they always did," she said wonderingly. "I've never known people like them. They really lived what they believed in. And then, one day, it all came down around our ears. The regimes changed so quickly." She hesitated.

He pulled her closer, sensing her feelings. "I've got you. You're safe. Tell me what happened."

"We were arrested for giving comfort to the enemy," she said, giving in to the terrifying memories. She pressed closer. "They locked us up overnight. Even then, my parents were sure that we'd be set free by the government troops when they arrived. But the next morning we were marched out of the village along with some other political prisoners and stood up against an ocotillo fence." She swallowed. "We could hear firing in the distance. I kept thinking, if we can just hold on for a few minutes, they'll come, they'll rescue us. Just as I thought it, the guns started firing. My father, and then my mother, fell beside me. I closed my eyes, waiting." She shivered and he held her close, bruisingly close. "A bullet whizzed past my head and I knew the next one was going to get me. But before it hit, gunfire erupted around the three of us who were still alive. I was taken out of the village by a priest we knew. He got me to safety, although how is still a blur. Of all the people I knew, Winnie was the only one I could trust, so I called her and she brought me here."

He thanked God that she was with him, that

he was holding her, that the bullets had missed and the soldiers had saved her. "So that's why you came here."

She nodded, staring across his broad chest toward the window. She sighed heavily. "It was a nightmare. Sometimes I still wake up crying in the night."

"If you wake up crying from now on, I'll be there to hold you," he said gently. "Starting tonight."

"But, Gene…!"

He put a finger over her lips. "I'll leave you before morning. No one will know except the two of us." He searched her soft eyes. "God, honey, it's going to be hell being separated from you even while I work, much less at night, do you know that? I don't want you out of my sight!"

Her lips parted on a rush of breath.

"Are you shocked?" he asked huskily, searching her rapt face. "I thought you knew by now that I'm hopelessly in love with you, Allie."

"Oh, Gene," she whispered, shaken.

"I never knew what love was," he said softly. "I'm not sure I was even alive until you came along."

"I feel the same way," she whispered. Her fingers touched his hard mouth tenderly. "I'd die for you, Gene."

His eyes closed and he shivered. He'd never felt anything so intense, or so special.

Allison kissed him softly, again and again. He looked as if he needed comforting. Incredible, for such an independent, self-sufficient man.

"What about your career, little one?" he asked later.

"I can't go back to it," she murmured, without mentioning the blemish on her reputation from the night in the line cabin that would cost her that career. There was no need to make him feel worse than he already did. "I couldn't ask you to leave here and follow me around the world. And I couldn't go without you. Besides," she said gently, "there's every possibility that I could be pregnant now. Today was the very best time for it to happen."

"Was it?" he murmured, and smiled tenderly, laying a big, lean hand on her belly. "Kids and cattle sort of go together, you know. It takes a big family to manage these days."

"I'd like a big family," she said drowsily, curling up in his hard arms. "I hope we can have one."

"If we can't, there are plenty of kids around who'd love to be needed by someone," he murmured, smiling. "Raising them makes people parents, not just having them."

She smiled back. "I'm sleepy."

His arms contracted. "Too much loving," he whispered. "I've exhausted you."

She opened her eyes and looked up at him. "Only temporarily," she whispered. "I love how it feels with you when you love me, Gene."

His jaw tensed. "So do I." He drew in a steadying breath. "We'd better get out of here before it happens again. You make me insatiable."

"I hope to keep you that way, when we're married," she said shyly.

"I'll hold you to it," he promised. He lifted her and got up, too. "I have something for you. In the heat of things, I forgot to give it to you." He opened his desk drawer and removed a felt-covered box. He opened it and slid a marquise diamond onto her engagement finger, leaving the companion wedding band in the box.

"Do you want me to wear a ring when we're married?" he asked seriously.

"Of course," she replied. "If I wear your brand," she said with a mischievous smile, "you have to wear mine."

He chuckled. "Nelson's brand, is that it? I like the sound of it. No trespassing allowed."

"And don't you forget it," she said.

She clung to his hand, wonderingly, astonished that her life could have changed so much in such a short period of time. All her nightmares were going to fade away now, she was sure of it.

Gene was equally sure of it. He'd laid his own ghosts to rest, including his worst one. Allison had said that environment played a big part in shaping a man's character. Perhaps it did. Maybe his real father had had a hard time of it and couldn't cope. Whatever the reason, it didn't have to affect his own life unless he let it. He could live with being an adopted Nelson. Marie and Dwight loved him, there was no doubt about that, and he and Dwight were going to work out the rest of the problems. He'd never been so certain of anything. He looked down at Allison and felt as if he were floating.

Dwight was able to go to the wedding the following week. He and Marie and Winnie witnessed at the small, quiet ceremony where Allison Hathoway became Mrs. Gene Nelson. She wore a simple white dress and carried a bouquet of daisies, and Gene thought he'd never seen anyone so beautiful. He said so, several times after they arrived at the hotel in Yellowstone National Park where they were spending part of their honeymoon.

"The most amazing thing is that nobody discovered we were sharing a bed until we got married," Allison said with a shy smile.

"Sharing it was all we did," he murmured ruefully, "because of your conscience. Not to mention my own. But it was sweet, honey. I never dreamed anything could be as sweet as holding you all night in my arms, even if we didn't make love."

"And now we never have to be apart again," she whispered, lifting into his arms as he began to kiss her very softly.

"Did you notice the reporter?" he asked against her mouth.

"The one you sent sprawling into the mud puddle?" she whispered, laughing involuntarily when she remembered the astonishment on the journalist's face. "Amazing that he finally found me, and by the time he did, it didn't matter anymore. They've started releasing all sorts of information through the international forces. I'm old news now."

"Thank God. He won't be hounding us anymore."

"I just wish my parents could have gotten out with me," she said, allowing herself that one regret.

"So do I, little one," he replied gently. "I'm just glad that you did."

She pressed close to him, drawing strength from his lean, powerful body.

"Make love to me this time," he whispered at her ear.

"But I don't know how," she said softly.

"No problem. I'll teach you."

And he did. He guided her, smiled at her reticence, laughed at her fumbling efforts to undress him. But when they were finally together on the big bed, softness to hardness, dark to light, the laughing stopped and they loved as they never had before. From tenderness to rough passion, to lazy sweetness and sharp demand, they didn't sleep all night long. By morning they lay exhausted in each other's arms, too tired to even move.

It was lunchtime before they stirred. Allison opened her eyes to find Gene sitting on the bed beside her, watching her as he toweled his hair dry.

"Good morning, Mrs. Nelson," he said softly.

She opened her arms, smiling as she dislodged the sheet and felt him lift her against his bare chest while he kissed her tenderly.

"Was it good?" he whispered.

"I thought I was going to die," she replied huskily.

"So did I. And I still may." He groaned, sitting upright, and then he laughed. "I think my back's broken."

"Married twenty-four hours, and you're already complaining," she moaned.

"That wasn't a complaint," he chuckled. He kissed her again and pulled her out of bed, his eyes sliding possessively over her soft pink nudity. "God, you're beautiful. Inside and out. You're my world, Allison."

She pressed close against him. "You're mine. I'll never live long enough to tell you how much I love you."

"Yes, you will." He smoothed her hair. "Now get dressed. I don't know about you, but I'm starved!"

"Come to think of it, so am I," she said, blinking. "Gene, we never had supper! Not to mention breakfast or lunch!"

He chuckled. "We didn't, did we?"

"No wonder we're hungry!"

"Amen. So get moving, woman."

She got dressed, with his dubious assistance, which took twice as long. They had a leisurely supper and then went out to see Old Faithful erupt. Later they drove up to the mud volcano, past the fishing bridge, and sat beside a little stream that cut through towering lodgepole pines with the jagged Rocky Mountains rising majestically in the distance and Yellowstone Lake in the other direction.

"Tomorrow's Sunday," he said when they were back in the hotel room, curled up together in bed.

"So it is," she replied.

He sighed softly and pressed her cheek to his bare chest. "They have church services nearby," he said. "I asked. Suppose we go?"

Her breath caught. She sat up, looking at him in the light from outside the room. "Do you mean it? You really want to?"

"I mean it," he said quietly.

She had to fight tears. "Oh, Gene," she whispered, because she knew what a giant step it was for him to make.

He brushed away the moistness from her eyes. "I love you," he said. "From now on, we go together—wherever we go."

"Yes." She laughed, so full of happiness that it was all but overflowing. "Oh, yes!"

He pulled her close and rested his cheek on her soft hair. Minutes later, he heard her breathing change as she fell asleep. He watched her sleeping face with quiet wonder for a few minutes before he pulled the covers over them and settled down beside her, with her cheek resting on his broad, warm shoulder.

Outside, a bird was making soft night noises, and his eyes closed as he relaxed into the mattress. He'd been looking for a place in life, somewhere he belonged, somewhere he fit. Now he'd found it. He fit very nicely into Allison's warm, soft arms—and even better in her gentle heart. She made him complete. He closed his eyes with a slow smile. He'd have to remember to tell her that in the morning.

* * * * *

To professional bull rider Tater Porter,
for taking the time to answer my many
questions and for sharing his experience and
knowledge with me.
Thanks, Tater. You're one of the best.

To Dr. Tandy Freeman and physical trainer
Dave Lammers, for giving me a tour of a
PBR training room and for explaining how
they assist injured riders.

And a special thank-you to the
Professional Bull Riders for showing me a
behind-the-scenes look at this exciting sport.
Without their help, the Lonetree Ranchers
series would not have been possible.

LONETREE RANCHERS: COLT

USA TODAY Bestselling Author

Kathie DeNosky

KATHIE DENOSKY

lives in her native Southern Illinois with her big, lovable Bernese mountain dog, Nemo. Highly sensual with a generous amount of humor, Kathie's books have appeared on the *USA TODAY* and Waldenbooks bestseller lists and received a Write Touch Readers' Award and a National Readers' Choice Award. Kathie enjoys going to rodeos, traveling to research settings for her books and listening to country music. Readers may contact Kathie at P.O. Box 2064, Herrin, Illinois 62948-5264 or email her at kathie@kathiedenosky.com. They can also visit her website at www.kathiedenosky.com.

Chapter One

As Kaylee Simpson arranged rolls of gauze and tape on a cart in the training room, the sudden hushed silence in the arena sent a numbing fear straight through her. There was only one reason an arena full of Professional Bull Riders fans became that quiet—one of the riders was down and not moving.

Closing her eyes, she held her breath and tried not to think as she waited for the applause that would signal the rider was being helped to his feet. But with each passing minute the likelihood of that happening dwindled considerably. When she heard several sets of boots hurrying down the corridor toward the training room, she knew they were bringing the rider in on a stretcher.

Dear God, please don't let it be anyone I know, she prayed.

"Get his vitals," Dr. Carson ordered as he entered the room followed by several other men carrying a stretcher. They hoisted it onto the examining table.

Grabbing the needed equipment, Kaylee's hands shook as she stepped up beside the unconscious cowboy. But the moment she gazed down at the handsome face of the fallen bull rider, her heart slammed against her ribs and she felt the blood drain from her cheeks.

"Colt," she whispered out loud.

The blood pressure cuff fell from her trembling hands to the floor. She barely noticed.

"You know this guy?" one of the paramedics asked, picking up the cuff on his way back to the arena.

Apparently he had no idea who the bull riders were. But Kaylee knew.

Unable to get words past the huge lump clogging her throat, she took the cuff from him, closed her eyes and nodded. She'd grown up around most of the cowboys on the PBR circuit, and until three years ago, most of them had been like brothers to her.

But the one lying on the table in front of her had always been different. She'd known Colt Wakefield from the time he was sixteen years old and she was ten. He'd been her brother's best friend, the love of her young life and the man who had broken her heart.

"Kaylee, if you're not going to take his blood pressure, step aside and let one of the others do it," Dr. Carson said impatiently as he ran clinical hands over Colt's scalp.

The doctor's sharp tone snapped her out of her shocked state and she moved to follow his directive. Placing the cuff on Colt's arm, she pumped it full of air, then listened with the stethoscope. "His blood pressure is one ten over seventy."

"Good. Help me get his riding gear off and his shirt open so we can see what we have here," Dr. Carson instructed.

Kaylee took a deep breath and unzipped the front of the protective black leather vest with trembling fingers, then released the heavy-duty Velcro closure at Colt's right shoulder while Dr. Carson unfastened the left side. Forcing herself to continue, she pushed the heavy leather out of the way and unsnapped his chambray shirt for the doctor to take a closer look.

But when she parted the garment, the sight of Colt's well-developed chest and rippling stomach muscles sent a shiver straight to her core and brought back memories that she'd worked for three long years to forget. Without thinking, she touched his smooth, warm skin with her fingertips. The last time she'd seen him without a shirt—the last time she'd seen him, period—had been the night after her brother's funeral. Devastated by Mitch's death, they'd turned to each other for comfort and support, and ended up…

"K-Kaylee?"

The sound of Colt's voice caused her to recoil. He'd regained consciousness without her realizing it.

Glancing down into his incredibly blue eyes, she felt as if she might not be able to draw her next breath. "Hi, Colt."

When she'd met him fourteen years ago, she'd decided he was the cutest boy she'd ever seen. But his good looks back then had only been a hint of the devilishly handsome man he would become. With raven hair and brilliant blue eyes, he'd always taken her breath away. Unfortunately, it appeared time hadn't lessened his effect on her.

Deciding to revert to the teasing relationship they'd shared before the events that changed her life forever, she added, "I see you're still doing your famous header dismount."

His lean cheeks flushed a dull red. "And I see you're still the same smart-mouthed little brat you've always been," he said, the mischievous light dancing in his eyes taking the sting from his words.

"That's where you're wrong, cowboy," she said, smiling sadly. Unable to stop herself, she added, "If you'll remember, I had to grow up pretty fast about three years ago."

Colt felt as if he'd been punched in the gut by Kaylee's cryptic comment. He wasn't sure if she was referring to Mitch's death or how he'd walked away without looking back the morning after the most incredible night of his life. Either way, the guilt that had plagued him for the past three years welled up inside until he felt as if it might choke the life out of him.

"How have you been, Kaylee?" he asked, unsure of what else to say. He watched her tuck a strand of silky auburn hair behind her ear as if trying to figure out how best to answer his question.

"I've survived. I finally finished my degree last year."

He frowned. "What took you so long? A few years ago you only had one more year left."

She seemed to avoid looking directly at him. "Something came up and I had to take time off from school." She wiped the dirt from his face with a damp cloth. "What about you, Colt? How have you been?"

He started to shrug, but the grinding pain in his left shoulder shot up the side of his neck and caused a low groan to echo throughout the training room. Humiliated at having Kaylee see him in such a weakened condition, he gritted his teeth and said the first thing that came to mind. "I'd be a hell of a lot better if you weren't standing over me like a vulture."

As soon as the words were out, Colt cursed himself for being a dirty lowlife snake. He'd rather cut off his right arm than to hurt Kaylee more than he knew he already had. But from the expression that fleetingly crossed her pretty face, he could tell that was exactly what he'd done.

Before he could apologize for being a total jerk, Dr. Carson broke the tension filling the small room. "It looks like you've got a broken collarbone in addition to a slight concussion, Colt. To be sure, I'm sending you to the hospital for a set of X-rays."

Colt stared at the man as the gravity of the

diagnosis sank in, along with an overwhelming amount of frustrated disappointment. "How long will I be out of commission?"

"Depending on how bad the break is, I'd say you're looking at eight to twelve weeks before you make it back," Carson answered.

It was the very last thing Colt wanted to hear. Ranked number three on this year's PBR tour, he was close enough to the top that he had a damned good shot at the season championship. Missing the last part of the regular season events would all but end his hopes of winning the title. The best he could hope for now was to make it back in time for the finals in November.

"I've called the ambulance crew for transport to the hospital," he heard Kaylee say from somewhere across the room.

She'd made good her escape and had moved away from the examining table while the doctor talked to him. Colt couldn't say that he blamed her. He should be horsewhipped for the way he'd talked to her and he needed to apologize.

"Kaylee?"

A man in a navy-blue paramedic jumpsuit with the name of Forrester embroidered on the breast pocket stepped close. "Are you wanting the cute little chick with the great set of—"

"Watch it, pal," Colt warned angrily. As long as he was around, he wouldn't tolerate anyone talking about Kaylee like that. She deserved the utmost respect and Colt intended to make sure she got it. "That girl just happens to be my best friend's sister."

Knowing Colt was in no shape to do anything about his comment, the man shrugged. "That's funny. She didn't look like much of a girl to me."

Colt ground his back teeth at the guy's lascivious expression. "And just what *did* she look like to you, Forrester?"

"One hundred percent all woman," the man answered, grinning suggestively.

If Colt hadn't been flat on his back and in pain, he'd have knocked the guy into the middle of next week. But as much as he wanted to teach the jerk a lesson in respect, he knew it would be some time before he was up to a good old-fashioned fistfight.

"Don't worry, cowboy. She was on her way out when we came in," the man went on as he and his rotund partner lifted Colt to the gurney they'd rolled up beside the examining table. "She'll most likely meet us at the hospital."

Colt didn't say anything as they transported him out of the training room to the ambulance. He knew damned good and well that Kaylee wouldn't be there when they arrived at the hospital.

After what happened three years ago, combined with the way he'd talked to her this evening, he'd be lucky if she ever spoke to him again.

A month after seeing Colt at the Professional Bull Riders event, Kaylee still found herself thinking about their encounter. He'd been the last person she'd wanted to see. From his reaction, it had been crystal clear that he'd felt the same way about seeing her.

She poured herself a fresh cup of coffee and wandered into the living room of her small apartment to curl up in a corner of the couch. Their run-in had dredged up some painful memories that she thought she'd worked through. Apparently she'd been wrong.

Over the years, cheering for Colt and her brother, Mitch, had become a tradition. She'd been on hand that fateful weekend three years ago for the PBR event in Houston. But what had started out as a typical Saturday evening of watching the two men she loved most in the world compete in the first round of bull riding had suddenly turned horribly tragic.

Colt had successfully ridden the bull he'd

drawn, then helped Mitch pull his rope to get ready for his ride. But the moment the chute gate opened, Kaylee had known Mitch was in serious trouble. The bull's first jump had been violent, whipping Mitch forward and slamming his face into the back of the bull's head, knocking him out. Bullfighters had moved in immediately, but before they could even distract the animal, Mitch had landed on the ground in front of the angry beast.

Tears welled in Kaylee's eyes as she relived the horrific events. The bullfighters had distracted the bull enough to keep it from hooking Mitch with its horns, but as the animal jumped over Mitch to go after the bullfighters, its back hooves had come down full-force in the middle of Mitch's chest.

With no regard to his own safety, Colt had vaulted the back of the chute and run to protect her brother. After he'd made sure someone was helping Mitch, he had come looking for her in the crush of people behind the chutes. He'd accompanied her to the hospital to wait while Mitch was in surgery. Then later, he'd held her when they received the news that her only brother—her only living relative—had died on the operating table.

"M-mommy!" a little voice cried from down the hall.

The sound of her daughter awakening from her afternoon nap was a welcomed release from the disturbing memories. Setting her coffee cup on the end table, Kaylee rose from the couch. As she walked down the hall to see about Amber, Kaylee wiped away the last of her tears. She had Amber to think about now. She didn't have time to worry about a past she couldn't change.

"Did you have a bad dream, sweetie?" she asked, lifting the little girl from her small bed.

Amber shook her head sleepily, put her finger in her mouth and buried her face in her mother's neck.

"It's all right. Mommy won't let anything hurt you," Kaylee said, hugging her daughter close.

She started into the living room to sit in the rocking chair with Amber, but the ringing doorbell had her detouring to see who the current salesman was and what he was trying to sell today. Turning on the CD player she kept by the door, she smiled at Amber as the sounds of a snarling German Shepherd filled the room.

"One of these days, Mommy's going to get a real dog with enormous teeth and an insatiable appetite for door-to-door salesmen." Making sure the security chain was in place, Kaylee took a deep breath and reached for the doorknob. "Until then, let's see how fast we can send this joker on his way."

As Colt waited at the door to the second-floor apartment, he adjusted the sling holding his left arm snug against his body and looked around at the shabby building. What was Kaylee doing here instead of living on her ranch up in the Oklahoma panhandle?

While he'd been recuperating last month, he'd done a lot of soul-searching and had come to the realization that he had to find her and make things right. He shook his head. He'd been ready to jump on that paramedic for his lack of respect toward her, yet, to his chagrin, he'd realized that he hadn't acted any better. He'd snapped at her for no other reason than the fact that she'd witnessed him give in to the pain of a broken collarbone like some little kid.

But when he'd gotten back on his feet, he'd gone to the Lazy S only to find that Kaylee had sold the ranch and moved to Oklahoma City shortly after Mitch had died. He'd had to resort to searching through the phone book to find her. Fortunately there'd only been one Kaylee Simpson listed in the area.

The door suddenly opened as far as the security chain would allow. "I don't care what you're selling. I don't want—" Kaylee stopped abruptly. "Colt?"

Pushing the wide brim of his Resistol up with his thumb, he rocked back on his heels, chuckling at the sound of a snarling dog. "Does that recording of Kujo really chase off door-to-door salesmen?"

She stared at him through the narrow opening as if she couldn't quite believe her eyes. "W-what are you doing here?"

He winced at her blunt tone. She sure didn't seem very happy to see him. All things considered, he couldn't say that he blamed her.

Hoping to tease her into a better mood, he grinned. "Well, hello to you, too, brat. You want to shut off Kujo, now that you know it's me and not somebody trying to sell a vacuum cleaner?"

She turned away and the sound of the snarling dog ceased. "I'm sorry. Hello, Colt."

"Me see," a little voice said a moment before a set of tiny fingers appeared around the edge of the door in an effort to open it wider.

Colt frowned. "Do you have company?"

"No, but this really isn't a good time," Kaylee said, prying the baby's fingers from the door.

The panic suddenly filling her violet eyes bothered him. A lot. "Are you all right, Kaylee?"

She nodded. "I'm fine."

"Me see, Mommy," the little voice insisted. "Me see."

"Not now, sweetie," Kaylee said gently.

Colt felt as though he'd been sucker punched. Kaylee had a child? Was she married?

"We need to talk," he said seriously.

He told himself that Mitch would want Colt to make sure she was doing okay. But the truth was, he wanted to know what was going on.

"I can't imagine what you think we need to talk about." She gave him a one-shouldered shrug, but he could tell from the tone of her voice that she was nervous as hell about something.

"Come on, Kaylee," he said, watching her closely. "I drove all the way down here from the Lonetree just to talk to you. The least you can do is give me five minutes."

Her defeated expression caused the air to lodge in his lungs. Something was definitely going on, and Colt had every intention of finding out what is was.

"Kaylee?"

She closed the door, released the chain, then swung it wide for him to step into the tiny apartment. "I'm sorry about the mess," she said, pointing to the toys scattered on the floor in front of the couch. "I wasn't expecting anyone."

Colt turned to tell her he was used to seeing toys scattered all over his two brothers' homes, but the words died somewhere between his vocal cords and opened mouth. The baby riding Kaylee's hip was a little girl with raven curls. Her face was buried shyly against Kaylee's neck, but something about the child caused his scalp to prickle and his pulse to race.

"Is she yours?" he asked cautiously.

Kaylee stared at him for what seemed like an eternity before she slowly nodded. "Yes. This is my daughter, Amber."

At the sound of her name, the baby looked up, but when she saw him staring at her, she stuck one tiny index finger in her mouth and once again hid her face in Kaylee's shoulder.

The glimpse Colt had gotten hadn't been much, but it was enough to see that the little girl's eyes were blue. A vivid blue. His sisters-in-law, Annie and Samantha, called it "Wakefield blue."

His heart pounding against his ribs like a jungle drum, he had a hard time drawing air into his lungs. The child had to be around the same age as his brother Brant's little boy, Zach. From there it didn't take much for Colt to do the math.

Swallowing hard, he asked, "She's mine, isn't she, Kaylee?"

Colt watched her bite her lower lip to keep it from trembling. He knew the answer, but he needed to hear her tell him.

"Kaylee?"

She took a deep breath, then defiantly met his gaze. "Yes, Colt. Amber is your daughter, too."

Chapter Two

"Dammit, Kaylee, why didn't you tell me?" Colt demanded. Conflicting emotions twisted his gut and he had to force himself to take several deep breaths in an effort to stay calm. "Didn't you think I had the right to know about my own daughter?"

Anger flashed in her violet eyes. "No."

Colt wasn't sure how he'd expected her to answer, but the vehemence in her tone surprised him. He'd never seen her this angry before.

"Why not?" he asked, his own anger flaring.

If anyone had the right to be pissed off here, it

was him. Kaylee had been the one who kept him from knowing about his child.

The baby started to whimper and clutch at her mother. Apparently their raised voices were upsetting her.

"Would you like to have some juice, sweetie?" Kaylee asked, her voice once again soft and gentle as she rubbed the little girl's back.

The child nodded.

"Let me get her settled down." Kaylee's voice was calm, but the look she gave him was pure defiance. "Then we'll talk."

"You're damned right we will," he muttered, watching her carry her daughter—his daughter—into the kitchenette.

His daughter.

Colt's chest swelled with a feeling he'd never before experienced. He was the daddy of a two-year-old child—a little girl who looked just like him. The thought caused a lump to form in his throat and made it hard as hell for him to drag air into his lungs.

As the knowledge sank in, questions flooded his mind. How could Kaylee have done this to him? Why hadn't she let him know that their only night together had made her pregnant?

He wasn't sure what her reasons had been, but

he had every intention of finding out. Removing his cowboy hat, he set it down beside a CD player on a shelf by the door. He wasn't going anywhere until Kaylee gave him some answers. And, he decided as he ran a frustrated hand through his thick hair, they'd better be damned good ones.

Kaylee brushed past him to set Amber on the floor with her toys. He waited until she handed the toddler a small plastic glass he'd heard his sisters-in-law refer to as a sippy cup before he asked, "Were you ever going to tell me about her?"

Kaylee picked up a mug from the coffee table. "No."

Shocked, Colt started to ask her why, but she stopped him by motioning for him to follow her into the kitchen. Walking behind her, he tried not to notice that her cutoff jeans hugged her cute little rear to perfection, or the fact that they exposed a lot more of her long, slender legs than they covered. When she reached up to get another coffee cup out of the cabinet for him, he swallowed hard. Her hot-pink tank top pulled away from the waistband of her cutoffs and gave him more than a fair view of her smooth, flat abdomen.

He shook his head. What the hell was wrong with him? Kaylee had not only kept his only child a secret from him, she was Mitch's little sister. And although Colt had given in to temptation once, he couldn't—wouldn't—let it happen again.

Pouring them both a cup of coffee, she indicated that he should sit at the small table. When he lowered himself into a chair, she seated herself across from him so that she could watch their daughter play with a small teddy bear.

"As far as I'm concerned, you never needed to know about Amber," she said, glaring at him.

Anger and confusion raced through him and he had to wait a moment before he could speak. Losing his cool wouldn't net him the answers he needed.

"Being pregnant was the reason you took that year off from school, wasn't it?" he asked, suddenly understanding her evasive answers in the training room the night he'd been injured.

"Yes."

"You should have told me," he said, trying to keep his voice even. "I would have helped."

"I didn't want or need your assistance." Her voice shook with emotion. "I never wanted you to know about Amber."

"Why, Kaylee?" He'd never seen her this stubborn. But then, he was just as determined. "What made you think I didn't have the right to know that I'd fathered a child?"

"You gave up the right," she said without looking at him. Her voice was a little more calm, but her words couldn't have held more resolution.

His own irritation won over his vow to remain coolheaded. "How the hell do you figure that?"

"The morning after Mitch's funeral I got the message loud and clear." She met his gaze head-on and the mixture of hurt and resentment sparkling in her eyes stopped him cold. "You wanted nothing more to do with me. When I discovered I was pregnant, I assumed those feelings would encompass my baby, as well."

The guilt that had plagued him for the past three years increased tenfold. He'd not only slept with his best friend's sister the night after they'd laid the man to rest, he'd taken her virginity. Colt knew that he'd handled things badly the morning after he'd made love to her, but he'd been so ashamed of his actions, he hadn't been able to face himself let alone her.

"Kaylee, that's not the way it was. I—"

"Oh, really?" she interrupted hotly. "Just how many times in the past three years have you tried to get in touch with me, Colt?"

He didn't think it was possible to feel lower than he already did, but Kaylee had just proven him wrong. "I know that if they handed out prizes for tactless jackasses, I'd win hands down. But there's a reason—"

"Too little, too late," she said, rising to her feet. "I'm really not interested in hearing why you left that morning without waking me or even leaving a note." She picked up his untouched coffee and poured it down the sink.

"Hey, I'm not finished with—"

"Yes, you are." She walked to the door. "I'd appreciate it if you'd go now. All I'm interested in is you leaving Amber…and me alone. We've done just fine…without you."

He detected the hitch in Kaylee's voice and knew she was fighting tears. The thought that he'd caused her such emotional pain made him feel physically ill.

Taking a deep breath, he rose and followed her. He needed time to come to grips with everything that he'd learned in the past hour, as well as to figure out how to make Kaylee listen to him.

"I think it would be best if we continue this conversation after we've both had a chance—"

"No, Colt," she said, shaking her head. "You gave up that chance three years ago when you left me behind without a backward glance. You got what you wanted, now let me have…what I want."

The single tear sliding down her pale cheek just about tore him apart. "What do you want, Kaylee?"

She took a deep breath and impatiently wiped the droplet away with a trembling hand, then pointed toward the door. "I want you to walk out…the way you did that morning three years ago and…never look back."

"I can't do that, honey," he said, reaching out to wipe another tear from her satiny skin with the pad of his thumb. "I'll be back tomorrow after we've both calmed down."

"Please…don't." Tears coursed down her cheeks unchecked as she stepped away from his touch. "It would be best…if you went back…to the Lonetree Ranch in Wyoming and forgot…we exist."

"That's not going to happen," Colt said gently.

He picked up his Resistol and placed it on his head, then looked over at Amber playing quietly with her toys. She was curiously watching him. But the moment she realized he was looking back at her, she smiled shyly and hid her face behind the teddy bear in her tiny hands.

He fell in love with his daughter right then and there.

"I'll see you tomorrow." Turning to open the door, he didn't think twice about leaning down to place a kiss on Kaylee's tear-stained cheek. "We'll get all of this worked out, honey. I promise."

The next day Kaylee nervously sat at the kitchen table awaiting Colt's return. She dreaded the upcoming confrontation, but at the same time, a small part of her looked forward to seeing him again. And that was a huge problem.

She'd fallen in love with Colt Wakefield almost the moment she'd met him. Her mother had called it a schoolgirl crush and told her that she'd grow out of it in time. But Kaylee had always known better. Over the years her feelings for him hadn't diminished, they'd only grown stronger.

But after that fateful morning when she'd awakened to find him gone, she'd forced herself to forget about him and to move on. She'd had to. She wouldn't have survived the past few years if she hadn't.

Unfortunately she'd discovered yesterday afternoon that he still affected her in ways she thought she'd put behind her. When Colt touched her, she'd felt the familiar racing of her heart, the jolt of excitement that being near him had always caused. But the most disturbing discovery of all had been the fact that he still had the power to cause her emotional pain.

"Mommy, see!"

Kaylee looked up to watch Amber laugh and point to the animated vegetables dancing and singing their way across the television screen.

Smiling, she walked into the living room to join her daughter. "You like that, don't you, sweetie?"

"No," Amber said, her soft shoulder-length curls bouncing as she nodded her little head affirmatively.

Kaylee grinned. One of these days Amber would get the words and the body language synchronized. As she gazed at her daughter, Kaylee was once again struck by how much Amber looked like Colt. The resemblance was amazing, and she had known the minute he saw Amber that he'd realize she was his child. She had the same dark hair and vivid blue eyes that all the Wakefields shared.

Lost in thought, the ringing doorbell caused her to jump and sent Amber scurrying to wrap her arms around Kaylee's legs. Amber wasn't used to strangers and tended to be extremely shy.

Picking her daughter up, Kaylee didn't bother turning on the snarling dog recording as she moved to answer the door. There was no need. She knew who would be waiting on the other side.

"Hi," Colt said when she opened the door. He picked up a shopping bag sitting at his booted feet.

"Sorry I'm a little late, but I stopped by a toy store to get something for Amber."

Amber's face was already buried in Kaylee's neck and the sound of Colt's deep baritone saying her name caused her to tighten her little arms around Kaylee's neck.

Stepping away for him to enter, Kaylee patted Amber's back in an effort to soothe her. "I see you didn't bother listening to me yesterday when I asked you to leave us alone."

His smile sent a shiver up her spine. "Did you really expect me to?"

"No." She sighed heavily. Why did he have to be so darned good-looking? So charming?

"Amber, I brought you something," he said softly.

"She's not used to strangers," Kaylee said when Amber continued to keep her face hidden. "And especially men."

Colt's piercing blue eyes met hers and she could tell that he was speculating about her social life—specifically her social life with men. "She hasn't been around a lot of men?" he finally asked.

"Not really," Kaylee answered evasively.

If circumstances had been different, she might have laughed out loud. She hadn't been out on a date in the past three years. But Colt didn't need to know that.

The cad had the audacity to look relieved. "That's going to change," he said, sounding quite confident. "She'll get used to me being around all the time."

All the time?

Kaylee's heart skipped a beat. She definitely didn't like the sound of that. She'd done a lot of thinking since yesterday afternoon and she'd conceded that she couldn't deny Amber the chance to get to know the man who was responsible for her existence. But there were going to be limits set.

"Colt, I don't think that would be a good idea."

"Why not?" he asked, wincing as he adjusted the sling holding his left arm immobile.

"Do you still have a lot of pain from the broken collarbone?" She hoped to divert the conversation into safer territory.

"Not really." He removed his Resistol and placed it on the shelf with her CD player. "But I anticipate that will change when I start physical therapy."

"If the therapy is done right, and you don't overwork your shoulder too soon, you shouldn't have anything more than a little minor soreness."

When she felt Amber begin to loosen her hold, signaling that she was becoming accustomed to Colt's presence, Kaylee walked over to sit her daughter down in front of the television. "When do you start therapy?"

"In another week or two," he answered. "I've been doing some simple range-of-motion stuff, but that's about it."

She heard him rummage through the shopping bag and, when she turned around, watched him struggle to pull out a large rag doll. Unable to use both of his hands, he'd gotten the doll tangled in the bag handles.

"Let me," she said, walking over to help him. Reaching to work the doll's leg free, his hand touched hers. Kaylee jerked back from the scorching contact and handed the doll to him. "A-Amber will like this."

He stared at her for several long seconds before he cleared his throat and asked, "Do you think it would frighten her if I gave it to her now?"

The look on his handsome face took Kaylee by surprise. It was the first time she ever remembered seeing Colt look uncertain.

"Maybe in a few minutes. She's just getting adjusted to you being here." Kaylee's heart went out to him even if she wasn't particularly comfortable with the feeling. It was clear Colt wanted to get to know Amber, but didn't want to do anything that would upset her. "Let's sit in the living room. You'll be close to her, but not so much that she'll feel threatened."

"Okay. We can talk while Amber gets used to me." He followed her over to sit on the couch, and she could feel his gaze on her backside just as surely as if he touched her.

When they were settled on the sagging blue cushions, Kaylee found it hard to breathe. Glancing at her daughter to keep from looking at Colt, she noticed Amber looking at them curiously.

"It's all right, sweetie. Colt is a friend."

"I'm your daddy," he said, his voice gentle. Turning to Kaylee, he firmly added, "I don't want her to ever doubt that."

Amber didn't seem to pick up on the sudden tension between the two adults as she turned her attention back to the television.

But Kaylee did, and it only served to increase her apprehension. Hoping to take the lead in what she knew would be a difficult conversation, she said, "Colt, I've done a lot of thinking about our situation—"

"I haven't been able to think of anything else,"

he said, nodding. "And this isn't something that can be resolved overnight."

"No, it's not. It's going to take time for us—"

"I'm glad you agree," he said, smiling. "It will make everything a lot easier on all concerned."

Where was he going with this? And why did he keep interrupting her?

"What's going on, Colt?" she asked, not at all sure she wanted to know.

"I doubt that you're going to like what I'm going to suggest."

She doubted that she would, either. His tone was relaxed, but from the serious look on his face, she could tell he was anything but nonchalant about what he was going to say.

"Tell me what you have in mind and we'll see," she said cautiously.

"I want you and Amber to come back to the Lonetree with me."

She couldn't believe he'd come up with something so outlandish. "You can't be serious."

"I'm very serious, Kaylee." The determination in his brilliant blue eyes startled her. "I intend to get to know my daughter."

"You can get to know Amber right here," she argued. There was no way she would agree to go to his ranch in Wyoming.

"No, I can't." He turned his gaze to watch Amber play quietly with some of her toys. "If I tried to get to know her here, I'd just end up being some guy who stopped by once in a while and who she'd end up forgetting between visits."

"It works for other fathers," Kaylee insisted, feeling desperate. She had to make him see reason. "It would work for you and Amber."

Colt shook his head. "Maybe if I'd been part of her life from the beginning, but not now." He glanced back at Amber. "I'm going to be her daddy, not just a man who claims to be her father."

Kaylee shook her head. "I can't take time off at the hospital. I'd lose my job."

"No, you won't." His knowing grin sent a chill slithering up her spine. "I've already talked to your superior."

"You did what?" Her temper flared and she had to concentrate hard on keeping her voice even so as not to upset Amber. "You couldn't possibly have talked to anyone about my taking time off. It's Sunday. The physical therapy unit is closed."

"I have my ways," he said, sounding so darned smug that she was sorely tempted to belt him one.

But thinking about what he said, Kaylee suddenly felt cold all over. "What did you do?"

He casually rested his right arm along the back

of the couch. "I got in touch with Dr. Carson and had him find out which hospital sent you over to work the PBR event last month. He also gave me the name and phone number of your boss."

Kaylee couldn't believe Colt's arrogance. "You called Brad at home?"

Grinning, Colt nodded. "Once I explained the situation—"

She felt the blood drain from her face. She'd made it a point not to discuss anything about her private life with her co-workers. "Please, tell me you didn't—"

He shook his head as he played with a lock of her hair. "No, honey, I didn't tell him the whole story. That's nobody's business but ours. But I did tell him there was a family crisis that needed your attention and asked if you could get a couple of months off." He smiled. "All you'll have to do is stop by the office tomorrow to sign the papers for your leave of absence."

Anger so intense that she actually started shaking ran through her. "How dare you?" Unable to sit still, Kaylee rose to pace the length of the small living room. "It's one thing for you to walk in and start telling me you want to be a part of my daughter's life, but—"

"Our daughter," he corrected.

Upset by the angry voices, Amber started to cry. She crawled over to Kaylee and wrapped her arms around her mother's leg. "M-mommy!"

Ignoring Colt, Kaylee picked up the baby and held her close as she continued. "You can't take matters into your own hands and make a decision like that for me." She stopped to glare at him. "I can't afford to take time off. I have rent, a car payment and—"

"I'll take care of it."

"Oh, no, you won't." She clutched Amber. "I don't want anything from you."

Standing, he walked over to her. "Be reasonable, Kaylee. The way I see it, I owe you a little over two years of back child support, and besides, I'd like to hire you to help me get back in shape for the PBR finals the first part of November. You can return here after we get back from Vegas."

"I don't want your money," she said stubbornly. "And I won't help you regain your strength just so you can go back into an arena and risk your life riding a bull for eight seconds' worth of thrills."

"When I come to pick up you and Amber tomorrow morning, I'll stop by the manager's office and take care of the rent, as well as having him see that the utilities are shut off," Colt went on as if he hadn't listened to a word she'd said. "Besides, Kaylee, you owe me."

"Oh, really? How do you figure that?" she asked hotly.

His intense blue gaze held hers captive. "You deprived me of Amber's first two years. You owe me the right to get to know her now."

Kaylee felt her life spinning out of control with no way to stop it. She had a frightened baby screaming in her ear and an infuriating, sexy-as-sin cowboy standing over her, telling her that he was taking over her life. It was enough to wear the Rock of Gibraltar down to an insignificant pebble.

"Please, don't do this to me, Colt," she whispered, feeling more trapped than she'd ever felt in her entire life.

He reached out to cup her cheek. "I love Amber, and I want her to love me. Please give us the chance to develop a relationship, Kaylee."

The weight of guilt settling over Kaylee's shoulders couldn't possibly have felt heavier. As much as she disliked having to admit it, she had been unfair to both Colt and Amber by keeping her secret. Kaylee knew beyond a shadow of doubt that no matter how much he wanted to forget their night together had ever happened, he would have loved and cared for his child from the very moment he learned of her existence.

Tears filled Kaylee's eyes. She'd kept Colt from knowing about his child because of her own hurt feelings and disillusion. In the process, she'd deprived Amber of a daddy who cared deeply for her.

"What do you say, Kaylee?" he asked, wiping a tear from her cheek with his thumb. "Will you and Amber come home with me to the Lonetree?"

She gazed up at the man she'd once loved with all her heart and soul. He was right. She did owe him and Amber the time together. But it was going to take everything she had in her to keep her wits about her while she was with him. If she didn't, she wasn't sure she wouldn't end up falling under his magnetic spell all over again. And that was something she couldn't allow herself to do. Her survival depended on it.

"I can't believe I'm actually going to say this," she finally said, feeling her insides shake like a bowl full of Jell-O.

"You'll go?" he asked hopefully.

Taking a deep breath, Kaylee felt as if she was stepping out onto a tightrope with no safety net below. "Yes, we'll go to the Lonetree with you. But only until you get ready to leave for the season finals. Amber and I won't be going to Las Vegas with you."

"We'll see about that."

The smile he sent her way curled her toes and already had her regretting her decision to go to the Lonetree Ranch with him for the next two months.

Chapter Three

"Dammit all," Colt muttered, cursing the fact that he still couldn't use his left arm. Not being able to use both hands made installing Amber's car seat in his truck extremely difficult.

"Problems?" Kaylee asked.

Turning, he watched her walk toward him. She held Amber in her arms.

"I could use another hand getting this car seat secured," he said, hating that he looked helpless and inadequate in front of her.

Kaylee set Amber on her feet. "Stay right here, sweetie, while Mommy helps Colt with your seat."

"Daddy," he said firmly. "I'm her daddy, Kaylee."

She stared up at him a moment before she gave a quick nod. "I'm going to help your...daddy, Amber."

Her reluctance to acknowledge him as Amber's father cut like a knife, but Colt ignored it. Once they got to the Lonetree they'd have plenty of time to sort things out and, hopefully, to rebuild the friendship they'd once shared. It would make their raising Amber together a whole hell of a lot easier.

A small sound caught Colt's attention. Glancing down, he noticed his daughter curiously watching him. But the moment she saw him look at her, she ducked behind Kaylee's leg.

"How long do you think it will take for her to be comfortable with me?" he asked, wondering the same thing about Kaylee. Would she ever again be at ease when she was around him?

"I'm not sure." She stared at him for endless seconds before she added, "This is new territory for all of us. It's going to take time."

Colt knew she was referring more to herself than their daughter. Deciding not to push for more, he reached into the truck to position the car seat. "Are you about ready to leave? I'd like to get on the road. We have a long drive and I'd like to get as far as we can before we stop for the night."

"Stop?"

When she turned to look at him, Kaylee's breast brushed his arm. His mouth went as dry as a pile of sawdust. "I—" he had to stop to clear his throat "—thought it would probably be best for Amber if we broke the trip into two days."

It took everything Colt had in him not to groan out loud when Kaylee's tongue darted out to moisten her perfect coral lips. "You're probably right," she finally answered. Backing away from him, she picked up Amber and started toward the stairs leading to the second floor of the apartment building. "I'll go check to make sure we brought all of the luggage down and grab Amber's bag of toys."

Colt waited until Kaylee climbed the steps and disappeared into her apartment before he finally managed to take another breath. Glancing at his scuffed boots, he kicked a pebble and watched it skitter across the asphalt parking lot. He hated that he'd had to resort to making her feel guilty to get her to go to the Lonetree with him. But, dammit, he needed time to get to know Amber, time to work out some kind of shared custody agreement, and time to make amends with Kaylee for what had happened three years ago.

He ran his hand around the back of his neck in an effort to ease some of the tension that had knotted his muscles since Saturday afternoon and his discovery that he'd fathered a child. How was he ever going to convince Kaylee that she wasn't the reason he'd walked away that morning? How was he going to explain that he'd felt as if he'd betrayed Mitch's friendship? And how was he going to make her understand that he'd been so ashamed of his actions, he hadn't been able to face himself, let alone face her?

"If they gave medals for screwing up, you'd win hands down, Wakefield," he muttered disgustedly.

He wasn't quite sure how to go about doing it, but he was determined to straighten everything out with Kaylee. He had to. His, hers and Amber's future happiness depended on it.

"Out, Mommy, out," Amber said, impatiently tugging on the harness holding her in the car seat.

"Just a few more minutes, sweetie," Kaylee answered as she watched Colt enter the motel lobby. "Colt…your daddy is going to get a couple of rooms for us to sleep in tonight."

Amber blinked and nodded her head. "Not seepy."

"I know you're not sleepy right now," Kaylee said, smiling. "But you will be later."

She absently watched Colt as he talked to the desk clerk. He'd decided to stop in Hays, Kansas, for the night even though it was early and they could have driven for several more hours. His excuse had been that he didn't want the trip to be too tiring for Amber. But Kaylee suspected his collarbone bothered him. She also knew that if that was the case, he'd never admit it. For Colt and most of the other cowboys on the PBR and professional rodeo circuits, admitting any kind of weakness was unheard of.

"Did you get rooms on the ground floor or the second level?" Kaylee asked when he got back into the truck.

"Ground floor." He put the truck into gear. "I figured it would be easier."

She didn't have to ask what he meant. She already knew. He intended to carry what few bags they took to their rooms himself, just as he'd insisted on carrying all of her luggage from the apartment to his truck this morning. Unable to use his left arm, it had taken him several trips to get everything downstairs, but he wouldn't hear of her helping.

"I'll carry our bag to mine and Amber's room," she said firmly when he pulled into a parking space at the side of the stucco building.

"Our room."

Kaylee stopped unbuckling Amber's shoulder harness to stare at him. "You rented only one room?"

"Yep."

Her heart hammered against her rib cage. "There weren't any more available?"

"I don't know how many they had available," he answered, sounding so darned unconcerned she wanted to throttle him. "I didn't ask."

When he moved to get out of the truck, she took hold of his arm to stop him. "You want to give me a reason for not getting the second room?" she asked, doing her best to keep her voice level.

The feel of Colt's rock-hard muscles beneath his red shirt sent a tingle arrowing up her arm. She immediately let go of his bicep to rub her palm on her jeans-clad thigh.

For the first time since getting back into the truck, Colt looked uncertain. "I don't like having to admit this, but I'm probably going to need your help tonight and in the morning."

"With your sling?" Kaylee asked, surprised that he'd admit needing assistance with anything. Because of her training she knew he probably did have trouble trying to put the restraint on with one hand, but she could help him without them spending the night in the same room.

He nodded. "I have a hard time getting it adjusted." He looked thoroughly disgusted. "Trying to get it comfortable is a pain in the—"

Kaylee loudly cleared her throat and nodded toward Amber. "She picks up certain words faster than others."

His charming grin sent a shiver straight up her spine. "I was going to say, it's a pain in the butt."

"I just assumed—"

"The worst," he finished for her as he opened the truck door. When he walked around to open the passenger door, he smiled. "Since Morgan's and Brant's kids came along, we've all learned to watch what we say."

"How are your brothers?" she asked, turning to lift Amber from her car seat.

Colt grinned. "Ornery as ever."

Kaylee smiled. She'd always liked Colt's older brothers. "How many children do they have now?"

"Morgan and his wife, Samantha, have two boys," he said, placing his palm to her back to steer her toward their room. "Brant and Annie have one son and, if the sonogram is correct, another one on the way."

"H-heaven help us. Another generation of Wakefield boys," Kaylee said, feeling as if she'd been branded by his warm touch. She quickly put distance between them.

"Yes, but now there's a Wakefield girl," he said, gazing down at Amber as he fit the key card into the lock.

Kaylee swallowed hard at the look of genuine affection on his handsome face. No matter what he felt for her, she knew for certain that he'd fallen head over heels in love with their daughter.

Feeling guilty for keeping Amber from him, she quickly stepped into the motel room and looked around to distract herself. She was relieved to see there were two beds.

"Which bag did you want me to bring in?" Colt asked from behind her.

She set Amber down. "I'll get it."

"No, you won't." He'd already turned to go back outside to the truck.

"Don't be ridiculous, Colt," she said, following him. "With your arm in a sling you'll have to make two trips. I'm perfectly capable of carrying one small overnight bag. It just makes more sense—"

When he spun around to face her, her breath caught at his deep scowl. "I may need help getting this da—dumb sling adjusted, but I'm not helpless. I'll carry the luggage. Now, which one do you want?"

She blew out a frustrated breath. "The red one."

"Wed one," Amber repeated from behind Kaylee's leg.

Colt's expression softened instantly. "Was she actually talking to me?"

"Maybe." He looked so hopeful, Kaylee didn't have the heart to tell him that, like most two-year-old children, Amber parroted a lot of what she heard.

Bending, he asked, "Do you want Daddy to get the red one, Amber?"

Amber smiled up at him a moment before she clutched Kaylee's leg and hid her face.

"Did you see that?" he asked incredulously. He straightened to his full six-foot height. "She actually looked at me for a second or two before she dived for cover."

Kaylee could tell from his expression that the small gesture meant the world to him. "I'd say you're making progress."

"It's a start," he agreed, opening the door to go out to the truck for their overnight bags.

When he closed the door behind him, Kaylee scooped Amber up into her arms. "Colt may be new to this father business, but I think he's going to be a good daddy, don't you, sweetie?"

To Kaylee's astonishment, Amber stared at her for a moment then, pointing to the door, nodded as if in complete agreement.

Sweat beaded Colt's forehead and upper lip as he braced himself on the motel-room desk with his right hand, bent slightly forward and let his left arm dangle in front of him. Taking a deep breath, he gritted his teeth and started another set of range-of-motion exercises. He was supposed to stop after the third set, but he figured if three were good, five had to be better.

"Colt, how many sets of those have you already completed?" Kaylee asked, walking out of the bathroom with Amber.

"Four," he answered without looking up.

He'd wanted to be done with the exercises before she finished giving Amber a bath. Apparently he'd miscalculated the time it would take for the extra sets.

Kaylee's eyes narrowed. "You weren't supposed to do more than three sets, were you?"

"Nope. But three sets, twice a day just isn't

enough," he said through gritted teeth. He took a deep breath. He hadn't anticipated the extra exercises taking this much out of him.

"Stop right now!"

At the sharp rise of her voice, he stopped to look up at her. "What?"

"By doing more than is recommended, you could do more damage," she said, sitting Amber in the middle of the bed. Turning back to face him, she propped her hands on her shapely hips as she glared at him. "You're just as stubborn as you always were. Are you even supposed to be in a sling yet, or should you still be wearing a Figure 8 splint?"

"I hated that splint." Careful to keep his shoulder in the same position, he slowly straightened. "I wore that dam—danged thing for about two weeks before I threw it away. I couldn't manage it by myself and I was tired of asking for Morgan and Brant's help."

"So you just took it upon yourself to graduate to a sling, instead of waiting for an orthopedist to say you're ready?" She gave him a look that clearly said she thought he was a few bricks shy of a full load. "Have you been using the sling day and night, or have you been trying to go without it, too?"

He bent his left elbow and held his arm close to his body while he tried to unsnap his shirt with his right hand. "Unless I'm taking a shower, I wear it all the time."

She stepped forward to help him with the snaps on his Western-style shirt. "Have you experienced any excess pain since you stopped wearing the splint?"

"No, and I'm not having a whole lot of discomfort now." *At least, not the painful kind,* he added silently.

"Only because I stopped you," she said sternly.

He felt his body spring to life as her delicate fingers worked each one of the grippers open. "Would you mind telling me what you think you're doing, Kaylee?"

"I'm helping you take your shirt off for your shower." When she reached the snap just above his belt buckle, she stopped to tug the tail of the garment from the waistband of his jeans.

Her hand brushed his stomach and it felt as if a charge of electricity ran straight through him. It took everything he had in him not to groan out loud.

"I can do this myself," he said through clenched teeth.

"Oh, really?" She stopped to give him a

withering glare. "Wasn't it your idea to get *one* room because you needed my assistance?"

"Well, yes, but—"

"Then stop arguing and let me help you."

Unsnapping his right cuff, she reached up to slide the sleeve off his shoulder. Her soft hands on his skin sent heat streaking through his veins and he found it hard to pull air into his lungs.

"I meant…" He had to stop to clear his suddenly dry throat. "—I'd need help with the sling."

She ignored his protest and started to unfasten the cuff at his left wrist. "And I suppose it's easy to get your shirt off and on by yourself."

Her fingertips feathered over his pulse and he had to concentrate hard on what she'd said. "I didn't say…it was easy."

"Could you please tell me something?" she asked, easing his shirt off his left shoulder and down his arm.

The room suddenly seemed warmer with his shirt off than it had with the garment on. "What's…that?"

"Tell me why men can't accept help when they need it, or ask for directions when they have no idea where they're going," she said, draping his shirt over the desk chair.

"We don't—" He stopped abruptly when she

brought her hands to his waist and started to work his belt through the metal buckle. "W-what are you…doing, Kaylee?"

"You said you'd need my help," she said, pulling the leather strap from the belt loops of his jeans. "And that's…just what you're going to get."

She sounded angry, but the hitch in her voice suggested she was as affected by helping him out of his clothes as he was by having her take them off him.

"Kaylee—"

He wasn't sure what he was about to say, but he stopped short at the sound of Amber's giggles. Turning his attention to his daughter, Colt didn't think he'd ever seen anything as precious as her happy expression.

"You think seeing your mommy yell at Daddy is funny?" he asked, grinning.

Giggling delightedly, the baby grabbed the doll he'd bought her and hid behind it.

Distracted by Amber's laughter, it took a moment for him to realize that Kaylee was working the metal button free at his waistband. Heat shot through his veins and made a beeline straight to his groin.

"I think…" His voice cracked like a kid going through puberty. "…I can handle it from here."

She gave him another one of those looks that a woman gives a man when she thinks he's being a stubborn fool. "Oh, for heaven's sake, I'm a trained medical professional and I've assisted dozens of people with their clothes." She reached for the tab of his zipper. "Besides, we both know you're no more attracted to me than I am to you, so it's not an issue."

From the heightened color on her cheeks and the hesitation in her voice, he knew her statement that she wasn't attracted to him was an outright lie. But at the moment, that wasn't an immediate concern. If he didn't stop her—and damn quick—it wouldn't take more than another second or two and she'd see the evidence of just how alluring he found her.

Grabbing her hand, Colt shook his head. "I said I'd take care of it."

"Fine." She pointed to the chair. "Have a seat and I'll take off your boots."

"I can—"

She arched one perfect eyebrow. "How long does it take you to get them on and off by yourself?"

"I manage," he said defensively. He hated to admit that he struggled more with his boots than anything else.

"Sit down and raise your foot."

Amused by her authoritative tone, he did as she said and lowered himself onto the chair. But his enjoyment quickly faded and his mouth went bone-dry when she turned, straddled his leg and began tugging on his boot. As she worked to remove it, her cute little rear bobbed in front of his face and sent his blood pressure into stroke range.

He closed his eyes and tried to think of something—anything—to get his mind off of how close Kaylee was and how much he'd like to prove her theory wrong that he didn't find her attractive. But by the time she'd removed both of his boots, Colt felt as if he had enough adrenaline pumping through his veins to bench-press a bulldozer and he was hard-pressed to suck air into his lungs.

"Do you want help with anything else?" she asked, turning to face him.

"No."

He wanted help all right, but it wasn't the kind of aid she was offering. Rising to his feet, he quickly turned to get a change of clothes from his duffel bag before she saw the evidence of the assistance he needed.

"After your shower I'll put the sling back on," she said as she picked up Amber. "Tell your daddy good-night, sweetie."

Grinning, Amber shook her head, hugged

Kaylee around the neck and buried her little face in her mother's shoulder.

"At least, she's smiling at me a little more," Colt said, wishing Amber would allow him to hold her.

"More progress," Kaylee said, sounding a little less angry.

Nodding, Colt turned to walk into the bathroom. Slowly but surely, he was winning over his daughter. Now if he could just regain the friendship he once shared with her mother, maybe they could work things out where everyone would be happy.

Long after Kaylee and Amber had fallen asleep, Colt lay in bed thinking about what Kaylee had said while helping him with his clothes. She didn't think he found her attractive.

He turned his head on the pillow to look over at the woman and child sleeping peacefully in the bed next to his. The light they'd left on in the bathroom illuminated the room enough for him to make out their delicate features in the semidarkness.

The idea that any man with a pulse wouldn't be drawn to Kaylee like a bee to honey was so damn ludicrous it was almost laughable. She was intelligent, witty and so damn sexy that every time he was around her, he found himself fighting a constant state of arousal. Hell, he could even remember the exact moment four years ago when he'd realized that Mitch's younger sister had grown from a skinny, bratty little kid into a beautiful, desirable woman.

It had been a couple of weeks before her twentieth birthday and she'd met him and Mitch at the PBR event in St. Louis, just as she'd always done. But when she'd breezed into the hotel where they'd been staying, Colt had taken one look and it was as if he'd seen her for the first time. He'd suddenly found himself noticing how her silky auburn hair framed her heart-shaped face, how her violet eyes sparkled with life, and how she seemed to light up a room with her smile.

He'd never allowed himself to act on his attraction to her, though. He hadn't dared. If things hadn't worked out between him and Kaylee, Colt might have lost the best friend he'd ever had. And that was something he hadn't been willing to risk.

But everything was different now. Mitch was gone—taken from this world way before his time. And, because of Colt's one night of weakness, he and Kaylee had a child together.

He closed his eyes against the guilt he still felt over the night Amber had been conceived. Due to the devastating blow they'd both suffered from losing Mitch, they'd turned to each other for emotional support. He'd been old enough to know better, and should have called a halt to it, but having Kaylee in his arms had been more temptation than he'd been able to resist. Like a damned fool, he'd allowed comfort to turn to passion and they'd ended up making love.

Colt sighed heavily. She had every right to despise him for taking her virginity and leaving her alone with a baby to care for. God only knew he hated himself enough for what he'd done. But he didn't think Kaylee felt that way. She might try to deny it, but he could tell the chemistry between them was just as strong, if not stronger, than it had ever been.

Unfortunately he wasn't sure that exploring it now, or in the future, would ever be an option for them. They had Amber to consider. And her welfare came first.

His gaze straying to his child, Colt's chest tightened. She looked like a cute little pixie curled up next to Kaylee, and although he'd only known about his daughter a few days, he loved her more than life itself.

Looking back at Kaylee, a deep sense of loss twisted his gut. If they tried for more than friendship and failed, it would only complicate an already complex situation and make raising Amber together extremely difficult.

He took a deep breath and tried to will himself to forget the idea completely. It just wasn't a risk he could afford to take.

But as he drifted off to sleep, Colt dreamed of holding Kaylee's delectable body to his, of having her call his name as he brought her to the brink of ecstasy, and of a future with her that he knew he could never have.

Chapter Four

"Colt, is this another way to get to the Lonetree?" Kaylee asked, looking around. She'd been to the ranch several times with Mitch before he died, but they'd never used the road Colt was driving down now.

Steering the truck around a tight curve, he grinned. "Honey, we've been on Lonetree land for the past fifteen minutes."

"I keep forgetting how big this place is," she said, not at all surprised by his answer.

Her family's ranch had been a nice size, but the Lonetree was one of the largest privately owned ranches left in the United States. Most of the other ranches of comparable acreage had been sold off to corporations or divided up into smaller tracts as one generation inherited the land from another. But the Wakefield brothers had decided after their father passed on to keep the Lonetree Ranch intact and to work it together.

"In case you're wondering why we aren't headed north to the homestead, it's because I don't live there anymore," he said matter-of-factly.

Kaylee swallowed hard. She'd been counting on Morgan and his wife to provide a buffer between her and Colt. "If you don't live there, just where *do* you live?"

"Two and a half years ago I decided to build my own place three miles northwest of the homestead," he said, smiling.

She narrowed her eyes as anger swept through her. "You purposely left that little detail out when you asked me to come here."

His easy expression faded. "I didn't think you'd agree if you'd known we wouldn't be staying with Morgan and Samantha."

"You're right." Blowing out a frustrated breath, she folded her arms beneath her breasts. "That's fine. You can take Amber and me to the bus station tomorrow and we'll go back to Oklahoma."

Colt's mouth flattened into a tight line, but he remained silent until they topped a rise overlooking a peaceful-looking valley. "That's my place down there," he said, pointing to the far end of the basin.

Kaylee's breath caught at the sight of a gorgeous two-story log home with a split-rail fence surrounding the yard. Several horses grazed contentedly in the pastures surrounding the structure and a beautiful black stallion pranced in the corral at the side of the big barn.

"Do you like it?" he asked.

"The word 'like' doesn't even begin to describe it," she said as she tried to swallow around the huge lump clogging her throat. Until Mitch's death, she'd lived on a ranch all of her life, and she missed the quiet solitude of an uncluttered landscape. "This is absolutely beautiful, Colt."

"Thanks." He seemed pleased that she liked his home as he steered the truck off the road and onto a narrow gravel lane leading up to the house. "I still have a storage shed I'd like to build next spring, and eventually I'd like to add an indoor arena with a couple of bucking chutes."

At the mention of his wanting to construct an area where he could practice riding bulls, a chill raced through her. She'd lost her enthusiasm for bull riding when she lost her brother to the sport.

Parking the truck beside the house, Colt grinned. "Welcome to my part of the Lonetree, ladies."

Amber giggled and hid her face behind her hands.

"You like Daddy's house?" Colt asked.

Shaking her head, she kept her face hidden but continued to laugh.

Colt's grin widened. "More progress."

Kaylee's chest tightened at the love she saw in Colt's expression when he gazed at Amber. No matter what had taken place between her and Colt, Kaylee knew for certain that Amber had a daddy who loved her with all his heart.

She sighed wistfully. There had been a time when she'd dreamed of coming home to the Lonetree with Colt and their child. Only, in her fantasy, they'd been married and hopelessly in love.

She almost laughed at her own foolishness. That had been several years ago—before she'd grown up to realize that the world wasn't made of fairy tales and not every story had a happy ending.

"Kaylee? Are you all right?"

Looking up, she saw that Colt had gotten out of the truck and was standing with the passenger door open. "I'm fine." She unbuckled Amber's shoulder harness, then lifted her daughter from the car seat. "I was just thinking about how many things have changed over the years."

He stared at her for a moment before he offered his hand to help her from the truck. He smiled sadly, and she knew he was thinking about Mitch. "Some things do change, honey. We don't always like it, but we can't stop it." When he met her gaze, the look in his vivid blue eyes took her breath. "But some things stay the same, even if it doesn't seem that they have."

She had no idea what he meant by his last comment, but deciding it was time to lighten the mood, she set Amber on her feet, then took hold of her hand. "Does the inside of your house look as good as the outside, or did you decorate in modern bachelor?"

Colt laughed as he guided her up the front porch steps. "It's actually a combination of modern bachelor and cast-off Wakefield."

Kaylee grinned. "Let me guess. You raided the attic at the homestead."

"Yep." Opening the front door, he stepped back for her and Amber to precede him into the house. "I do have a new recliner and a kick-butt entertainment system, though."

"That would be the modern bachelor part of

the decor, right?" she asked, leading Amber into the foyer. Before he could answer she caught her breath at her first glimpse of the great room. "Colt, it's absolutely perfect."

The golden hue of the log walls and wood floor were perfectly accented by the bright red, blue and yellow Native American print upholstery on the couch and matching chairs. Grouped on a huge braided rug in front of the stone fireplace, it made the room very warm and inviting.

"I love the colors and the Western accents," she said, noticing several pieces of vintage leather tack and Native American artifacts hanging on the walls, along with a pair of spurs and a bronze sculpture of a bull and rider on the mantel.

"Samantha and Annie really got into helping me decorate it," he said, sounding pleased. "Annie bought a do-it-yourself book on reupholstering, then coerced Brant and Morgan into helping her with some furniture she and Samantha found in the attic at the homestead. While they recovered the couch and chairs, Samantha made drapes. I came home after a PBR event in Colorado Springs and didn't recognize the place."

"They did a wonderful job," Kaylee said, meaning it. She looked around. "But I thought you said you had a lounger and an entertainment system."

"They're in the family room just off the kitchen," he said, pointing toward one end of the great room. "And there's a weight room back there, too."

Kaylee glanced in the direction he indicated and felt compelled to take a closer look. She wasn't interested in the other rooms as much as she was the kitchen. She loved to cook and had always felt that it was the heart of any home.

Holding Amber's hand so she wouldn't wander off, Kaylee walked past the snack bar separating the two rooms and immediately fell in love with the light oak cabinets, highly polished black-marble countertops and terra-cotta-tiled floor. Everything about the room appealed to her.

"Like it?" Colt asked, leaning one hip against the end of the snack bar.

"What woman wouldn't like it?" she asked, smiling.

A sudden thought caused her smile to fade and a deep sadness to fill her soul. One day Colt would be sharing this beautiful home with a woman, and it wouldn't be her.

"Up, Mommy, up," Amber said, rubbing her eyes with one little fist.

Thankful that she'd been distracted from the disturbing thought, Kaylee picked up her daughter. "It's about time for your nap, isn't it, sweetie?"

Amber shook her head, then laid her cheek on Kaylee's shoulder.

"I don't think she likes admitting that she's sleepy," Colt said, smiling.

Kaylee nodded. "She's afraid she'll miss something." She glanced toward the family room. "Is there somewhere I could lay her down once she goes to sleep?"

"I guess the couch in the family room would be best," he said, looking thoughtful. "I think the first order of business will be to borrow a crib from Morgan or Brant, and a couple of those gates they put up to keep their kids away from the stairs."

When Kaylee nodded her agreement, then carried Amber into the family room, Colt released a relieved breath. He couldn't believe how good it felt to know Kaylee liked his home. He really hadn't expected her opinion to mean so much to him.

But at the moment he had a more pressing concern than Kaylee's approval. He hadn't been prepared for a toddler, and the house needed to be child-proofed for Amber's safety.

He took a deep breath, then crossed the great

room to enter the study. He wasn't looking forward to the phone call he was about to make. No matter which brother he called to borrow the items needed to make the house safe, he was going to get the third degree.

Deciding Brant was the less intense of his two brothers, Colt picked up the phone and punched in the number. "Hey, bro," he said when Brant answered. "I need a favor."

Twenty minutes later, when Colt parked the truck in his brother's driveway, he wasn't at all surprised to see Brant standing on the porch waiting for him.

"Okay, little brother, spill it," Brant said as soon as Colt opened the driver's door. "Why do you need all of this baby stuff?"

"Hello to you, too, bro," Colt said, stalling.

He'd told his brother he would explain everything when he arrived to pick up the portable crib and other items he'd requested. But he sure as hell wasn't looking forward to it.

Both of his brothers liked Kaylee a lot. They'd known her almost as long as Colt had, and from the time they'd figured out that she had a huge crush on him, they'd warned him not to hurt her, unless he wanted to answer to both of them. Now, meeting his grim-faced brother's stormy gaze, Colt knew for certain Brant wasn't going to like what he was about to hear any more than Colt liked having to tell him.

Deciding there was no better way to break the news than straight-out, Colt took a deep breath. "I need the crib for my daughter, Amber."

Clearly dumbfounded, it took a moment for Brant to respond. "Let me get this straight. You have a daughter named Amber, and she's staying with you?"

"Yep."

"Her mom is with her?" Brant asked, his frown darkening.

"She's getting Amber down for a nap," Colt said, nodding. "That's why I need to get the stuff and get back."

Brant shook his head. "You're not getting off that easy, little brother. You left out a whole bunch of real important details. Like, how old Amber is, how long you've known about her and her mother's name."

Pushing his Resistol back with his thumb, Colt sighed heavily and sat on the porch steps. "You might want to have a seat."

"I don't like the sound of this," Brant said, sitting beside him.

"Well, I'm none too wild about having to tell you about it, either," Colt said, staring out across the pasture. He should have known Brant wasn't going to settle for a bare-bones account of what was going on. "Amber is a couple of months younger than Zach," he finally said, referring to Brant's little boy. "And I didn't know anything about her until four days ago."

Brant whistled low. "That's unfair," he said, his voice filled with understanding. "I'm sorry to hear the woman didn't see fit to let you know. Do I know her?"

"Yeah." Colt glanced at his brother from the corner of his eye. "Kaylee is Amber's mother."

From his stunned expression, Brant looked as though he'd been treated to the business end of a cattle prod. "Kaylee Simpson?"

Nodding, Colt didn't say anything as he waited for his brother to digest the news. It didn't take long.

"What the hell were you thinking?" Brant demanded, his dark scowl formidable. "Besides the fact that Morgan and I both warned you not to hurt Kaylee, why didn't you make sure you protected her?"

Colt rubbed at the tension gripping the muscles at the back of his neck, then readjusted his sling to a more comfortable position. "Neither one of us was doing a whole lot of thinking that night. We were both too torn up over losing Mitch." He took a deep breath and met his brother's gaze head-on. "I swear I didn't intend to sleep with Kaylee that night. But as soon as I saw my little girl, I knew I wasn't sorry that I had."

Brant's deep frown faded as his eyes filled with understanding. "I felt the same way the first time I looked at Zach. But that doesn't explain why Kaylee didn't tell you when she found out she was pregnant."

Staring out across the pasture, Colt shrugged his good shoulder. He wasn't proud of his actions, nor was he eager to share the details. "Let's just say she had her reasons, and leave it at that."

Brant nodded. "I guess that explains why none of us has seen or heard from Kaylee since Mitch died."

"Yeah." Colt sighed heavily. "It also explains why she turned down Morgan's request last year when he emailed to see if she'd teach horseback riding at Samantha's camp for underprivileged kids."

"How *did* you find out about Amber?" Brant asked suddenly.

"I stopped by Kaylee's place to see how she's

been. When she opened the door, she was holding Amber." Colt met Brant's questioning gaze. "All it took was one look and I knew Amber was my little girl."

"She looks like a Wakefield?"

"Same black hair and blue eyes," Colt said, nodding.

They sat in silence for some time before Brant asked, "Are you going to marry Kaylee?"

Colt whipped his head around to stare at his brother. "Did you work the PBR event this past weekend?" One of the best rodeo bullfighters in the country, Brant worked most of the PBR events plus several of the major professional rodeos.

Brant looked puzzled. "Yeah, but what does that have to do with—"

"You must have taken a pretty good hit and ended up landing on your head," Colt said disgustedly. "How do you figure Kaylee would want to marry me if she wouldn't even tell me she was pregnant?"

"Have you asked her?"

"No."

"Then how do you know she wouldn't?" Brant asked seriously.

"I just know," Colt said, shaking his head.

He'd already thought about asking Kaylee to

be his wife when he first found out about Amber. But it had taken him all of about two seconds to come to his senses. Even if Kaylee was willing to marry him, which he knew for certain she wasn't, they had Amber's happiness to think of. Getting married for the wrong reasons could prove disastrous.

What would happen if their marriage didn't work? Amber could be hurt worse by a breakup than if they never married at all.

"But you are going to make things right between the two of you?" Brant asked.

Colt nodded. "That's why I brought Kaylee and Amber home with me. First and foremost, I'm going to do some major fence-mending."

"Good idea," Brant said. "I don't know what happened between you, but I do know Kaylee. Whatever it was had to be pretty bad for her not to tell you about your daughter."

"It wasn't one of my prouder moments," Colt admitted, his gut twisting when he thought about how badly he'd handled the situation. "But after I make amends for being a real bonehead, I want to see if we can't rebuild our friendship, as well as come to an agreement about how we want to raise Amber."

"You've got a lot to accomplish," Brant said.

"How long will Kaylee and Amber be staying with you?"

"Until the end of October," Colt said, rising to his feet. "And unless I want to do more groveling, I'd better get the crib and other stuff loaded and get back to them."

"Well, congratulations on being a father, little brother," Brant said, standing. "And best of luck with straightening things out with Kaylee."

"Thanks," Colt said, following him into the house. "I have a feeling I'll need all the luck I can get."

Standing in the bedroom she would be sharing with Amber, Kaylee watched Colt as he tried to put the portable crib together with one hand. "I know you like to do things for yourself," she said diplomatically, "but I think you're going to need a little help with that."

"I think you're right." He didn't look happy. "I can't hold it up and lock these braces in place without using both hands."

"I'll support it while you secure it," she said, moving to help him.

"Son of a bi—buck!" Colt stood, slinging his hand.

"What happened?" Kaylee asked, rounding the

crib to take his hand in hers. She examined his thumb as she tried to ignore the tingling sensation zinging up her arm. "It doesn't appear to be cut."

He shook his head. "I just pinched the—" he glanced over at Amber sitting in the rocking chair watching them "—heck out of it."

Amber giggled and grabbed the doll Colt had given her, but didn't hide behind it when she noticed them watching her.

"She thinks you're funny," Kaylee said, smiling fondly at her daughter.

"Do you think Daddy's funny?" Colt asked, grinning at Amber.

When Amber broke into a fresh wave of giggles, Kaylee laughed. "I'd say she finds you very amusing."

"I remember a time when I used to amuse you, too," Colt said, suddenly serious.

Needing to put distance between them, Kaylee tried to release his hand, but his fingers tightened around hers. "That was a long time ago," she said, hating that she sounded so breathless.

"Not that long ago, honey."

When she looked up at his handsome face, his expression caused her heart to stutter. "Colt?"

"Hush," he said, lowering his lips to hers.

Before she could come to her senses and push

him away, he released her hand to put his arm around her shoulders and pull her close. Mesmerized by the feel of his firm mouth, his musky male scent and the strength of his hard body pressed to hers, Kaylee didn't even think to protest. Instead her eyes drifted shut and she brought her hands up to rest on his wide chest.

Colt traced her lips, seeking entry to the sensitive recesses beyond, and Kaylee opened for him without hesitation. He touched his tongue to hers to engage her in a game of advance and retreat, sending heat streaking through her veins and making her heart skip several beats. But when he slid his hand down her back to cup her rear, then pull her lower body to his, Kaylee felt as if she'd gone into sensory overload. His burgeoning arousal pressing against her lower stomach, the taste of his passion and the sound of his deep groan made her knees wobble and her head spin. Gripping the front of his denim shirt, she wasn't sure she could keep herself from melting into a puddle at his big, booted feet.

"Mommy, up," Amber said, slapping Kaylee's leg with her little hand. "Up."

Brought back to her senses, Kaylee would have jerked from Colt's embrace, but he held her close as he slowly broke the kiss. "I think a certain little pixie is jealous," he murmured, his words vibrating against Kaylee's lips.

Stepping back, Kaylee shook her head. "That shouldn't have happened."

Colt stared at her for endless seconds and she felt as if she just might drown in the depths of his incredibly blue gaze. "Maybe not, but I'll be da—darned if I'm sorry it did," he finally said.

Kaylee swallowed hard and leaned down to pick up Amber. If she had any sense she'd take her daughter and run as hard and fast as she could back to Oklahoma City.

"Colt, I don't think—"

"Shh, honey," he said, placing his finger to her lips. He stared at her a moment longer, then, turning toward the door, motioned for her to follow him. "I need your help with something else."

Thankful that Amber had interrupted the kiss, Kaylee walked on shaky legs out into the hall. Had she lost her mind? Why had she allowed him to kiss her? Hadn't she learned anything three years ago?

Colt was the man who'd broken her heart. The man who—if she wasn't extremely careful—could do the same thing again.

"I'd like for you to decorate this room for Amber," he said, crossing the hall into another bedroom. Completely empty, the room was like a blank canvas waiting for an artist to bring it to life. "Anything you want to do is fine with me. Buy furniture, wall decorations, toys—whatever you want or need to make it hers."

"Are you sure about this?" Kaylee asked, setting Amber down. She watched her daughter wander around the room as if surveying what was needed to make it comfortable. "That's a lot of expense. We haven't even discussed how often she might be visiting the Lonetree."

"I don't care what it costs," he said, shaking his head. Turning his attention to Amber, he grinned. "I want her to like it."

Kaylee watched his expression as he gazed at Amber toddling around the room. Colt Wakefield might not have ever loved her, but he certainly cared for their daughter and wanted to do whatever he could to make her happy. He was going to be a wonderful father, and just knowing that caused Kaylee's chest to tighten with emotion.

"Kaylee, are you all right?" Colt asked, sounding concerned. He moved closer to wipe a drop of moisture from her cheek with the pad of his thumb. "What's wrong, honey?"

Unaware that she'd been crying, Kaylee's cheeks burned and she impatiently wiped away her foolish tears. "I—I guess it's just one of those moments when a mother realizes how fast her baby is growing up," she said, hoping her excuse didn't sound as lame to him as it did to her. Needing to put distance between them to collect herself, she started backing from the room. "If you don't mind, I think I'll…see what I can make for supper."

He stared at her curiously. "Sure. Do whatever you like. I want you and Amber to feel like this is your home, too."

Holding a shaky hand out to Amber, Kaylee coaxed, "Come on, sweetie. Let's go downstairs to the kitchen."

Amber looked up with a grin on her face. "Eat."

Colt laughed. "That's my girl. She knows what's important." Smiling, he asked, "Do you think she'd let me watch her while you cook?"

"Maybe," Kaylee said, leading Amber across the loft area of the upper floor. "Do you get the children's television network?"

"I'm pretty sure I do," he said from behind her. "I have a satellite system with about a zillion channels. Surely one of them caters to kids."

"You have that to watch the Rockies baseball games," she said, descending the stairs.

His low chuckle sent a shiver up her spine. "Think you know me pretty well, huh?"

She shrugged as she walked into the kitchen. "At one time I thought I did, but it turned out I was wrong."

He took a step toward her. "Kaylee, we need to talk about—"

"Not now, Colt." She pointed to the entertainment center in the family room. "Why don't you see about tuning in a children's show? Amber might be tempted to watch it with you."

He opened his mouth as if he wanted to argue, then, giving her a short nod, walked into the other room and switched on the big-screen television.

Relieved that he hadn't pressed further, Kaylee breathed a sigh of relief. She wasn't ready to talk about that night three years ago, wasn't sure she ever wanted to hear his reasons for walking away.

As she watched Amber tentatively enter the room where Colt sat, Kaylee bit her lower lip against the deep sadness settling into every cell of her being. Agreeing to come to the Lonetree with Colt had been a big mistake. For the next couple of months she was going to be with him day-in and day-out, watching him and Amber bond, getting a glimpse of the way life might have been if only Colt could have loved her the way she'd loved him.

Giving herself a mental shake, Kaylee turned to the cabinets and busied herself with finding something to make for supper. What was wrong with her? She'd gotten over him some time ago and had moved on with her life.

But as she peeled potatoes and carrots for a pot roast, she couldn't help but wonder how she was ever going to survive the next couple of months without losing the last scrap of what little sanity she had left.

Chapter Five

Colt smiled as he tested the way his shoulder and upper chest felt without the sling. There was a little soreness, but no pain.

"It's about damn time," he muttered.

He tossed the sling on top of the dresser as he walked out of his bedroom and down the hall. As far as he was concerned, he didn't care if he never saw it again. But he knew Kaylee would raise hell with him if he threw it away.

Of course, if she gave him a lecture, it would be an improvement over the silent treatment he'd been getting for the past couple of weeks. Ever since he'd kissed her the day they'd put the crib together she'd been pensive, and although they'd spent a lot of time together, she'd kept her distance both physically and emotionally. He wasn't sure what was running through that pretty little head of hers, but he had every intention of finding out.

The smell of fresh coffee and fried bacon beckoned, and Colt quickened his step. Since Kaylee and Amber arrived, he'd been eating better than he had in ages. At the bottom of the stairs he stepped over the child-safety gate they kept in place to block Amber's access and followed the enticing smell into the kitchen.

"Morning," he said cheerfully as he entered the room. "Something smells mighty good."

"Good morning." Kaylee stopped filling their plates. "Where's your sling?"

"On the dresser in my room," he said, seating himself beside Amber's high chair at the snack bar. He grinned at his daughter and whispered loudly, "Do you think Mommy will yell at Daddy in front of you?"

"Mommy," Amber said, pointing to Kaylee.

"Can you say 'Daddy'?" Colt asked, hoping to hear his daughter use the word for the first time.

Amber nodded her head and picked up a handful of scrambled eggs to put in her spoon.

He and Amber had come a long way. She still wouldn't let him hold her, but she'd stopped hiding her face every time he looked her way and giggled whenever he talked to her. She'd also started jabbering at him. Not a lot. But he suspected as time went along she'd be a regular little chatterbox.

"No, I'm not going to yell at you," Kaylee said, placing a heaping plate of eggs, bacon and hash browns in front of him. She seated herself on the other side of Amber. "If you say it doesn't hurt, then it's probably safe to go without the sling." She handed Amber a sippy cup, then gave him a warning look. "But if it starts causing you discomfort, you'd better put the sling back on or I will give you the talk I give my patients who foolishly try to push for too much, too soon."

Colt grinned. It wasn't exactly what he'd had in mind when he decided to draw Kaylee out, but it was a start. "Yes, ma'am."

"Yes, Mom," Amber repeated.

His daughter's laughter sounded like the tinkling of a small wind chime on a gentle breeze and he found himself laughing with her. He loved hearing her mispronounce words. It was just so darned cute. Of course, as far as he was concerned, everything about his little girl was precious.

"Would you two lovely ladies like to join me this morning for a tour of my part of the Lonetree?" he asked.

The day after he'd brought them to the ranch the weather had turned cold as an early winter front had settled over the area. But today was supposed to be a lot warmer.

"No," Amber said, nodding her head affirmatively.

Colt laughed as he glanced at Kaylee. "Is that a yes or a no?"

Kaylee smiled and he felt like a kid at Christmas. It was the first genuine smile he'd seen from her in quite a while. "I think if you rephrase it so that you're asking if she wants to go outside you might get a more definitive response."

"Would you like for Daddy and Mommy to take you for a walk outside after breakfast, Amber?"

Grinning, the little girl shook her head so hard her raven curls swung back and forth. "Ouside. Now."

"No, sweetie, you have to eat first," Kaylee said gently.

They ate in silence for several minutes before

Colt asked, "Have you decided what you're going to do with Amber's room?"

"Not really." Kaylee shrugged one shoulder. "I thought I might do an internet search to see what's available."

"Good idea." He finished the last bite of his eggs, then rose from the bar stool to carry their empty plates to the sink. Rinsing them, he placed them in the dishwasher. "You might even give Annie and Samantha a call. I'm sure they'd be more than happy to go shopping down in Laramie with you."

"I'll think about it," Kaylee said, wiping Amber's face and hands with a damp cloth, then lifting her from the high chair. "What time did you want to give us that tour?"

"Anytime you're ready."

Taking Amber by the hand, she nodded. "We'll be down as soon I get her changed out of her pajamas."

He watched her lead Amber upstairs. Even though Kaylee had seemed in better spirits this morning, there was a sadness about her that twisted his gut. To know he was the cause of her unhappiness made him feel like the biggest jerk the good Lord ever blessed with the breath of life. How was he going to make things right? What could he do to bring the smile back to Kaylee's pretty face?

She wouldn't allow him to explain why he'd left her alone the morning after he'd made love to her, didn't want to hear his lame excuses. And he couldn't say he blamed her.

For the past few years he'd been telling himself that he was ashamed of taking advantage of her, felt as if he'd betrayed Mitch's trust. But the real reason he'd run like a tail-tucked dog was because of the way Kaylee had made him feel that night. He'd never felt more emotionally connected to another person in his entire life. And it had scared the living hell out of him.

Colt sucked in a sharp breath. Had he been on the verge of falling in love with Kaylee?

He rejected the notion immediately. Emotions had been running high that night, they'd both been hurting from Mitch's loss, and they'd turned to each other for comfort and support.

"You're losing it, Wakefield," he muttered disgustedly.

Shaking his head at his own foolishness, he crossed the great room to the foyer and grabbed his Resistol from one of the hooks by the door. He needed to find a way to make amends for his actions three years ago and to get back the easy friendship he'd once shared with Kaylee, not confuse the issue with a lot of self-analyzation.

"How old is the stallion?" Kaylee asked when Colt walked them over to the enclosed paddock where the black horse she'd seen the day they'd arrived stood munching on a flake of hay.

"He'll be five this spring."

Colt stood so close she could feel the warmth from his much larger body, smell the clean, woodsy scent of his aftershave. Holding Amber's hand, Kaylee stepped closer to the fence to put a little space between them. Her breath caught when he followed her.

"I miss having a horse," she said wistfully.

"What happened to your buckskin mare?"

"I had to sell her at the same time I sold the ranch." It still hurt whenever she thought of having to get rid of the horse Mitch had given her for her twentieth birthday.

"Why did you sell the ranch, Kaylee?" The gentle tone of Colt's deep baritone sent a wave of goose bumps shimmering over her skin.

They hadn't discussed her reasons for selling the ranch. In fact, they hadn't talked about much of anything personal for the past couple of weeks. But telling him why she'd sold the ranch seemed like a safe enough topic.

"I couldn't afford to keep it," she finally said, still hating the fact that she'd had to part with the ranch that her family had owned for more than seventy-five years.

Clearly confused, Colt frowned as he propped his forearms on the top rail of the fence. "But Mitch told me he'd been investing all of his winnings since before your parents died."

"He had been." Turning to face him, she smiled sadly. "Mitch put everything he had into improving the ranch."

"He didn't leave anything in savings?" Colt asked incredulously.

She shook her head. "No. He closed out his account when he started raising Red Brangus cattle."

"He was really proud of that breeding program," Colt said, nodding.

"With good reason." Kaylee stared at a golden eagle tracing lazy circles in the sky above. "But what he didn't tell you, me or anyone else was that he'd not only wiped out his savings, he'd taken a mortgage on the ranch to get the program up and running."

"I had no idea, honey." Colt reached out to cup her cheek and the feel of his calloused palm on her skin sent a tiny spark of electric current to every nerve in her body.

"I didn't, either. I was away at school and didn't find out about any of it until I started going over Mitch's accounts the week after he died." She swallowed around the lump in her throat. Talking about the ranch had been a bad idea, but the conversation had gone too far to turn back now. "Everything would have been fine once he got everything established, but he…died before that happened." Tears flooded her eyes. "And without his PBR winnings to help supplement the ranch, I couldn't keep it going."

"I'm so sorry, honey," Colt said, reaching out to take her into his arms.

Kaylee told herself she should move away, that she needed to put distance between them before she did something stupid. But the feel of his strength surrounding her, the steady beat of his heart beneath her ear, were too comforting to resist.

"Mommy, up," Amber said, tugging on her hand.

Releasing her, Colt bent to pick Amber up, but she pushed his hands away. "No! Mommy."

Kaylee wiped her eyes, then swung her daughter up to hug her close. Amber immediately threw her arms around Kaylee's neck and buried her face in Kaylee's shoulder.

"It's all right, sweetie," Kaylee crooned. "Mommy was just being a big baby and feeling sorry for herself."

"Honey, you have every right—"

"I think I'll take Amber inside now," she interrupted, backing away from him.

Kaylee felt Colt's gaze follow her as she hurried toward the back door. Pride was about all she had left, and she needed time to collect herself before she faced him again. She'd spent three years fighting to keep from lamenting all that she'd lost, and she was embarrassed that he'd seen her give in to it.

Colt watched Kaylee disappear into the house before he let loose with a string of blistering curses, and every single one of them was self-directed. How could he have left her alone to deal with everything she'd had to face after Mitch died? Why hadn't he picked up the phone and at least called to inquire how she was doing?

But as he castigated himself, he knew she would have never admitted needing help—wouldn't have accepted it from him even if he'd known about her circumstances and offered his assistance. He shook his head. When it came to stubborn pride, Kaylee had enough for a dozen people.

"What the hell were you thinking, Mitch?" he murmured out loud.

The shrill cry of the eagle circling above the pasture had him absently gazing skyward. He couldn't change the past—couldn't bring Mitch back to ask him why he'd left Kaylee without any resources and no recourse but to sell the ranch—and there was no sense spending time wishing that he could.

Staring at the big bird soaring overhead, Colt decided that the past might be over and gone, but the future was a clean slate—wide open and ready for him to start making things easier for Kaylee. In the process he fully intended to see that she was a lot happier than she'd been in a long time.

He grinned suddenly. And he knew exactly where he wanted to start making that happen.

He headed for the house and didn't stop until he was seated behind the desk in his office. Dialing the phone, he didn't bother with a greeting when his oldest brother answered on the third ring.

"Morgan, I need you and Brant to find a buckskin mare for me."

"Colt, I'm only going to tell you this one time," Kaylee said sternly. "If you don't stop trying to push your progress, you're on your own." She pointed to the weight room door. "I'll walk out and you'll have to find someone else to help you with your physical therapy."

"It won't hurt if I do an extra set of the isometric exercises." He frowned. "Besides, if I don't push myself, I won't be ready in time for finals."

"I could care less if you make it to Las Vegas," she said, unable to stop herself from telling him exactly how she felt. "I'm not helping you regain the strength in your arm just so you can go back into an arena again and get hurt, or…worse."

"Calm down, honey," he said, taking a step toward her.

"I'm perfectly calm," she lied, taking a step back. She wasn't, but he didn't need to know that the very thought of him climbing onto the back of a bull sent a chilling numbness all the way to her very soul. "I have no intention of helping you risk your life for an eight-second adrenaline rush."

"You've always known that I'm a bull rider." He gave her a measuring look as he advanced. "Why don't you want me in the arena now, Kaylee?"

She swallowed hard and took another step back. How could she tell him that although she knew they had no future together, she wasn't sure she'd be able to go on if something happened to him?

Before she could think of an excuse without telling him the truth, he walked up to stand in front of her. Placing one finger under her chin, he tipped her face up until their eyes met. "Is it because of what happened to Mitch? Are you afraid something like that will happen to me?"

"Yes...I mean no." Kaylee shook her head. "That's not it at all." She tried putting more distance between them, but she found that he'd backed her up against the wall.

"Which is it, Kaylee?" he asked, gazing down at her from his much taller height. "Does the idea of my getting hurt frighten you?"

"I don't like to see anyone injured," she said evasively.

She suddenly found it hard to take a breath with him so close. Colt had taken his shirt off for the therapy session and the well-developed muscles of his chest and abdomen glistened with a fine sheen of perspiration from the exercises she'd had him doing. She'd never seen him look better.

"You know what I think?" he asked, leaning down to whisper in her ear.

Kaylee shook her head. She couldn't have formed words if her life depended on it.

"I think you're more worried about me than you'd like to admit," he said, his warm breath stirring the hair at her temple. "Whether you like it or not, I think it would matter a great deal to you if I got hurt." His lips skimmed the sensitive skin along the column of her neck. "Am I right, honey?"

She closed her eyes and tried to regain control of her senses. How was she supposed to respond when her heart was racing ninety miles an hour and her knees were threatening to collapse?

When his arms closed around her, Kaylee's eyes flew open and she brought her hands up to his chest to push him away. "C-Colt, I—"

"It's okay, honey," he said a moment before his mouth descended to hers. "All I'm going to do is kiss you."

From the first featherlight touch of his lips on

hers, Kaylee was lost. If she'd had the ability to think, she might have protested, but feeling his strong arms surround her, the warmth of his hard, muscled chest beneath her palms, and she was lucky to remember her own name.

Her eyes drifted shut, and as he coaxed her to open for him, the last traces of her will to resist dissipated like mist beneath the rays of a warm summer sun. She knew she was playing a dangerous game, but as Colt's tongue stroked hers, her body tingled to life and she shamelessly melted against him. She wanted to taste him, wanted to once again experience the thrill of his kiss.

Her heart pounded and her breathing became shallow as he explored her thoroughly, eliciting responses from her that she'd kept buried for three long years. When he brought one hand up to cup her breast, the sensation of his thumb chafing her hardened nipple through the layers of her clothing caused her stomach to flutter and deep need to pool in the pit of her stomach. No other man had ever made her feel the way Colt did, never caused her to lose the ability to think straight.

He shifted his hips and the feel of his arousal sent heat streaking through her with an intensity that robbed her of breath. He wanted her as she wanted him.

The realization that her feelings for Colt could very easily come back full-force hit like a physical blow and helped to clear her head. If she didn't put a halt to things, and very quickly, she was in danger of making a fool of herself. Hadn't past experience taught her that the physical desire he had for her wasn't the same as an emotional bond?

The thought brought back some of her sanity and she whimpered as she pushed against him. She couldn't—wouldn't—allow herself to fall for him again.

"Please…Colt. Let me go."

He leaned back to stare at her. "We need to talk."

Kaylee shook her head as she pulled from his arms. "I have to get Amber up from her nap. Annie called this morning and asked if we would go shopping with her."

He caught her by the arm. "You're going to have to listen to me sometime, Kaylee."

Looking down at his strong hand holding her captive, she pried his fingers from her wrist and stepped away from him. "There's really no point, Colt." She turned toward the door. "We've never been on the same page, and I seriously doubt we ever will be."

Colt watched her walk from the room, head high, her damnable pride wrapped around her like some kind of protective armor. How the hell was he going to get through to her? How could he explain about that night three years ago if she wouldn't listen to him?

He sat heavily on the weight bench and stared off into space. What he needed was Kaylee's undivided attention. But how was he going to get that?

The only time they were alone was when Amber took a nap, and Kaylee insisted on conducting his therapy sessions during that time. He'd tried a couple of times over the past week to talk to her while she put him through the exercises, but each time she'd turned into a no-nonsense physical trainer with all the personality of an army drill sergeant.

Short of putting a gag in her mouth and tying her up, Colt didn't have any idea how he was going to get her to listen to him.

"You look like your mind is about a million miles away, Colt. Is something wrong?" his sister-in-law Annie asked from the doorway.

Looking up, Colt started to shake his head, but ended up nodding instead. "I've got a hell of a problem and her name is Kaylee."

Annie gave him an inquisitive look. "Anything I can do to help?"

Colt blew out a frustrated breath. "You wouldn't happen to have some rope and a gag with you?"

"No, those aren't items I normally carry around in my purse," she said dryly. She walked over to sit beside him on the weight bench. "Although, come to think of it, there are times when I could use them on your brother to get him to listen to me."

"He is a stubborn cuss, isn't he?" Colt asked, grinning.

"No more so than you and Morgan." Annie smiled. "Now, what can I do to help?"

"Do you and Brant have plans for tomorrow night?" he asked as an idea began to take shape.

To Colt's relief Annie shook her head. "No. Brant doesn't have a rodeo or PBR event scheduled this weekend, so we're free. What do you need us to do?"

"I think Kaylee could use a night out. Would you and Brant bring Zach over and watch Amber while Kaylee and I go down to Laramie?"

Annie smiled. "Sure. I'll call Morgan and Samantha and have them bring Timmy and Jared over, too. I think it's time the Wakefield cousins got to know each other."

Colt nodded. "Could you keep this under your hat while you and Kaylee are out shopping today? I'd like to surprise her."

"Are you sure about this?" Annie looked skeptical. "Take it from me. Women like a little advanced notice when they're being taken out on a date."

He shook his head. "This isn't a date."

She gave him a knowing smile. "Whatever you say, Colt." She rose to her feet when they heard Kaylee and Amber coming downstairs. "Where are you taking her?"

Where was he taking Kaylee?

"Probably out to eat," he finally said. "And maybe a movie."

His sister-in-law grinned. "If that isn't a date, what would you call it?"

"I—" He stopped to consider what he would call his night out with Kaylee. "I'm not sure, but it's definitely not a date."

When he followed Annie into the great room, he watched Kaylee smile and reach to hug his sister-in-law. "It's so good to see you again, Annie."

"It's good to see you, too," Annie said, hugging Kaylee back. She bent down. "And you must be Amber."

Grinning, Amber nodded and held up her arms for Annie to pick her up.

Envy stabbed Colt's gut when Annie picked up his daughter. In the three weeks since he'd found out about her, Amber had gotten to where she jabbered at him and laughed at just about everything he did, but still wouldn't allow him to hold her.

As Kaylee gathered her purse and jacket, the two women started talking about making a stop at Baby World so Annie could look at something called a layette for the baby she was expecting in a couple of months. Fishing his wallet from the hip pocket of his jeans, Colt held his credit card out to Kaylee.

"Buy whatever you want or need." When she started to refuse, he hurried to add, "If you find the furniture you want for Amber's room go ahead and buy it. I'll drive down tomorrow to pick it up."

Kaylee finally took the plastic card from him, but he noticed that she was careful to keep from touching his fingers. "Hopefully they'll have a sale," she said, tucking it into her shoulder bag.

He shrugged. "Doesn't matter to me what it costs. Get whatever you like."

Annie set Amber on her feet. "Are you ready to go spend your daddy's money, Amber?"

"Daddy," Amber said, nodding and pointing at him.

Colt's chest tightened, and he couldn't have stopped his ear-to-ear grin, nor could he have strung two words together to save his own life. It was the first time his little girl had called him "Daddy," and he couldn't believe what an incredible feeling it gave him.

Chapter Six

"Colt, keep your elbow straight and your shoulder elevated so that your arm is parallel to the floor," Kaylee said, stepping close. "Now bring it across your body."

Taking hold of his arm to lift it to the proper position, she did her best to ignore how hard his bicep was, how being so close to him affected her breathing. She quickly placed one end of a long narrow strip of thin rubber in his left hand, then took the other end and stood at his right side.

"Keeping your arm straight, pull this back as far as you can without pain," she instructed.

"That should be easy," he said, testing the stretchy band.

When he actually started the exercise, Kaylee noticed him wince when he had the band stretched almost even with his shoulder. "That's far enough. Now, slowly let it retract." She waited until he had returned his arm to the rest position. "Next time, don't go quite as far as you went the last time. I don't want you experiencing any pain."

"No pain, no gain," he said, pulling on the rubber again.

When she noticed sweat popping out on his forehead and a muscle jerk along his lean jaw, she calmly took the band from his hand and started for the door. "That's it."

"Hey, I wasn't finished," he said, frowning. "You told me I needed to do two sets of ten. I only finished seven out of the first set."

She spun around to face him. "I also told you to stop before you felt any kind of pain."

"It didn't hurt that much," he insisted, his expression belligerent.

Anger swept through her and, stepping forward, she poked his bare chest with her finger. "Look, Mr. Macho Cowboy, I told you absolutely no pain. What part of that statement don't you understand?"

He picked up a towel to wipe the perspiration

from his forehead. "I understand it fine. I just don't happen to agree with it."

"Then you'll have to find another P.T." She walked down the short hall to the great room before he caught up with her.

"I don't want another physical therapist," he said, taking her by the upper arm.

She looked down at his big hand, then met his determined gaze head-on. "I don't work with patients who refuse to follow my instructions."

They stared at each other for several long seconds in a silent battle of wills before he finally nodded and let go of her arm. "All right. I'll do what you say, but only on one condition."

"*You're* going to set conditions?" She laughed at his audacity. "You certainly are a piece of work, aren't you?"

His charming grin sent her pulse into overdrive. "Yeah, but that's what you've always liked about me."

"Give me a break," she said, rolling her eyes. "So what's the condition?"

"I want you to go down to Laramie with me to pick up Amber's furniture this afternoon," he said earnestly. "We'll leave around five."

She looked at her watch. "By the time we get finished with your exercises it's going to be too late. The store will be closed before we could get there."

He shook his head. "I called earlier. Baby World doesn't close until eight on Friday nights."

"But I really should stay here and—"

"Please?"

He looked so hopeful, she found herself nodding before she could stop herself. "All right. But remember your end of the bargain."

"What's that?" he asked, frowning.

She lightly tapped his shoulder with her finger. "No pain."

"Oh, yeah." He grinned. "Not a problem."

Kaylee thought he'd given in a little too easily, but she didn't have time to wonder about it when the sound of her daughter waking from her nap came from the baby monitor clipped to her belt. "I'll go get Amber and be back down to finish your strengthening exercises."

"Why don't we knock off for today?" he asked, draping the towel around his neck.

She narrowed her eyes. "You just spent the last ten minutes arguing with me about how you want to push yourself, and now you want to quit for the day?" She frowned. "Are you in pain?"

He laughed as they started up the stairs. "Nope.

I just thought you might want to start getting ready to go out."

When she stopped dead in her tracks, he bumped into her from behind. A sizzling thrill ran from the top of her head to the soles of her feet. Quickly putting distance between them, she turned to face him. "We're just going to pick up a youth bed, mattress and chest. This isn't a date."

"Nope." He shook his head. "It's definitely not a date."

"If this isn't a date, Colt Wakefield, what would you call it?"

Colt glanced at Kaylee from the corner of his eye as he steered the truck onto the main highway toward Laramie. He didn't think he'd ever seen her quite this angry. But at least she was talking to him again. It sure as hell beat the dead silence he'd endured from the time Brant, Annie and Zach had shown up to watch Amber. For a few minutes when they'd first arrived, Colt hadn't been sure Kaylee wouldn't refuse to go with him.

"It's just a night out," he said calmly.

Maybe Annie was right. Maybe women didn't like being surprised about things like this.

"You set this up, didn't you?" Kaylee accused.

"It wasn't just a coincidence that Annie and Brant dropped by as we were getting ready to leave."

Setting the cruise control, he leaned back for the hour's drive to Laramie before he answered her. "I'm not going to lie to you. I did arrange for them to watch Amber this evening." He checked his watch. "And by now, Morgan, Samantha and their boys are there, too."

She glared at him across the truck cab. "Why?"

"Because I thought you could use a break," he answered honestly. "You've been busy cooking and helping me with therapy, and I wanted to show my appreciation. That's why I decided to treat you to supper and a movie."

"Don't you think it would have been more considerate to ask me, instead of arranging everything first?" She still sounded irritated, but not quite as angry as she had only moments before.

"I wanted to surprise you," he said defensively. He purposely failed to mention that he'd known she wouldn't have gone otherwise.

"You certainly achieved your goal. I feel like I've been blindsided." She gazed out the passenger window for several long seconds before she spoke again. "Could you promise me something, Colt?"

"What's that, honey?" he asked, tensing. From

the tone of her voice, he wasn't sure he wanted to hear what she was about to ask of him.

"Please, don't play games with me. I've never been good at them."

The emotion he detected in her quietly spoken request had him disengaging the cruise control and steering the truck to the shoulder of the road. He killed the engine, then turned to look at her. She was staring down at her hands, which were clasped tightly in her lap.

"Kaylee, look at me." When she shook her head, he cupped her chin and gently turned her head until their gazes met. "I give you my word, I'm not playing games. A lot has happened in the past three weeks and I thought you could use a little time to relax." The feel of her satiny skin against his calloused palm quickly had his temperature rising. Dropping his hand to keep from pulling her into his arms, he took a deep breath. "Tonight is about two old friends getting together to catch up and have a few laughs. That's all."

She stared at him a moment longer, then, looking resigned, she nodded. "All right. But I'd like to get back to your place early. I know Amber is satisfied with Annie watching her, and she's going to love playing with Zach, and Morgan's boys, but she's used to me putting her to bed. She might be frightened if I'm not there."

"That works for me," he said, starting the truck and pulling back onto the road. It wasn't the evening he'd planned, but he'd take what he could get. "We'll pick up the furniture, then stop at the Broken Spoke Steakhouse on the way back."

"Is that the place offering a free meal to everyone at the table if one person orders and manages to eat their biggest steak?" she asked, sounding a little more relaxed.

"That's the one. It's a thirty-two ounce piece of prime Black Angus beef. But the kicker is, you have to eat a huge pile of fries along with it. Whenever Mitch came home with me, we'd stop there." Colt chuckled. "And they lost money on the deal every time."

"It doesn't surprise me," she said, shaking her head. "Mitch was a bottomless pit. He could eat more than any person I've ever known."

Colt grinned. "It amazed me that he never gained weight."

"I know," she said, laughing. "I used to think that was so unfair. Mitch ate like a horse and stayed thin, while I dieted and gained weight."

When their laughter faded, Colt stared at the

road ahead. "Mitch and I had a lot of good times over the years."

"He really loved you, Colt," she said quietly. "You were like a brother to him."

Colt's gut clenched painfully, as it always did when he thought of losing the best friend he'd ever had. "I felt the same way about him."

They rode in silence for several miles as Colt wrestled with his conscience. He wasn't sure if he was about to ruin what little friendship they had left, but they needed to clear the air about what happened three years ago.

"Kaylee, I know you don't want to talk about it, but I think it's time we stopped walking on eggshells around each other, talk over what happened the morning after we made love, and move on."

Her quick intake of breath was the only sound she made for several tense moments. "I'm not sure I can do that, Colt." Her voice shook and he could tell this wasn't going to be easy for either of them.

"We have to, honey," he said, reaching over to take her hand in his. "We have a little girl depending on us to work this out between us. Her happiness depends on it."

Kaylee remained silent so long, he wasn't sure she was going to agree. "All right," she finally said, sighing. "Say what you feel you have to and get it over with."

He stared at the road ahead as he tried to put his thoughts into words. "First off, I want you to know there hasn't been a day gone by that I haven't regretted the way I handled the situation." Taking a deep breath, he figured it was better to say it outright and get it over with. "I left without waking you that morning because I was so ashamed of what I'd done, I couldn't face you, Kaylee. I know it was the coward's way out, but I knew I couldn't stand seeing the regret or the hatred in your eyes for what I'd done."

"What on earth gave you the impression that I'd feel that way?" She sounded shocked.

"Because you turned to me for comfort and I let things go too far." He swallowed down his own self-disgust. "I should have called a halt to things before it got out of hand."

"Excuse me? What makes you think you were the only one who could have stopped what happened?" she asked incredulously. She shook her head. "Let me clue you in on something, cowboy. You weren't alone in that bed. I could have—"

"No, Kaylee." He heard what she was saying, but he couldn't let her take any part of the blame for what had happened. "Mitch was my best friend, and the night after his funeral I was taking his sister's virginity." Colt shook his head. "Do you really think that's something I'm proud of?"

She reached out to put her hand on his arm. "Colt—"

"If I could go back and change things, I swear I would, Kaylee," he said seriously.

They remained silent for some time before she spoke again. "There's something that I wouldn't change about what happened three years ago even if I could," she said quietly.

"What's that, honey?"

There was no hesitation when she answered. "Amber. She's my life now."

Colt swallowed hard as he digested what Kaylee had just told him. She didn't regret having his child. Did that mean she had no regrets about making love with him?

"I have to ask you something, and I want you to be completely honest with me," he said, his heart pumping so hard he wasn't sure she couldn't hear it.

"I think we've gone over—"

"I wouldn't ask if it wasn't important to me, Kaylee," he said, taking her hand in his.

She looked as if she was going to refuse, then

finally nodded. "All right. What do you want to know?"

"You said you weren't sorry you had Amber." He took a deep breath. He'd probably gone completely around the bend, but he had to know. "Do you have any regrets about making love with me that night?"

She remained silent a moment, then shook her head. "No. I've never been sorry about what happened that night."

Two hours later, as they left the Broken Spoke Steakhouse and turned onto the road leading back to the Lonetree, Colt was still thinking about Kaylee's admission. Hell, he hadn't been able to think of anything else the entire evening.

Had he been wrong all this time about what happened that night?

For three years he'd convinced himself that he'd taken advantage of her, that he'd seduced her when she'd been the most vulnerable. But had that really been the case? Or had she been just as desperate as he'd been to escape the emotional trauma of losing Mitch with the life-affirming act of making love with someone she really cared for?

"Colt, are you all right?" Kaylee asked, dragging his attention back to the present.

He shook off his disturbing speculation as he glanced at her across the truck cab. "Sure. Why do you ask?"

"You've been distracted all evening," she said, looking concerned. "And when we were eating, you kept staring at your steak like you expected it to moo. I've never known you to lose your appetite before."

"Well, it was pretty rare."

"It was definitely that," Kaylee said, grinning.

The appearance of her smile and the sound of her velvet voice caused his heart to thump hard against his ribs. He didn't think he'd ever seen her look prettier, or more desirable.

But he was determined to keep things light. He wasn't willing to jeopardize the easy mood that had developed between them over the course of the evening.

"Did you enjoy yourself tonight?" he asked as he casually stretched his arm along the back of the bench seat.

"Yes, I did." She hesitated a moment before she added, "But I owe you an apology."

"For what?" He couldn't think of anything that she'd need to apologize for.

"I'm sorry for the way I acted earlier," she said,

her voice small. "You know, about your surprising me this evening."

Her silky hair brushed his hand, sending tiny currents of electricity streaking through him. He couldn't stop himself from tangling his fingers in the auburn strands.

"I'm just glad you had a good time, honey."

"But I shouldn't have overreacted the way I did," she insisted. "You were just trying to be nice and—"

"I think we both learned something about each other tonight," he interrupted.

She turned her head to give him a questioning look. "What would that be?"

"I'm not nearly as devious as you thought." He chuckled as he steered the truck onto the lane leading to his house. "And you don't like surprises."

She shook her head. "That's not entirely true. It depends on the surprise." Grinning, she added, "Sometimes they can be very nice."

Parking the truck, he got out and walked around to open the passenger door for her. "I'll remind you of that the next time I decide to surprise you."

Even though she was smiling, she looked a bit apprehensive. "Next time?"

"Sure." When she got out of the truck, he

shut the door then draped a companionable arm across her shoulders and started walking toward the house. "Didn't you know, life is nothing more than a series of astounding events, punctuated by stretches of monotonous boredom?"

"That's pretty deep for a cowboy," she said, laughing.

"Watch it, brat." He gave her a playful hug as he pressed a kiss to the top of her head. "I'll have you know I made straight A's in my college philosophy courses."

"You actually attended classes?" She shook her head in mock amazement. "I'm impressed. I always thought you and Mitch were there to meet girls."

"Well, there was that, too," he said, grinning. As they climbed the porch steps, he chuckled. "But there's a funny thing about those scholarships they give out for college rodeo teams."

"What's that?"

"They actually expect you to pass a few classes."

"Imagine that," she said laughing.

Reluctant for the evening to end, when they reached the front door Colt turned her to face him. "I know that you don't like surprises," he said, using his thumb to push his hat back on his head.

With the brim out of the way, he took her into his arms. "So I think I'd better warn you. I'm going to kiss you now, Kaylee."

She gazed up at him, and just when he thought she was going to tell him to buzz off, she nodded. "I think I'd like that, Colt."

Lowering his head, he told himself to keep the kiss simple. But the moment his mouth touched hers, the spark of desire that had been flickering inside him all evening ignited into a flame. He couldn't have stopped himself from pulling her to him any more than he could stop the changing of the seasons.

When her lips parted on a soft sigh and he slipped his tongue inside, the sweet taste that was uniquely Kaylee made his pulse pound and his temperature soar. As he stroked her tongue with his, a tiny moan escaped her and she put her arms around his neck. The feel of her nails lightly raking the sensitive skin at his nape and her eagerness to get closer to him sent shock waves to every cell in his body and liquid fire racing through his veins.

Her supple body molding to his quickly worked its magic and his arousal was not only predictable, it made him light-headed with its intensity. Sliding one hand down to cup her delightful little bottom, he pulled her forward. He wanted her to feel the need she'd created in him, to let her know how wrong she'd been about his not being attracted to her.

Bringing his other hand up under her jean jacket and along her side, he cupped her breast and chafed her puckered nipple through the layers of her pink T-shirt and bra. The bud tightened further and his own body hardened in response. He'd never wanted a woman more than he wanted Kaylee at that very moment.

Slowly breaking the kiss, he held her close as he tried to bring his breathing under control. How on God's green earth had he managed to talk himself into believing that he and Kaylee could return to the easy relationship they'd once shared?

Hell, nothing could be further from the truth. With sudden clarity, Colt realized that he and Kaylee had crossed a line three years ago and there was no turning back. The only thing they could do now would be to move forward and try to build something new.

"Colt, I…we—" She shook her head. "This can't happen again."

"It's all right, honey."

Easing back, Colt found the sight of her perfect lips slightly swollen from his kiss and the rosy blush of desire on her pale cheeks absolutely fascinating. Her luminous violet eyes were filled with questions that at the moment he couldn't even begin to answer. And he wasn't fool enough to try.

"Don't be frightened of what's happening between us, Kaylee." He smoothed her silky auburn hair with a shaky hand. "We're not going to rush into something before we're both ready. This time we're going to take it a step at a time and see where it leads us." He kissed the tip of her cute little nose. "Now, let's go inside and listen to my brothers and their wives tell us how adorable our daughter is and how much fun she had getting to know her cousins."

As Kaylee gazed up at Colt, she knew beyond a shadow of doubt that her feelings for him were as strong, if not stronger, than they had ever been. The realization caused her breathing to stall and her heart to skip several beats.

For the past few years she'd convinced herself that she'd gotten over him, that she'd moved on with her life. But it was past time she stopped lying to herself and faced the truth. She'd never stopped loving Colt—could never stop loving him.

She bit her lower lip against the panic threatening to swamp her. But before she had the chance to come to grips with her discovery and what it might mean to her sanity, Colt stepped back, took her hand in his and opened the front door.

Dazed and feeling as if she was moving through a heavy fog, she allowed him to lead her through the house to the family room. Standing just inside the doorway, she watched Amber put her arms around a baby boy, who appeared to be about a year old, as she kissed his chubby little cheek.

"Baby," she said, grinning at Annie and another woman sitting on the couch.

When the woman Kaylee assumed to be Morgan's wife, Samantha, turned to smile at Amber, she noticed Kaylee and Colt. "Look who's home, Amber."

"Mommy!" Amber said, her grin widening as she ran over for Kaylee to pick her up.

"Did you have a good time with your cousins?" Kaylee asked, swinging her daughter up into her arms.

"No," Amber said, nodding affirmatively. She immediately began to wiggle as she pointed to the floor. "Down."

"Hey there, Kaylee-Q," Brant said as he and Morgan both rose from their chairs. He wrapped her in a bear hug. "It's good to see you again."

"It's nice seeing you, too, Brant," she said, meaning it.

She'd missed seeing Colt's brothers. They'd always treated her and Mitch like they were members of their family.

When Brant released her, Morgan took his place. "It's been way too long, Kaylee. We've missed having you around."

She hugged the oldest of the Wakefield brothers. "You've just missed having someone around to tease unmercifully."

"I see you can still hold your own with us," Morgan said, laughing as he released her. He held out his arm for the pretty, brown-haired woman to step into his embrace. "Kaylee, this is my wife, Samantha."

"It's nice to finally meet you, Kaylee," Samantha said, smiling. "I've heard so much about you, I feel like I've known you for years. In fact, Annie and I were just talking about taking you with us down to Laramie next week for lunch and shopping."

Annie grinned. "We thought a girls' afternoon at the mall would be nice."

"I'd like that," Kaylee said, noticing Brant and Morgan simultaneously wink and grin at their wives as if they shared a delightful secret.

Before she had a chance to speculate on what was going on, a little boy walked over to them and held his arms up to Colt. "Unca Colt, I gots a new watch."

"You sure do, Timmy," Colt said, picking the child up to sit on his right forearm.

"No," Amber said, shaking her head vigorously.

Shocked at the uncharacteristic vehemence in her daughter's voice and the correct use of the negative gesture, Kaylee turned to watch Amber run across the room toward the adults. When she stopped in front of Colt, she held up her little arms for him to pick her up.

"Up, Daddy," Amber insisted. "Up."

Chapter Seven

Colt's heart stopped then took off at a gallop at Amber's insistence that he pick her up. It was the first time his daughter had wanted him to hold her and he wasn't about to miss the opportunity. Unfortunately, he still couldn't lift anything with his left arm, and if he set Timmy on his feet, Colt ran the risk of hurting the little boy's feelings. And that was something he just wouldn't do.

"Let me take him," Morgan said, apparently sensing Colt's dilemma.

"Thanks," Colt said, handing the three-year-old to his dad.

With his right arm free, he bent to lift his daughter up to sit on his forearm. She immediately wrapped her little arms around his neck to give him a hug before she turned to glare at Timmy.

"Mine Daddy," she said as if staking her claim.

Colt's chest tightened with emotion and he felt as if he had a lump the size of a basketball clogging his throat. The feeling of finally holding his daughter, of knowing that she'd accepted him, was overwhelming.

He felt Kaylee touch his elbow. Being careful not to move his shoulder farther than was comfortable, he put his left arm around her waist and pulled her to his side. Gazing down at her, he suddenly felt as if he held everything in his arms that he'd ever wanted. It should have scared the hell out of him. Instead, it filled him with a sense of completion like nothing he'd ever known.

Unaware that she'd given Colt a moment he'd never forget as long as he lived, Amber began to pull on the wide brim of his hat. "Me wear. Me."

He couldn't have denied her if his life depended on it. Removing his Resistol, he set it on her little head so that it didn't cover her eyes. "There you go, pixie."

"I think Amber is going to be a Daddy's girl," Annie said as she wiped a tear from her cheek.

"I think so, too," Samantha agreed, sniffling. When Colt's youngest nephew, Jared, whimpered and lifted his arms for his mother to pick him up, Samantha smiled. "I hate to cut the evening short, but I think we need to take the boys home and get them ready for bed."

Annie nodded. "Brant and I need to do the same with Zach."

"Come on, partner," Brant said, catching his son around the waist to swing the little boy up and onto his shoulders. "Mommy said it's time for us to head home."

Colt held his daughter as he and Kaylee walked his brothers and their families to the door. "Thanks for watching Amber this evening."

"It was our pleasure," Samantha said, raising on tiptoe to kiss Amber's cheek. "Bye-bye, Amber."

Amber raised her hand and waved, then laid her head on Colt's shoulder. The gesture was so trusting that he thought his heart might burst from the love filling it.

"You have a sweet little girl there, Colt," Morgan said. Turning to Kaylee, he smiled. "If this joker gives you any problems, don't hesitate to call me. I'll straighten him out in a hurry."

"And if you can't get hold of Morgan, call me," Brant added with a grin.

"Thanks for the votes of confidence," Colt grumbled as he watched Kaylee accept hugs from both of his brothers.

"I'll call you tomorrow about our afternoon at the mall, Kaylee," Annie said before giving Colt a knowing grin.

Now what was that all about?

He'd noticed the bemused expressions on both of his brothers' and their wives' faces each time the trip to the mall had been mentioned. But before he could ask what was going on, Annie gave Amber a little wave, then hurried across the porch and down the steps.

When he closed the door behind his family, he turned to see Kaylee watching him. She looked a bit uncertain, and he knew she was mulling over what he'd said about them taking things slowly.

"Kaylee, I—"

"I think it's time this little lady got ready for bed," she said, interrupting him. She held out her hands to take Amber. "It's been a big evening."

Realizing that Kaylee was talking about herself as much as she was Amber, Colt hugged and kissed Amber's baby-soft cheek. "Sleep tight, pixie." Reluctantly handing her to Kaylee, he asked, "Do you need help?"

Kaylee shook her head. "She's normally easy to

get to sleep." Starting toward the stairs, she turned back. "I'm, um, pretty tired. I think I'll turn in for the night, too. Thank you for the evening out. I'll see you at breakfast tomorrow morning. Good night."

"'Night," Colt said, watching Kaylee hurry up the stairs with Amber.

He shook his head when she disappeared down the hall. Kaylee needed time to come to the same conclusion he'd reached earlier in the evening. They would never—could never—be "just" friends. Thinking back on it, he wasn't sure they ever had been.

Kaylee handed Colt a small weight. "I'm going to warn you before we start the next phase of your therapy, I won't tolerate your trying to lift anything heavier than this. Understand?"

"I can lift more than this thing with my little finger," he said, testing the three-pound weight in his left hand.

"You'd better not," she said sternly. She knew if she didn't lay down the law now, he would push for more and end up reinjuring himself.

"Aw, come on, honey. I know I can lift twice this much." His charming grin caused her pulse to take off at breakneck speed. "The least you can do is let me try."

She hardened herself to his supplicating expression and shook her head. "Not until we see if doing the biceps curls are going to bother you."

"They won't."

"Do three sets of ten with these weights, then we'll talk," she said, refusing to budge.

He stared at her with narrowed eyes as if trying to intimidate her. Fortunately she wasn't that easily coerced.

"Oh, all right," he finally said, glaring at her as he plopped onto the weight bench.

Watching him begin the exercise, Kaylee tried to remind herself that he was like any other patient she'd worked with. But she knew she was only fooling herself. Colt could never be just another person to her. Ever.

If she hadn't known that before, she would have after last night. He'd kissed her before, but never like he had after they returned home from their evening in Laramie. When he'd pressed his lips to hers, then deepened the kiss, it had felt as if fireworks had been ignited in her soul. And if that hadn't been enough to convince her, what he'd told her afterward certainly would have. He'd said not to be afraid of what was happening between them, that they were going to take things slowly and not rush into anything they weren't ready for this time.

This time.

Two very simple little four-letter words with the power to scare her as little else could. She shivered at the thought of what they implied.

Colt had indicated, in a roundabout way, that he wanted them to explore a relationship that went well beyond friendship. But could she do that? Would she be able to survive if it didn't work out for them?

Three years ago, the only thing that had kept her going after losing her brother and having Colt walk away had been Amber. Kaylee had focused on her pregnancy, then after Amber's birth, she'd concentrated all of her energy into being the best mother she could be. And it had worked. She'd picked up the pieces of her life and moved on because Colt hadn't been around to remind her that she'd put her heart on the line and lost.

But this time, everything would be different. Now that he knew about their daughter, Kaylee would see him on a regular basis when he came to visit Amber.

And what would happen if things *did* work out between them? Would she be able to accept what he did for a living?

When she'd lost Mitch to the sport of bull riding, she'd lost her only living relative, and it had very nearly been the end of her. But how would she survive if something happened to Colt? The thought was so frightening she had to wrap her arms around herself to ward off the chill.

"Kaylee, are you okay?"

When she glanced up, she was surprised to see that Colt was standing right in front of her. "Y-yes, I'm fine. I was…thinking about the next phase of your therapy," she lied.

He stared at her a moment before shaking his head. "No you weren't." Tracing his finger down her cheek, he gave her a smile so tender that her toes curled inside her cross-trainers. "We both need to stop dancing around what we're really thinking, Kaylee. Being up front and honest with each other is the only way we're going to have a chance of making it work out this time around." He leaned forward to lightly brush her lips with his. "And I want that chance, honey."

A shiver of longing coursed through her at his touch. "Really, I was just—"

She stopped abruptly to stare into his brilliant blue eyes. He was right. If they were going to attempt a relationship, it had to be based on complete honesty. She'd already admitted to herself that she still cared for him—had never stopped caring for him—but did she have the courage to tell him? Did she dare open herself up to the possibility of more heartbreak?

"What do *you* want, Kaylee?" he asked, his voice gentle. "Tell me what's really going on in that pretty little head of yours."

Staring up at him, she knew what she wanted—what she had always wanted. "I—I'm afraid, Colt."

He immediately wrapped her in his arms and pulled her to his wide chest. "Honey, I know it's scary. But anything worth having is always risky." His hands caressed her with a reverence that brought tears to her eyes. "And we'll never know what we could have together if we don't give it a try."

The feel of his strength surrounding her, the soothing sound of his deep baritone and the steady beat of his heart beneath her ear gave her the courage she needed to tell him what was in her heart. "The thought of failing scares me to death, but I'm even more frightened of never knowing what we could have together." Leaning back to look up into his handsome face, she took a deep breath. "Yes, Colt. I'd like to see where this leads us."

* * *

As Colt flipped through the channels, Amber sat up in his lap and pointed at the television. "Mato!"

"You want to watch this?" he asked as an animated tomato and cucumber scooted across the screen.

"Yes, yes, yes," she said as she shook her head in a negative gesture.

"Okay, pixie," he said, kissing the top of her head and settling back in his recliner. "We'll watch this until Mommy says it's time for you to go to bed."

He frowned as he watched the vegetables sing, dance and crack jokes. Cartoons sure had changed a lot since he was a little kid. Whatever happened to the good old days when cars, trucks and airplanes transformed into robots, or lions, tigers and panthers talked and fought skeleton-like villains?

But several minutes later, Colt found himself laughing out loud at a talking stalk of broccoli. "This is pretty good stuff, pixie."

Giggling, Amber scrambled up his chest, placed her little hands on his cheeks and gave him a sloppy baby kiss.

"How are you two doing?" Kaylee asked, walking into the family room from the kitchen.

"I can see now why you decorated Amber's room with these characters," Colt said, grinning. "She loves this show."

"From the way you were laughing, I think you're getting just as big of a kick out of it," Kaylee said, smiling back at him.

Colt swallowed hard. How in the name of Sam Hill was he going to keep his hands to himself if she kept turning that killer smile on him?

After their talk this afternoon, he'd told himself it was more important than ever for them not to rush into anything. They needed to let their feelings for each other build slowly in order to be certain that when they made love it was right for both of them.

But now he wasn't sure that was going to be an option. Not when he found everything Kaylee said, every move she made, sexy as hell. And just knowing they would eventually be exploring the chemistry that had always simmered between them was enough to keep him in a constant state of arousal.

"Colt, did you hear me?" she asked, picking up Amber.

He shook his head. "Sorry, I was thinking about something I need…to do."

"I asked if you would mind watching Amber on Monday morning while I go to the mall with Annie and Samantha," Kaylee said patiently.

"Sure." Turning the television off, he rose from the chair. "But I thought you were supposed to go some afternoon."

Kaylee nodded. "We were. But Annie has an early doctor's appointment and wondered if Samantha and I would like to go shopping afterward and then have lunch."

When she started toward the stairs, he followed her. "Do you want to take my credit card?"

"No."

"Wait a minute," he said, taking hold of her arm. He removed his wallet from his hip pocket. "I want you to get some more stuff for Amber's room."

"What kind of *stuff*?" she asked, frowning as she accepted the plastic card.

He shrugged. "Toys, stuffed animals, clothes, whatever you think she'd like." Leaning down, he kissed Amber's cheek. "Sleep tight, little pixie." He brushed Kaylee's lips with his, then added, "After you get her to bed, come back downstairs."

The phone rang before she could answer. "You'd

better get that while I get Amber into bed," she said, turning to go upstairs.

Cursing the caller's timing, Colt watched Kaylee's delightful little bottom as she climbed the stairs. When the phone rang for the third time, he marched into his office and snatched the cordless unit from its base. "What?"

"Did I interrupt something, little brother?" Morgan asked without missing a beat.

Colt blew out a frustrated breath. "Did anyone ever tell you how lousy your timing is?"

Morgan's hearty laughter echoed in Colt's ear. "I seem to remember Brant saying something similar the first time he brought Annie to the Lonetree."

"Well, he was right," Colt said, his anger over the interruption beginning to cool. "What's up, bro?"

"I've got some news about that buckskin mare you wanted me and Brant to find."

Colt perked up immediately. "Is she for sale?"

"Not anymore," Morgan said, sounding quite pleased. "Unless, of course, *you* intend to sell her."

"Nope." Relieved that Kaylee's horse had been found, Colt grinned. "Where did you find her?"

"Down in the Texas panhandle. When the guy at the sale barn Kaylee had used to sell the Lazy S livestock told us the buyer was from down that way, Brant got in touch with his old rodeo buddy Cooper Adams." Morgan chuckled. "Two hours later we knew who owned her, and how much it would take to buy her."

"I've always liked Coop," Colt said, grinning. "How soon can I go down to pick her up?"

"You don't have to," Morgan answered. Colt could hear the smile in his brother's voice. "Cooper's sister, Jenna, and her husband, Flint, are heading up to Denver for a horse show anyway. They're going to load the mare in their horse trailer and bring her with them. Brant and I are going to drive down Monday morning to get her."

Colt couldn't have asked for more. "I owe you and Brant one."

"We were glad to help you find the mare," Morgan said seriously. "We knew Mitch gave it to Kaylee and how much the horse meant to her."

"Thanks, Morgan."

After they said goodbye, Colt walked out of the study and, taking the stairs two at a time, strode purposefully down the hall to Amber's room. He couldn't wait to let Kaylee know about her horse.

"Kaylee, I've got something to tell you," he said, entering his daughter's dimly lit bedroom.

He found Kaylee sitting in the rocking chair on the far side of the room, slowly rocking Amber.

She placed her index finger to her lips to silence him. "She just went to sleep," she whispered.

"Sorry," he mouthed, walking over to stand next to them.

As he watched Kaylee cuddle Amber to her, his chest tightened and he forgot all about the reason he'd sought her out. If he lived to be as old as Methuselah he didn't think he'd ever see a more beautiful sight.

When Kaylee moved to get up from the chair, Colt reached out to take his sleeping daughter from her. His hand brushed Kaylee's breast as he lifted Amber into his arms and he barely managed to suppress a groan.

"I told you this afternoon not to lift anything heavier than the three-pound weight," Kaylee whispered hotly.

He chuckled. "And I told you I could lift that much with my little finger," he said just as quietly.

He wasn't going to tell her about the little twinge he'd felt in his shoulder. It wasn't anything significant and he'd much rather savor the moment of helping Kaylee put their little girl to bed.

Laying Amber down, he smiled as Kaylee covered her with a colorful quilt. "Thank you, honey."

Straightening, she frowned. "What for?"

Colt took her into his arms. "For giving me the most precious gift a woman can give a man—his child."

Kaylee rested her head against his chest and wrapped her arms around his waist as they both stared down at their sleeping daughter. "I should be thanking you," she said softly. "Amber is the best thing that's ever happened to me. From the moment I suspected I was pregnant with her, I was thrilled."

Her quiet statement seemed to rob him of breath. All things considered, most women would have been fit to be tied by an unexpected pregnancy. But Kaylee had been happy about him making her pregnant?

"Why, Kaylee?" he asked, needing to know. "Why were you happy at the prospect of having a baby?"

She leaned back to stare up at him. Uncertainty clouded her violet gaze a moment before she took a deep breath and whispered, "Because I knew the baby was a part of you."

Colt's heart stalled, then took off at a dead run. Kaylee had welcomed his child, loved and nurtured her, even before she'd known for sure that Amber was growing in her belly.

His knees threatened to buckle and he had a

hard time expressing how much her admission meant to him. Groaning, he simply lowered his mouth to hers, letting her know without words what he was feeling.

At the first touch of Kaylee's sweet lips to his, Colt's temperature shot skyward and a lazy warmth began to gather in the pit of his stomach. But when he deepened the kiss, every nerve in his body sparked to life and a shimmering heat began to race through his veins.

Bringing his hand up along her side, he gently cupped her breast and was rewarded by her soft moan vibrating against his mouth. The sound sent his pulse into overdrive and his good intentions right out the window.

He'd told her they would allow their feelings to build before they took the next step in their relationship. But it had been three long years since he'd made love to her, and the need to once again make Kaylee his tightened his body to an almost painful state and clouded his mind.

Taking things slowly was no longer an option for them. As she melted against him, Colt wasn't sure that it had ever been. He wanted Kaylee with a need that staggered him and he sensed that the same hunger that had seized him, had her in its grips, as well.

When he broke the kiss and lifted his head, he glanced at their daughter, then at the woman in his arms. "I want to make love with you, Kaylee. I want to be buried so deeply inside of you that we both lose sight of where I end and you begin." He brushed a lock of auburn hair from her satiny cheek. "Is that what you want?"

Indecision crossed her lovely features, and just when he thought she was going to tell him she wasn't ready to take that step, she closed her eyes and nodded. "I've never wanted anything more in my life than to be loved by you, Colt."

Chapter Eight

Kaylee watched Colt's vivid blue gaze darken. Then, releasing her, he stepped back to take her by the hand. "Let's go to my room, honey."

Her stomach fluttered as if a thousand tiny butterflies had been unleashed inside of her and her knees felt like rubber as she let Colt lead her out of Amber's room and down the hall. A tiny part of her was frightened that she could very easily be making the biggest mistake of her life, that she might be setting herself up for more of the same shattering disappointment she'd experienced three years ago. But her heart told her that she'd never really had a choice in the matter. From the moment she'd first laid eyes on Colt Wakefield fourteen years ago, she'd loved him.

When they entered his bedroom, he walked over to the bedside table and switched on the lamp, then turned to face her. "Kaylee, I don't want you feeling pressured." He gently cupped her cheeks with his hands. "If you're not ready for this, I want you to tell me now. I don't ever want you to regret making love with me."

She took a deep breath as she gazed into his eyes and told him what she knew in her heart to be true. "I won't regret making love with you, Colt."

He stared at her for endless seconds, then pulled her to him. She felt a shudder run through his body at the same moment a groan rumbled up from deep in his chest. "You can't imagine how much that means to me, honey."

Before she could respond he covered her mouth with his and Kaylee felt as if the butterflies in her stomach had gone absolutely berserk. But when he traced her lips with his tongue, then entered her mouth to stroke her with a rhythm that left her breathless, the fluttering sensation spread to every cell of her being.

Tasting Colt's passion, feeling his strong arousal pressed to her soft lower belly, made her knees wobble and she found that she had to cling to him to keep from melting into a puddle at his feet. She'd always thought his kiss was devastating, but this time she could tell that he held nothing back, and she felt branded by the extent of his hunger.

When he raised his head, his breathing was labored. "I'm going to try to take this slow. But I've never wanted a woman as much as I want you."

"I want you, too," she said, feeling just as breathless.

"Are you on the pill or the patch, honey?"

Kaylee's cheeks grew warm. Discussing something so intimate was slightly embarrassing. But not addressing the issue a few years ago was the very reason she was at the Lonetree now.

"I, um, haven't had to worry about birth control," she said, shaking her head.

He sucked in a sharp breath. "Kaylee, I know I have no right to ask, but—"

"There hasn't been anyone else since that night with you," she said quietly.

Colt's heart slammed against his ribs and he felt as if he might never breathe again. Kaylee had been a virgin three years ago, and the knowledge that he'd been the only man she'd ever made love with sent his blood pressure into stroke range.

He closed his eyes, took a deep breath, then opened them to gaze down at her. "I promise this time you don't have to worry, honey." Giving her a quick kiss, he bent to remove her tennis shoes and his boots, then straightened to tug her T-shirt from the waistband of her jeans. He slid his hands beneath the hem to lift the garment up and over her arms. "I'll take care of protecting you."

With a smile that sent a surge of heat straight to the region south of his belt buckle, she began to unfasten the snaps on his chambray shirt. When she peeled it back and placed her warm palms on his heated skin, Colt felt as if a slow-burning fuse had been ignited deep inside him.

"Did anyone ever tell you what a gorgeous body you have, cowboy?" she asked, running her hands over the muscles of his chest and abdomen.

"Honey, I've been called a lot of things, but I don't ever remember the word 'gorgeous' being used to describe me," he said, chuckling. He started to tell her that she was the one who was beautiful, but she lightly grazed his flat nipples with the tips of her fingernails and a strangled groan came out instead.

Her busy little hands stilled. "Do you want me to stop?"

Unable to get his vocal cords to work, he shook

his head and watched as she continued to trace the now puckered flesh.

When they'd made love before, it had been an urgent coupling—a desperate attempt to escape the pain of losing Mitch. But this time was different. This time they were exploring, learning what was pleasing and what brought the most pleasure.

No longer willing or able to keep from touching her, Colt reached behind Kaylee to unhook her plain white bra, then slid the straps from her shoulders to toss it on top of her shirt. His hands shook slightly as he cupped her firm breasts in his calloused palms, then chafed the tight tips with the pads of his thumbs.

A soft moan escaped her lips. "Mmm."

"Feel good?" he asked as he continued to tease her.

"Y-yes."

He leaned down to kiss one perfect coral bud, then took it into his mouth to taste her sweetness. When she swayed, he wrapped an arm around her waist to support her while he turned his attention to her other nipple.

Raising his head, he kissed her forehead, her eyes and the tip of her nose. "So sweet. So perfect."

She moved to ease his shirt from his shoulders. "I think you're overdressed, don't you, cowboy?"

"Not for long," he said, reaching for his belt buckle.

To his delight, she shook her head and shooed his hands away. "Let me take care of that for you."

"The last time you unfastened my belt, you were mad at me," he said, remembering the night they spent in the motel on the way to the Lonetree.

"You deserved that. You were running the risk of reinjuring your collarbone by doing too much, too soon," she said, making short work of freeing the leather strap from the buckle.

"But you're not upset with me now?" he asked, grinning.

She shook her head and started to release the button at his waistband. "At the moment, anger is the last thing I'm feeling."

Her fingers brushed his lower belly and he felt as if a surge of heat shot straight to his groin. Taking a deep breath, he reached for the belt encircling her small waist. Making quick work of unbuckling it, he released the button at the top of her jeans, unzipped them, then slid them and her sensible white cotton panties down her slender legs.

When she stepped out of them, her gaze met his and the look in her violet eyes damn near brought him to his knees as she reached for the metal tab at the top of his fly. He held his breath as she eased the zipper down over his arousal straining insistently at the fabric of his boxer briefs. But when she placed her hands just inside the elastic band, and shoved them and his jeans down his legs, Colt felt as if he just might go into total meltdown.

Suddenly looking uncertain, she stepped back. Noticing the direction of her gaze, he gave her a reassuring smile before pulling her to him. But the contrast of her soft femininity against his hard male flesh, the feel of her pebbled nipples pressing into his skin, hastened the sizzling fuse burning inside him and he had to take several deep breaths to hang on to his rapidly slipping control.

"You feel so damned good," he said through clenched teeth.

"Colt—"

Gazing at her pretty face, he noticed the blush of passion on her porcelain cheeks, and he could tell she was feeling the same burning need that he was. "Do you trust me, Kaylee?"

"Yes."

He smiled. "It's going to be okay."

"I-it's been so long, Colt."

"I know, honey. But I promise this time there won't be any discomfort." He kissed her forehead.

"I'm going to make sure that it's nothing but pure pleasure for you."

He slid his hands down her back to cup her delightful bottom and pulled her to him. The feel of his arousal nestled against her soft warmth had him gritting his teeth and praying for the strength to go slow.

"Don't ever doubt that I'm attracted to you, Kaylee," he finally managed to say. "Or that I want you."

He felt her tremble, then, without a word, she took his hand in hers and led him over to the side of his king-size bed. Pulling back the covers, she laid down, then smiled at him.

"I'll be right back, honey," he said, walking into the adjoining bathroom.

When he returned, he tucked a foil packet beneath his pillow and stretched out beside her on the bed. Taking her into his arms, he kissed her until they were both gasping for breath.

"I want you to tell me what feels good," he said, sliding his hand along her side.

Kaylee's skin tingled from Colt's touch and heat flowed through her veins, threading its way to the very core of her being. A coil of need began to form in the pit of her stomach as his lips nibbled a path from the pulse fluttering at the base of her throat, over her collarbone and down the slope of her breast. He took the tight tip into his mouth, then flicked it with his tongue, causing her heart to skip a beat and her breathing to become shallow.

Tangling her hands in his thick raven hair, she held him to her as wave after wave of pleasure swept over her and the coil in her belly tightened. The first time they'd made love, it had been hurried and reckless as they both tried to forget their grief. But this time they were taking their time as they explored each other and the compelling magnetism pulling them together.

When Colt raised his head to gaze down at her, the look in his eyes stole her breath. "Honey, I want you so damned much I ache from it."

He lowered his head to kiss her as he slid his hand down to her hip. The feel of his firm lips on hers, his calloused palm on her skin and the insistence of his arousal pressed to her thigh caused Kaylee to bite her lower lip in an effort to stifle the moan threatening to escape. But when he moved his hand to the apex of her thighs, she shivered with a need like nothing she'd ever before experienced. His fingers searched for and found her pleasure point and she couldn't hold in the sound of her passion any longer.

"What do you want, Kaylee?" he whispered close to her ear.

"I want…you, Colt," she said, barely recognizing the throaty voice as her own. Wanting to touch him as he touched her, she reached down to stroke him with infinite care. "Only you."

She felt a shudder run through his big body a moment before he groaned and buried his head in the curve of her neck. He caught her hand in his and brought it to his chest.

"Honey, if you keep that up I'm not going to make it past the eight-second whistle."

"Then make love to me, Colt," she said, wanting him more than she'd ever dreamed possible.

He kissed her, then reached under his pillow. Once he had the condom in place, he took her in his arms and nudged her knees apart.

Looking up into eyes so blue she felt as if she might drown in their depths, Kaylee was lost. His smoldering gaze held her captive as without a word, he gathered her close and slowly, gently, pressed forward to make their bodies one. She tensed and held her breath at the exquisite stretching.

"Just relax, honey," he said when he'd completely filled her.

She felt his body quiver as he fought for control.

A muscle jerked along his lean jaw and she could tell what his restraint was costing him.

Touching his cheeks with trembling fingers, she pulled his handsome face down to kiss his firm, warm lips. "Colt, I need—"

He opened his eyes and gave her a look that caused her pulse to race. "Kaylee, I want to make this last, but it's been so long and you feel so damn good."

She felt the same way. But unable to find the words to express what she needed, she simply wrapped her legs around his narrow hips as she tried to get closer.

"Honey, I think you're going to kill me," he said, groaning.

He threaded his fingers in her hair and kissed her passionately as he pulled back then moved forward. Her body responded with an answering motion and together they found the rhythm that would take them to a place only lovers go.

Her heart swelled with emotion as he cradled her in his arms and her world was reduced to just the two of them—one man, one woman coming together in the age-old dance of love. Surrounded by Colt, being filled by him, quickly had Kaylee climbing toward the peak, reaching for the unknown. Heat flowed through her and she moaned from the tightening of the coil deep inside her.

Apparently sensing her readiness, Colt quickened the pace. "Let it happen, Kaylee. I'm right here with you, honey."

Suddenly feeling as if stars had burst within her soul, she spun out of control, her universe reduced to the man holding her body to his. Light danced behind her closed eyes and pleasure shimmered over every cell in her being as with one final thrust Colt joined her and together they soared on the current of perfect fulfillment.

Drifting back to reality, love so pure it brought tears to her eyes filled her and she held him close, reluctant for the moment to end. She wasn't sure where their relationship was headed, or if they had a future together. But the one thing that would never change, no matter what happened between them, was the depth of her love for him.

At the age of ten she'd loved him with a child's innocent adoration. But at twenty-four, she loved him with a woman's passionate heart. And she knew beyond a shadow of doubt that she always would.

"We have one more stop to make before we start back home," Annie said.

Grinning, Samantha nodded. "We always save the best for last."

As they all walked out of the restaurant where they'd had lunch, Kaylee watched the two women exchange a knowing smile. She'd seen that look before. It was the same amused expression they'd worn the night they baby-sat Amber.

"What's going on?" She looked from one woman to the other. "Is there something I should know about?"

"It's nothing really," Samantha said, shaking her head. "Annie and I just need to buy some new, um, under things."

Kaylee laughed. "Since when is buying underwear special?"

"It's where we shop that makes the difference," Annie and Samantha said in unison.

Kaylee frowned. "Where do you—" She stopped suddenly. "Oh, dear heavens! You two shop at the—"

"Sleek and Sassy Lady Lingerie Boutique," Annie said, laughing.

Samantha suddenly looked uncertain. "Kaylee, I, uh, that is, we don't know what your relationship is with Colt, and it's none of our business. If you'd rather not go shopping for lingerie, we'll understand."

"Absolutely," Annie said, nodding.

Kaylee nibbled on her lower lip. She remembered the expressions on Brant's and Morgan's faces when the shopping trip was mentioned. The two men hadn't been able to hide their anticipation for what their wives might bring home.

"I've never worn anything but plain white cotton," she said, thinking out loud. Her cheeks heated as she tried to decide how to ask a question that might be a little too personal. "I don't mean to be nosy, but do your husbands really like what you buy?"

Looking relieved that Kaylee hadn't been offended, both women laughed.

"There are four things that the Wakefield men have in common," Annie said. "Black hair, blue eyes, their love of the Lonetree Ranch, and…they have a deep appreciation for the Sleek and Sassy Lady Lingerie Boutique."

"We're betting Colt is no different," Samantha added, grinning.

"I…oh, heavens," Kaylee stammered, blushing.

Did she really have the nerve to buy sexy underwear? Would Colt like seeing her in provocative undies? Something told her that he would be just as enthusiastic about it as his older brothers.

"Maybe this was a bad idea," Samantha said, frowning.

Annie shook her head. "Forget we mentioned it, Kaylee."

Kaylee took a deep breath, then smiled at her two friends. "Actually, I think..." She giggled nervously. "...I'd like to see if Colt has the same appreciation for lingerie that his brothers have."

Samantha laughed. "Then let's go see what we can find that will knock that man's socks off."

An hour later Kaylee walked out of the mall carrying several bags with the Sleek and Sassy Lady logo on them. Colt had given her his credit card, but she'd used her own money for the lingerie. She wasn't about to use his card for her underwear. Some things were highly personal and sexy undies were one of them.

"I really like that white lace teddy you bought," Annie said, juggling her own bags as she dug for the keys to her SUV. "As soon as I have the baby I think I'll go back and buy one in royal blue."

"I like that emerald camisole and matching thong," Samantha added. "With your peaches-and-cream complexion and auburn hair, it's really going to look nice, Kaylee."

"I just hope I have the nerve to wear this stuff,"

Kaylee said, laughing. "It's all so different from my white cotton—"

"Granny panties," Samantha and Annie said at the same time.

"Well, I wasn't going to call them that," Kaylee said, laughing. "But I'd say that's a pretty accurate description."

"When are you going to spring your new look on Colt?" Samantha asked as they stored the packages in the back of Annie's SUV.

"I'm not sure, but it'll have to be soon." Kaylee felt a pang of sadness knife through her. "I'm due back at my job soon."

"You're not staying?" Samantha asked, clearly shocked. "But I thought—"

Kaylee shrugged one shoulder. She and Colt hadn't discussed what would happen when it was time for her to return to Oklahoma. "It's complicated."

"Are you going to the PBR finals with Colt?" Annie asked.

"I…can't." Kaylee shook her head and took a deep, steadying breath. "Not after what happened to Mitch."

Annie reached out to hug her. "I hope you're able to work it out between you two."

"I do, too," Samantha said, hugging Kaylee

when Annie released her. "We want you to stay on at the Lonetree."

Kaylee fought her threatening tears as they got into the SUV and drove from the mall parking lot onto the highway. She wanted nothing more than for her, Colt and Amber to be a family and to live on the Lonetree Ranch together.

But Colt was a bull rider, and although she couldn't bear the thought of something happening to him, she wouldn't ask him to give that up. It would be like asking him to give up who he was. And that was something she just couldn't do.

Chapter Nine

Colt waited impatiently while Kaylee went upstairs to put away some laundry she'd done as soon as she'd returned from shopping with Annie and Samantha. "This is one surprise I think your mommy's going to like," he told Amber as he helped her into her little jean jacket.

He frowned as he glanced toward the stairs. What could be taking Kaylee so long? She'd told him she'd be right back, but that had been fifteen minutes ago.

When she finally walked across the loft area, then started down the stairs, she was smiling. "You both look quite smug. Were you waiting on me for a reason?"

Nodding, Colt caught her around the waist and pulled her to him. "We've missed you something awful," he said, giving her a quick kiss.

"I missed you, too." She smiled. "What did you two do while I was gone, watch television the whole time?"

He shook his head. "Nope. We visited with Morgan and Brant for a while this morning—"

"But I thought they were supposed to be watching the boys," Kaylee said, frowning.

"They had Bettylou Milford baby-sit while they brought…er, ran an errand for me." He shrugged nonchalantly in an effort to dismiss the importance of their visit.

"Doggie," Amber said, grinning.

"Did you see a doggie?" Kaylee asked, smiling at their daughter.

"Yes," Amber said, shaking her head negatively.

Colt was thankful Kaylee had no idea that Amber was referring to the horse his brothers had brought over earlier. To keep her from asking questions, he hurried on. "After Brant and Morgan left, Amber and I made peanut butter and jelly sandwiches and watched the veggie show."

"Mato," Amber said, holding out her arms for him to pick her up.

Colt swung her up to sit on his right forearm. Holding Kaylee and his daughter, he was once again struck by the feeling that his life was more complete than it had ever been.

"Why does Amber have her jacket on?" Kaylee asked suddenly. "Were you two going somewhere?"

"Yep." He couldn't stop his ear-to-ear grin. "And we're taking you with us."

Kaylee laughed. "Where are we going?"

Colt winked at Amber as he put her down then took her little hand in his. "Oh, just out to the barn."

"Born," Amber said, giggling. "Doggie."

Reaching for Kaylee's hand, he led them out the door and down the porch steps. "I want you to close your eyes, Kaylee."

"Another surprise?" she asked, raising one perfect eyebrow.

"Yes. But this time, I promise you're going to like it."

She gave him a smile that made him weak in the knees. "You're that sure, huh?"

"Yep." He rocked back on his heels. "Now, close your eyes." He waited until she'd done as he'd requested, then started leading her toward the barn. "Don't open them until I tell you to."

"This isn't something that's going to jump out at me, is it?" she asked, her tone cautious.

"Nope." When they entered the barn, he led her and Amber over to the two saddled horses, standing tied to the outside of a stall. "Okay, honey, you can open your eyes."

He couldn't stop grinning as he watched Kaylee apprehensively open one eye, then the other.

She blinked as if she couldn't quite believe what she was seeing. "Oh my God, Colt!" She covered her mouth with both hands, then turned to stare at him, her eyes wide. "Where did you get…I mean how did you find…" Her voice trailed off as her eyes filled with tears. Throwing her arms around his neck, she kissed his cheek. "I can't believe you found my horse."

He put his arm around her waist and held her to him. "I take it you like the surprise?"

"Oh, Colt, thank you for finding her," Kaylee said, kissing him again before she pulled away to approach the buckskin.

"Doggie," Amber said, pointing to the horses.

Picking Amber up, Colt laughed as he untied the buckskin mare and the bay gelding, then handed the mare's reins to Kaylee. "No, pixie. These are horses, and when you get old enough, Daddy's going to get you one, too."

"I can't wait to ride my horse again," Kaylee said, patting the mare's neck as they led the two animals out of the barn. When she turned and kissed him again, he decided it would have been worth twice what he'd had to pay for the mare just to see Kaylee this happy.

"Go ahead and mount up," he said, unable to stop grinning. "Amber and I are right behind you."

Lifting his daughter onto the back of the gelding, he put his boot in the stirrup and swung up onto the saddle. Settling Amber on his lap, he wrapped his arm around her little body, then flicked the reins. The bay took off at a slow walk, sending Amber into a fit of giggles.

"You like riding with Mommy and Daddy?" Colt asked as he and Kaylee rode out of the yard and into the pasture to the west of the barn.

"No," Amber said, nodding her head.

"Colt, would you mind if I—"

"Go right ahead, honey," he said, knowing that Kaylee wanted to put the mare through her paces.

Kaylee immediately nudged the mare into a canter, then, giving the horse her head, raced across the open meadow toward the slow-moving stream on the other side of the valley. She was a very accomplished horsewoman and it was clear she was having the time of her life. And he was having the time of his life watching her.

Her long auburn hair was in attractive disarray and her cheeks were pink from the wind in her face. But it was her obvious happiness that tightened his chest with emotion. She was happier than he'd seen her since before Mitch died.

Colt smiled. He could spend an entire lifetime and never get tired of making Kaylee happy.

Sucking in a sharp breath, he pulled the bay to a halt. Had he fallen in love with Kaylee?

His heart pounded against his ribs. He'd always liked her and when he'd realized that she'd grown into a beautiful woman, he'd desired her. But love?

He'd known for years that she'd had a crush on him, and although he'd been extremely attracted to her, he'd always put a clamp on his feelings. That is, until that night three years ago.

Thinking about that night, he'd convinced himself that he'd taken off the next morning because of feeling guilty and ashamed for taking advantage of her. But had he really been running from himself? Had he been in love with her then?

As he continued to stare at Kaylee riding the mare, a slow grin spread across his face. Hell, truth to tell, he'd always loved her. He'd just been too damned blind to see it.

"Amber, your daddy's been a fool," he said, kissing the top of her little head. "But now that he's come to his senses, he's going to make up for lost time with your mommy."

Amber pointed to Kaylee, riding toward them. "Mommy, doggie."

Feeling younger and happier than he had in a long time, Colt laughed out loud. "One of these days I'll get you a horse and a dog, too, little pixie. But right now, Daddy's got to find the perfect time to tell your mommy what an idiot he's been and how he'd like to spend the rest of his life telling her how much he loves her."

"I can't believe how out of shape I am," Kaylee muttered as she straightened the kitchen.

It seemed as if every muscle from her waist down had decided to rebel. But as much as she hurt, it had felt absolutely wonderful to be riding her mare again. She hadn't realized how much she'd missed feeling the wind in her hair and the graceful power of a horse moving beneath her.

Tears filled her eyes when she thought of how considerate Colt's gesture had been. He'd known how much the horse meant to her. It had been the last thing Mitch had given her before his death and it had broken her heart to have to sell the animal. But now that Colt owned the mare, maybe she'd get to ride the horse occasionally, whenever she brought Amber to the Lonetree for a visit.

Thoughts of going back home caused her chest to tighten. She hadn't wanted to come to the Lonetree because she'd feared falling in love with Colt again. She almost laughed out loud. The truth of the matter was, she'd never stopped loving him.

But even if, by some miracle, he'd fallen head over heels in love with her, Kaylee didn't see them having a future together. Not as long as he continued to ride bulls. Just the thought of him being hurt or…

A chill ran through her. She couldn't bring herself to think about the worst that could happen.

Two strong arms suddenly wrapped around her from behind and pulled her back against a wide chest. "What are you thinking about, honey?"

She closed her eyes to block out the disturbing thought before she turned in the circle of Colt's arms to smile up at him. "I'm thinking about how much I appreciate you finding my horse, and how wonderful it was to be riding her again." She winced when her calf muscle cramped. "Even if my legs don't agree."

His deep blue gaze held her captive. "Pretty sore, huh?"

Groaning, she nodded. "I'm discovering muscles I forgot I had."

"Why don't you go upstairs and soak in the Jacuzzi?" he asked, brushing his lips lightly over hers.

Time in a whirlpool sounded like heaven to Kaylee, but she still had things to do. "I wish I could. But I need to get Amber ready for bed."

"Why don't you relax this evening and let me get her settled down for the night?" he asked, nuzzling the column of her neck.

Shivers of excitement coursed through her from the feel of his warm breath and lips moving over her sensitive skin. "D-do you think you can handle her bath?" she asked, trying to form a coherent answer. She was tempted by the idea of soaking some of the soreness from her aching muscles, but Colt had never dealt with a two-year-old at bath time. "There are times when giving her a bath can be a real trial."

"Hey, I ride bulls for a living." He chuckled. "How hard can it be to get one little girl into bed for the night?"

"It might prove more difficult than you think," Kaylee said, ignoring his reference to his job. She didn't want to think about that now. He was holding her and that was all that mattered.

"Up, Daddy."

Colt bent to pick up Amber. "Why don't we get her ready for bed together?" Grinning, he added, "Then I can help you with your bath."

Kaylee's cheeks heated and her insides felt as if they'd turned to warm pudding at his suggestion. "We'll see."

"Hey, no fair, pixie," Colt said, looking down at the wet spot spreading across his shirt.

"Daddy wet," Amber said happily. She gave him a grin that melted his heart, then slapped the top of her bathwater again with her hand.

This time the splash covered Colt's face. "Kaylee!"

"Problems?"

He turned to see her casually leaning one shoulder against the door frame, a big smile on her pretty face. "Why didn't you tell me our daughter likes water sports?" he asked, reaching for the fluffy towel hanging on a rack beside the tub.

"And miss the fun of watching Amber teach her daddy what bath time is like with a two-year-old?"

Grinning, she shook her head. "I don't think so, cowboy."

He wiped the water dripping off his face. "Is it always like this?"

"Oh, sometimes it's even worse," Kaylee said, laughing.

He gazed down at his happy daughter. "You wouldn't splash me more than you already have, would you?"

As if in answer, Amber kicked both legs and slapped the water with both hands, proving just how much worse giving her a bath could get.

"Okay. Okay. I get the idea," he said, laughing.

By the time Colt lifted his happy little girl from the bathtub and handed her to Kaylee, there wasn't a dry thread on him from his collar to his belt. "I'm soaked to the bone."

"I'll take pity on you and rock her to sleep," Kaylee said, toweling Amber dry, then pulling a pink nightgown over her little head. "Why don't you go find a dry shirt to put on?"

"Sounds good to me." He got to his feet and kissed Amber. "'Night, little pixie." Walking to the bathroom door, he turned back to grin at Kaylee. "I think from now on, I'll let you give her a bath and I'll do the rocking."

As he walked down the hall to his room, her

laughter sounded like music to his ears. She was having a grand old time at his expense. And he loved every minute of it.

By the time he entered his room, Colt had his shirt unsnapped. It was drenched and, entering the master bath to drape it over the towel rack, he eyed the oversize Jacuzzi. What was the use of having a bathtub two people could fit into if he didn't share?

Without hesitation, he turned on the polished gold faucet, set the dimmer switch on the lights to a muted setting, then sat on the side of the tub to pull off his boots. Shucking his jeans, socks and boxer briefs, he turned on the jets, climbed into the water and lounged against the back.

A few minutes later, he smiled when he heard Kaylee softly call his name as she entered his bedroom. "Colt, where are you?"

"In here, honey."

When Kaylee walked into the bathroom, he motioned for her to join him. "I decided to get the water ready for you."

"I thought I was the one getting the use of the Jacuzzi this evening," she said, giving him a smile that made him feel as if the water temperature had risen by about ten degrees.

"I'm a man of my word, honey," he said,

grinning. "I told you I'd help you with your bath, and that's just what I intend to do."

He watched her nervously nibble at her lower lip for a moment before she took a deep breath and reached to pull her T-shirt from the waistband of her jeans. "Have Morgan or Brant ever mentioned Samantha and Annie's shopping trips?"

"No, but they sure seem to like when the women mention a trip to the mall." Frowning, he shook his head. "But I don't want to talk about—"

He stopped short and sat up straight when Kaylee pulled her purple shirt over her head and tossed it aside. Until now, when he'd taken her clothes off of her, she'd worn a plain white bra with no frills. But tonight she was wearing the skimpiest scrap of black lace and satin he'd ever seen.

"Is that—" he had to stop to clear the rust from his throat "—something you bought today?"

She nodded. "Do you like it?"

"Hell, yes."

He started to tell her that he'd like it better off of her, but her smile promised that the show wasn't over yet. Settling back against the tub, he looked forward to what she had planned next. To his delight, he didn't have long to wait.

Watching her unbutton the top of her jeans, then

slowly slide the zipper down was heaven and hell rolled into one for him. His eyes widened and he knew for certain he'd never seen anything quite as provocative as the look she gave him when she pushed the denim down her slender legs. But catching sight of the triangle of lace and satin barely covering her feminine secrets, Colt wasn't sure his eyes weren't going to pop right out of his head. Made to match her bra, the set was enough to bury a man with any kind of heart problems.

"H-honey, where did you get those?" he finally managed to ask.

"The Sleek and Sassy Lady Lingerie Boutique."

"I think that's my favorite store," he said, meaning it.

"Annie and Samantha said Brant and Morgan have a deep appreciation for the items the store carries," she said, making a slow turn for him to get the full effect of what she was wearing.

"Oh, yeah. I'm appreciating the hell out of it right now." He swallowed hard when he realized the little triangle showed more of her delightful bottom than it hid. "Damn, Kaylee, that little patch of satin could be considered a lethal weapon."

She smiled. "Now do you understand why your brothers like for their wives to visit the mall?"

Feeling as if his blood pressure was reaching the danger zone, he nodded.

As he watched, she touched the clasp between her breasts. "I have several new sets of matching under things—" she unfastened the closure, then slipped the thin straps down her arms and tossed the minuscule scrap on top of her shirt "—in various colors and styles."

If he could have found his voice, he would have told her that he was looking forward to seeing her model each set. Unfortunately he couldn't seem to get his vocal cords to work. But when she hooked her thumbs in the waistband of the panties and slowly pulled them down, a groan rumbled up from deep in his chest and his heart damn near thumped a hole right through his rib cage.

Colt closed his eyes and tried to drag some much needed air into his lungs. He was so turned on that if he didn't slow down, he was going to blow a gasket right then and there.

"Those stores should get some kind of special award for being a man's best friend," he said, breathing deeply in an effort to hang on to his control.

When he felt Kaylee step into the tub, he opened his eyes and helped her to sit between his legs. Wrapping his arms around her, he pulled her back to lie against him. He gritted his teeth at the feel of her smooth skin pressed to his chest, her bottom nestled against the part of him that was changing so rapidly it made him light-headed.

She sighed. "The Sleek and Sassy Lady Lingerie Boutique chain might be a man's best friend, but this whirlpool is mine."

He kissed the side of her head as he put his hands on her thighs and massaged her tight muscles. "Is that feeling a little better, honey?" he asked when he felt her begin to relax.

"Mmm."

The water made her smooth skin slippery and he easily slid his hands up her thighs and over her abdomen to cup her full breasts. His body throbbed from the feel of her pressed against the most vulnerable part of him. The tightening of her nipples as he teased them only increased his arousal.

"Kaylee?"

When she turned her head to look up at him, he captured her mouth with his and, tracing her lips with his tongue, he slipped it inside to taste the sweetness that was uniquely Kaylee. He loved holding her, kissing her. Hell, he just plain loved everything about her. And he fully intended to tell her so when he had enough of his wits about him to form words.

But at the moment he was lost to anything but the feel of her filling his hands, the taste of her passion and the sound of her labored breathing. The knowledge that she wanted him as much as he wanted her fueled the fire building within him.

Leisurely sliding one hand down her wet body to the apex of her thighs, he parted her to gently stroke the tiny nub nestled within. Her moan of pleasure vibrating against his lips heightened his own excitement, and Colt felt blood surge through his veins, tightening his body, urging him to once again make her his.

Breaking the kiss, he whispered, "Turn around, Kaylee. I want to love you."

"But—"

He chuckled. "Trust me, honey. It can be done."

To his satisfaction, she didn't even hesitate as she maneuvered herself around to face him. He scooted forward, then helped her drape her legs over his thighs.

"See, it's not as difficult as you thought," he said, pressing a kiss to her perfect lips, her chin and her collarbone.

When he continued to nibble his way down the slope of her breast, Colt felt a tremor run through her a moment before she circled his neck with her arms and curled her legs around his hips. Her head fell back to give him better access. Taking advantage of the position, he took her nipple in his mouth to suck her gently.

"Colt, I…need—"

Lifting his head, he watched her slowly open her eyes. The passion and love he saw in the violet depths robbed him of breath.

Without a word, Colt lowered his mouth to hers as he lifted her to him and in one smooth motion joined their bodies. The feel of Kaylee surrounding him, the sound of her soft sigh and the taste of desire on her sweet lips blocked out all reason and left him with nothing but the ability to complete the act of loving her.

He held her hips and guided her in a rocking motion that quickly had him gritting his teeth against the urgent need to race for the peak. His body throbbed and his heart pounded, but he refused to give in to his own satisfaction before he was assured he'd helped Kaylee find hers.

When he felt her inner feminine muscles tighten around him, signaling that she was close to finding her completion, he reached between them to stroke her. The moment his finger touched her, she went completely still, then, whispering his name, he felt her body quiver around him as she was released from the exquisite tension inside her.

Only then did he give in to the storm raging inside him and surrender the tight hold he had on his control. Surging into her one final time, he groaned as he emptied his essence deep within her warm depths.

As the whirlpool jets worked their magic and lulled them back to the realm of reality, he held Kaylee close. He'd done the unthinkable. He'd failed to protect her. Much the way he'd done three years ago, he'd let his need to brand her as his override his good sense.

But as he caressed her soft body, it came as no small surprise that he wasn't sorry. Nothing would please him more than to create another child with Kaylee, of seeing her belly grow round as his baby grew inside her.

Unfortunately he wasn't sure how she felt about giving Amber a little brother or sister. Nor had they discussed their future together.

He was sure she loved him and there wasn't a doubt in his mind that he loved her. But knowing how he made his living, would she be willing to marry him?

"Kaylee?"

"Mmm."

"Do you have any idea how much I love you?"

He heard her soft intake of breath a moment before she leaned back to gaze up at him. "Y-you love me?"

Unable to stop grinning, Colt nodded. "I always have. I was just too big of a fool to admit it."

Tears filled her pretty violet eyes. "Oh, Colt. I've loved you from the first minute I set eyes on you."

His heart soared. Everything was going to be all right. They'd work something out. They had to. There was no way he was going to take a chance on screwing this up a second time.

Kissing her creamy shoulder, he smiled. "Let's get out of the tub, honey. We need to talk."

Chapter Ten

"Kaylee, I want you and Amber to go with me to the PBR finals in Vegas."

Sitting in the middle of Colt's bed, Kaylee gazed into his vivid blue eyes and fought the urge to tell him that she would go with him. Pulling her chenille robe more tightly around her, she shivered violently. She loved him more than life itself, but he was asking something of her that she just couldn't do.

"Colt, I love you. I'll always love you." She shook her head. "But I can't watch you ride bulls."

He took her hands in his. "Honey, I know you're

afraid something might happen to me. But you've always known what I did for a living and you accepted it."

"Th-that was before." She pulled away from him and got out of bed before his touch and the beseeching expression on his handsome face caused her to weaken.

"Honey, I'm close to winning the championship," Colt argued. "I can't quit now."

Pacing the length of his room, she tried to explain how she felt. "Colt, I would never ask you to stop being a bull rider. It's a part of you—it's who you are." Feeling as if she might choke on the emotions welling up inside of her, she stopped to catch her breath. "But I can't bear the thought of watching you being taken out of an arena like Mitch was that night in Houston."

"Kaylee, you know I'm always careful. I keep myself in good shape and—"

"Mitch was in as good a shape as any of the riders and he was always careful," she said, impatiently wiping at a tear running down her cheek. "And look what happened to him."

"But—"

She shook her head. "Colt, I couldn't survive standing in another hospital waiting room while some doctor tells me there's nothing he could do to save your life." Chills racked her body and she couldn't stop shaking. "I just can't…do that again," she whispered.

He got out of bed and, walking over to her, wrapped her in his strong arms. "Kaylee, life doesn't come with any kind of guarantee. Something could happen to me no matter what I do for a living."

"I…know that," she said, trying desperately to stop her teeth from chattering. "But we both know the high price that riding bulls can cost." The feel of his warm chest pressed to her cheek and the steady beat of his heart should have been reassuring, but her fears were too strong and ran too deep.

"Honey, I love you and Amber and I want you both with me," he said, rubbing his hands soothingly up and down her spine. "It's important to me for you to be there with me." He kissed the top of her head. "Besides, you won't be alone. Morgan, Samantha and Annie will be sitting in the stands with you, and Brant will be down in the arena with me."

Tears ran down her cheeks as she pulled from his arms and started to back out of the room. "Colt, don't you understand? It doesn't matter who's with me or how many people there are around me, they couldn't stop something from happening to you."

"Kaylee, honey, wait—"

"No." She stood in the doorway, her knees feeling as if they were going to buckle at any moment. "You've always been, and will always be, my biggest weakness, Colt. I love you more than you'll ever know. But I can't watch you ride." She took a deep breath, then rushed on before she had a chance to change her mind. "Your shoulder is healed now, and you really don't need me—"

"I'll always need you, Kaylee," he said, taking a step toward her.

"I told you I would help you regain the use of your arm," she said quietly. "And I've done that. But I also told you I wouldn't help you get ready for the finals."

"Kaylee, don't do this," he said, taking another step toward her.

She could tell by his expression that he'd anticipated what she was about to say next. But she couldn't let that sway her. Her survival depended on it.

"Amber and I will be leaving tomorrow to go back to Oklahoma City. I'll get Annie or Samantha to drive me down to Laramie to catch a commuter flight to Denver."

Before he could respond, she turned and walked down the hall to the room she'd shared with Amber. She knew she was being a coward. But she really didn't have a choice.

She would be devastated if something tragic happened to Colt at any time. But Kaylee knew for certain that if she had to witness him being fatally injured the way she had Mitch, she'd never be able to survive. And surviving was something she had to do at all costs.

She had a little girl to think of now. Amber was depending on her. And Kaylee wasn't about to let Amber down.

Colt stood behind the bucking chutes as the bulls were being loaded into the enclosures on the last day of the Professional Bull Riders championship. He'd had an exceptional finals and was currently tied with another rider to win the season title.

But even if he achieved his goal and won the damn championship, he knew for certain the victory would be a hollow one. Hell, his whole life had been nothing but an empty void for the past two weeks—ever since Kaylee and Amber had gone back to Oklahoma.

"You ready to go out there and kick Kamikaze's

butt once and for all?" Brant asked, referring to the bull Colt had never been able to ride.

Colt shrugged as he buckled his bat-wing chaps. "It's just another ride."

Dressed in the bullfighter's uniform of shorts and matching jersey, Brant rotated his shoulders to stay loose. "Just keep your head out there, little brother. You can take off for Oklahoma City tomorrow morning to see if you can straighten things out with Kaylee."

"What makes you think I'll be going to Oklahoma?" Colt asked, pulling on his riding glove.

"Two reasons," Brant said, sounding so certain that Colt felt like belting him one.

"What would those be?" he asked, knowing his brother would tell him anyway.

"Number one, you've been like a bear with a sore paw ever since Kaylee left. You might as well give it up and admit that nothing is more important than being with the woman you love," Brant said, bending to adjust his knee pads. When he straightened to his full height, he wore a knowing expression. "Take it from me, bro, if you don't come to that conclusion your mood is only going to get worse."

"Since when did you become an expert on affairs of the heart?" Colt asked sourly.

Brant grinned. "If you'll remember, I went through something similar with Annie before I came to my senses. I was one miserable SOB until I decided there was nothing more important than being with her."

Colt glared at his brother. "That was different. You had some stupid idea that you and Annie didn't have anything in common."

Brant grinned and went on as if Colt hadn't said anything. "And the second reason I know you'll be going to Oklahoma City is because if you don't go on your own, Morgan and I are going to stuff you on the plane ourselves."

Before Colt could respond, Brant turned and jogged out into the arena.

As Colt watched his brother take his place in front of the bucking chutes, he thought about what Brant had said. He was miserable without Kaylee and Amber. They were his life, and a hell of a lot more important than riding two thousand pounds of pissed-off beef.

He shook his head. Kaylee had told him a bull rider was who he was, and he'd pretty much agreed with her. But they'd both been wrong. There was a hell of a lot more to him than that.

Instead of looking at winning a championship buckle to define who he was, he should have considered what else he had going for him. He was a damned good rancher, the father of a precious little girl and the man who loved Kaylee Simpson with all of his heart and soul.

Climbing the steps behind the chutes, Colt gazed down at the back of his old nemesis Kamikaze. He'd drawn the brindle bull many times in the past several years, and so far, the score was Kamikaze three, Colt zero. In fact, the bull had been the one Colt had been bucked off of the night he'd broken his collarbone.

"As far as I'm concerned, we might as well make it four to zero," Colt said, deciding that riding bulls wasn't worth losing Kaylee. "Hey, Jim?"

"What's that, hotshot?" Jim Elliott, the time-keeper asked.

"I'm not going to—"

"Colt," a familiar female voice called from somewhere behind him.

He stopped short of telling the man that he wouldn't be riding Kamikaze. Turning, he scanned the crowd of people milling around behind the chutes. Just when he thought he'd imagined hearing her, he spotted Kaylee and Amber standing not twenty feet away.

Afraid he might be hallucinating, he jumped down from the platform and rushed over to wrap his arms around them. "What are you doing here, honey?"

"Daddy," Amber said, poking her little finger into his protective black leather vest.

"That's right, little pixie," he said, kissing her baby-soft cheek.

"I couldn't stay away," Kaylee said, hugging him back. "If something happened and I wasn't with you, I don't think I could live with myself."

He shook his head as he gazed down into her pretty violet eyes. "It's no longer an issue," he said, brushing his lips over hers, then kissing the top of Amber's head. He couldn't get enough of holding them, of letting them know how much he loved them. "I was just getting ready to tell Jim that I'm turning out. I'm not going to ride Kamikaze."

She looked confused. "Why would you do that?"

"Because I love you," he said honestly. "You and Amber mean more to me than anything else and I know it upsets you to think about me riding."

"Colt, I love you, too." She gave him a kiss that damned near knocked him to his knees, then shook her head. "I can't believe I'm going to say this, but I don't want you to turn out. I want you to ride that bull."

It was his turn to look incredulous. "What made you change your mind, honey?"

"I want you to ride because I love you and I don't ever want you to have any regrets." She shook her head. "I don't want you to wonder if you could have won the championship if you'd only taken this ride."

"Wakefield, you're up next," Jim called.

Colt held up his hand. "Just a minute, Jim." Turning back to Kaylee, he searched her face. "Are you sure, honey? Say the word, and I'll take the turn-out."

He watched her take a deep breath, then meet his questioning gaze head-on. "Yes, Colt. If Mitch were here right now, he'd kick your buns if he heard you were about to turn down a bull you could win it all on."

"Last call, Wakefield," Jim shouted above the noisy crowd.

Colt stared at Kaylee for a moment longer, then, pressing his lips to hers, he smiled. "I'll be right back, honey."

He took the steps to the raised platform behind the bucking chutes two at a time, then stepped over the side of the tubular steel enclosure. Slipping his mouth guard into place to protect his teeth during the jarring ride, he settled himself onto the brindle bull's broad back and put his gloved hand, palm up, into the bull rope's grip.

Kamikaze tensed beneath him in anticipation of making Colt sorry he'd ever been born, but he ignored the animal's building rage. As he and some of the other riders pulled the flat braided rope snug around the bull's thick body, he was more determined than ever to keep himself from being hurt or worse. Kaylee was counting on him, and he'd go through hell and back before he let her down.

Once Colt was satisfied that the binding was as tight as it was going to get, he placed the long end of the rope in his palm and wound it around his hand several times, effectively tying himself to Kamikaze's back. Closing his fingers into a fist around the wrap, he pushed his Resistol down on his head with his free hand, took a deep breath and gave a quick nod to signal that he was ready for the ride to begin. Just as he expected, when the gate swung wide, Kamikaze exploded from the chute and out into the arena with all the energy of a keg of dynamite.

With his left arm extended above his head for

balance, he gripped the animal's sides with his thighs and concentrated on staying with the bull jump for jump. True to style, Kamikaze took two high leaps, then circled to the left and settled into a tight, bucking spin.

Every lurching move of the two thousand pounds of pure fury pulled mercilessly on his right arm and made Colt feel as if someone had lifted him high into the air then slammed him down with the force of a wrecking ball. Directing all of his energy toward hanging on to the rope and keeping his body aligned with the center of the bull's back, Colt tried to anticipate Kamikaze's next move.

Adrenaline raced through his veins as he focused on every nuance of the ride and he knew the moment the eight-second whistle blew that he'd finally bested his nemesis. Reaching down between his legs, he released his hand from the bull rope and jumped clear of the angry animal.

Kaylee clutched Amber and held her breath as she watched Colt successfully ride Kamikaze. She prayed that he wouldn't hang up in the rope or fall as he landed on the dirt floor of the arena when it came time for his dismount. But to her relief, Colt managed to stay on his feet and sprint to safety, while Brant and the other two bullfighters distracted the big, ugly bull.

Watching Brant wrap Colt in a congratulatory bear hug, then seeing the ear-to-ear grin on his face, she knew she'd made the right choice in coming to the finals. She'd spent two agonizing weeks vacillating between staying in Oklahoma City or being at his side. And in the end, she'd known that she really never had any choice in the matter. When you loved someone as much as she loved Colt, you simply accepted that person and didn't try to change them.

She wasn't sure how she was going to manage watching Colt climb on the back of a bull every weekend for the next several years, knowing that at any time something could go terribly wrong. But in the past two weeks she had quickly reached the conclusion that living with the fear was something she was going to have to get used to. It couldn't be worse than the debilitating loneliness of living without him in her life at all.

"Daddy," Amber said, holding her arms out to Colt when he slipped through the arena gate and made his way to them through the crowd of well-wishers.

Happy for him, Kaylee's eyes filled with moisture as he lifted Amber to sit on his forearm, then put his other arm around her shoulders. "You did it, Colt. You won."

Still grinning, he nodded. "I guess I did." When a tear slipped down her cheek, Colt's smile disappeared instantly as he wiped it away with his finger. "Honey, are you all right?"

She nodded. "I'm just happy you won and relieved you're all right."

"Kaylee, there's something I want to tell you—" At the sound of his name being announced over the loudspeaker, he smiled apologetically. "Dang, I need to—"

Reaching up to kiss his lean cheek, she smiled and reached for Amber. "Go accept your award. You've earned it. We'll be right here waiting for you."

"Honey, you don't know how good that sounds to me." He gave her a quick kiss, then turned and walked back out into the arena for the presentation of the trophies.

Kaylee listened as the announcer presented the championship cup and an oversize check to the bull rider who had the most points for the season. The cowboy thanked the good Lord above for blessing him with an injury-free season and the fans for their support. Then the announcer turned to Colt and handed him a big gold buckle and a check for a huge amount of money for winning the finals. Colt thanked everyone, then asked the man holding the microphone if he could make an announcement.

"Well, sure...I guess that would be okay," the man said, wearing a bewildered expression.

"I've had a great career with the PBR," Colt said, his voice booming across the now eerily quiet arena. "And I couldn't have asked for this season to have ended any better." Kaylee watched Colt take a deep breath. "That's why I'm going out a winner. It's time to hang up my chaps and spurs and join the ranks of the retired."

The crowd seemed to emit a collective gasp a moment before they gave him a standing ovation.

Tears blurred Kaylee's vision. Colt was giving up his career as a bull rider. He was no longer going to tempt fate.

By the time he pushed his way through the crowd and made it back to her, she couldn't stop trembling. "Why, Colt?"

Smiling, he hugged her and Amber. "Because you two are more important to me than anything else."

She shook her head. "Please don't quit because of me," she said, shaking her head. "I don't want you having any regrets."

"I don't, honey." He took Amber from her, then draped his arm across her shoulders and started walking toward the staging area behind the bucking chutes. "I've won the finals and made a good showing every year since I joined the PBR. I have nothing left to prove to anyone, but how much I love you and our daughter." He bent his head to kiss her cheek. "Besides, I don't want to be so banged up that I miss one night of making love with you for the rest of my life."

Kaylee's heart skipped a beat. "For the rest of your life?"

"Yep." When he stopped walking and turned to face her, the love she saw shining in his incredible blue eyes stole her breath. "Will you do me the honor of being my wife, Kaylee Simpson? Will you live with me on the Lonetree Ranch, allow me to be a full-time daddy to Amber and let me give you more babies?"

"Y-yes," Kaylee said, closing her eyes to the light-headed feeling sweeping over her.

"Honey, are you okay?" Colt asked, taking hold of her arm to support her.

"I seem to get kind of woozy when I get excited lately," she said, frowning. "The only other time I was like this was when I got pregnant with…" Her voice trailed off as she stared up at the man she'd loved all of her life.

"The whirlpool," he said, grinning. He pulled her forward and kissed her until her head swam.

"Daddy, Mommy," Amber said, wrapping her little arms around both of their necks.

"Would you like a new baby brother or sister, little pixie?" Colt asked.

"Yes," Amber said, nodding her head affirmatively.

"Hey, she got it right," he said, laughing. His expression suddenly turned serious. "Kaylee, how do you feel about having another baby?"

Smiling, she gazed up at the man and child she loved with all her heart. "I'd love to have another baby with raven hair and Wakefield blue eyes."

His grin returned. "Let's go find a chapel and make it official."

"No," she said, shaking her head.

"What do you mean, no?" he asked, looking as if that was the last thing he'd expected her to say. "No, you've changed your mind and you don't want to marry me? Or, no you don't want to get married in Vegas?"

She reached up to smooth the frown marring his forehead. "No, I don't want to get married in Las Vegas. If you don't mind, I'd like to have our wedding at the Lonetree. That's where we'll live, and where I'd like to start our life together."

"I like the sound of that, honey." He brushed his lips over hers. "I love you, Kaylee."

"And I love you, cowboy. More than you'll ever know."

Epilogue

Christmas Eve

"I feel like I'm about to choke to death," Colt said, tugging at the collar of his dress shirt.

Brant chuckled. "You're just being paid back for making fun of me and Morgan when we stood at the bottom of these stairs a few years back, waiting for our brides."

"What could be taking so long?" Colt asked, ready to climb the steps and escort Kaylee downstairs himself.

"It's my guess Annie and Samantha are fussing

over Kaylee's dress, or her hair, or anything else they can think of to fuss over." Brant shrugged. "Once you're married awhile, you'll come to realize that women like to make a fuss over the least little detail."

"They should have had plenty of time to get things ready," Colt said, frowning.

Annie and Samantha had insisted that Kaylee and Amber spend last night at the homestead with them, while Colt, Brant, Morgan and his nephews spent the night at Colt's. They'd said it was necessary because the groom wasn't supposed to see the bride until she walked down the aisle. He didn't know anything about that kind of wedding protocol, he just missed the hell out of Kaylee and couldn't wait to see her again.

When Samantha appeared at the top of the stairs, holding Amber's hand, Colt smiled. His daughter looked like a little pixie in her red-velvet-and-white-lace dress.

"Daddy," she said, pointing to him as Samantha helped her down the steps. Once they got to the bottom she held up her arms for him to pick her up. "Up, Daddy. Up."

Without hesitation, Colt bent and swung her up to sit on his forearm. It thrilled Colt at how fast Amber had become a Daddy's girl.

"Are you ready to help Mommy and Daddy get married?" he asked, kissing her cheek.

Nodding, she smiled. "Yes."

"Get ready, little brother," Brant said when Annie walked across the loft area and stopped at the top of the stairs. "You're about to join the ranks of the blissfully hitched."

Colt grinned. "I never in a million years thought I'd ever say this, but it can't be soon enough for me."

Samantha turned on the CD player, and as she herded his nephews over to stand by the large Christmas tree on the other side of the fireplace, the country group Lonestar's lead singer began to sing about being amazed by the woman he loved. Watching Annie descend the stairs, Colt waited until Brant offered his arm, then escorted her over to stand in front of the big stone fireplace where Preacher Hill from the Methodist church down in Bear Creek stood, waiting to perform the marriage ceremony.

"Mommy pitty," Amber said suddenly, pointing to the loft.

When he glanced up, Colt sucked in a sharp breath. Kaylee stood at the top of the stairs, her hand tucked in the crook of Morgan's arm. Dressed in a white satin-and-lace wedding gown, her shiny auburn hair piled in soft curls on top of her head, she was absolutely beautiful.

"Yes, Amber," Colt said, stepping forward. "Your mommy is the prettiest woman I've ever seen."

At the bottom of the steps, Morgan smiled and placed Kaylee's hand in Colt's. He kissed Kaylee's cheek, then patted Colt on the shoulder.

"Take good care of each other," he said, then took his place with Samantha and the boys by the Christmas tree.

"Are you ready to become Mrs. Colt Wakefield?" he asked, grinning.

The smile Kaylee gave him sent his temperature sky-high. "I've been ready for this moment all of my life."

Colt grinned. "So have I, honey. I just didn't realize it."

With Kaylee on one arm and Amber in the other, Colt walked them over to the big stone fireplace for Preacher Hill to make their union complete.

Three hours later, after putting Amber to bed upstairs, Kaylee and Colt sat on the couch in their living room, holding each other. A cozy fire blazed in the fireplace, but other than the twinkling lights on the Christmas tree, the room was romantically dim.

"Colt?"

"What, honey?"

"I have an early Christmas present for you," she said, rising to retrieve a brightly wrapped box from beneath the tree.

"But I thought we were going to wait until tomorrow morning to exchange presents," Colt said, frowning.

Kaylee shook her head. "I'd rather give this to you now."

She nibbled on her lower lip as he turned the box over in his hands then shook it. "It's pretty light," he said, grinning. When he tore the wrapping away and lifted the box lid, he frowned. "What's this?"

"That's a copy of the ultrasound," she said, unable to stop smiling. "You know I had my second prenatal check yesterday."

Until the wedding, they hadn't seen each other since she, Annie and Samantha had returned from Laramie the afternoon before. And news like this just couldn't be shared over the phone.

"What did the doctor have to say?" Colt asked, frowning as he gazed at the paper in his hand. "Is everything all right?"

Grinning, she reached up to smooth the frown

from his brow with her fingertips, then pointed to the picture. "He said I'm as healthy as a horse. And so are the...babies."

"That's a re—" He stopped short. "What do you mean *babies?*"

Kaylee laughed at his shocked expression. "The doctor did this early ultrasound because he said I was getting pretty big for only being a couple of months along." She kissed his firm male lips. "We're having twins, cowboy."

A slow grin began to spread across his handsome face as he took her hand in his and kissed the wedding band on the third finger of her left hand. "Besides getting married, this is the best Christmas present I've ever received."

They held each other for some time before Colt spoke again. "If the twins are boys, would you mind if we named one of them Mitch?"

Tears filled her eyes at Colt's thoughtfulness. "I'd like that." She raised her head from his shoulder to gaze up at him. "I love you, Colt."

"And I love you, honey."

"I think this is the best Christmas ever," Kaylee said, snuggling closer.

"It's just the first of many special days, honey." Colt gave her a kiss that turned her insides to warm pudding, then stood and, smiling, held out his hand to help her up from the couch. "Now, let's go upstairs and let me show you how special the nights are going to be."

Without hesitation Kaylee put her hand in his, anxious to start their lives together as man and wife on their part of the Lonetree Ranch.

* * * * *

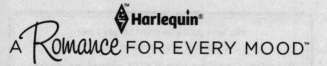

♦™ Harlequin®

A *Romance* FOR EVERY MOOD™

Discover more great romances from Harlequin® Books.

Whether you prefer romantic suspense, heartwarming or passionate novels, each and every month Harlequin has new books for you!

Use the coupon below and save $1.00 when you purchase 2 or more Harlequin® Books.

Available wherever books are sold, including most bookstores, supermarkets, drugstores and discount stores.

- ✂

$1.⁰⁰ OFF the purchase of 2 or more Harlequin® series-romance books.

Coupon valid until October 24, 2011. Redeemable at participating retail outlets in the U.S. and Canada only. Limit one coupon per customer.

52610022

Canadian Retailers: Harlequin Enterprises Limited will pay the face value of this coupon plus 10.25¢ if submitted by customer for this product only. Any other use constitutes fraud. Coupon is nonassignable. Void if taxed, prohibited or restricted by law. Consumer must pay any government taxes. Void if copied. Nielsen Clearing House ("NCH") customers submit coupons and proof of sales to Harlequin Enterprises Limited, P.O. Box 3000, Saint John, NB E2L 4L3, Canada. Non-NCH retailer—for reimbursement submit coupons and proof of sales directly to Harlequin Enterprises Limited, Retail Marketing Department, 225 Duncan Mill Rd., Don Mills, ON M3B 3K9, Canada.

65373 00076 2 (8100)0 11764

U.S. Retailers: Harlequin Enterprises Limited will pay the face value of this coupon plus 8¢ if submitted by customer for this product only. Any other use constitutes fraud. Coupon is nonassignable. Void if taxed, prohibited or restricted by law. Consumer must pay any government taxes. Void if copied. For reimbursement submit coupons and proof of sales directly to Harlequin Enterprises Limited, P.O. Box 880478, El Paso, TX 88588-0478, U.S.A. Cash value 1/100 cents.

and TM are trademarks owned and used by the trademark owner and/or its licensee.
2011 Harlequin Enterprises Limited

He was just the man to give her
what she was looking for....

New York Times and **USA TODAY** bestselling author

DIANA PALMER

returns with a classic tale of love, redemption
and new horizons.

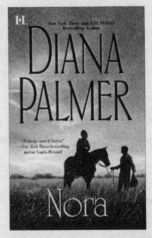

When innocent, wealthy Nora Marlowe came to visit the
Wild West, she was as wide-open to adventure as the vast Texas
horizon. Its rugged individualism—and dashing cowboys—suited
her romantic spirit. That is, until a certain cowboy decided to
take the elegant heiress down a notch!

Available now.

www.Harlequin.com

PHDP631

REQUEST YOUR FREE BOOKS!

2 FREE NOVELS
FROM THE ROMANCE COLLECTION
PLUS 2 FREE GIFTS!

YES! Please send me 2 FREE novels from the Romance Collection and my 2 FREE gifts (gifts are worth about $10). After receiving them, if I don't wish to receive any more books, I can return the shipping statement marked "cancel." If I don't cancel, I will receive 4 brand-new novels every month and be billed just $5.99 per book in the U.S. or $6.49 per book in Canada. That's a saving of at least 25% off the cover price. It's quite a bargain! Shipping and handling is just 50¢ per book in the U.S. and 75¢ per book in Canada.* I understand that accepting the 2 free books and gifts places me under no obligation to buy anything. I can always return a shipment and cancel at any time. Even if I never buy another book, the two free books and gifts are mine to keep forever.

194/394 MDN FELQ

Name _____ (PLEASE PRINT)

Address _____ Apt. #

City _____ State/Prov. _____ Zip/Postal Code

Signature (if under 18, a parent or guardian must sign)

Mail to the **Reader Service:**
IN U.S.A.: P.O. Box 1867, Buffalo, NY 14240-1867
IN CANADA: P.O. Box 609, Fort Erie, Ontario L2A 5X3

Not valid for current subscribers to the Romance Collection
or the Romance/Suspense Collection.

Want to try two free books from another line?
Call 1-800-873-8635 or visit www.ReaderService.com.

* Terms and prices subject to change without notice. Prices do not include applicable taxes. Sales tax applicable in N.Y. Canadian residents will be charged applicable taxes. Offer not valid in Quebec. This offer is limited to one order per household. All orders subject to credit approval. Credit or debit balances in a customer's account(s) may be offset by any other outstanding balance owed by or to the customer. Please allow 4 to 6 weeks for delivery. Offer available while quantities last.

Your Privacy—The Reader Service is committed to protecting your privacy. Our Privacy Policy is available online at www.ReaderService.com or upon request from the Reader Service.

We make a portion of our mailing list available to reputable third parties that offer products we believe may interest you. If you prefer that we not exchange your name with third parties, or if you wish to clarify or modify your communication preferences, please visit us at www.ReaderService.com/consumerschoice or write to us at Reader Service Preference Service, P.O. Box 9062, Buffalo, NY 14269. Include your complete name and address.

BESTSELLING AUTHOR COLLECTION

CLASSIC ROMANCES IN COLLECTIBLE VOLUMES

New York Times and *USA TODAY* bestselling author

JOAN JOHNSTON

Harriet Allistair was determined to prove that she could be a successful rancher—without Nathan Hazard. But could she? And did she really want to?

A Wolf in Sheep's Clothing

Available in August wherever books are sold.

PLUS, ENJOY THE BONUS STORY
***TELL ME YOUR SECRETS...* BY ACCLAIMED AUTHOR CARA SUMMERS, INCLUDED IN THIS 2-IN-1 VOLUME!**

www.Harlequin.com

NYTJJ0811

TM ♦ **Harlequin**®

A *Romance* FOR EVERY MOOD™

Experience the variety
of romances that
Harlequin has to offer...

CATINTROR

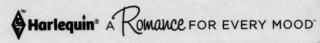

Harlequin® A *Romance* FOR EVERY MOOD™

HEART & HOME

Heartwarming romances where love can
happen right when you least expect it.

Harlequin® American Romance®
Lively stories about homes, families
and communities like the ones you know.
This is romance the all-American way!

Harlequin® Special Edition
A woman in her world—living and loving.
Celebrating the magic of creating a family
and developing romantic relationships.

Harlequin® Superromance®
Unexpected, exciting and emotional
stories about life and falling in love.

Look for these and many other Harlequin romance books wherever books are
sold, including most bookstores, supermarkets, drugstores and discount stores.

tryharlequin.com

HHCATR11

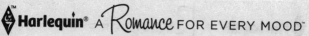

Harlequin® A *Romance* FOR EVERY MOOD™

PASSION

For a spicier, decidedly hotter read—
these are your destinations for romance!

Harlequin Desire®

Passionate and provocative stories
featuring rich, powerful heroes and
scandalous family sagas.

Harlequin® Blaze™

Fun, flirtatious and steamy books
that tell it like it is, inside and outside
the bedroom.

Kimani™ Romance

Sexy and entertaining love stories
with true-to-life African-American
characters who heat up the pages
with romance and passion.

Look for these and many other Harlequin romance books wherever books are
sold, including most bookstores, supermarkets, drugstores and discount stores.

tryharlequin.com

PASSCATR1

SUSPENSE & PARANORMAL

Heartstopping stories of intrigue and mystery—
where true love always triumphs.

Harlequin Intrigue®
Breathtaking romantic suspense. Crime
stories that will keep you on the edge of
your seat.

Harlequin® Romantic Suspense
Heart-racing sensuality and the promise
of a sweeping romance set against the
backdrop of suspense.

Harlequin® Nocturne™
Dark and sensual paranormal
romance reads that stretch the
boundaries of conflict and desire,
life and death.

Look for these and many other Harlequin romance books wherever books are
sold, including most bookstores, supermarkets, drugstores and discount stores.

tryharlequin.com

SUSCATR